The GENERAL'S WIFE

SUZANNE DANA

Copyright © 2025 by Suzanne Dana

All rights reserved.

No part of this book may be reproduced or transmitted in any form or by any means, electronic or mechanical, including photocopying, recording, or by any information storage and retrieval system, without the written permission of the author, except for the use of brief quotations in a book review.

This book is a work of fiction. Names, characters, places, and incidents either are products of the author's imagination or are used fictitiously. Any resemblance to actual persons, living or dead, events, or locales is entirely coincidental.

Cover Designer: Monika MacFarlane, Ampersand Book Covers

Editor: Caroline Tolley

Editor and Interior Designer: Jovana Shirley, Unforeseen Editing

Published by Zen House Ink.

For Marie, my mother and my favorite general's wife.

To know someone here or there with whom you can feel there is understanding in spite of distances or thoughts expressed ... That can make life a garden.

—Johann Wolfgang von Goethe

Chapter One
WHERE MARINES ARE MADE

August 2008
Marine Corps Recruit Depot
San Diego, California

BRIGADIER GENERAL GEORGE E. STONE had recently taken command of the Marine Corps Recruit Depot (MCRD), the basic training camp for Marine recruits in San Diego. After thirteen weeks of rigorous training, the newly trained Marines and their drill instructors participated in a formal graduation ceremony on the parade deck before family and friends.

Margaret Stone sat in the bleachers of the reviewing stand, cursing herself for forgetting to bring her wide-brimmed straw hat to shield her fair-skinned face and shoulder-length auburn hair from the piercing rays of the sun. She instinctively rechecked her phone—no new messages. Relief and dread twisted through her stomach in equal measure.

Overhead, an American Airlines 757 roared as it descended into Lindbergh Field—a constant sight and sound at MCRD, given its proximity to downtown San Diego Airport and Naval Air Station North Island. George liked to call that "the sound of freedom." For Maggie, lately, freedom had felt like a luxury slipping through her fingers.

Maggie gazed across the parade field at the historic Spanish mission-style buildings with terra-cotta rooftops and beautiful archways. Palm trees swayed gently in the subtle summer wind. Long branches danced gracefully as a backdrop to the beat of the United States Marine Band marching across the parade deck. Directly behind the band, platoons of recruits stood in perfect formation.

The narrator's voice boomed out from the public address system. "Ladies and gentlemen, I'm pleased to introduce Brigadier General George E. Stone, Commanding General, Marine Corps Recruit Depot, San Diego."

George stood up from his seat beside Maggie and moved to the podium.

"Welcome to this morning's graduation ceremony," he remarked. "Those graduating today have earned the right to the title United States Marine. I want to personally thank you for entrusting us, the Marine Corps, with your Marine. Generation after generation of Americans have given the title United States Marine special meaning. These men and women live by a set of enduring core values, which form the bedrock of their character. Honor—the quality that guides Marines to exemplify the ultimate in ethical and moral behavior. Courage—the moral, mental, and physical strength to do what is right, to adhere to a higher standard of personal conduct, and to make tough decisions under pressure and stress. Commitment—the promise and pursuit to complete a worthy goal, objective, or mission. I hope you enjoy the remainder of your visit to San Diego and take time to tour our Recruit Depot. Thank you for supporting your Marine, and welcome to our Marine Corps family. Semper fi!"

George took his position on the parade deck. Each platoon proudly passed in front of the reviewing stand with a sharp salute to the general.

The Marine Band, the last to pass, played the familiar tune. *"From the halls of Montezuma to the shores of Tripoli. We fight our country's battles in the air, on land, and sea ..."*

Goose bumps rose on Maggie's arms, and her heart pumped with pride as she gazed at her husband, who was saluting the recruits as they marched on. This was the man she had married. She had experienced both good and bad times with him, including the numerous deployments and separations, as well as the multiple moves to twelve different duty stations, two of which were outside the continental United States. Her eyes darted to the crowd, scanning faces almost unconsciously. The familiar knot of anxiety tightened in her chest—the one that had been her constant companion these past weeks.

What would George think if he knew? The question haunted her daily, weighing heavier with each passing hour.

George looked exceptionally sharp. He stood six feet tall, with a lean yet muscular build. His salt-and-pepper hair was freshly clipped to Marine regulations. The silver stars on his uniform shirt collar caught the August sun, sending a brilliant flash across Maggie's vision. The metallic glint instantly transported her back to that first night, when a much younger George, nicknamed Rocky, had sat across from her in a Las Vegas hotel, wearing his squadron logo T-shirt. The memory washed over her as clearly as the notes of "The Marines' Hymn" as it still echoed across the parade ground.

She clenched her jaw, pushing away the nagging thought that everything they'd built together was suddenly precarious. Some things from the past were better left buried, but Maggie knew that secrets had a way of surfacing, like bodies in water. Her smile remained fixed, practiced over years of military functions, while her mind raced with thoughts of impending jeopardy beneath it.

Chapter Two
G-LOC

September 1988
San Diego, California

"Let's go, Maggie." Karma's voice rang out as she honked the horn of her red Volkswagen (VW) Bug. "We've got fighter pilots waiting."

Maggie stood in the doorway of Alpha Chi Omega—her sorority house—steps from the campus of San Diego State University (SDSU). It had been her home for the past six years—three as an undergrad and three more as house mother. The familiar white AXΩ letters of Alpha Chi Omega loomed above on the upper landing, catching the morning sunlight. Maggie adjusted her floppy straw hat, shielding her eyes from the glare, and hefted her duffel bag over her shoulder.

Fighter pilots. Just the thought sent a flutter through Maggie's stomach. After weeks of wrangling fifth-graders as a teacher at Hardy Elementary, she was more than ready for this Vegas adventure.

Maggie tossed her bag into the back seat of the Bug and hopped in, settling behind Karma. Barbara sat primly in the passenger seat, her blonde hair perfectly in place, as always. She watched Karma grab her trusty Aqua Net from the glove box, step out, and perform her ritual hair-spraying performance.

Karma was a "big" girl. Five-seven, full-figured, with curly fiery-red hair.

"You know you're killing the environment with that stuff," Barbara said.

"Calm down, doll," Karma replied. "Worse things are being done to the environment."

Maggie smiled to herself. *Some things never change.*

Maggie, Karma, and Barbara had been doing this dance since the fifth grade. They met at Bud Kearns Memorial Pool in North Park, where all three girls participated in the local youth swim team. Karma with bold energy, Barbara with measured caution, and Maggie somewhere in between. Now, years after graduating from college, their paths had diverged, but their friendship remained constant.

Karma had graduated from San Diego State with a degree in psychology. She was still trying to establish her foothold in the pharmaceutical sales industry. Pfizer was her dream job. In the meantime, she had moved back home and was waitressing at a Chili's restaurant.

Barbara had attended SDSU on a Navy Reserve Officers' Training Corps Scholarship. She majored in nursing. After graduation, she was stationed as an emergency room nurse at Balboa Naval Hospital in San Diego. She shared an apartment with another Navy nurse in Mission Hills—an upscale area overlooking downtown and San Diego Bay.

Karma gazed at the sorority house. "If these walls could talk," she said.

"Oh ... the stories they could tell," remarked Barbara. "Like the time you messed with the president of Lambda Chi Alpha."

Maggie remembered that incident vividly. The two-way mirror in the bathroom at the fraternity house. Karma's brilliant revenge with that English Beat song, "Mirror in the Bathroom." Good times indeed.

"Hey," said Maggie, suddenly aware of her growling stomach, "how about a square meal deal at Square Pan Pizza or some fish tacos at Rubio's before we hit the road?"

The VW Bug headed north.

Vegas, here we come!

G-LOC—the abbreviated term for G-force-induced loss of consciousness—and the three-day convention for Navy and Marine Corps pilots took place in Las Vegas. The girls had heard a great deal about it during their summer circuit adventures in San Diego.

Wednesday nights kicked off the week at the Officers' Club at Naval Air Station Miramar. The club promised naval aviators in military-green flight suits. Thursday nights, it was McP's Irish Pub on Coronado Island, the off-duty home of the United States Navy Sea, Air, and Land Teams—commonly known as Navy SEALs. Friday nights were spent sweating on the dance floor with Marines at the Officers' Club at MCRD in downtown San Diego. After a Saturday break, unless one of them scored a date, they'd end their weekends at the open-air top deck of The Pennant, followed by the Beachcomber next door in South Mission Beach. The beach bars were a mixture of Navy and Marine Corps officers belting out sing-alongs, like "Sweet Caroline," "Brown Eyed Girl," and "Margaritaville."

The clubs had the same thing in common—no cover charge, cheap booze, and a plentiful sea of military men. Lured by the prospect of free drinks, food, and attractive men, the girls decided to attend the convention in the fall.

"I can't believe we're doing this," said Maggie. "We're going to G-LOC. We've been surrounded by these men all summer, and now we'll see them in their element. Listening to their stories, their fascinating experiences—it's clear that their world is full of discipline and purpose. It's certainly a different world from the organized chaos of my elementary school classroom."

"These men *are* very disciplined," said Barbara. "But you might find one who needs a spanking."

"Or better yet," said Karma, "he might need some one-on-one tutoring."

Karma and Barbara laughed. Maggie shook her head and gazed out at the passing desert landscape. The VW Bug pulled into the driveway of the Las Vegas Hilton. The thirty-story Y-shaped building looked majestic against the panoramic desert skyline. The marquee sign read, *Welcome, G-LOC '88.*

Maggie felt the excitement building inside her. Everywhere she looked, the hotel was abuzz with twenty-five to thirty-five-year-old men. All the men were physically fit and clean-shaven with short, cropped hair. Her eyes darted from one to the other as the girls stood in line to check in to their room. One of the men approached Barbara and handed her a business card.

"Hope to see you later, ladies," he said confidently.

Barbara read the card: *A-6 Intruders—all-weather attack. We stay up longer … and deliver bigger loads. Please join the intruders for an evening of imbibing, chicanery, and debauchery—Suite 307.*

"Looks like the party's on the third floor," said Barbara.

Maggie felt her cheeks flush slightly at the suggestive message.

This weekend was going to be an interesting one.

The girls' nerves tingled with anticipation as they took the elevator to the hotel's third floor. The doors opened to reveal a raucous crowd of men, mostly wearing shorts and T-shirts. Maggie took a deep breath before stepping out of the elevator.

"Whoa," said Karma. "A woman in a bikini is being passed hand over hand overhead down the hallway."

Maggie watched, wide-eyed, as the crowd chanted and yelled.

This was much wilder than their typical nights at the Officers' Club.

The girls ducked into the VF-124 suite, Fightertown. The suite was packed with pilots from the Fighter Squadron based at Naval Air Station Miramar in San Diego. A disc jockey spun music in one corner while an X-rated movie flickered on a large screen. On the coffee table, people were doing belly shots.

Ever the adventurer, Karma immediately headed to the coffee table and lay down on her back. Maggie watched, half amused and half appalled, as a guy named Chainsaw performed the ritual.

"I'm going to rub a wedge of lime on your upper thigh, then sprinkle it with salt," said Chainsaw. "Next, I'll place a lime wedge between your luscious breasts."

He then poured tequila from a bottle into her navel.

"Now comes the fun part," he said.

Chainsaw placed his tongue on Karma's thigh and licked the salt off. He moved on to her belly button and slurped up the tequila. He finished the shot off by placing his mouth between her breasts and retrieving the lime wedge. The crowd erupted.

Maggie, Karma, and Barbara moved on to the Marine Corps Air Station, El Toro suite, based in El Toro, California, where a Marine lieutenant introduced himself to Maggie as Hurl.

"How did you get *that* name?" asked Maggie, genuinely curious about these call signs she'd heard all night.

"As a second lieutenant, I got liquored up one night and puked all over myself," he explained matter-of-factly.

"What's with all the squadron logo stickers stuck on women's *delicate* body parts?" Maggie asked.

"As you can see, popular zapping zones are the breasts, butt, and crotch," explained Hurl. "Zapping happens when we visit other squadrons and they zap our aircraft with their squadron logo. This is a new take on zapping I haven't seen before."

Military culture, up close and personal.

Karma and Barbara returned from the bar with margaritas. As Barbara handed Maggie her drink, she accidentally brushed up against the guy standing behind her. She glanced over her shoulder and noticed the guy's testicles were exposed.

"Oh my God!" Barbara shrieked.

Her shocked reaction caused Hurl to look over toward the guy.

Hurl casually explained, "It's called ball walking; some guys think it's a manly thing to do. See the T-shirts?"

Maggie looked around the room and saw guys wearing T-shirts that read, *Hang 'em if you got 'em.*

This is getting out of hand.

Maggie grabbed her friends, and they hurried out of the suite. The three ventured into the Rhino suite next. In the center of the suite, a large, hand-painted mural of a rhinoceros stood. Strategically placed in the rhino's crotch was a dildo, rigged as a drink dispenser. A squadron member named Nasty called out to the girls. Nasty was wearing headgear made of rhinoceros horns.

"Well, if it isn't Charlie's Angels!" he shouted. "Angels … right this way," said Nasty, directing the girls toward the rhino.

He pulled on the appendage, releasing a frothy white liquid, called Rhino Spunk, into plastic cups that he then handed to the girls.

"It tastes like a sweeter version of a white Russian," said Karma. "Rum, Kahlúa, and cream?"

"You're quite right," responded Nasty. "See … you *are* detectives."

Maggie hesitantly took a sip. *It is just a white Russian with a crude name*, Maggie reminded herself, trying to stay levelheaded amid the increasingly wild atmosphere.

The girls lingered a bit longer and questioned Nasty about the history behind his call sign.

"Well, that was a memorable event when we pulled into Subic Bay in the Philippines," he said.

"I already feel like I'm going to need to be sanitized after hearing this story," said Barbara.

"Antibiotics," said Nasty. "Let's just say, I had a nasty eye infection when I boarded the ship."

Karma glanced down at her frothy drink. "I'm going to be sick," she exclaimed.

"Amen, sister," said Maggie. "Let's head outside."

The heat from so many bodies packed into the suites was becoming overwhelming. Maggie's face flushed, and sweat trickled down her back. She headed out to the pool patio for some fresh air, with Karma and Barbara following behind. Each girl grabbed a lounge chair next to Hurl. Maggie looked up at the windows overlooking the pool and saw eight bare buttocks pressed against the glass, mooning the crowd below. In the pool, women in bikinis sat on aviators' shoulders, engaging in "chicken fights" as they tried to remove the bathing suit tops of other women. Maggie's eyes drifted to a banner on the sliding glass doors of a suite—*Free Leg Shaves! VMA-214.*

That seemed like a quiet reprieve from the chaotic energy out where they lounged.

"I'm going to check out that suite," she yelled to Karma and Barbara, who opted to remain on the patio with Hurl.

Just inside the sliding glass doors, Maggie saw several booths set up. Each booth consisted of a chair for the person being shaved, an equipment table, and a stool for the aviator performing the shave. Maggie sat down in an open chair, curious about the process.

A six-foot-tall, heavily muscled man with Mediterranean features and severely cropped black hair approached her. He offered her a plastic cup filled with beer and introduced himself as Rocky.

Maggie gazed into his hazel eyes, admiring his strong Roman nose.

"Rocky, as in you're rough around the edges?" she asked.

"Not that clever," he said with a smile. "My last name is Stone, and I'm from Philadelphia. You know, Rocky Balboa from the boxing movie?"

"Yes," she said. "I assume you're Italian."

"On my mother's side, Saccucci."

As he placed a hot towel on Maggie's legs to steam them up, she noticed the logo on the upper-left corner of his T-shirt—a black sheep, surrounded by a circle of twelve stars, crowned with the image of an aircraft, and superimposed with a diagonal black bar.

"What's VMA-214?" she asked.

"The Black Sheep. We're a Marine Attack Squadron based in Yuma, Arizona. Right now, we fly A-4s, but we're transitioning to AV-8B Harriers," he explained, his voice filled with passion.

"How are the Harriers different from the A-4s?" asked Maggie, genuinely interested in his enthusiasm.

Rocky's eyes lit up. He shifted back on his stool.

"To begin with," said Rocky, "Harriers have a Rolls-Royce 23,400-pound-thrust turbofan engine, a range of 2,416 miles, and two 25-millimeter cannons, plus 9,200 pounds of bombs, rockets, missiles, or extra fuel tanks."

"Wow," said Maggie, impressed by his knowledge. "A man who knows his specs."

"And then there's the vertical and short takeoff and landing," he continued excitedly. "It's one of the most maneuverable combat aircraft in service, allowing it to zoom out of range of enemy fire extremely quickly."

"Well, you certainly sound excited to fly it," said Maggie, finding his passion contagious.

"Hell yeah!" he shouted.

This guy is incredible, Maggie thought. *He's intense about flying his aircraft. He's confident, but not arrogant.*

Rocky applied baby oil to her legs, massaging them with firm yet gentle hands.

Oh my God ... I could sit here all night, Maggie thought as his fingers worked their magic.

He tenderly picked up the razor and ran it up her leg, performing his craft slowly and meticulously.

The entire process took about twenty minutes. When finished, he licked her leg with his tongue.

"To ensure quality control," he said with a sly smile.

"Do you accept tips?" asked Maggie, feeling a connection she hadn't expected.

"No," he replied, looking into her eyes. "But I'll take your phone number."

As Maggie returned to the pool patio, she felt like she was floating.

"I just met the most amazing guy," she told her friends excitedly. "Only bad thing is … he lives in Arizona."

It was close to midnight, and the girls were ready to return to their room. The passage to the elevator was through the dimly lit hallway on the third floor. Since their arrival earlier in the evening, it had become extremely crowded, with men drinking and socializing.

"This will be a challenge to get through," said Maggie, eyeing the mass of bodies.

As the girls approached the hall, they heard someone cry, "Clear deck."

Approximately two hundred men lined up along the hallway wall on cue, providing a clear passage down the center. Maggie led the way through the funnel, followed by Barbara and Karma.

The men began pounding on the walls, repeatedly chanting, "Gauntlet, gauntlet, gauntlet!"

Maggie felt hands grabbing at her breasts, and someone pinched her ass several times. Adrenaline surged through her veins as she pushed through the hall. She felt her dress begin to lift. Furious, she spun around and threw her cup of beer at the offender's face. She felt nauseous from the disgusting smell of spilled beer, vomit, and urine soaked into the carpet.

Looking back, she saw Barbara experiencing the same treatment. Maggie saw the color drain from Barbara's face as she began dry-heaving. She immediately grabbed her hand and pulled her forward to the broader, subdued area in front of the elevators.

They waited anxiously for Karma, fighting and biting through the crowd. Karma arrived at the elevators with her rainbow-striped tube top pulled down around her hips, exposing her breasts. As she adjusted her clothing, she noticed a sign taped to the wall: *Gauntlet—Enter at Your Own Risk.*

"Son of a bitch," Karma exclaimed. "They want Charlie's Angels. We're not coming back here unless we have black belts in karate."

Maggie stood, shaking with anger and violation, the evening's magical moment with Rocky now tainted by this awful experience.

What kind of world have we entered? Maggie wondered as she embraced her friends, and they stepped into the elevator.

The elevator dinged and opened to the girls' floor. As they walked down the hallway to their room, they passed a man fumbling for his room key while simultaneously trying to keep an intoxicated woman from falling.

"Evening, Angels," said the man as they passed by.

"Oh my God," said Maggie. "That's Nasty."

"Living up to his name," said Karma.

"Let's quickly get to our room," said Barbara frantically.

Maggie locked the door and turned to her friends, their shared trauma hanging in the silence between them, and at that moment, she knew their innocence about this world was gone forever.

Chapter Three

HAPPY BIRTHDAY, GENERAL

November 2009
Quarters One, MCRD

EARLY DAWN LIGHT CREPT IN through the window of Quarters One at MCRD. The beautiful, historic home echoed the rustic grandeur of Spanish colonial architecture, with arched doors and windows, a white stucco exterior, balconies, and a red clay rooftop. Behind the estate, palm trees, flowers, and exotic foliage flourished. Large koi fish swam in the garden's center in a long, rectangular pond painted with lily pads. Just beyond the pond stood a wisteria-covered terrace.

Inside the home, the dark wooden ceiling beams, stucco walls, hand-painted tiles, and decorative wrought iron exemplified the traditional warmth of a Spanish hacienda. Just inside the house's entrance was the Kennedy Room. Its walls were covered with photos of President Kennedy's visit to the Depot in 1963. Memorabilia were scattered about the room, including Brigadier General Smedley D. Butler's sword, which hung triumphantly on the wall.

On the morning of Tuesday, November 10, a tradition was taking place upstairs in the bedroom. George lay sleeping on his right side, his left arm resting gently against his body.

Maggie studied his face for a moment—the lines around his eyes that deepened when he laughed, the strong jawline. He was still the handsomest man in any room, even after all these years.

Maggie kissed his forehead and gently positioned him on his back. She thought, *Another year, another birthday*, as she carefully slid down to the base of the bed, separating his legs on the way down. *Some traditions are worth keeping, especially with you.*

Brigadier General Stone rose to the humming sound of "The Marines' Hymn."

"From the halls of Montezuma to the shores of Tripoli."

Maggie gazed up at her husband with her mouth securely wrapped around his penis. With an internal smile, she mused about the things they did for love and country.

She continued humming, *"We fight our country's battles in the air, on land, and sea."*

In addition to her stroking his testicles, her mouth moved in a constant battle rhythm. *"First to fight for right and freedom and to keep our honor clean."*

If only he knew what she had done to keep their honor clean.

Maggie's tongue wiggled for the grand finale. *"We are proud to claim the title of United States Marine.* Happy birthday, General."

"Well, Maggie, that's the kind of birthday greeting that makes you want to live to be one hundred," remarked George.

His eyes, still heavy with sleep, met hers with a tenderness that made her heart skip a beat. He reached for her hand and pulled her up beside him, kissing her deeply.

"I love you," he whispered against her ear. "Nineteen years, and you still surprise me."

And I'd surprise you even more if you knew everything, she thought, resting her head against his chest, listening to the steady beat of his heart. But some surprises would break even a Marine.

"I love you too," she said, meaning it more than he could know.

Their relationship had weathered every hardship, from lonely nights during deployments to difficult moves to new bases or countries. She had chosen him time and again, and he had chosen her.

The invitation for the two hundred thirty-fourth birthday of the United States Marine Corps rested on the round reception table in the front foyer. It featured a white card with black cursive lettering and an embossed one-starred United States Marine Corps flag centered at the top. George and Maggie would be hosting the ball that evening at The US Grant hotel in downtown San Diego.

Maggie lifted the stack of morning mail off the receiving table. She flipped through the envelopes and stopped suddenly at a letter addressed to Mrs. George E. Stone with no return address. *That's odd.* Her heart quickened with an instinctive wariness she couldn't explain.

She ripped open the letter, her fingers suddenly clumsy with inexplicable dread. As her eyes scanned the contents, she felt a knot form in her stomach.

Dear Maggie,

Congratulations on George's recent selection for promotion to major general. I'm sure you will agree that you want to ensure nothing comes to light that would prevent those second stars from appearing on his shoulders. It's time for you to make monthly payments. Your secret is safe with me!

Yours truly,

Swimbuddy1980

No. No. No. She had been making the quarterly payments for over a year, since George's promotion to brigadier general. Now they were demanding more. Why? Because George had been selected for promotion to major general?

You bastard.

Maggie shoved the letter into her pocket and tossed the rest of the mail back onto the table, her hands trembling slightly. She looked around the pristine foyer of their home—this sanctuary they'd built together—and suddenly felt it transform into something fragile and vulnerable.

This would not end well if she didn't find out who this person was. She felt the panic rise within her, but years of practiced calm as a military wife took over. Why unveil the secret now? A secret that had been haunting her for twenty-nine years. Everything she and George had built together—his career, their marriage, their life—could all crumble if her secret came to light.

She took a deep breath and straightened her shoulders, just like she'd seen George do countless times before facing a challenge. She briefly closed her eyes, recalling George's face from only moments ago—trusting, loving, unaware. She would not let this coward destroy what they had. Swimbuddy1980 had no idea who they were dealing with.

Chapter Four

THE RENDEZVOUS LOUNGE

THE BLACK SEDAN IDLED AT the curb in front of Quarters One as five o'clock chimed somewhere in the distance. Maggie watched as Corporal Smith opened the back passenger door for George. He slid into the car with practiced military precision. Then Corporal Smith circled to open the door for Maggie on the driver's side.

"Remind me, Corporal Smith," Maggie asked, settling into the leather seat, "why do I sit behind the driver?"

"Yes, ma'am," Corporal Smith replied with that perfect military formality. "If I take a bullet on the driver's side, we want to ensure the general remains safe, ma'am."

Maggie caught George's eye across the back seat. "The things I do for you, my love," she said, trying to keep her voice light despite the grim reminder of danger that always shadowed their lives.

The sedan pulled away, gliding down Broadway toward downtown. Maggie's gaze drifted to the storefronts passing by until an enormous black lion's head on a white background caught her attention. Her breath caught in her throat. That sign. After all these years, The Lion's Den tattoo studio was still there, sandwiched between Little Darlings go-go bar and Raul's Bail Bonds.

Maggie quickly wiped away the tear that had formed before George could notice. The memories flooded back—her first and only tattoo and her first love. Even now, just seeing that sign made her heart ache with a dull, familiar pain.

Ian …

After all these years, he still has that power over me, Maggie thought, staring at the lion's face until it disappeared behind them. *I wonder what it would have been like if he had never walked through those doors. I wouldn't be dealing with this torment.*

The car slowed as they approached 326 Broadway. Maggie gathered herself, pushing those thoughts away. Tonight wasn't about old ghosts.

George looked magnificent in his evening dress uniform— the single star on each shoulder, three rows of shiny gold medals over his heart.

The Distinguished Flying Cross from Desert Storm, Navy Commendation Medal with Combat V for valor in Somalia, and Legion of Merit with Combat V for his service in Iraq. Each one told a story of the man she'd married. Brave and dedicated.

Maggie smoothed her off-the-shoulder navy-blue ball gown as Corporal Smith opened the door. The cool evening air brushed against her shoulders as she stepped out, George following behind her.

As they entered, the Rendezvous Lounge glowed with warm light. The neon sign above the entrance cast colored shadows across the threshold of what had once been a Prohibition-era speakeasy. Inside, stained-glass windows filtered the light, wood-paneled walls absorbed sound into a comfortable murmur, and the rich mahogany bar stretched a hundred feet along one wall.

Maggie's eyes scanned the room. There they were—Karma and Hurl, seated in a private wooden booth in the back. Maggie nudged George, and they made their way over, sliding into the bench seats beside them.

A tuxedoed waiter approached with a bar trolley. "Can I offer anyone a cocktail this evening?" he asked.

After everyone ordered—Karma a Vieux Carré, Maggie a dry vodka martini with an olive, George and Hurl both Manhattans—Maggie took a moment to study her friends.

Karma and Hurl. Their relationship had been explosive from the start after the encounter in Las Vegas years ago. Tall, thin Hurl, with his big heart and mild manner, was the perfect counterbalance to Karma's fiery nature. They'd dated for six months and married when she was six months pregnant on March 17, 1989. By June, they were Captain and Mrs. John "Hurl" McCauley with a beautiful baby daughter named Erin.

George and Maggie had followed their example. In the summer of 1990, their wedding was at Mission Basilica San Diego de Alcala in the hills of Mission Valley. Three hundred guests, a full Catholic Mass. She could still feel the moment during their vows when a sudden gust of wind had lifted her veil—she'd known immediately it was her mother's presence.

Oh, how I miss you, Mom. She imagined her smiling down from heaven on that special day. The memory was vivid—magenta bougainvillea popping against the white adobe church, the three tiers of mission bells, the sun glinting off the steel Mameluke swords, held in an arch by white-gloved Marines in their dress whites. Hurl led the sword detail.

George and Maggie passed through that arch, and at the end, the last two Marines lowered their swords to block their way.

"Give this Marine a kiss!" Hurl had ordered.

Maggie complied, of course.

"Captain and Mrs. George E. Stone," Hurl had announced as the swords rose.

As Maggie stepped forward, she had felt a gentle swat on her behind from Hurl's lowered sword, followed by, "Welcome to the Marine Corps, ma'am."

The Marines' enthusiastic, "Ooh-rah!" still echoed in her memory.

Now, here they were, nineteen years later—Colonel and Mrs. McCauley and Brigadier General and Mrs. Stone, best friends, stationed together at MCRD. George was the commanding general, anxiously awaiting his confirmation announcement to major general, and Hurl was his chief of staff.

Maggie gazed at her husband across the table, watching how his eyes crinkled at the corners when he laughed at something Hurl had said. The memory of their early days together flooded her suddenly, as vivid as if it were yesterday.

Their first date was nothing special—Filippi's Pizza Grotto in Little Italy. George had traveled from Yuma for the weekend. She remembered how nervous he'd been.

This confident fighter pilot fumbled with his silverware, nearly knocking over his water glass when she asked about his call sign.

"So, why do they really call you Rocky?" she asked, genuinely curious about this man sitting across from her.

He hesitated, that half smile that she would come to love playing at the corners of his mouth. "Well, officially, it's because I'm solid as a rock in the air."

"And unofficially?" Maggie prompted, leaning forward slightly.

"And unofficially," he admitted with a self-deprecating chuckle, "it's because I'm about as graceful as one on the ground."

And then he proved his point by dropping his fork with a clatter.

"I swear I'm normally more coordinated than this," he said, his cheeks flushing slightly as he retrieved it.

"I don't mind," Maggie replied. "It's refreshing to meet someone who isn't trying to impress me."

"Oh, I'm trying to impress you." He laughed. "I'm just terrible at it."

They'd taken things slowly at first—weekend trips to Catalina Island, long sunset beach walks, and surf lessons. When George had mentioned he'd never surfed, Maggie couldn't believe it.

"You fly multimillion-dollar aircraft through enemy fire, but you've never tried surfing?" she asked as they walked along the shoreline one evening.

He shrugged, looking almost sheepish. "Never had the right teacher, I guess."

"Well, you do now," Maggie declared. "Tomorrow. Zero seven hundred. Del Mar Beach. Don't be late, Captain."

He snapped a mock salute. "Yes, ma'am."

The next morning dawned perfectly for beginners—gentle, rolling waves, minimal wind, and enough sun to burn off the marine layer early. Maggie laid two boards on the sand—a shortboard and a longboard, the one she'd learned to surf on.

If he only knew the story behind this board. Her mind flashed back to Ian coaching her to surf with his wild intensity, which had thrilled and frightened her at the same time.

"Lesson one," she said, "starts here on the sand."

"I thought surfing happened in the water," he replied with that crooked grin.

"With that attitude, Captain, you're bound to wipe out," Maggie retorted. "Now, lie down on the board and show me your paddling form."

George followed her instructions perfectly, practicing pop-ups on the sand until his movements looked fluid. The real test came in the water. Surprisingly, his confidence in the air translated well to the ocean. His balance was excellent. His military training had served him well.

After catching his first real wave and riding it back to shore, he jogged over to Maggie like an excited kid.

"Did you see me?" he called, grinning wildly. "I did it!"

"Not bad for a flyboy," Maggie conceded. "But don't get too cocky. That's when the ocean will humble you."

A larger set rolled in.

George looked at it and said, "That one. I'm going to try that one."

"George, wait . . ." Maggie called, following behind him.

What happened next was spectacular and disastrous. He caught the wave but misjudged the drop, sending him cartwheeling through the air before disappearing under the whitewash. Maggie paddled over quickly. Before she reached him, he surfaced, still clutching his board, laughing so hard that he could barely speak.

"I get it now," he spluttered. "You don't have to conquer the wave. You have to work with it."

"Exactly," she said, relieved he wasn't hurt. "Just like I'm learning from you."

"Me? What did I teach you?" George asked, genuinely surprised.

"To let go sometimes," Maggie admitted, suddenly feeling vulnerable. "To learn to trust."

He looked at her then, water droplets clinging to his eyelashes. "Teach me more about waves," he said quietly. "And I'll teach you more about letting go."

Maggie thought at that moment that she was falling in love with this man. Beneath his military precision and confidence, George wasn't afraid to be a beginner, fail, laugh about it, and see the parallel between surfing and life. She fell in love with how he looked at her, like she was the only person who mattered.

"Deal," she said, and they sealed it with a salty kiss in the morning sun.

And then came that day at Torrey Pines, when they hiked along the cliffs above the Pacific. Maggie should have known something was up—George was never jittery. He couldn't seem to stand still. He kept checking his pocket and looking at his watch.

"You're acting strange," Maggie said as they climbed the trail. "Is everything okay?"

"Everything's perfect," he replied. "Just enjoying the day."

"When do you check your watch every thirty seconds to enjoy the day?"

"You notice everything, don't you?" George laughed nervously.

"About you, yes," Maggie said, squeezing his hand.

When they reached the overlook, the ocean stretched endlessly before them. George fell silent, staring out at the horizon. Then he turned to Maggie.

"You know, I've flown over oceans worldwide," he said softly. "Always looking for that line where the sky meets the water, using it to stay level, to find my way home."

"That's very poetic for a Marine," Maggie teased.

George smiled, then suddenly dropped to one knee. Maggie's heart nearly stopped.

"I had this whole speech prepared," he said, pulling out a small red box with trembling fingers, "about how you're like the horizon out there— beautiful, constant, something to navigate by."

"Oh, George," Maggie whispered, tears forming.

"But now all I can think to say is that I love you, Maggie," he continued, his voice steady. "You're my horizon. You're my home. I want to build a life with you." He opened the box, revealing the ring inside. "Will you marry me?"

The ring had been his grandmother's, a simple diamond solitaire, nothing flashy. When he slipped it on her finger, it felt so right.

"Yes," Maggie said through tears. "Yes, of course I'll marry you."

George rose to his feet. "You're sure? Even knowing what you're signing up for? The moves, the deployments, the—"

"I'm not marrying the Marine Corps, George Stone. I'm marrying you."

"Well," said George, suddenly serious, "we kind of come as a package deal."

"Then I'll take the package," Maggie replied. "I love you, George."

George lifted Maggie off her feet and spun her around as she laughed and cried at the same time.

"I love you, Maggie," he whispered against her hair. "I'll spend the rest of my life trying to deserve you."

A family taking photos nearby captured the moment—the spinning, the laughter, and the absolute joy on both of their faces.

That photo still sat framed on their dresser at home, a perfect moment frozen in time.

Returning to the present, Maggie sipped her martini, and an overwhelming sense of gratitude came over her. George caught her eye across the table and gave her that same warm smile that had won her over all those years ago.

How did I get so lucky?

Chapter Five

THE CRYSTAL BALLROOM

THE CRYSTAL BALLROOM AT THE US Grant hotel was a formal and refined venue, highlighting stunning architectural details. It featured a black-and-gold travertine floor, towering columns, a beautiful hand-painted mural on the ceiling, and nine crystal chandeliers that illuminated the space, creating a truly historic and regal ambiance.

Maggie's stomach churned as the guests were told to take their seats. *Just breathe*, she reminded herself. *No one knows. Everything looks normal on the outside.*

She and Anna—Sergeant Major Reed's wife—were escorted to the head table, with Karma and Hurl following behind. George and Sergeant Major Reed waited at the back of the room for their part in the upcoming ceremony.

While waiting, Maggie turned to Anna, hoping the conversation would calm her nerves. "Anna, how did you meet Sergeant Major Reed?"

Anna's face softened with the memory. "I left Texas and followed my high school boyfriend to Camp Lejeune, North Carolina. He deployed to Beirut and was killed in the terrorist bombing of the Marine Corps barracks."

"Oh, Anna, I'm so sorry," Maggie said, genuinely moved by the story she hadn't expected.

"I stuck around for a while, deciding whether to return to Texas," Anna continued. "I worked selling cars at the Sanders Ford dealership in Jacksonville. I sold Roy a car, and that was it. We dated for a few months, and then we got married."

"Wow, he saved you," Maggie said, thinking about her relationship with George. *Did he save me too? And now I might be destroying everything we've built.*

"Yes. He came along at the right time. He's a blessing and a comfort," Anna replied, her eyes drifting to where her husband stood.

"You seem so close," Maggie observed. "What's kept you together all these years?"

Anna turned back to Maggie, her expression serious. "The most important thing in maintaining a strong relationship is trust. No secrets. It isn't easy, especially if you've always had to protect yourself. You must be open and admit mistakes. With deep trust, you have a sense of peace and security."

It's easy for her to say. She's not being blackmailed, Maggie thought bitterly. *How can I tell George? What would happen if he knew the truth?*

The Marine Corps Birthday Ball ceremony began, and Maggie found herself only half present, her mind wrestling with guilt and fear. She watched the traditional elements unfold, her eyes frequently seeking George, standing proud and respected.

He doesn't deserve this, she thought.

All he'd ever done was serve with honor, and she might be the one to bring him down.

During a somber moment, honoring fallen service members, Maggie's thoughts drifted to friends lost in training exercises and the Iraq War. *Cheeks, Fester, Merlin, Smurf.* The women who married Marines understood that their lives could be shattered in an instant. It took a special woman to travel a path with a husband who prided himself on his mission and steadfast dedication to the Corps and country. And what kind of wife was she? One who was keeping secrets that could destroy everything.

After the formal ceremony, Brigadier General Stone approached the podium for his address. Maggie blew him a kiss, hiding her inner turmoil with the practiced smile of a military spouse.

"Good evening, Marines!" George's voice boomed through the ballroom. "My wife, Margaret, and I are honored to be here. First thing … for everyone with a date or spouse here this evening, I ask you to look this person in the eye and tell them how squared away—or as civilians say, fabulous— they look tonight. Trust me, I've been married for nineteen years. This is important."

Nineteen years, Maggie thought.

After almost two decades of building a life together, they could lose it all because of her recklessness.

George's speech continued with pride and passion as he spoke about the history of the Marine Corps and what he would tell President Grant if he could.

"If I were lucky enough to have a beer with President Grant, I'd tell him three things," George said, his voice carrying throughout the room. "First, this generation of Marines is the best I've seen in twenty-seven years of service. You're intelligent, patriotic, and very talented."

As Maggie watched her husband speak, she felt a swell of pride mixed with her fear. George was so good, so dedicated. He believed in honor and service with every fiber of his being. How would he react if he knew what Maggie had done?

When George returned to his seat amid applause, his chief of staff leaned toward him. "Sir," said Hurl, "I think you'll want to see this email from the inspector general at Headquarters Marine Corps."

Maggie watched George's face change as he read the message. Her heart pounded as he shared the screen with her. The email informed George that suspicious monetary transactions had been identified during a review of his financial disclosure report—part of his confirmation process for major general—and that he was under investigation.

With trembling fingers, Maggie reached for his hand under the table. "Oh, George, I'm so sorry. This must be a misunderstanding," she said, her voice barely above a whisper, even as guilt consumed her from within.

This is all my fault, she thought desperately.

George's career would be over if he didn't get this promotion, and their marriage would be over if George didn't forgive her. Her purpose had been to support George and take care of military families. If she lost either of them, she would lose everything.

"It has to be a mistake," George said quietly, his brow furrowed in confusion. "I've always been careful with our finances."

If only you knew, Maggie thought, fighting back tears.

Karma leaned over from her seat. "Is everything okay?" she whispered, noticing the change in atmosphere.

"Just work stuff," Maggie managed to say, forcing a smile. "Nothing that can't wait until tomorrow."

But she knew tomorrow would bring no relief. The clock was ticking, and she would have to decide whether to continue hiding the truth and hope the investigation would go nowhere, or confess everything to George and face the consequences.

Chapter Six
THE CRASH

September 1978
North Park, San Diego

THE NOTORIOUS SANTA ANA WINDS kicked up, bringing restless energy and fear of fires to San Diegans. Maggie scurried around the house, getting ready for school. She glanced in the mirror a bit longer this morning to look at her new Dorothy Hamill haircut—a short wedge bob with bangs. Her puka shell choker felt too tight around her neck in the hundred-degree heat.

I look just like her, Maggie thought, adjusting her bangs and tilting her head from side to side. *Mom says I'll regret it when the style changes, but Dorothy Hamill won Olympic gold with this hair, so how bad could it be?*

There was a knock at the door. It was Karma and Barbara.

Maggie, Karma, and Barbara had been friends since Maggie had moved into the neighborhood five years earlier, when Maggie's parents divorced.

Maggie, an only child, lived with her mother, Mary, in a quaint 1950s-style Craftsman bungalow northeast of Balboa Park in the North Park neighborhood. Her father, Ed "Curly" White, lived in an apartment in downtown San Diego, only a few miles away. Maggie rarely saw her dad who, when he wasn't working as one of America's Finest—a San Diego police officer—could be found at Star Bar on E Street, drinking one-dollar Busch pints; singing Irish drinking songs at The Blarney Stone on Fifth Avenue; or in a poker game at The Follies Theater, also on Fifth Avenue.

Ed was a Navy Vietnam veteran. He'd returned home a changed man—a functioning alcoholic without a hair on his head, hence the nickname Curly. Ed and Mary moved out west for a fresh start. Unfortunately, it didn't take long before the drinking, gambling, anger, and rage got the best of him.

Mary left with Maggie. Mary was a nurse who worked full-time at Mercy Hospital in Hillcrest, northwest of Balboa Park. Mother and daughter had settled into their new home on Dwight Street in North Park.

"Bye, Mom," said Maggie.

She knew her mom couldn't hear her, but it felt wrong to leave without saying it. She paused briefly at her mother's closed bedroom door, hand hovering, as if to knock, then decided against it. She needed her sleep more than she needed to hear Maggie say goodbye.

Mary had switched to nights when Maggie started high school. The money was much better, and Maggie was proud that she felt confident and could contribute by being mature enough to be left alone for the night. Mary always packed Maggie's lunch, tucked a note inside it, and left it on the counter before she went to bed after her night shift.

Maggie grabbed her lunch off the counter, smiling as she felt the shape of the folded note through the brown paper bag. The girls headed to the bus stop, schoolbooks tucked in their arms and brown leather purses hanging from their shoulders.

"It's too blazin' hot to go to school today," said Karma, her wild and wavy red locks blowing in the warm wind. "And besides," she added, "it's Monday. Come on. Let's head to Mission Beach for the day. Better yet, Mexico … *arriba, andale!* Up! Let's go! You must admit, Coronas on the beach would be sweet right now."

"Karma, you're such a bad influence on us," said Maggie. "I have a test in English today. If this weather doesn't break by the weekend, I promise we'll go to Mexico with you. I'll even buy you a bucket of Coronas and a cabana boy at the Rosarito Beach Hotel."

"She might need her own personal security detail," said Barbara. "Last time we were down there, we thought she'd been kidnapped. We found her hours later, smoking weed and drinking tequila with the local boys."

"Okay, okay." Karma nodded. "I'll behave this time."

"Right," said Barbara and Maggie in unison.

"Give me a break," said Karma. "My mother had just finished her last round of chemotherapy."

"Sorry," said Maggie. "We're so glad your mom is a survivor, Karma. That was a scary time for all of us. What would any of us do without our moms?"

"Breast cancer is a bitch," said Barbara.

"It was a hard time for all of us," said Karma tenderly. "But you dolls helped me through it. I love you both so much."

The trio embraced and hopped on the bus. Fifteen minutes later, the bus pulled up to the front entrance of San Diego High School. When Karma exited the bus, she pulled an aerosol can of Aqua Net out of her purse, stepped to the side, flipped her head over, and sprayed her entire head of hair.

"Good God, Karma!" exclaimed Barbara.

"I swear you are single-handedly destroying the ozone layer," said Maggie, waving away the cloud of hair spray. "But that hair isn't going anywhere in this wind."

"Are you the environment police?" replied Karma. "See you dolls at lunch!"

Thirty minutes into the English test, one of the students in Maggie's class yelled, "Check out the falling plane!"

The class jumped up to the window and looked out to see a plane with its wing on fire heading down and heard the screaming sound of a jet engine. The students watched as the aircraft dropped to the ground and exploded. Maggie's heart pounded as she pressed her face against the window and realized the downed plane was near her neighborhood, her street.

Minutes later, Ed White arrived at the school in uniform and signed out Maggie, Karma, and Barbara. His face was ashen, his hands trembling slightly as he filled out the forms. When he looked up at Maggie, his bloodshot eyes betrayed both fear and the lingering effects of last night's drinking.

"Dad, what's going on?" Maggie's voice quavered.

Ed cleared his throat, struggling to maintain his professional composure. "Not sure, Maggie," he said, his voice cracking slightly. "I heard on the radio that two planes collided and went down around Dwight and Nile Streets."

He reached out and squeezed her shoulder—an unusual gesture from a man who rarely showed physical affection. Maggie realized, with a jolt, that her father was scared.

Ed's squad car approached the Stop sign at Landis and Boundary Street. Dark, thick black smoke rose in the air. Police personnel blocked off the area. Ed parked the car and spoke with a policeman, who allowed them to enter the scene. All four set out on foot to reach Dwight Street. They headed down Boundary, and as they approached Dwight and Nile, the smell of diesel fuel permeated the air. The street was engulfed in flames, and body parts were strung in trees like Christmas ornaments.

"Wait here," said Ed, his voice commanding but strained. His face had gone from ashen to green, and sweat beaded on his bald head despite the hot wind. "What was Mom doing when you left for school?"

"Sleeping," Maggie whispered, feeling suddenly cold despite the heat. "Oh my God, I hope she's all right."

Please be okay, Mom, Maggie silently pleaded. *Please have woken up and gone somewhere. Please.*

Moments later, Ed walked back to the girls. His shoulders were slumped, his entire body seeming to have aged years in just minutes. Tears streamed down his face, cutting clean tracks through the soot that had settled on his skin.

"I'm so sorry, Maggie," he choked out, his voice breaking completely. He reached for her hands, holding them tightly in his own. "The officers say this is the point of impact for both planes. Many homes were demolished. Your house was one of them."

"That's not true," said Maggie.

He's wrong. He has to be wrong. Our house is fine. Mom is fine. This isn't happening.

She pushed past her father. Her eyes scanned the street. After a moment, she realized her house was no longer there. Feeling dizzy and nauseous, she fell to her knees.

"No, no, no!" she screamed amid heavy sobbing.

She wrapped her arms around herself and rocked back and forth. The lunch note was the last thing her mother had written to her. She hadn't had a chance to read it. She would never have the opportunity to say goodbye.

Ed dropped down beside her, wrapping his arms around his daughter. His body shook with sobs as he held her tight against him. For the first time in years, he was fully present, the alcohol haze burned away by the horror before them. His voice was hoarse as he whispered, "I've got you, Magpie. I've got you." It was the nickname he hadn't used since Maggie had been a little girl.

Chapter Seven

IN BETWEEN THE FOXY
AND THE FOLLIES

AS THE SUN SET, HIGH ATOP a hill overlooking the Pacific Ocean, a Navy color guard marched across the grass at Rosecrans National Cemetery. Though divorced, Ed felt Mary should have a special ceremony with sailors and law enforcement present.

Maggie sat in the front row, her body tense and rigid, clutching a crumpled piece of paper in her trembling hands. Everything around her felt distant, as if she were viewing it all through a foggy window. As she glanced down at the eulogy she had written and rewritten a dozen times, she questioned her ability to stand before everyone and deliver the speech successfully.

As the Navy flag lowered, a bugler off in the distance played "Taps." The mournful twenty-four notes played to commemorate the mother, the wife, and the nurse who had perished in the prime of her life.

Day is done, gone the sun, from the lake, from the hill, from the sky; All is well, safely rest, God is nigh.

Maggie felt Karma squeeze her hand.

"You can do this," her friend whispered.

With leaden feet, Maggie approached the podium. The paper shook in her hands as she smoothed it against the wooden surface. She looked out at the sea of faces—some familiar, many not. She spotted her father, his eyes bloodshot and watery, his uniform immaculate for once.

He cleaned up for you, Mom, she thought. *He's trying.*

Maggie cleared her throat, then took a deep breath.

"A remembrance of Mary is a story about love," she began, her voice surprisingly steady. "It's a story about laughter, strength, courage, humor, and fun. It's a story about commitment—to a man who would serve two tours in Vietnam as a United States sailor and return home to join the San Diego Police Department."

I'm doing this for you, Mom. I hope you can hear me.

"My dad, Ed 'Curly' White, met my mom, Mary, at a United Service Organization dance in their Bayonne, New Jersey, hometown. She was eighteen, and he was six years her senior. Dad tried to impress her with pictures of his dog, Clancy, a brindle boxer."

Maggie paused, looking directly at her father. A flicker of a smile crossed his face as he nodded slightly. She knew this part of the story was always his favorite.

"I'm told the St. Patrick's Day parties at our home were quite a sight. Mom, the ideal hostess, danced the jig with the best of them and spoke with an Irish brogue all night." Maggie's voice cracked slightly.

She only remembered two of those parties before things had taken a turn and her dad started drinking too much.

"Unfortunately, my parents divorced after twelve years of marriage. If there was a silver lining, it was that Mom and I moved to North Park and found a new community—people who welcomed us with open hearts."

Maggie paused, swallowing hard and struggling to hold back tears. She knew that if she began to cry now, she would lose all control.

"Mom was one of those mothers who was a mom to everyone, but also one of the girls. She loved to be included in everything we did. She would chauffeur us past the newest hottie's house so that we could catch a glimpse of him." This drew a gentle laugh from Karma and Barbara in the front row. "She was one of the girls, but always a step ahead. She was in the thick of it … always in the know … always knowing best. She was cool."

You were the coolest, Mom. I don't know how to be without you.

"Love is the easy part to describe. You could see how much she loved me—loved all of us—anytime you were with her. The sense of humor? That's easy too. Have you ever known someone whose eyes *actually* twinkled? If you knew my mom, you knew that mischievous Irish twinkle in her eye. You'd recognize that bright, hearty laugh, always waiting to surface; she found the laughter in every situation. She taught us to make the best of it, whatever *it* might be. Her incredible inner beauty made us all feel like part of her family. She made us feel loved, and we loved her in return."

Maggie paused, taking another deep breath as tears threatened. *Keep it together. Just a little longer.*

"Mom's strength is more difficult to describe. She handled every situation in the same easygoing, unflappable way. A single mother, working full-time as a nurse, she inspired us with her courage."

You never complained, Mom. Not once. Even when it was hard.

"She was cheerful, encouraging, and always saw the good in everything. And it was so easy for all of us to see the good in her. Mom left us too early, but we will remember the life, the love, that great laugh, and the twinkle in those blue eyes. She gave us a legacy of love, laughter, strength, and beauty that we will never forget."

Maggie stepped away from the podium, her legs wobbly. As she returned to her seat, she felt a strange emptiness.

I did it, Mom. I hope I made you proud.

Six uniformed law enforcement officers approached, carrying the casket. Solid black mourning bands were tightly wrapped straight across their badges. Maggie stared at the casket being lowered into the ground. Not exactly sure what she was feeling—a swirl of shock, disbelief, and anger. She didn't know. What she did know … she felt numb.

This can't be real. They're putting you in the ground, and I'm supposed to just go on living. How am I supposed to do that?

Her father's hand found hers, squeezing gently. She didn't pull away.

"You did good, Magpie," he whispered, his voice rough with emotion. "Your mom would've been proud."

"Thanks, Dad," she murmured, not looking at him. *Would she be proud? Or would she be terrified, knowing I'm left with you?*

Seemingly overnight, Maggie's world had undergone a seismic shift—from a cozy suburban bungalow to a shitty one-bedroom downtown apartment. She had to take a city bus to get to school, but it was one of the few normal things left in her life.

Home was now a squalid single-resident occupancy hotel called the Yuma Building, or the YB, located between the Foxy and the Follies—adult theaters on Fifth Avenue in the Gaslamp District of downtown San Diego. The Foxy took pride in its magnificent Art Deco marquee. Neon letters advertised XXX-rated adult films and an air-conditioned theater that was open all night. The underside of the marquee flaunted a sensual display of peep-show art. Neon-lit circles with dots in the center resembled nipples while ovals with short middles and long, squiggly tails resembled traveling sperm. She knew her mother would have been horrified to know she walked past porn theaters to get home.

The Follies was more understated than the Foxy, a cave-like establishment that screened mostly silent porn loops. When the door opened, a distinct foul odor greeted visitors, smelling of decades of filth and sex that had seeped into the wooden floors and walls. Behind the main theater was a utility room that served as a card room, where mostly older men, including Curly, played poker. Though a "straight" theater, many "casual encounters" took place there, primarily involving closeted men who were married. Cops frequented the place, yet there were never any arrests. How did this degenerate cinema escape any hint of suspected criminal activity? One had to consider that Curly and his band of merry uniformed men contributed to the business-as-usual atmosphere.

When Curly showed Maggie the apartment, the first thing she saw upon entering was a tattered, blue-checkered couch, an end table littered with empty beer bottles, horse racing forms, an ashtray overflowing with ashes, girlie magazines, and a mustard-yellow rotary phone.

Well, that certainly sums up my father's life …

"The bedroom's a bit small," said Curly, shuffling awkwardly as he watched her take in the squalor. "But it's all yours. I'll sleep on the couch."

"You didn't have to give up your room," Maggie said quietly, guilt mingling with her disgust. She knew he was trying, in a messed-up way.

"Course I did," Curly replied, rubbing his bald head. "You're my daughter. You need your space."

Maggie glanced at the bedroom, which was the size of a small closet. It had a single bed with a military-green wool blanket serving as a bedspread and a wooden crate doubling as a nightstand.

"I know it's not much," Curly said, noting her expression. "I bought some new sheets. They're, uh … they're pink. Thought you might like that."

Pink sheets. Like I'm still ten years old, Maggie thought, but she nodded. "Thanks, Dad."

Outside the bedroom, there was an arm's-length coat rack and a sink with a metal-rimmed mirror above it.

"Where's the bathroom?" Maggie asked, dreading the answer.

"Down the hall," said Curly, not meeting her eyes. "Showers, baths, and toilets are shared by the occupants on our floor."

"Dad," Maggie said hesitantly, "how long do you think we'll live here?"

Curly sighed, running a hand over his face. "I don't know, Magpie. Money's tight. But I'm going to try to save up and get us something better before you graduate. Bear with me, okay?"

Maggie knew he wouldn't save a dime, not with the drinking and gambling, but she nodded. "Okay."

"Hey," Curly said, perking up slightly. "The lobby's not half bad. Lou—he's the manager—he keeps it clean. And there's a TV. Big one. I'll show you around."

Curly led her back into the hallway and down the stairs to the only inviting place in the YB—the high-ceilinged, train-station-styled lobby with an enormous black-and-white honeycomb porcelain tiled floor. An assortment of dark brown mission-style rocking chairs and high-back easy chairs with paddle arms and slat backs faced the communal television. The usual suspects—a handful of middle-aged men, mostly veterans—gathered daily to smoke and watch *The Six Million Dollar Man*, *Baretta*, and *Barney Miller* reruns.

"Afternoon, Curly," one of the men called. "Is this your girl?"

"Yeah, this is Maggie," Curly said, a hint of pride in his voice. "My daughter."

"She's a looker," another man commented, and Maggie felt herself shrink into her father's shadow, desperately seeking to avoid being left alone with these men.

"Watch yourself, Donny," Curly said, his voice taking on an edge Maggie had rarely heard. "That's my daughter you're talking about."

Old mission benches with dark brown leather seats lined the walls, separated by half a dozen coin-operated vending machines. Twenty-four hours a day, anyone could purchase anything—from condoms and cologne to a Coke and chips. Large-framed landscape oil paintings of various scenes adorned the walls—the Pacific Ocean, the Grand Canyon, rugged mountains, and Torrey Pines, to name a few.

Around the corner from the foyer stood a trio of wooden pay phone booths. A solitary antique switchboard. A wall-mounted black cast iron post box with *Letters* embossed at the top. Above, in the ceiling, was the pièce de résistance—sixteen tiles of floral stained glass. A border of peach, orange, red, and blue poppies burst with color—a circle of red poppies in the center with swirling vines, ending in bright blue buds.

Maggie paused, gazing up at the stained glass. She wondered how something so beautiful could find itself in a place like this.

"Pretty, ain't it?" Curly said, following her gaze. "The building's over sixty years old. Used to be fancy, I guess."

Maggie felt the building's struggle within itself. Was it a historical structure with artistic and vintage treasures or a sad workingmen's club, where the broken and injured waited to die? Either way, Maggie didn't belong here.

"Well, well! This must be the famous Maggie!" A booming voice interrupted her thoughts.

Lou, the building manager, approached from his registration desk. An African American in his early fifties, he was the heart and soul of the YB. His signature look was a fedora hat and black canvas Converse All-Star sneakers.

"Lou, this is my daughter," Curly said almost formally. "Maggie, this is Lou. He runs this place. Anything you need, you ask him."

"Nice to meet you, sir," Maggie said politely, extending her hand.

Lou's laugh was warm and genuine as he shook her hand. "Sir? You hear that, Curly? This girl's got manners! You sure she's yours?"

"Ha-ha," Curly said dryly, but there was a hint of a smile on his face.

"I'm real sorry about your mama, honey," Lou said, his voice softening. "Curly told me what happened. That's a tough break for a young lady."

Maggie felt tears threaten. She could handle anything but kindness at the moment. "Thank you," she managed.

"You need anything—anything at all—you come find me," Lou said. "I'm usually right here or"—he winked at Curly—"at the track with your old man."

Lou loved his liquor, his smokes, and his ponies. His off days were spent at the Del Mar Racetrack. His off-hours were spent at the hole-in-the-wall bars in the Gaslamp … usually accompanied by Maggie's father, Curly.

"Let's get your stuff unpacked," Curly said, guiding her back toward the stairs. "I got a shift tonight, but I thought maybe we could grab a burger before I go?"

The offer took Maggie aback. She couldn't recall the last time they had shared a meal.

"Sure, Dad," she said. "That would be nice."

As they ascended the stairs, Maggie felt the weight of her new reality pressing down on her. Her mother was gone, and her home was gone. Everything familiar had been stripped away—her cherished books sat on shelves in a house that was no longer there, her clothes hung in a closet she would never see again. Even the Italian inlay musical jewelry box her mother had given her for her fifteenth birthday was now lost to her. She arrived at her father's doorstep with nothing but the clothes on her back and a grief so heavy that it felt like she was carrying stones.

Everything had been replaced by this strange, seedy world inhabited by her father. She wasn't sure how to fit in or if she even wanted to try. She promised herself that, by graduation, she would be gone. She just had to survive until then.

Chapter Eight
THE LION'S DEN

June 1980
Gaslamp Quarter, San Diego

WHAT A DIFFERENCE NEARLY TWO years made.

In the summer of '78, Maggie's mother had been alive. She lived in a stable, structured home in the peaceful suburbs. She worked as a lifeguard at Bud Kearns in Balboa Park with Karma and Barbara. On her days off, she frolicked on Mission Beach, drank beer around a beach bonfire, and flirted with surfers. Life had been simple then. Uncomplicated.

In the summer of '80, her mother was dead. She lived in a cramped, one-bedroom apartment in the seediest part of downtown San Diego. She worked the counter at The Lion's Den tattoo studio. On her days off, she drank beer and smoked weed at G Street Mole Park, next to the Navy Pier and the commercial fishermen's basin on San Diego Bay.

How had she gotten here? Sometimes, she would wake up and, for a split second, forget. Then reality would crash down on her like a wave.

Her meaningless conversations were with street people and hookers. Here, she could allow herself to let her guard down, not pretend everything would be all right. She could feel sad, surrounded by the reeking aroma of piss, dead fish, and the body odor from drunks passed out on the grass, mixed with the smell of cheap perfume from women selling their bodies to make ends meet. It was the perfect environment to match her shitty life as she knew it now. No one here expected her to be okay. No one asked, *How are you doing?* with that pitying look. They were all just trying to survive, like her.

At least there was the beauty of San Diego Bay. Blue water lapped against the rocks as seagulls shrieked overhead. The whoosh of speedboats and the flutter of sailboats passed by the pier. Rainbow-colored kites danced in the cloudless sky, above children playing on the grassy knoll, where families picnicked and lovers romanced.

Her mother had always said, "Beauty finds a way to shine through, even in the darkest places."

Maggie wondered if she could see it now, wherever she was.

Maggie struggled to make it through each day without crying, trying to put on a happy face. She knew she wasn't fooling anyone, especially not herself.

She wanted to believe it when friends said, "You'll be okay. Everything will be okay."

How the hell would they know? Their mothers were still alive. Their lives hadn't shattered overnight.

Triggers happened in unexpected ways. While walking down Market Street, Maggie caught the aroma of a woman wearing her mother's scent—Estée Lauder Youth Dew. The smell knocked her back. For a second, she thought, *Could it be?* But no. Never again.

As she entered San Diego Hardware on Fifth Avenue, she heard "Love Will Keep Us Together" by Captain & Tennille on the radio—one of her mother's favorite songs. She used to dance around the kitchen to it, with a wooden spoon as a microphone. Maggie would roll her eyes but secretly loved it.

After getting off the bus to school, she saw a 1972 Oldsmobile Vista Cruiser station wagon—her mother's car.

For a heartbeat, she thought she'd come to pick her up. That everything had been a terrible mistake.

Out of seemingly nowhere, her eyes would fill with water. Tears streamed down her face. She could feel the discomfort of salt and liquid burning down the back of her throat. Sometimes, she could reel it in.

Deep breaths, Maggie. Not here. Not now. You're stronger than this.

Sometimes, she could keep it short and simple. Other times, it was gut-wrenching sobs. A pain so deep inside that it felt like her soul was being ripped apart. A painful wail, more like a howl. Deep breaths in. Deep breaths out. A release, but simultaneously, a profound sadness that life would never be the same. Was this what they meant by heartbreak? Because it felt like her chest was being torn open. Had this happened? Maybe it was all a dream, and she would wake up in the North Park house. Not so alone. Not so heartbroken. Not so lost.

Please, just let me wake up. Let me hear her voice one more time.

Sometimes, she would pull out a slip of paper from her pocket. In black cursive letters, it read, *M, Good luck on your English test today! I love you to the moon and back. Mom,* ending with a smiley face.

Maggie traced her finger over her mother's handwriting before tucking the note back into her pocket, cherishing the last one she'd ever received. Her handwriting was so beautiful. Flowing and confident, just like her.

This was real. This was her life now. This emptiness that nothing seemed to fill.

To make matters worse, she rarely saw Karma or Barbara. Karma was working full-time as a lifeguard at Bud Kearns, and Barbara was busy with the Navy Junior Reserve Officer Training Corps (NJROTC). Barbara had decided she needed to find a way to attend college, so she joined the NJROTC program at the high school. The program offered physical and mental challenges and a competitive advantage when applying for a ROTC full-ride college scholarship.

Everyone else was moving forward, while Maggie was stuck in this moment, this pain. They had plans and futures. What did she have?

"Good afternoon, Bobby," said Maggie as she entered The Lion's Den.

At least this place felt real. No pretending. No pity.

Bobby, his American name, was the principal owner and operator.

A Vietnamese refugee, loyal to South Vietnam, he had fled due to fear of political persecution following the fall of Saigon in 1975. One of the original boat people, Bobby, was a staff member at the US Embassy in Saigon. In the wee hours of the morning on April 30, 1975, Bobby and his partner, Hai, boarded a military transport barge. The barge, crammed with three hundred refugees, navigated its way down the Mekong Delta. The bobbing barge was a slow-moving target for the Viet Cong. As the barge drifted out to sea, Bobby hugged Hai tightly.

"Take a good look at our country," he'd said. "It will be the last time you see it."

Bobby was a hard worker. He loved America and the opportunity it had given him to achieve his dream of owning his own business. In America, Bobby didn't have to hide his sexuality and love for Hai. Back in Saigon, it was illegal to be gay. Every moment together had required caution—no holding hands in public, no stolen kisses on street corners. They had been forced to retreat to private, underground bars to enjoy time together.

Bobby understood loss too. Different, but still a loss. Maybe that's why Maggie felt safe here.

Entering Bobby's studio was like entering Walt Disney's version of a tattoo paradise. Cartoon-colored pictures plastered the studio walls with significant square clusters of design options. Everything from religious symbols, insects, birds, dragons, flowers, military insignia, and Asian ladies to skulls and then some. A couple of tattered black leather club chairs and a round metal floor fan were in the waiting area. Maggie loved the chaos of the place.

All these symbols people choose to make permanent. What does that say about us? Do we need to mark our pain, our loves, and our beliefs on our skin to make them real?

During the week, the shop was mostly quiet. On the weekends, when the Navy ships docked at the pier, it was a bustling beehive of activity. Enlisted young sailors and Marines stumbled in, asking for anchor and bulldog tattoos, respectively.

"Maggie," said Bobby on a slow Monday afternoon, "now's a good time to give you your eighteenth birthday present."

"Really?" exclaimed Maggie. "I've had this design picked out for months. It signifies my love for my mother, my trust and confidence in my friends—Barb and Karma—and my desire for good things to come my way. It's my trinity, I suppose."

Maybe this would help. A permanent reminder on her skin when everything else seemed so temporary. Something she chose when so much had been taken from her.

Maggie lowered the dentist-style chair to a flat position. She then climbed on the chair face down and pulled down her denim shorts to expose the upper portion of her right butt cheek. Her mom would have probably freaked out if she knew.

"Bobby," said Maggie, "what do you think my mother would have said about my tattoo?"

"I don't know much about the Christian religion and Irish tradition," said Bobby. "But I know you're a feisty young lady with a tender heart who deserves good things to come her way. I think your mother would be proud of you."

"Thank you, Bobby," said Maggie. "That means a lot to me."

Maggie hoped he was right. She hoped her mother would understand why she needed this.

Bobby cleaned her skin with rubbing alcohol. He then used a disposable razor to remove any hair from the area. He cleaned the area again to ensure it was smooth and ready for the image transfer. Maggie tried to remain still as he pressed the stencil. When he pulled the paper away from the skin, it left a purplish-blue likeness of a shamrock. Next, tiny white cups were filled with ink. The needles and tubes were removed from their sterile pouches and placed in the machine. Ointment was applied to the design.

"It's time," said Bobby. "Take a deep breath and try to relax."

"Good God, Bobby," said Maggie. "Are you trying to seduce me?" Deflect with humor—her go-to defense.

"Yes," said Bobby. "But only with my needle."

"It feels like you're using an X-Acto knife on my skin," said Maggie.

"Well, it's a needle," said Bobby. "Stay still while I finish the outline. I'm switching to the Magnum for the coloring."

"Bobby," said Maggie, "I didn't know you were so big!"

Her jokes would mortify her mom. Or maybe she'd laugh. Maggie would never know.

Bobby finished his work and took a picture with his Polaroid camera to show Maggie. A voice boomed behind the counter as he waited for the camera to spit out the image.

"Well, I'll be damned," said a gentleman, speaking with an Irish brogue. "I think I found my lucky charm!"

Bobby and Maggie snapped their heads to look toward the voice. Great. Just what she needed. Another man who thought he was God's gift.

"The name's Ian Murphy," said the voice. "If you're interested in getting to know me, I hang out at McP's Irish Pub on Coronado on Sunday afternoons."

Arrogant prick, Maggie thought, rolling her eyes internally.

And just like that ... he disappeared. As if she would chase after some random guy. As if she had room in her life for that kind of complication. But the accent … her mom would have laughed about *that*.

Chapter Nine

SUMMER OF IAN

MAGGIE HAD TO WAIT TWO weeks for her tattoo to heal before plunging back into the pool to swim laps. Two weeks too long. Swimming was the only time her mind shut off completely. She tried to make it to Bud Kearns at least once a week to swim and catch up with Karma. The pool was in a charming 1930s building, situated at the north end of Balboa Park. It possessed a Spanish-Mediterranean vibe, characterized by its clay tiled roof, decorative wrought iron, and ornamental tiles. The atmosphere had an open-air, tropical feel to it.

The nearly Olympic-sized pool was outdoor, and the roof above the lockers and showers was also open. Palm trees surrounded the pool, and the multifaceted scent—with hints of mint, honey, and citrus from the eucalyptus trees—was abundantly fragrant. This smell always reminded Maggie of summer. Of before. Before everything had changed.

Karma climbed down from her lifeguard post for her fifteen-minute break and sat on the side of the pool, reading a book, while she waited for Maggie to finish her laps.

Maggie pushed herself harder, feeling the burn in her muscles. Faster. To keep going. To not have to think. She reached the side of the pool after her final lap, lungs burning pleasantly. She removed her goggles and swim cap, hoisted her body out of the water, and sat down to catch her breath.

"What're you reading?" she asked Karma, squeezing water from her hair.

"*Tales of the City*, Armistead Maupin. It's set in San Francisco in the '70s."

"What's it about?" Maggie leaned over to look at the cover, genuinely curious.

"Tenants in an apartment complex. The landlady is a hoot. She grows her marijuana."

"A woman after your own heart," Maggie said, nudging Karma with her elbow.

"The main character is Mary Ann. It's about her escapades in the city. Bisexuals, bathhouses, gays, infidelity, blackmail … all the good stuff."

"Sounds like you're getting your fill of hippie pleasure."

Always the wild one, Karma.

"Speaking of that … I've been seeing Levi."

"Levi," said Maggie, her eyes widening. "As in Levi Siegel, the pool cleaner?"

No way. The guy who smells like chlorine and patchouli?

"Yes," said Karma, a mischievous smile spreading across her face.

"Jesus!" exclaimed Maggie, sitting up straighter. "He's twice your age. Plus, he's a major Deadhead. He sings an entire concert in a day's work. Off-key, I might add." Maggie had heard enough "Sugar Magnolia" to last a lifetime.

"That's true," said Karma. "He's an avid Grateful Dead fan."

"What *is* the attraction?" asked Maggie, genuinely bewildered.

"Besides the tie-dye, long hair, groovy bandanna, and his endless supply of weed and pharmaceuticals?" asked Karma.

"Yes!" said Maggie, leaning forward.

"His dick," responded Karma with an enormous laugh.

"Well, okay then," said Maggie, joining in the laughter. She hadn't laughed like this in weeks. God, she had missed this. Just being silly with Karma. "Can he get us some fake IDs? I have a bar we should check out."

"Since when are you interested in bars?" Karma raised an eyebrow. "Wait, is this about that Irish guy from the tattoo studio?"

Maggie shrugged, trying to appear nonchalant. "Maybe. I'm just curious. He said he hangs out at McP's on Coronado. What's the harm in checking it out?"

"Maggie White, actually interested in a guy. This I have to see," Karma said, closing her book. "I'll ask Levi tonight."

The following Sunday afternoon, the girls took their bikes on the ferry from Broadway Pier to Coronado. The ferry ride was breezy and refreshing, with the skyline of San Diego growing smaller behind them.

"What if he's not even there?" Maggie said, nervously adjusting her hair as they approached the pub. "This was probably a stupid idea."

"Then we have drinks and enjoy the view," Karma replied. "Look at you, all worried about your hair. You do like this guy."

"Shut up," Maggie muttered, but she couldn't hide her smile.

As they walked inside the cozy pub, laughter filled the air. Framed photos of naval aircraft, military awards and plaques, SEAL posters, squadron and unit patches, and other military memorabilia lined the walls of the entire room.

It's like a testosterone museum, Maggie thought, taking in the scene.

The extremely well-stocked bar filled up the whole left side of the room. Military and law enforcement patches and stickers were plastered on the wall below the ceiling and down the center beam of the bar. The ceiling glistened with rows of hanging glass beer mugs, each with a white shamrock key chain denoting the owner. Maggie's mom would've loved the place—all the Irish kitsch.

About a dozen men stood at the bar, holding various brands of bottled beer or pint glasses. They all wore shorts, tank tops, T-shirts, and flip-flops. They varied in height, with some sporting mustaches and longer hair, while others were clean-shaven with military-regulation haircuts. All had lean bodies and beyond-basic toned muscles. These men displayed hulking, well-defined curves in their forearms, biceps, and chests. Was this what all that SEAL training did to them? It resembled a calendar shoot.

B.W. Stevenson's "My Maria" blasted over the sound system. All the men were focused on the petite, dark-haired Italian woman in the center of the bar. She wore red-and-white striped dolphin shorts with a white cotton tank top. Her dark, curly hair was pulled up in a side ponytail with a sparkly pink scrunchie. In unison, the men sang the song's lyrics.

"This is like some weird mating ritual," Maggie whispered to Karma. "Should we leave?"

"Are you kidding? This is the best show in town, and we have front-row seats," Karma whispered back.

When the song ended, most of the men disassembled from the bar area, allowing the girls to reach the bar to order drinks. Karma stood next to the petite, dark-haired girl who had recently been the center of attention.

"Maria, I assume," said Karma.

"It's Julia," she answered.

"Come here often?" Karma inquired.

"I do," said Julia. "I live just down the street."

One of the men stepped in next to Julia. "New York," he said, "your friends?"

"I don't know," she responded. "I just met them."

Karma extended her hand to the six-foot-four man with sandy-blond hair and piercing blue eyes. Maggie's heart skipped a beat when she recognized him—the arrogant prick from the tattoo studio. And, damn, he looked even better up close.

"Ian Murphy," said the gentleman, grabbing Karma's hand.

"I'm Karma," she said. "This is Maggie."

"Well … my lucky charm has finally arrived," he responded, his eyes finding Maggie's.

Cheesy line, Maggie thought, feeling her cheeks warm.

"Karma," said Maggie, nudging her friend, "this is the gentleman who observed my tattoo at The Lion's Den."

"Observed? Is that what we're calling it?" Karma whispered with a smirk.

Maggie stepped forward, deciding to take control of the situation. "So, you told me to come find you here, and I did. What now, Ian Murphy?"

Ian's eyebrows shot up, but his smile widened. "Now I buy you and your friend a drink, and we get to know each other properly."

"We'll each take a beer. Whatever's on tap," Maggie said, returning his smile.

Ian and Julia joined the girls outside at a table on the Paddy-O, an outdoor space adjacent to the bar. Kelly-green market umbrellas added color to the square pub tables and rusted metal barstools. During the conversation, Julia explained that she had come to Coronado on vacation from Long Island, New York, the previous summer and had never returned home. The guys had nicknamed her New York. She worked as a hairdresser at the Orange Avenue Beauty Salon and rented a room in a house on the island that she had found in *The San Diego Reader* newspaper.

"So, you just … stayed?" Maggie asked, fascinated. "Left everything behind?" What would that be like? To start over completely somewhere new?

"Best decision I ever made," Julia replied. "Sometimes, you have to trust your gut."

Ian talked about his SEAL training at the Naval Special Warfare Training Center on the island. He had just finished his first and most challenging phase, Hell Week, and was now on his second phase, seven weeks of combat diving.

"Is it as brutal as they say?" Maggie asked, leaning forward with genuine interest. "Hell Week?"

"Worse," Ian said with a grin. "Five and a half days of constant physical activity. We get about four hours of sleep total."

"Why would anyone voluntarily do that to themselves?" Maggie asked, shaking her head.

"To find out what you're made of," Ian replied, his eyes meeting hers with surprising intensity.

"Where did you grow up, Ian?" Maggie asked, wanting to know more about him.

There was something about him that felt ... familiar somehow.

"I was born and raised outside of Boston, Massachusetts. My father died of a heart attack at the age of fifty-five. My mother and three older siblings raised me. After high school, I knocked around in Quincy, Massachusetts, working on commercial fishing boats."

He had lost a parent at a young age, like *her*. Maggie was struck by the realization, which created an unexpected connection.

"I'm sorry about your dad," she said softly. "I lost my mom recently. It's ... hard."

Ian's expression softened. "It is. Changes everything, doesn't it?"

Maggie nodded, surprised at how easily the words had come. She hadn't talked about her mom with anyone new in months.

"When did you decide to be a SEAL?" Maggie asked, wanting to steer the conversation back to safer ground.

"I was also working charter boats on my days off from the lobster boats," said Ian. "I met Declan Fitzgerald, who told me about his days in the Navy SEALs. He enlisted in the SEALs in the mid-1960s. He served two tours in Vietnam and the rest in the reserves. I loved listening to his stories of brotherhood, camaraderie, and demanding mental and physical training. He inspired me to be like him and, of course, to serve my country."

A lean six-foot-three gentleman with sun-bleached brown hair approached the table.

"Is this your twin, Ian?" Maggie asked, noting the newcomer's similar build and confident stance.

"Ladies, this is my training partner, Lance Barlowe. He and I made a pact to push each other through our training and receive our Trident insignia together."

"Hi, Lance," Maggie said, extending her hand. "I'm Maggie, and this is Karma."

Lance had grown up in Hermosa Beach, Los Angeles County, north of San Diego. He was an avid surfer who had turned pro at age seventeen and won four consecutive championships between 1973 and 1977.

"A pro surfer turned SEAL?" Maggie said. "That's quite a career change."

"What made you want to become a SEAL?" Karma asked.

"Whenever we surfed in San Diego, we'd usually end up here at McP's. I got to know the owner. Like Ian's mentor, he shared stories with me about his time in the Navy SEALs and three tours in Vietnam. I respected him for his discipline, his bravery, and his integrity. I went into pro surfing to make money. I want to become a SEAL and be part of a team of like-minded men. To be part of something bigger than myself."

"Hear, hear," said Julia. "Another round of drinks, everyone? What can I get you, Lance?"

"Water's fine," Lance replied.

"Our friend Lance is as clean as they come," said Ian. "He doesn't drink, smoke, or do drugs. He doesn't even drink soda. No vices that I can find."

"Interesting," said Maggie, giving Lance an appraising look.

"What about you, Maggie?" Ian asked. "What's your story?"

"Not much of a story," Maggie replied, suddenly self-conscious. What could she say that wouldn't sound pathetic? *My mom died, I work in a tattoo studio, and I'm just trying to survive each day.* "I work at The Lion's Den. That's where you saw me getting my shamrock."

"And before that?" Ian pressed. "You seem like someone with interesting stories."

"I used to be a lifeguard with Karma," Maggie said, gesturing to her friend. "At Bud Kearns in Balboa Park. But things changed. Life changed."

"It has a habit of doing that," Ian said, his eyes understanding.

"Hey," Maggie said, suddenly wanting to change the subject. "You guys surf, right? I'd love to watch you sometime. Is there a good spot around here?"

"The best," Ian said, his face lighting up. "We could show you tomorrow morning if you're free. The Outlet, near North Island. Dawn patrol's the best time."

"Dawn patrol?" Maggie raised an eyebrow.

"Surfing at sunrise," Lance explained. "Best waves, fewer people."

"I'm in," Maggie said, surprising herself. But she couldn't deny the pull she felt toward Ian, the first genuine interest she'd had in anything or anyone in months.

"Karma?" she asked her friend.

"Sorry, doll. Morning shifts at the pool all week," Karma replied. "But you go have fun."

Ian and Maggie started spending more time together on their days off from training and working. Maggie loved watching Ian and Lance surf at The Outlet in the mornings.

There's something hypnotic about watching Ian out there, she thought. *So free, so in control.*

"There are some rad barrels out there today," said Ian, emerging from the water. "Must be the hurricane swells coming up from the Baja."

Ian plopped down on the towel next to Maggie. He was dripping from head to toe in cool saltwater. Maggie was mesmerized by his gorgeous body. Wet muscles glistened in the sunlight. An intense magnetic attraction pulled her toward him.

Get a grip, Maggie, she told herself, but couldn't look away.

"You should try it sometime," Ian said.

"Surfing? No way." Maggie laughed. "I'm a pool swimmer. I like my water chlorinated and wave-free."

"You'd be a natural," Ian insisted. "Strong swimmer, good balance … I could teach you." His blue eyes lit up with an intensity that caught Maggie off guard.

"I don't know …" Maggie hesitated.

"Come on," Ian said, jumping to his feet with sudden energy. He extended his hand to her. "Right now. The waves are perfect for beginners."

"Now? I don't even have a suit," Maggie protested, but Ian was already pulling her up.

"You're wearing shorts and a T-shirt. That'll work." His enthusiasm was infectious, almost manic. He was like a force of nature when he got excited about something.

"I didn't agree to this," Maggie said, but followed him to where the surfboards lay on the sand.

"Life's too short to wait for permission," Ian said, grabbing a slightly longer board. "This one's more stable. Better for learning."

Is he always like this? Maggie wondered. *Zero to sixty in two seconds flat.*

Ian spent ten minutes showing her the basics on the sand—how to paddle, how to position herself on the board, and how to pop up. His hands were firm on her shoulders, adjusting her stance, and his voice switched between patient instructor and drill sergeant.

"Keep your back foot angled! Weight centered! Eyes forward, not down!" he commanded, then softened. "That's it. You're a natural, just like I said."

Before she could properly process what was happening, they were wading into the ocean, Ian guiding her board through the breaking waves.

"I'm not ready," Maggie said, the cold water sending a shock through her system.

"You'll never be ready," Ian replied, his eyes wild with excitement. "That's the point. The ocean doesn't wait. Neither should you."

This is insane, Maggie thought as she lay on the board, feeling the rise and fall of the swells beneath her.

Ian was beside her, his hand steadying her board.

"When I say paddle, you paddle hard. Like your life depends on it," he instructed.

"Does it?" Maggie asked, only half joking.

Ian grinned, a flash of white teeth against his tanned face. "Maybe. That's what makes it worth doing."

A wave approached, and Ian's grip on her board tightened. "This one. Start paddling. *Now!*"

Maggie dug her arms into the water, feeling the wave catch the board. Ian let go, and suddenly, she was moving, faster than she'd expected, the shore rushing toward her.

"Stand up!" Ian's voice called from behind her.

Maggie pushed herself up, swaying unsteadily, her heart racing. She stood on the wave for two glorious seconds, experiencing a rush that was unlike anything she had ever felt. She plunged into the swirling whitewash as the board slipped out from under her.

The wave tumbled her, completely disorienting her. Her lungs burned. Panic set in. Then strong hands grabbed her, pulling her to the surface. Ian's face was inches from hers.

"You did it!" he exclaimed, oblivious to her fear. "You stood up on your first wave!"

Maggie gasped for air, pushing wet hair from her face. "I nearly drowned!"

"But you didn't," Ian remarked, his eyes glimmering with excitement. "Dancing on the edge is the rush."

"You're crazy," Maggie said, but couldn't help smiling at his infectious enthusiasm.

"Crazy enough to know you need to get right back out there," Ian said, pulling her board toward them. "The longer you wait, the harder it gets."

He was right, Maggie realized.

Three waves later, Maggie managed to ride to the shallow water, wobbly but upright, Ian whooping from deeper water. She collapsed on the sand, exhausted but exhilarated.

Ian jogged up, dropping down beside her. "You're fearless," he said, his voice filled with admiration. "Most people quit after the first wipeout."

"I'm not like most people," Maggie panted. "It feels … good. Being scared is better than feeling nothing."

Ian's expression grew serious. "That's it exactly. That's how I live." He touched her cheek gently. "That's how you have to live after losing someone. Either feel everything or nothing at all. I choose everything."

Even the bits that hurt? Maggie pondered.

However, she recognized the allure as she gazed at Ian, his eyes brimming with passion, his entire being exuding intensity. He never took a half-hearted approach. He threw himself wholeheartedly into everything—life, love, suffering, and happiness.

"I do like being in the water," Maggie admitted. "It's where I feel most … normal."

"Normal?" Ian questioned.

"Free," Maggie corrected. "Like nothing else matters for a while." *Like I'm not broken.*

She wanted to know as much as possible about him, as quickly as possible. He was the perfect package and beautifully wrapped. On the outside, a gorgeous specimen of male perfection. On the inside, a warm soul. Friendly, honest, loyal, and trustworthy. They had so much in common. A deep connection. Both had lost a parent at an early age. Their Irish heritage. Their love of water.

"What was your dad like?" Maggie asked suddenly. "Do you remember much about him?"

"He was loud." Ian smiled at the memory. "A booming voice you could hear across the neighborhood. Tough but fair. Worked on the docks his whole life. Hands like sandpaper."

"My mom was the opposite," Maggie said softly. "Gentle. Always humming or singing around the house. But strong in her way."

Lance emerged from the water, dropped his surfboard, and lay before Maggie and Ian in the sand.

"You looked great out there, Lance," said Maggie.

"Surfing is very much like making love," said Lance. "It always feels good, no matter how often you've done it."

"Nice quote. Yours?" Ian asked.

"Paul Strauch," Lance answered. "The surfer in the iconic film *Endless Summer*."

"I think we found your vice." Maggie laughed. "So, the clean-living SEAL has a dirty mind after all."

"Nothing dirty about it," Lance replied with a straight face. "Just natural. We should head down to Ensenada, Mexico, and catch the swell where it starts. Check out the blowhole. Drinks on me at Hussong's Cantina."

"Lance, that sounds like a great idea," said Maggie. When was the last time she had done something just for fun? "Let's stop for lunch in Puerto Nuevo on the way down. They have the best lobster I've ever tasted. I used to head down there all the time with Karma and my other childhood friend, Barbara."

"It's settled then," Ian said, squeezing her hand. "This weekend?"

"This weekend," Maggie agreed, squeezing back.

"My lucky charm is full of surprises," Ian said with admiration.

Maggie glanced at Ian, gesturing broadly with his hands, his eyes filled with excitement. He was talking animatedly with Lance about their plans for Mexico. There was something both magnetic and frightening about his intensity—the way he attacked life head-on without hesitation or fear. It was so different from how she'd been living since her mother died, cautious and withdrawn.

He's like touching a live wire, Maggie thought. *Thrilling but risky.* She wasn't sure if she was prepared for someone who felt everything so intensely and lived entirely in the present. However, it was possible that she needed someone who could help her return to society, even if it meant taking a chance on getting hurt again.

Chapter Ten
BAJA CALIFORNIA

"OH MY GOD, ARE WE going to die?" Maggie shrieked, clutching the door handle as Lance swerved around yet another taxi.

Lance drove his iridescent, dark blue GMC Suburban down Highway 5 South. Surfboards strapped to the top, a cooler full of beer in the back, and passengers, Ian and Maggie, belting out songs on the radio as the SUV crossed the border into Mexico. Lance navigated the Suburban effortlessly through Tijuana traffic and the many chaotic traffic circles without set rules.

"Just jump in and keep moving," said Lance, cutting off a pickup truck with casual confidence.

Is he insane, or is this normal? Maggie wondered, her knuckles white as she gripped the seat.

She had often been to Mexico, but always with Karma driving her VW Bug. Even Karma's driving was more cautious.

"Don't we need to stop for Mexican car insurance?" asked Maggie.

"No need," said Lance. "I'm a careful driver."

"It's not you I'm worried about," said Maggie, flinching as a scooter zipped past them with inches to spare. "Everyone else on this road seems to think traffic laws are optional suggestions."

Her head spun from the third traffic circle and ached from honking horns.

"Want to hit Revolution Avenue and drink *cervezas* at the Long Bar?" Lance asked.

"First stop, Puerto Nuevo," said Ian, reassuringly reaching back to squeeze Maggie's knee. "We promised Maggie lobster, remember?"

"My hero," Maggie said, leaning forward to kiss the back of Ian's neck. "Saving me from starvation and Lance's driving, all at once."

After fifteen minutes on Mexican coastal Highway 1, occasionally stopping for livestock crossing, the Suburban passed the town of Rosarito. Maggie shared stories of times spent with Karma and Barbara as young teenagers on the patio of La Calafia, drinking tequila and catching a glimpse of the gray whales migrating to the warm waters of Mexico from the cold waters of Alaska at the end of summer. As they passed the Rosarito Beach Hotel, she laughed.

"See all the loungers and straw umbrella huts?" Maggie pointed. "So many fun memories here. We'd come down for the day and sit on the beach, and the cabana boys would deliver us food and buckets of Corona beer. Once, Barbara convinced this poor waiter she was a famous American actress, and he kept bringing us free drinks all day."

"Should I be jealous?" Ian asked, turning to face Maggie.

"Of course not. You're my cabana boy now," she said, moving close to kiss Ian, feeling happier than she had in a long time.

"Okay, lovebirds," said Lance. "We're approaching Puerto Nuevo."

Lance drove the Suburban through the red brick arch, entering the cobblestone seaside hamlet. The sun shone brightly in a cloudless blue sky over the deep blue ocean. Lance parked, and everyone exited the vehicle. Two young boys approached Lance and Ian in the parking lot. Ian handed them a Mexican peso. Maggie watched as Lance and Ian popped something into their mouths.

"Whatcha got there?" Maggie asked, peering suspiciously at the small brown objects.

"Crickets covered in Tajin, a Mexican seasoning," said Ian, offering her one.

"They're not bad," said Lance.

"You guys are disgusting." Maggie laughed, but impulsively reached for one. *When in Mexico.* She popped it in her mouth and crunched. The spicy, limey flavor hit first, almost masking the earthy insect taste. "Actually ... that's weirdly okay."

Casa de la Langosta, or the Lobster House, was perched high on the bluffs, offering sweeping views of the Pacific Ocean. Upon entering, Lance spoke to the attendant in Spanish.

"*Impresionante vista, no? Queremos una mesa junto a la ventana, por favor,*" Lance said fluently.

"You speak Spanish?" Maggie asked, genuinely impressed. "That's how you got us this table by the window with this incredible view."

"It's just one of my many talents." Lance laughed. "I've been coming down here to surf for years. You pick up a lot."

"Pick up a lot, huh?" Maggie repeated, raising an eyebrow. "Is that how you *picked up* all those women at McP's last weekend? With your Spanish skills?"

Lance grinned, unembarrassed. "Works every time. Ladies love a man who can order them tequila in two languages."

"I'll stick with the one gringo, thanks," Maggie said, sliding her arm through Ian's.

The waiter delivered their entrées—pan-fried split lobster, rice, beans, and handmade flour tortillas.

"Oh my God," Maggie moaned after her first bite. "This is even better than I remembered."

"I checked the surf report," said Lance. "High tide is at six nineteen tonight. We'll check out the blowhole first, then head to San Miguel."

"Is the surfing really that good?" Maggie asked.

"Best in Baja," Ian said enthusiastically. "You should try it here. The waves are perfect for beginners in some spots."

"After last time? I nearly drowned," Maggie protested, but without conviction. She had loved that rush though. That moment of standing on the board …

"I'll stay with you the whole time," Ian promised. "You'll love it."

Before getting back into their vehicle, Ian ran over to a vendor. He climbed back into the SUV and presented Maggie with a sterling silver oval cuff bracelet.

"Something to remember the trip by," said Ian.

"How could I forget?" whispered Maggie. "It's beautiful." So, this was what it felt like to be special to someone again.

An hour and a half later, they reached La Bufadora, the blowhole, the second-largest geyser in the world. According to local legend, a gray whale had been transformed into stone.

"Come on. I want the full tourist experience!" Maggie declared, grabbing both men by the hands and pulling them through the vendor stalls.

She tried on oversize sombreros, haggled for a painted ceramic sun, and bought them all churros dusted with cinnamon sugar.

The three walked past several vendors and taco stands down a dusty trail to a platform built eighty feet above the sea cave. Ian and Lance hopped over the platform barrier to stand on the rocks above the hole.

"Are you crazy? Get back here!" Maggie shouted, but they just waved her over.

"Don't be scared," Ian called. "Come on!"

Maggie thought they were out of their minds, but something in her—that same something that had made her stand up on the surfboard—made her jump over the barrier and join them on the slippery rocks.

Moments later, waves hit the cave, pressurizing the water. A thunderous sound was heard as the waves crashed into the cave and exploded back out one hundred feet in the air. Cascading water drenched all three.

"Holy shit!" Maggie screamed, laughing as the cold spray soaked her completely.

The adrenaline, the danger, the beauty of it—she felt fully alive.

"C'mon, adrenaline junkies," said Maggie, still laughing. "Hop back over the barrier before we get arrested or killed."

The three climbed back into the Suburban, soaking wet, and headed toward San Miguel. Lance explained that San Miguel was where surfing in Ensenada had begun. The site of the '66 Baja Surf Club International had sparked SoCal's finest surfers to put it on the map for surf missions.

"The spot is a tribute to the Lower Trestles," said Lance. "The shoulders peel and curve right into the inside of a south-facing headland, usually nicely pitched for the action of the lip; occasionally, it hollows for a bit of tube."

"I'll take your word for it," said Maggie with a questionable look and a laugh. "Is surfer your third language?"

"You don't have to just take his word for it," Ian said, looking at her. "You're going to see for yourself."

"Wait, what?" Maggie's eyes widened.

"We brought the long board," Lance said. "The one you've been using."

"I don't have a wetsuit or anything," Maggie protested weakly.

"It's Mexico in summer." Ian laughed. "The water's warm enough for shorts and a T-shirt."

"I don't think—"

"Stop thinking," Ian interrupted, his eyes bright with that wild intensity. "Just feel."

Just feel. The words echoed in her mind as they pulled up to the beach. It was what she'd been avoiding for months—feeling anything too deeply.

Minutes later, Maggie was paddling out into the ocean, Ian beside her. Her arms ached, and her heart pounded with a mix of fear and excitement.

"This one," Ian called as a perfect, smooth wave approached. "Remember what I taught you. Paddle hard, then push up and stand in one motion."

I can't believe I'm doing this, Maggie thought as she dug her arms into the water, feeling the wave lift her.

Everything slowed down. She pushed up, wobbled, found her balance, and then …

She was standing. Flying. The wave carried her toward the shore, water rushing beneath her, wind in her hair. She heard Ian whooping behind her. Pure joy bubbled up from somewhere deep inside her.

"I'm doing it!" she screamed, raising her arms triumphantly—and promptly wiped out, tumbling into the warm water.

When she surfaced, Ian was there, grinning. "You were amazing! You rode it almost all the way in."

"I want to go again," Maggie said, surprising herself.

They surfed until the sun set, Maggie improving with each wave. By the end, she was exhausted but exhilarated, saltwater and happiness coursing through her veins.

As night fell and surfing ended, the Suburban headed into town. Their destination was Hussong's Cantina, reportedly the oldest cantina in Mexico and the birthplace of the margarita.

"I've seen the bumper stickers at home, but I've never actually been here," said Maggie, shifting uncomfortably in her still-damp clothes. Her muscles ached pleasantly from the surfing.

Lance opened the door to an old wooden building, revealing the aroma of stale beer, cigarette smoke, and the sound of loud, rowdy cheers.

"Welcome to Hussong's," said Lance. "Where the tide ebbs and flows with the drunk."

"Poetic." Maggie snorted, but she was already catching the infectious energy of the place.

To the right was a long wooden bar, the room's length, with leather-covered barstools. The rest of the room was filled with square tables and metal chairs. Caricature sketches of Americans wallpapered the walls. Waiters buzzed about the room with trays of tequila bottles and shot glasses.

"You're not going to believe this place," Ian shouted over the noise, leading her to a small table. "It's famous for a reason."

Ian motioned a waiter over to the table and purchased a bottle of tequila and two shot glasses for him and Maggie.

"To new experiences," Ian said, filling her glass. "And fearless women who stand up on surfboards."

"To adrenaline junkies who make me do crazy things," Maggie countered, clinking her glass against his before throwing back the shot. The tequila burned down her throat, warming her from the inside.

Three shots later, Maggie was feeling wonderfully lightheaded, the last of her inhibitions melting away. She leaned against Ian, watching the colorful characters around them.

"Check this out," said Lance, pointing to a man in a suit with a box contraption hanging around his neck. "He calls himself Juice Man. For two hundred pesos, he attaches electrodes to participants at the table. Everyone joins hands, and Juice Man cranks his box. The faster he cranks, the stronger the voltage. Whoever breaks the chain first buys a round of drinks."

"That can't be legal," Maggie said, but she was already standing up. "I'm in. Ian?"

"Are you serious?" Ian looked at her with surprise and delight.

"Deadly serious," Maggie said, pulling him up. "I've already surfed in Mexico today. Might as well get electrocuted too."

The Juice Man attached small metal clips to her fingers. Five minutes and a considerable shock later, Maggie was buying a round of drinks for their table and three strangers who'd joined their game. Her fingers still tingled, but she was laughing harder than she had in years.

Lance stepped up from the table. "I'll be back in about forty-five minutes," he said.

"Where are you going?" Maggie called after him.

"To make us some money." Lance winked and disappeared into the crowd.

Ian and Maggie remained at their table and watched as people of all types came and went—men, women, young, old—all drunk or on their way to get there.

"I like who I am when I'm with you," Maggie said suddenly, the tequila loosening her tongue. "I feel … alive."

Ian's eyes softened. "You were always this person, Maggie. You just forgot for a while."

Just before ten p.m., Lance returned to the cantina, wearing a souvenir sombrero. He threw down a wad of Mexican pesos on the table.

"Holy shit!" Maggie exclaimed, her eyes widening at the pile of money. "Where have you been?"

"The Foreign Bookie. On Saturday and Sunday nights, you can bet on horse races at Agua Caliente in Tijuana."

"You did well," said Maggie, picking up some bills. "Ian, did you know Lance was an expert gambler?"

"No. He appears to be a Renaissance man," Ian replied, eyeing the money with amusement.

"Let me try," Maggie said, grabbing a handful of pesos. "Take me there."

"It's getting late." Lance hesitated.

"Come on," Maggie insisted. "I'm feeling lucky. Must be all that surfing and electrocution."

What am I doing? she thought, but the rush of the day— surfing, the tequila, the shocks—had awakened something in her, a hunger for more sensation, more life.

Maggie stood in a smoky room full of men, watching a TV screen showing a horse race in Tijuana. She'd placed fifty pesos on a horse named, of all things, Lucky Charm at twenty to one odds.

"And it's Lucky Charm on the outside!" the announcer's voice crackled in Spanish over the speakers as her horse surged forward.

"Go, go, go!" Maggie screamed, jumping up and down, gripping Ian's arm so hard that he winced.

When Lucky Charm crossed the finish line first, Maggie's scream of triumph could probably be heard back in San Diego. She collected her winnings—a thousand fifty pesos—with excited hands.

"Let's find us the nicest hotel suite to spend the night with our winnings," said Maggie, her head spinning with tequila, adrenaline, and the strange, fantastic feeling that her life was finally moving forward again.

"I never want this day to end," Maggie whispered to Ian as they walked under the star-filled Mexican sky.

"It doesn't have to," he replied, pulling her close. "This is just the beginning."

Chapter Eleven

The Only Easy Day Was Yesterday

IAN WAS FINISHING UP HIS second phase of training. As usual, Maggie and Karma showed up at McP's on Sunday. Only this time, Karma brought along Levi. Surprisingly, Ian and Levi got along quite well.

"My older brother is a Deadhead," Ian said to Maggie. "I get his vibe. He's a little left of center, but so is Karma."

"Agreed," said Maggie, watching the two men talk animatedly about concert venues. It was nice to see different parts of her life come together, as if she were building something new, piece by piece.

Julia walked up to the table. "Does anybody have weed? I need to chill out. My parents keep calling me, begging me to return home."

Levi popped up from the table.

"Let me escort you to my office," he said, slinging his arm around Julia's shoulders and guiding her to the back of the building.

"Let's go to the bar and share a shot to celebrate the end of phase two," said Ian, his eyes holding a different intensity than usual when they met Maggie's.

"Karma, do you mind?" asked Maggie, feeling a flutter of anticipation in her stomach.

Something was different today. The way Ian was looking at Maggie …

"Of course not," said Karma, giving Maggie a knowing smile. "I'll enjoy my Guinness while I wait for Pablo Escobar to make his sale. You two go ahead. I feel magic in the air."

The two headed toward the bar. Ian's arm wrapped affectionately around Maggie's body. His touch felt electric through the thin fabric of her shirt, and she leaned into him, savoring the closeness. They had been together almost two months, but they hadn't … gone all the way yet.

Is tonight the night?

"Bartender," said Ian, "we'll have two shots of Sex on the Beach."

"What the hell?" responded Maggie, feeling her cheeks flush at the suggestive name.

"It's Chambord, green melon liqueur, lime, and pineapple juice," said Ian, his eyes twinkling mischievously.

"I'm in," said Maggie.

Was this his way of hinting? Subtle. Real *subtle*.

The bartender delivered the shots. Ian and Maggie each grabbed a shot glass.

"I propose a toast," said Ian. "To the future."

Our future, Maggie thought, a warmth spreading through her chest that had nothing to do with the alcohol. She was starting to believe in that again.

"It tastes sweet but a little bit sour," said Maggie. "Is that what our future has in store for us?"

"Of course not. Nothing but the best for us, baby," said Ian.

Maggie studied his face—the confidence in his eyes, the curve of his lips. She trusted him, she realized. *Completely.* When had that happened?

"How about we have sex … on the beach?" proposed Maggie with a giggle, surprising herself with her boldness.

Ian, his mouth breaking into a grin, grabbed his backpack, and the two walked out of McP's, hand in hand. They headed toward The Dunes, the closest beach to the bar. Palm trees swayed sensually in the breeze as the late afternoon sun kissed the crests of falling waves in the surf.

This is really happening, Maggie thought, her heart pounding.

She had never felt this way about anyone before. She'd follow him anywhere, trust him with anything—even *this*.

Once on the beach, Ian pulled out a blanket from his pack and laid it gently on the sand. The two sat down. Next, he pulled out a bottle of Veuve Clicquot Brut champagne. He popped the cork and poured champagne into two plastic glasses, handing one to Maggie.

"I get the impression this was preplanned, Seaman Murphy," said Maggie, taking the glass.

He'd thought about this. Prepared for it. For us.

"You've heard our motto …" said Ian.

"No, enlighten me," answered Maggie.

"No sky too high, no sea too rough, no muff too tough," he replied.

"Wow!" said Maggie. "You give Shakespeare a run for his money."

So much for romance, she thought, but she was laughing.

His irreverence was part of what she loved about him.

Ian started singing, "*Oh, sweet Maggie. Won't you lie with me tonight? The stars are out. It will be so right.*"

"Oh my! Eric Clapton just called. He wants his song lyrics back." But she wanted him to keep singing anyway. She loved the sound of his voice. She loved that Ian was trying to make this special.

As day turned into night, the sun fell into the Pacific Ocean, creating a deep, bright rusty-orange glow with a copper undertone. Ian and Maggie lay back on the sandy blanket. It was *perfect* as they looked up at the sky above them. It was like a scene from a movie, but not. It was her life.

Ian took off his shirt and leaned in to kiss her. Maggie could smell the salty sea on his chest, fresh from his morning surf. It was a scent she would never forget—salt and sun and Ian. A mixture of nervousness and excitement overwhelmed her.

Maggie wanted this—*him*. She had been waiting for the right person, the right moment. This was it. This felt right.

He gently removed her T-shirt and bra. Her nipples hardened as he blew air on them, making them sensitive to the touch.

No going back now, she thought, feeling suddenly vulnerable under the open sky. But there was no fear, only trust and desire.

He tenderly attached his mouth over each breast, alternating equally between them and caressing and sucking.

I never knew it could feel like this, Maggie thought, her mind spinning with new sensations.

Ian pulled down her skirt and bikini bottoms.

All of me. No barriers between us now. She felt a moment of shyness, then pride as she saw the appreciation in his eyes.

He slid down and put his mouth between her legs. Maggie could feel the wetness and warmth of her core. She could hear the lapping sounds of Ian's tongue inside her, licking and sucking.

Oh God, she thought, her mind barely able to form coherent thoughts. *Is this what everyone has been talking about all this time? Why didn't anyone tell me it would be this ... overwhelming?*

Ian flicked his tongue along her clitoris with precision. Her body felt like it had just been plugged into an electric circuit. The power and intensity of energy flowed through her from head to toe. Every nerve ending tingling. Her moist core screamed with desire.

It's like surfing, she thought wildly. That same rush, that same feeling of letting go completely.

Just at the right moment, Ian entered his large shaft inside her. The sudden pressure brought her back to reality.

"Go easy," said Maggie. "This is my first time."

She had wanted it to be with someone special. Someone who mattered.

Someone like you, Ian Murphy.

Ian pulled back, a little surprised but pleased at the same time.

"In the words of the Frogmen," he whispered, "the only easy day was yesterday."

So, this is what it means to give yourself to someone, Maggie thought as they moved together. *Not just your body, but your trust. Your vulnerability.*

The pain was there, but so was pleasure, building slowly.

My mom always said I'd know when it was right, she thought, tears pricking her eyes, not from pain, but from emotion. Maggie wished she could tell her she was right, that she had indeed waited for the right person.

As they moved together under the stars, Maggie felt something inside her shift and heal. Sex wasn't just physical; it was letting someone else in, trusting them with your body, your heart. After years of keeping people at a distance, of protecting herself from more loss, she was opening up again and taking a risk. Living.

This is what it means to move forward, she realized. *To build new memories. New connections.*

Her mom would want this for her …

And at that moment, with the waves crashing nearby and Ian's heartbeat against hers, Maggie was precisely that. Happy. Present. Alive.

Chapter Twelve

EMERSON WHO?

GOD, HE LOOKS DAMN GOOD in those shorts, Maggie thought, taking in Ian's athletic frame as he approached her in the YB lobby.

"Good morning, Lou," said Maggie. "I'd like you to meet Ian."

Lou extended his hand through the registration window. "Pleasure to meet you, Ian," said Lou.

"The pleasure is all mine," said Ian, shaking Lou's hand. "Maggie speaks highly of you."

"Well, I speak highly of Maggie," said Lou. "Where are you kids heading this fine morning?"

"Fiesta Island," said Maggie. "Heading to Over the Line."

"You an OTL virgin, Ian?" asked Lou.

"Yes, sir," said Ian.

"Oh boy. You're in for a treat! Cheer on my teams. Stop Laughing It Gets Bigger, Everybody's Gonna Touch It, and my favorite, Dixie Normous."

Lou broke into a raucous, belly-laughing fit.

Lou, Maggie thought with a mixture of affection and embarrassment. Always pushing the envelope. She did love him though.

"Maggie, stay hydrated," said Lou. "There's no shade out there. Remember, for every beer, a glass of water."

"Yes, Mother Lou," said Maggie.

He was always looking out for her, and she was touched by his concern despite his crass humor. Her dad was always too drunk to notice.

"And don't show your titties for a free drink," Lou counseled. "You are classier than that!"

Jesus, Lou! Maggie cringed internally, feeling her cheeks flush. She shot Lou a warning glance, though she knew it wouldn't stop him.

"This is going to be fun!" said Ian.

Maggie glanced at Ian, surprised by his easy acceptance of Lou's crude humor. Ian seemed to take it in stride.

"Have you seen my dad?" asked Maggie.

"Yes, ma'am," said Lou. "He came down about an hour ago. Said he was headed to Star Bar for the breakfast special."

Maggie rolled her eyes at Ian.

Of course he is—the "breakfast special" at ten a.m.

"Let's go, Ian," said Maggie. "Bye, Lou. Have a nice afternoon."

"I shall," said Lou.

Maggie and Ian walked out of the YB. Maggie stopped for a moment and glanced at Ian.

"Ian?" said Maggie. "Would you like to meet my dad?"

Her heart raced slightly as she asked. She hadn't introduced any man to her father, but something about Ian made her want to include him in more aspects of her life.

"Absolutely," said Ian. "Would love to meet the man, the myth, the legend."

"He's not a legend," said Maggie. "Unless you consider his drinking capacity. He's my dad. I want you to meet him."

Please don't be too drunk, Dad, she silently pleaded. *Just this once.*

"Destination: Star Bar," said Ian.

Star Bar was the quintessential dive bar located at 423 E. Street. Maggie and Ian entered the dimly lit bar, enveloped in a smoky haze and the sound of The Who's "Pinball Wizard" on the jukebox. The bar screamed red from the moment you opened the red front door. Inside were red leather seat covers on the barstools and booth seating, a red cloth on the pool table, red walls, and neon red Star Bar and beer signs. The red carpet on the floor and the year-round red tinsel and paper stars hanging from the ceiling completed the baroque, house-of-ill-repute distinction.

Maggie had practically grown up in the place. The familiar smell of stale beer and cigarettes brought back memories. Waiting for her dad after school; doing homework in the back booth while he nursed his fourth or fifth beer; Aurora, the bartender, slipping her Shirley Temples with extra cherries.

The left side of the bar resembled an altar to hard liquor, stacked high with any standard handle you could name. On the right were seventeen taps of mainstream beers and Curly smoking a cigarette.

"Good morning, Dad," said Maggie. "Hello, Aurora."

Aurora was a petite Filipina woman with long, dark hair and silicone-enhanced breasts. She'd started behind the bar in her early twenties. Aurora looked out for Curly. Many a night, Aurora ensured Curly returned to his doorstep after the bar closed.

Thank God for Aurora. She'd kept him alive all these years.

"Well, hey there, Maggie," said Curly.

Maggie studied her father's face. He seemed steady today, only a beer or two in. Relief washed over her.

"Dad … Aurora," said Maggie, "I'd like you to meet Ian."

Ian shook hands with Curly and Aurora.

"Love the breakfast special, sir," said Ian. "A pint of beer and chips."

Smooth, Maggie thought approvingly. *He's trying to connect with Dad.*

"Breakfast of champions," said Curly.

"Aurora," said Ian, "Maggie tells me you've been tending bar here for thirty-plus years. I'm sure you have some great stories."

"Ah, Ian," said Aurora. "That's part of the charm of this place. You might be sitting next to a San Diego Padres baseball player, a celebrity, or a homeless person. All are welcome here. Except that bitch!"

Maggie glanced over at the Vietnamese woman behind the hard liquor bar.

"That's Ling," said Maggie. "Aurora and Ling have a long-standing rivalry. It got so bad that the owner created a second bar to separate them. Their feud is the longest-running show in town. It's been going on since I was in elementary school."

"Rusty, stop pissing on the floor," yelled Ling to a disheveled customer sitting in a back booth.

"I come for the cheap beer," said Curly. "Plus, it reminds me of the bars in Vietnam."

And he comes to escape his memories, Maggie thought sadly. The ones he never talked about.

"Enjoy your nostalgia, Dad," said Maggie. "We're heading out."

"I'm going to hit the head," said Ian.

While Ian was gone, Curly leaned closer to Maggie.

"He seems like a good one," he said quietly.

Maggie was surprised by her father's approval. "You think?"

"Yes, I do," Curly said. "I hope he makes you happy. You deserve to be happy, Magpie."

Maggie smiled, touched by her father's observation. Maybe he paid more attention than she gave him credit for.

Maggie chatted with her dad and Aurora until Ian returned, and they left the bar.

"Interesting erotica dispenser in the restroom," said Ian.

"You should see what they have in the ladies' room." Maggie laughed.

"This will be the twenty-seventh edition of OTL," Maggie explained on the drive to the island in Ian's sunburned brown Silverado truck.

With the wind in her hair and the sun on her skin, Maggie felt a lightness while feeling anchored. She felt good, she realized. Easy.

"It's a boozy beach party, invented by the OMBAC—Old Mission Beach Athletic Club guys. They sponsor volleyball tournaments, rugby games, surfing contests, and OTL. You probably picked up that the more suggestive and risqué the team names for OTL, the better. Their offices are at The Pennant and Beachcomber, side-by-side neighborhood drinking holes in South Mission Beach."

The Silverado pulled into a parking space, joining the thousands of people who descended on the island for the tournament. On the way to the bar, they passed the spectator rules sign—*No bottles, bowsers (dogs), babies, bikes, or bad attitudes.* Three beautifully tanned and toned young ladies wearing bikinis walked past, one wearing red, one yellow, and one blue with an M&M on each breast. Two men walked by, one in a clown suit and the other dressed as the Tin Man. A woman also passed by, wearing a bikini and a sash that read *Miss Emerson 1979.*

To think, she had always wanted to be Miss Emerson when she was younger. Maggie had a nostalgic smile.

"What's Miss Emerson?" asked Ian.

"It's a competition to choose the spokesmodel for OMBAC," explained Maggie. "She's little sister to the OMBAC guys, and she gets to put up with their immature behavior. The winner also gets her name on the highly revered Titty Trophy."

The Titty Trophy was comprised of two squishy, jiggling, flesh-colored rubber boobies, perched atop the tower of past winner names. The history behind the name was that one of the OMBAC guys had passed a woman with large breasts at OTL and asked if she was Emerson.

He'd then proceeded to tell the knock-knock joke. "Guy says, 'Knock, knock.' The girl says, 'Who's there?' Guy says, 'Emerson.' The girl says, 'Emerson who?' Guy says, 'Emerson, nice titties.' "

This place was crazy, but she was smiling. She loved it.

Maggie and Ian sat down in the sand with beers and hot dogs to watch a game. Maggie felt Ian's arm brush against hers as they sat close together. The casual contact sent a pleasant shiver down her spine.

She explained how the game was played. "There are three players to a side," she said. "Like in baseball, each side bats while the other is in the field. A batter stands at the triangle's peak, drawn in the sand, and swings at softballs gently tossed to them by a teammate who kneels roughly one foot away."

"Where are the bases?" asked Ian.

"There are no physical bases to run," said Maggie. "The line is about fifty-five feet from the batter. The batter has to hit the large rectangle in the sand beyond the line, known as fair territory, without a fielder catching it. One run is scored after three hits in an inning. One more run is scored for each extra hit in the same inning. Home runs clear the bases."

"Are they doing Jell-O shots?" asked Ian, motioning to the team players.

"Yeah," said Maggie. "They're allowed to drink while playing. It gets a little dangerous as the day continues and the drinking continues. I've seen more than a few bloody noses and twisted ankles over the years. Not to mention sunburns and alcohol poisoning."

"As Good as We Once Was is up next," said the announcer.

"They're not English majors." Maggie laughed.

Ian's fingers intertwined with Maggie's, and she let them stay there, enjoying the warmth of his hand in hers. When he turned to smile at her, she felt her heart skip.

"Thanks for bringing me here," he said.

"It's not exactly high society," Maggie said, self-conscious of the obscene names and boisterous atmosphere.

"It's authentic," Ian said. "Like you."

"I'm not sure who the authentic Maggie is anymore," she admitted, surprising herself with the candor. "After my mom's death … I'm still figuring that out."

Ian squeezed her hand. "Well, I'm enjoying getting to know this version of you."

Maggie leaned against his shoulder, feeling a sense of peace she hadn't expected. Ian wrapped his arm around her.

"Want to grab another beer?" she asked.

"Sure," Ian said. "But first …"

He leaned in slowly, and Maggie drew closer to him. Their kiss tasted of beer and promise.

Chapter Thirteen

If Tattoos Could Speak ...

CUSTOMERS LINED UP OUTSIDE THE door of The Lion's Den. Servicemen were getting permanent reminders of their military experience and brotherhood. Maggie enjoyed watching as stories surfaced on their skin, revealing what was important to them, their backgrounds, and their interests. The names of fallen comrades, Bible verses, unit insignia, children's names, flags, rifles, and eagles all had profound personal meaning. Remembrance was a recurring theme, whether it was family love, patriotic expression, unit pride, or honoring a fallen comrade. Maggie watched a young Marine receive the emblem of his unit and thought there was something honest about tattoos. The marks represented deliberate choices to create something permanent. This mattered enough to carry forever.

Maggie finished cashing out a customer at the counter. When she looked up, Ian and Julia were the next customers.

"What a nice surprise!" she said. "What brings you guys downtown?"

Ian didn't mention he was coming by today. A mixture of pleasure and confusion cascaded through her. *And with Julia, of all people.*

"I'd like to get a tattoo," said Julia. "Ian offered to drive me since I'd had more than a few tequila shots to build up my courage."

Tequila, really? And Ian drove her?

Maggie felt an unexpected twinge of something—not quite jealousy, but discomfort.

"Well, you came to the right place," said Maggie. "As you can see, we're quite busy tonight. I can fit you in before we close at ten, but it will take a couple of hours. Why don't you get a bite to eat and come back?"

"Sounds great," said Ian.

Ian and Julia turned around and exited the shop. Maggie's eyes zoomed in on Julia's tight Jordache jeans. *The jeans look painted on.* She caught herself staring and quickly shifted her gaze back to the counter. *Why had she even noticed that?*

"Was that the arrogant Irishman?" asked Bobby.

"Yes, but he's not arrogant. We've been dating for over two months." It felt longer, somehow like she had known him forever.

"Who's the girl?"

"She's a friend. Her name is Julia."

"Hmm, Ian's friend?"

"Yes, of course." *Why did I say "of course" like that?* Maggie questioned herself.

They were allowed to be friends.

"I don't know, Maggie. Men have a hard time being friends with women—unless they're men like me. Gay men."

"Bobby, don't be silly. Julia's friends with all the guys at McP's."

"My point exactly."

Bobby's words lingered in Maggie's mind as she worked through the next few customers. She'd never given much thought to Ian and Julia's friendship before. Julia was just part of the McP's crowd—loud, fun, always the life of the party. But now, watching the clock and knowing they were out to dinner together, Maggie felt an unsettling feeling in her stomach.

Stop it, she chided herself. *Ian's been nothing but honest.*

Only one customer remained in the chair when Ian and Julia returned. Julia perused the many art options and selected a butterfly with Celtic vines for her lower back. Maggie locked the shop door and flipped the sign to *Closed*. Just as Julia was about to lie face down on the chair, Ian handed her a flask. Julia opened the top and took a long sip.

Maggie noticed the easy familiarity between them, the way Ian anticipated Julia's needs. How well did they really know each other?

"For reinforcement," Julia said with a laugh.

Bobby explained the procedures to Julia and started the job while Maggie and Ian sat in the club chairs at the opposite end of the room. Ian told Maggie about dinner at The Old Spaghetti Factory, where he and Julia had sat inside an antique trolley car.

"Julia, being from New York, was not impressed with the food," said Ian. "But she loved the ambiance."

They share inside jokes and memories I'm not a part of, Maggie thought, struggling to maintain her casual expression. Was she being ridiculous? *Two friends had dinner. So what?*

"How's work going, Julia?" asked Maggie, hoping to steer the conversation to neutral territory.

"Great! I've never done so many perms in my life. I don't understand the requests for the mullet and the rat tail though. Californians have strange ideas about hair. What do they say back home? *California is like granola. Take away the fruits and nuts; all you have left are the flakes.*"

Maggie forced a smile, though the joke grated on her. New Yorkers and their superiority complex. As if Julia were above it all.

"Karma says Levi's been delivering not only pot, but also cocaine and quaaludes to Julia twice a week. Seems like she's keeping Levi busy, if you know what I mean."

Why was she telling Ian this? She felt confident that Ian had no idea about the extent of Julia's drug use. Was she trying to make Julia look bad?

That's not like me.

She studied Ian's face for a reaction, but his expression remained neutral.

"Did she say anything else?" asked Ian.

The question struck Maggie as oddly specific. What else would there be? He didn't even question Julia's drug use.

"No. *Is* there something else?"

"No, not at all."

But his tone wasn't convincing. Maggie could hear the false note in his voice, the slight tension. Over the years, she'd developed a radar for half-truths, thanks to her dad. There was something Ian wasn't telling her about Julia. Why was he hanging out with Julia alone? Was Bobby right about men having a hard time being friends with women?

There was a story here she wasn't privy to, Maggie realized. Something more than friendship.

Bobby finished the tattoo and waited for the Polaroid photo to develop.

"I thought Julia was one hundred percent Italian," said Maggie, probing gently.

"She is," said Ian.

"I get the butterfly representing her freedom flight from New York to California, but why the Celtic vine?"

Why choose something Irish unless it's meaningful? Maggie wondered. *Unless it's about Ian.*

"She says McP's has a special place in her heart."

"Well, it now has a special place on her back." *Or maybe it's Ian who has a special place in her heart,* Maggie thought, but kept the words to herself.

Instead, she cleaned up while Bobby applied the bandage to Julia's newly inked skin.

As Julia stood up, slightly wobbly from the tequila and the endorphin rush from the tattoo, Ian steadied her with a hand on her elbow. The gesture was casual but intimate—the kind of touch that came from familiarity.

"We should get you home," Ian said to Julia. "You need to rest."

"My hero," Julia said with a grin that seemed, to Maggie's increasingly suspicious mind, a bit too adoring.

"I'll call you tomorrow," Ian told Maggie, giving her a quick kiss on the cheek.

"Sure," Maggie replied, her voice carefully neutral. "Drive safe."

After they left, Bobby raised an eyebrow at her. "You okay?"

"Fine," Maggie said automatically. Then, after a moment's hesitation, she asked, "Did you notice anything … off about them?"

Bobby's expression softened. "Honey, I've watched people's body language for twenty years. Those two have history."

"What kind of history?"

"I don't know. But there's something there that's not just McP's friends."

Maggie nodded slowly, processing this confirmation of her suspicions. "I'm probably overthinking it."

"Maybe," Bobby said, not sounding convinced. "Or maybe your radar is better than you think."

As Maggie locked up the shop, she replayed the evening—Julia's laughter, Ian's attentiveness, the Celtic vines winding around the butterfly on Julia's skin. For the first time since they'd started dating, Maggie felt a seed of doubt about Ian taking root.

Was she overthinking it? Or did she not want to believe it was real? Should she confront Ian about his relationship with Julia? She hadn't wanted to ask him about his relationship with Julia because part of her feared the answer. Confronting him might mean risking another disappointment, another heartbreak.

As she walked down Fifth Avenue under the dim streetlights, Maggie decided to talk to Karma tomorrow. Karma would tell her she was being paranoid. Ian was crazy about her. She had nothing to worry about.

Chapter Fourteen

BLIND NO MORE

MAGGIE AND IAN WERE INSEPARABLE. Ian had convinced her that she was his only love interest. His feelings for Julia were nothing more than those of a sister.

When she wasn't working at The Lion's Den, Maggie spent most of her time on Coronado Island. Her life was intoxicating. Free from the grime and filth of Fifth Avenue, she relished her mornings lying on the sand, watching Ian surf. Her evenings were spent on his couch, watching movies or reading, cuddling up next to the man who had turned her world right side up again.

He found me when I was drowning in grief, Maggie thought, watching him ride a wave to shore one morning.

After her mom died, she had been going through the motions. Ian pulled her back to the surface. He understood her pain as real and valid without trying to fix it. He had shown her the path back to the land of the living.

Sunday afternoons were always spent at McP's. Maggie enjoyed listening to Ian's fellow recruits discuss their training and pranks. How they found so much pleasure in punking their pals were beyond her comprehension. She supposed it was their way of blowing off steam. The rigorous program required more than just physical stamina; it also required mental grit. Olympic athletes had tried and failed. Sometimes, Karma and

Levi would join them on Sundays, but it didn't matter to Maggie. She was at peace. Ian got her. He had saved her. He gave her permission to laugh again. To enjoy life without feeling guilty that her mother couldn't.

On the last Saturday in August, Maggie was scheduled to work at The Lion's Den. A Navy ship docked at the pier was getting ready to set sail. Marines and sailors would be lined up outside, waiting to get their tattoos before leaving the city. When she arrived at the tattoo studio, a middle-aged man was sitting in the chair, and two college-aged boys were waiting in line.

"Where is everyone, Bobby?" she asked.

"Beats me," Bobby replied. "The ship must be in a security lockdown. There might be a firearm missing, a bomb threat, or an active threat against the shipyard."

Around nine p.m., it was clear that business would not pick up. Bobby told Maggie that she could take off for the night if she wished.

"Thanks, Bobby," she said. "With school starting next week, I want to spend as much time as possible with Ian."

She thought about phoning Ian to tell him she was coming over early, but decided to surprise him. He loved surprises, and she loved the look on his face when she showed up unexpectedly.

After taking the ferry from Broadway Pier, she rode her bike up to Ian's townhouse. The lights were not on in the upstairs living room.

Did he decide to go out with the guys? she thought, a slight frown crossing her face.

The light was on in Ian's downstairs bedroom. She propped her bike against the house, rounded the corner, and peeked in to see if he had fallen asleep. She took a step back in horror and disbelief. Lying on the bed, a man and woman were naked, arms and legs entwined. She recognized the tattoo on the small of the woman's back. She blinked her eyes and took another look. Yes, it was, in fact, Ian and Julia.

A knot seized her stomach like a tight cramp. Betrayal pierced and seared her heart.

No, no, no, her mind screamed. *Not this. Not him. Not when I've already lost so much.*

The Celtic vines. The butterfly. The tattoo she herself had watched Bobby ink onto Julia's skin. There was no mistaking it.

I should have known, she thought, bile rising in her throat. *Bobby was right. The signs were all there. History, he said. They have history.*

Her thoughts raced, each one a fresh wound. The flask. The inside jokes. How Julia was "friends" with all the guys at McP's. The way he'd steadied her after the tattoo.

Maggie had been so stupid. So willfully blind.

Think, Maggie. Think.

She took a moment to compose herself and then put her key in the door.

"Surprise!" she shouted. "Ian! Are you home?"

Let them scramble, she thought viciously. *Let them panic.*

Silence.

Her heart raced so hard that she thought it might burst from her chest. She dug her nails into her sweaty palms, feeling the pulse of adrenaline coursing through her veins. She was starting to feel whole again. The grief from her mother's death was becoming bearable.

You bastard.

She heard Ian's footsteps climbing the stairs. He turned the corner and walked into the kitchen. Julia was right behind him.

Look at them, she thought. *Not even a hint of shame. Do they think I'm blind? Stupid?*

"Hey, Maggie," said Ian. "You're here early!"

As if nothing had happened. As if she hadn't just seen them together.

"Yeah. It was a slow night," she said. "Bobby let me leave early. Julia, what a surprise to see you here at this late hour."

Play along, Maggie. Don't let them know you saw. Not yet.

"Actually," Julia stumbled to say, "I came over to see if the two of you would like to go for a night swim in the ocean. It's a full moon tonight, and it's been so stiflingly hot lately. I thought it might be a fun way to end the summer."

Quick thinking, Maggie thought.

But she saw right through them.

"Wow!" Maggie blurted. "That's a great idea. Let me go down and get my swimsuit. I assume you brought yours, Julia?"

How far would their charade go?

"I've got an idea," interjected Ian. "Let's go skinny-dipping."

Of course. Might as well be naked with both of them. Why choose?

The ride from the townhouse to The Dunes was an extremely long four minutes.

I should confront them now, she thought, staring out the window at the passing streetlights.

But no. Not here. Not trapped in the truck with them.

Maggie struggled to rein in her anger. She would play this out until the end, then have her say with Ian.

Keep breathing, she told herself. *Just keep breathing.*

Her mom had always said not to make decisions when angry.

Maggie was not angry. She was pissed.

The full moon spread its shine over the roar and rumble of the ocean as the trio entered the water, a mystic shimmer seemingly casting a spell over the evening. Maggie glanced curtly at Ian's perfectly chiseled form as the waves crashed against his body.

How could he? she thought as a fresh stab of pain cut through her chest. How could Ian do this to her when he knew how vulnerable she was?

She felt the strength of the ocean before her feet were completely wet. The waves were immeasurably bigger than usual. Out past the break of the waves, the three bobbed in the water. Trying to keep the conversation going, Ian rattled off the stats for the Padres. His passionate attempt failed. Finally, he conceded and told the girls he would body surf into shore.

Coward, Maggie thought. Running away when things got uncomfortable.

Once Ian was gone, Maggie stared intently at Julia.

"I know what's going on here," said Maggie. "I saw you two together."

"Of course you saw us together back at the townhouse," said Julia.

She was playing dumb. Testing to see what Maggie really knew.

"No!" Maggie spit. "I saw the tramp stamp you have on your lower back. I saw you in bed with Ian." *There. It's out now. No more pretending.*

Julia smirked. "It wasn't the first time. Where do you think he spends Saturday nights while you're working? Ian loves me. He's breaking up with you."

Every Saturday? The thought hit Maggie like a slap to the face. All those nights she had been at the shop … they were together?

"You are a lying bitch!"

But is she lying? a voice in Maggie's head wondered.

Or had Ian been playing them both?

Maggie started splashing and pushing Julia.

"Stop!" Julia cried. "I'm pregnant."

Pregnant? The word exploded in Maggie's mind like a grenade. *No. It can't be. He wouldn't …*

But even as she denied it, Maggie knew it could be true. The way Julia had been avoiding alcohol lately, except for that one night at the tattoo studio, and the whispered conversations that stopped when she approached.

Something snapped inside Maggie. She pounced on Julia and pushed down on her shoulders until her head submerged.

Shut up! Just shut up! her mind screamed.

Her hands, holding Julia underwater, felt as though they belonged to someone else, disconnected from her body. The raw grief of losing her mother, the betrayal from Ian—it all converged into a white-hot rage that pulsed through her veins.

Is any of this true? It couldn't be. Maggie refused to believe it.

A flash of clarity cut through her rage. *What am I doing? I'm drowning her. I'm actually drowning her.*

Maggie released Julia, glancing back to see her head pop above the water. She heard Julia gasp for air and plead with Maggie to help her back to shore. She caught the next wave. Vigorous and powerful, the water reflected her state of mind. Water rushed past her body, gravity pulling her down with relentless force. Swirling and spinning, Maggie was dragged toward the beach. Her body finally skidded onto the shore, and she lay face down, sand grinding against her, the sting of salt in her mouth and eyes. She felt exhausted, both physically and mentally, a wave of defeat washing over her.

Ian appeared and helped her to her feet.

"Where's Julia?" he questioned.

He doesn't know, she realized. *He didn't see what I almost did.*

"I left her alone," she said. "Something you should have done."

"Maggie, what did you do?" he pleaded. "Julia's not as strong of a swimmer as you."

Oh God, she thought.

What if she couldn't make it back? What if she was drowning right now?

"What did *I* do?!" screamed Maggie. "It's what you did. You fucked her."

And now Julia might be dead because of it. Because of her. Because she had lost control, just like her dad used to.

"Oh my God, Maggie," he said, panicking. "Go. Just go. I'll take care of this. You were never here."

He was protecting her, she realized with a sickening lurch. Even now, after everything, he was trying to protect her.

But it wasn't enough. Nothing would ever be enough to erase what had happened—what she had done.

Maggie approached her pile of clothing and pulled on her jeans and T-shirt, saltwater dripping from her body. She walked across the street to the pay phone outside McP's and made a collect call to Karma.

What should she tell her?

Maggie wondered if she might have killed someone because she had lost control.

"Hey, doll. What's up?" said Karma after accepting the call.

"Karma," she breathed into the phone. "Can you please come pick me up outside McP's?" She should tell her everything now. But the words wouldn't come. How did she explain to Karma what she'd done?

As she waited for Karma, Maggie's gaze returned to the beach. She could see Ian's silhouette, pacing the shoreline, wading back into the water, searching. Her heart hammered in her chest.

Please let Julia be okay, she prayed. *Please don't let me be a murderer. Mom, if you can hear me, I'm so sorry.*

The minutes ticked by with no sign of Julia emerging from the waves, and the horrible truth began to sink in. Three bodies had gone into the water that night. Only two came back out.

Chapter Fifteen
WHAT HAVE I DONE?

MAGGIE LAY IN BED, STARING at the ceiling of her room. Sleep wouldn't come. Whenever she closed her eyes, she saw Julia's face disappearing beneath the dark water. The look of shock in her eyes. The bubbles rising to the surface.

What have I done? The question echoed in her mind, unanswerable and damning. *Dear God, what have I done?* The thought pounded in her head like a hammer.

She'd pushed a woman—a pregnant woman—underwater in a fit of rage. Even after she let go, Julia was treading water when Maggie swam away. The ocean had been rough that night. The undertow strong.

She reached for the Sunday newspaper on her nightstand. The morning edition had arrived early, and she'd snatched it from the lobby before anyone else could see. Her hands trembled as she unfolded it, scanning the headlines.

Nothing. No mention of a drowning. No reports of a body washing up on shore.

That didn't mean anything. It could take days to find Julia. Or maybe she was still out there, somewhere in the ocean.

She rolled onto her side, hugging her pillow tightly. "I didn't mean to hurt her," she whispered to the empty room. "I was just so angry."

The image of Ian and Julia together flashed in her mind. The betrayal stung, but it seemed trivial now compared to what might have happened afterward.

Did Ian find her? Did he get to her in time?

Maggie considered calling Ian, but couldn't pick up the phone. What would she say? *Hey, just checking if Julia's still alive.* The thought made her stomach turn.

She got up and paced the small room, her bare feet silent on the wood floor. Outside her window, the first streaks of dawn were appearing. She'd been up all night, replaying the events over and over.

I'm not a murderer, she told herself.

She had let her go. She had stopped. But she left Julia out there. The ocean had been so dark, so angry that night.

Maggie paused at the window, pressing her forehead against the cool glass.

When Karma dropped her off at the YB last night, she found Lou sitting solo in the lobby, smoking a cigarette. He could tell by the distraught look on her face that something had happened. Still reeling from the shock of the evening, she slumped into a chair next to Lou.

"Do you want to talk about it?" asked Lou, intentionally not facing Maggie.

"No," said Maggie, fidgeting in her damp clothes.

"Bad things happen," said Lou. "It's how you deal with them that matters."

She needed to know what had happened. She needed to face whatever she had done.

With trembling fingers, she picked up the phone and dialed Ian's number, bracing herself for whatever news might come.

The phone rang five times before she hung up. *Chicken,* she thought to herself.

But there was something else gnawing at her—her bike. She'd ridden it to Ian's yesterday, left it leaning against his house when she discovered him with Julia. In her shock and the chaos that followed, she'd completely forgotten about it.

I need my bike, she thought, running her hands through her tangled hair. She couldn't just leave it at Ian's—a physical reminder of her presence there on that terrible night.

"You were never here." Ian's words echoed in her mind.

Maggie glanced at the clock—six fifteen a.m. Early enough that she might avoid running into Ian if he were even home. Maybe he was still out searching. Maybe he was at the police station, reporting what she'd done.

She pulled on jeans and a sweatshirt and slipped quietly out of her room, down the stairs, and out of the YB. The morning air was cool and damp with fog, and the streets were nearly empty. She took the ferry to the island and walked the fifteen blocks to Ian's house. She rehearsed what she would say if she were to encounter him.

I just came for my bike, she would say matter-of-factly—no questions about Julia, no accusations about their betrayal. *Just get the bike and leave.*

But as Ian's house came into view, her heart hammered in her chest. What if Julia was there? What if she was fine, and Maggie had spent the night torturing herself for nothing? Or worse, what if she wasn't fine, and the police were already looking for Maggie?

Maggie retrieved her bike without incident. Ian's house was quiet, with no car in the driveway. She pedaled away as fast as her legs could carry her, the morning fog providing a welcome cover.

The day passed in a haze of anxiety. She'd called in sick to work, unable to face anyone, spending the hours alternating between fitful naps and obsessively checking the local radio and news for updates. Nothing about a drowning. Nothing about Julia.

By evening, Maggie had convinced herself that everything must be okay. Julia had survived. Ian had found her. Maybe they were together right now, plotting their future without Maggie in it.

Three days later, Maggie sat in the YB's common area, pretending to read a magazine while the evening news played on the television. Lou and a handful of other residents were there, half watching the screen.

"And in local news tonight"—the anchor's voice suddenly cut through Maggie's thoughts—"the body of a woman was recovered from the ocean on Silver Strand State Beach, south of the city of Coronado, this afternoon. Police have identified the victim as a twenty-four-year-old woman."

The magazine slipped from Maggie's fingers. Around her, the conversation continued, no one paying particular attention to the news, but for Maggie, the room had gone silent, except for the anchor's voice.

"Authorities believe Julia Franco might have drowned while swimming after dark, which officials remind the public is extremely dangerous, especially given the strong rip currents in the area."

A photo of Julia appeared on the screen—a vibrant, smiling woman with curly, long, dark hair. Not the Julia that Maggie had last seen, face twisted in panic as the water closed over her head.

"The investigation is ongoing. Anyone with information is asked to contact the Coronado Police Department."

The room spun. She gripped the arms of her chair, trying to steady herself.

I killed her. I killed her.

"You okay, Maggie?" Lou's voice seemed to come from miles away. "You look like you've seen a ghost."

"I-I'm fine," she managed to say, though her voice sounded foreign to her ears. "Just tired."

She stumbled to her feet, needing to get away—away from the news, away from Lou's perceptive eyes. In her room, she collapsed against the closed door, sliding down until she sat on the floor.

What have I done?

When Karma picked her up that night, she recounted the events of the evening through tears of fear and apprehension—catching Ian and Julia in bed together, skinny-dipping, the pregnancy, and fighting with Julia in the water. The question echoed in her mind, but this time, there was no ambiguity, no maybes. Julia was dead. And Maggie felt responsible.

Chapter Sixteen
MAWTS-1

August 1999
Yuma, Arizona

MAWTS-1—Marine Aviation Weapons and Tactics Squadron-1–was located aboard the Marine Corps Air Station in Yuma, Arizona. MCAS Yuma lay midway between San Diego, California; Phoenix, Arizona; and the border of Algodones, Mexico.

Maggie and Karma had cried joyfully when they heard George and Hurl would be moving to Yuma. The two had been stationed separately for several years. Yuma, Arizona, boasted a thriving Mexican food scene, the historic Yuma Territorial Prison, two gambling casinos, numerous tattoo parlors and pawn shops, and the title of Hottest City in America due to its average summer temperatures of over one hundred degrees. It was indeed hell on earth.

Hell on earth is right, Maggie thought as she unpacked yet another box in their new home.

The dry heat had been relentless since they'd arrived, making her long for their previous station in coastal North Carolina. At least she'd had a beach there to cool off. Still, having Karma nearby again made it worthwhile. They'd been together for only one duty station before being separated.

The McCauleys and the Stones had purchased homes within blocks of each other in the Rancho Sereno neighborhood. Rancho Sereno, a subdivision of single-family homes in the Valley, was known as the off-base housing area, where most Marines stationed in Yuma resided.

At least the houses are nice, Maggie mused, admiring the spacious floor plan that cost half of what it would near Pendleton or Miramar. Maybe there were some perks to living in the middle of nowhere.

The newcomers attended their first MAWTS party just a few weeks after arriving. The block was packed with vehicles in front of the party house. Music pumped, and the buzz of conversation could be heard outside the beautiful two-story Mediterranean-style home. The foursome pushed through the sea of men dressed in Hawaiian shirts to find the bar. Standing behind the bar was the party host, Colonel "Sneaky" Pete Gibbons, the commanding officer of MAWTS. Colonel Gibbons reached into the cooler and handed over four chilled bottles of Heineken.

"My wife, Candace, is outside by the pool," said Colonel Gibbons. "She's petite with a blonde pixie."

Maggie approached the backyard while George, Karma, and Hurl chatted with the colonel.

Here we go again, she thought. *Another squadron, another round of wives to size up and politics to navigate.*

After nine years as a Marine wife, she'd developed a sixth sense for squadron dynamics—who to befriend, who to avoid, and how to protect her husband's career while maintaining her sanity.

Maggie closed the sliding glass door, leaving the coolness of the air-conditioned house behind her. The heat wrapped around her instantly, like stepping into an oven.

Sweet Jesus, it's after sunset and still ninety degrees, she thought, already missing the ocean breeze.

As she turned, a petite blonde woman reached out her hand to welcome her.

"You must be Margaret," she said. "I'm Candace."

"Oh, please, call me Maggie."

"You have a beer, so let's meet everyone."

Candace waved to a tall blonde girl wearing a cowboy hat.

"Come over and meet Maggie," beckoned Candace.

As the girl made her way through the crowd, Candace filled Maggie in on her background. "This is Rachel Carter. She's a fun gal. Teaches aerobics at the gym. Girl Scout leader. President of the Parent-Teacher Association. You know the type. Her husband, Chainsaw, is a good stick. The guys admire his skills in the air. He snores loudly. Hence his call sign—Chainsaw."

Perfect PTA mom meets Marine aviator. That would be an interesting dynamic to watch unfold. She'd seen these types before—women who threw themselves into community roles while their husbands were deployed. Sometimes, it worked beautifully; other times, resentment built like a pressure cooker.

"Look to your left," said Candace. "The Puerto Rican girl with the dark ponytail. That's Rosa. She teaches cooking classes at the local community college. She says she went to New York University and was a model. Maybe she was; maybe she wasn't. She met her husband, 'Nasty' Tom Wilson, in Manhattan. He was blowing his bonus money on wine and women," continued Candace. "That's him standing behind her."

"The last time I saw Nasty, he was wearing rhinoceros headgear at G-LOC," said Maggie. "Well, that's not true. The last time I saw him was in a compromising situation with a drunk woman."

"Not surprising," replied Candace.

"She's quite beautiful … Rosa," said Maggie.

And had a story she wasn't telling. She'd met enough squadron wives to know when someone was reinventing themselves. Not that she blamed Rosa—the military was the perfect place to start over.

Different squadron, same stories. Maggie had heard it all before—the call signs, the scandals, the rumors. Like a traveling circus, the chaotic, nomadic nature of military life provided a diverse cast of characters.

Suddenly, a loud sound erupted from around the pool.

The Commodores' classic song "Brick House" thumped over the speakers. A crowd had formed and was hooting and hollering poolside. Maggie and Candace pushed to the pool's edge to see what all the commotion was about. Straddling a surfboard in a red bikini bottom, a long-haired brunette Hispanic woman swayed from side to side as she swung her top in circles above her head.

"And that's Marcella Hammock," said Candace. "She goes by Marcie. She takes classes at Northern Arizona University's satellite campus. She's also a dancer at Platinum Cabaret, the only strip club in town. She's married to Banana."

Maggie's face lit up. "Banana Hammock?"

"Yep," replied Candace. "Matt Hammock."

"Oh, that's too funny." Maggie chuckled. "Banana hammock, like the old men wear in South Florida."

"He's a great guy," said Candace. "I don't know what he sees in her."

Gazing at Marcie's thin physique and large breasts, Maggie knew precisely what Matt saw ...

Every squadron has one, thought Maggie with a mixture of amusement and exasperation. The wife who pushed boundaries and kept the gossip mill turning. She'd seen her share of marriages implode over less.

Maggie made her way back into the house to find her group. They were still gathered around the bar, talking with the colonel.

"Maggie," said George, "do you remember Chainsaw? You met him at G-LOC."

Chainsaw extended his hand to Maggie.

"Chainsaw, as in belly-shot Fightertown Chainsaw?" asked Maggie. "I thought you were a Navy pilot."

"I did an interservice transfer to the Marine Corps," said Chainsaw. "I wanted to fly the Harrier."

"Welcome to the Corps," said Maggie. "I just met your wife, Rachel, out by the pool. Nasty, from the Rhino Suite, is here as well." Maggie rolled her eyes at Karma.

"You missed our conversation about bonus money," said Colonel Gibbons. "George has decided to buy a ski boat."

"You're kidding." Maggie laughed. "You do know we live in a desert?"

Here we go again, she thought—the bonus-money spending spree. Maggie had hoped they might save for their retirement fund instead of adding to George's collection of toys—high-end cars, motorcycles, and bikes. She knew better than to voice that thought here; besides, he worked hard, so why shouldn't he play hard?

"The colonel tells us that Martinez Lake lies along the Colorado River about thirty miles away," said George. "Everyone has boats and heads to the river to meet on the sandbars."

"Size matters," piped Hurl. "I'm getting a Malibu with a Corvette engine."

"Speaking of size," said Chainsaw, "I'm buying Rachel some tits. Double Ds are more than a mouthful."

Men and their toys. No matter what squadron they were in.

"This calls for another round," shouted the colonel.

Two weeks later, Maggie sat on her patio, nursing an iced tea and watching the sunset paint the desert sky in shades of orange and purple. Despite her initial misgivings, Yuma was growing on her. The dry heat was still brutal, but there was something peaceful about the desert landscape that soothed her soul.

Her phone rang with a call from Karma. "Hey, doll. Emergency wives' coffee tomorrow at Candace's. Drama with Marcie and Banana. You in?"

Maggie laughed. "Wouldn't miss it. What happened?"

"Not sure. I guess we'll find out tomorrow."

Maggie set down her phone and smiled. The squadron dynamics were already in full swing. It was a new base with the same stories but with different characters. Part of her found comfort in the familiar rhythm of military life, even in this desert outpost.

George came outside, wrapped his arms around her shoulders, and kissed the top of her head. "How're you settling in, love?"

"Better than I expected," she admitted. "It's hot as hell, but the people seem nice. Karma's already in the thick of squadron gossip, and apparently, there's drama with Marcie and Banana."

George laughed. "On the guys' side too. Word is, Banana caught Marcie with one of the instructors from the civilian contractor team."

Maggie shook her head. "That didn't take long."

"Welcome to MAWTS," George said, sitting beside her. "You know what they say—what happens in Yuma ..."

"Becomes squadron legend everywhere else," Maggie finished with a smile.

As the sun disappeared behind the mountains, a strange contentment settled over Maggie. Yuma might be hell on earth temperature-wise, but with George by her side, Karma just down the street, and a speedboat to escape on the water, it was starting to feel comfortable. Another chapter in their military life was about to begin, and despite the heat and drama, she was ready for whatever came next.

Chapter Seventeen
THE CROWN CITY

NEARLY ONE HUNDRED THOUSAND PEOPLE flocked to Yuma every year to avoid the harsh winter months in their hometowns. The sleepy little town in the desert doubled in population, and RV parks were full. Crowded restaurants and congested roads became the norm.

November was approaching, and the Marine Corps Ball season would be in full swing. Over coffee at Rachel's house one school morning, Maggie suggested the three girls head to San Diego to shop for ball gowns. Rachel mentioned that Chainsaw was off duty over the following weekend and would ask him to watch her girls and Erin. Maggie planned to contact Barbara and ask her to join them.

After several years as an emergency room nurse, Barbara had decided to commit more years to the Navy and attend the University of California, San Diego School of Medicine. After four years of medical school, she interned her first year at Bethesda Naval Hospital. Then she'd headed to Pensacola, Florida, for eight months of flight training and the Naval Flight Surgeon Course at the Naval Aerospace Medical Institute.

Maggie needed this escape. The desert was wearing on her, and seeing Barbara might be just what she needed to feel like herself again.

Early Saturday morning, a gold Chrysler Town & Country van pulled into Maggie's driveway, and the driver honked the horn. Maggie hurried out the door with her overnight bag slung over her shoulder.

"What the fuck?!" she exclaimed. "Karma, what happened to the VW Bug?"

The van is so … suburban, Maggie thought with a mixture of amusement and dismay. So unlike the free spirit she had always known Karma to be.

"What?" answered Karma. "You don't like my new ride? I'm a cool mom who drives a van."

Karma explained she still had the VW but needed a bigger vehicle for carpools now that Erin was playing competitive sports.

"Besides," said Karma, "it's a great trip vehicle."

They were all changing. Moving away from who they used to be. Was she the only one who felt stuck between her past and present?

The girls started their three-hour drive to San Diego, with Karma driving the van, Rachel riding shotgun, and Maggie in the second-row captain's chair. Once they reached the city limits, the van entered the distinctive curve and soaring sweep of the Coronado Bridge. A little over two miles long and two hundred feet in the air, the bridge captured panoramic views of the downtown skyline and the South Bay. Rachel pointed to the right as the van approached Coronado Island, the Crown City, where a multitude of anchored sailboats clustered near the bridge. Their masts stood vertical, like white sticks poking out of the deep blue water.

"We're not in Yuma anymore," said Maggie. "Karma and I will roll out the red carpet. You're in our hometown!"

After Karma paid the one-dollar toll, the van traveled down Ocean Boulevard. She pointed out the majestic Hotel del Coronado, boasting about its iconic Victorian beauty and the many celebrities who had stayed there during the roaring '20s and '30s.

"This was the party destination for Charlie Chaplin, Clark Gable, Mae West, Katharine Hepburn, Bette Davis, and Ginger Rogers back in the day," she fired off in rapid succession. "The Marilyn Monroe movie *Some Like It Hot* and, most recently, the Steve Martin movie *My Blue Heaven* were filmed here."

Maggie smiled. Karma always needed to be the tour guide.

The Town & Country drove down Orange Avenue. At the corner of C Avenue stood a white building with kelly-green trim. An American flag and an Irish flag hung above McP's Irish Pub, and a green shamrock with the number 1107 was in the center above the doorway.

Maggie's heart skipped a beat at the sight of the pub. *So many memories*, she thought, her throat tightening. *And a night that changed everything.*

"This watering hole, my dear Rachel," introduced Maggie, "is home to the legendary Navy SEALs."

"Tell me more!" Rachel burst out.

"We had some good times back here in the '80s," said Maggie. "Especially during BUDs—Basic Underwater Demolition training, also known as Hell Week. It's the last and hardest week of their basic training program. They're sleep-deprived, covered in sand and grit, and pushed to their mental and physical limits. Unfortunately, many reach their breaking point and ring the ship's brass bell three times to drop out."

The countless times I spent with Ian here, she thought, her mind flooding with images of Ian and his wild intensity. The beginning of everything ... and the end.

"Fortunately for us," Karma chimed in, "the ones who survived made their way to McP's, and one in particular found his way into Maggie's heart."

Karma's steel-blue eyes locked with Maggie's.

Good God. Why couldn't Karma keep it light? Why did she have to go dark? She knew how emotional this trip was for Maggie.

Maggie had shared the details with Karma during the car ride home that fateful night and later with Barbara. Both girls were supportive, convincing her that it was an accidental drowning. Barbara, with her cautious and measured tone, knew how to calm her. Karma, however, had known exactly how to push her buttons.

She always knew exactly where to press to make it hurt. A flash of anger sliced through her nostalgia. After all these years, Karma still couldn't let Maggie have her memories without reminding her of the pain.

Her past remarks: "I still can't believe you left that night," or, "Most people would have called 911." Or her subtle dig, disguised as concern: "Are you okay to drive?" Karma had asked after Maggie had one glass of wine. "I just worry about your judgment sometimes. You know how you get when you're not thinking clearly."

"We're at the gate," Maggie snapped.

Karma reached for her military-dependent ID card and handed it to the Naval Air Station North Island entrance gate guard.

"Good afternoon, ma'am," greeted the Navy petty officer.

"Thank you," responded Karma when the guard handed her ID back. "Can you tell me how to get to the Navy lodge?"

"Yes, ma'am," said the petty officer. "Just follow this main road till you get to the T. Take a left, and you'll see the lodge down by the beach."

Maggie's pulse quickened. Back on Coronado. Would it feel like slipping on an old, comfortable sweater or more like ripping off an itchy one? Was Ian still living on the island? Had he completed SEAL training? She'd had no contact with him since that fateful night.

The van pulled into a parking spot in front of the lodge. The girls unloaded their bags and headed for the lobby check-in counter. A freckled, strawberry-blonde twenty-something girl greeted them at the counter.

"Welcome, ladies," she said. "Where are you visiting from?"

"Yuma, Arizona," replied Maggie.

"In that case," said the girl, "welcome to Paradise!"

She is not wrong, Maggie thought with a smile. Compared to the desert, this was paradise.

The girls settled into their rooms, changed into heels and party clothes, and headed downstairs to the Breakers Tiki Bar.

Nestled on the beach below the lodge stood a thatched hut, surrounded by flaming torches and carved tiki poles with elongated faces, welcoming guests. Intimate, high-backed booths carved out cozy, hidden corners inside the dimly lit bar. Wicker chairs and bamboo tables abound. Salvaged divers' helmets, shark teeth, ships' wheels, and block pulleys were scattered around the walls and plastered over the ceiling.

Maggie breathed in the salt air. This was precisely what she needed. The ocean always had a way of soothing her, even still …

Karma, Maggie, and Rachel entered the bar.

"There she is," Karma pointed.

Barbara jumped up from her barstool and embraced her friends.

Barbara, Maggie thought, a surge of affection almost overwhelming her. Her constant. The one who never judged, never pushed, just accepted.

"You look great!" said Maggie. "Love the new bob haircut."

"I love the outfit!" said Karma. "Short skirt, halter top … and heels! Look at the good doctor now."

"Rachel," said Maggie, "I'd like you to meet Barbara. She grew up with me and Karma, not far from here."

Maggie's chest swelled with emotion. *Charlie's Angels, reunited at last.*

The past and present collided in this moment.

The four settled onto their barstools. Soothing waves from the Pacific Ocean crashed against the shoreline. In front of the girls, a row of sweet-smelling rum drinks—garnished with pineapple, cherries, and umbrellas—was lined up. Karma, Barbara, and Maggie shared their childhood stories with Rachel.

This feels good, Maggie thought, taking a sip of her drink and letting the warmth spread through her body.

"Barbara, tell us about your training," said Karma.

Barbara told the girls about her flight surgeon training program. She'd spent five weeks learning aerodynamics, weather, navigation, engines, flight rules, and regulations in the first phase. She'd learned how to fly planes and helicopters in the primary and second phases.

Maggie felt pride and a twinge of something like envy. Barbara had always been the ambitious one.

"What's been the most challenging so far?" asked Rachel.

"The dunker," said Barbara without hesitation. "It's a water survival component, where we must learn how to evacuate from a sinking helicopter."

"Oh my God … you go, girl!" shouted Karma.

"When helicopters sink, they turn upside down," explained Barbara. "We're about ten feet underwater, strapped into a helicopter simulator. We must get out, wearing our full gear … oh, and black-out goggles, so we can't see."

She's so brave.

How different their lives had become. Barbara was saving lives, and Maggie … what was she doing with hers?

"Talk about an adrenaline rush," said Maggie.

"I hope I never have to experience it for real," said Barbara. "You prepare for the worst. Hope for the best."

"What's been the best part?" asked Rachel.

"Riding in the back seat of an F-18," said Barbara. "Shooting a .50 caliber out the back of a helicopter. Watching jets catapult off an aircraft carrier. I love the rush … and heightened sense of living on the edge."

Maggie wistfully remembered that feeling. The thrill of being young and fearless before consequences meant anything.

"Oh … I almost forgot," said Barbara.

She dug into her black leather clutch and pulled out a winged, gold-plated oval with an oak leaf and acorn in the center.

"My wings!" Barbara exclaimed. "I'm officially a Navy flight surgeon. Lieutenant Commander Hunter, at your service. My first duty station as a flight surgeon will be VMA-214 in Yuma, Arizona. I'll be working two and a half days in the primary care clinic on base and two and a half days in the squadron."

Maggie's heart leaped at the news. Yuma? Barbara was coming to Yuma. She felt a surge of joy and excitement. Her life had felt out of balance without Barbara nearby.

The girls screamed, jumped off their barstools, and hugged Barbara.

"We're so incredibly proud of you, Barbara," said Maggie, fighting back unexpected tears. She was selfishly grateful that Barbara would be near her.

"I couldn't have done it without the support from you and Karma," said Barbara. Her pale blue eyes stared longingly at her friends.

They were growing up, but were still together. Maggie felt more hopeful than she had in months. The puzzle pieces of her life would be put back together with both close friends living nearby. She felt immediate comfort, knowing there would be inside jokes that needed no setup, conversations that picked up mid-sentence after years apart, and the luxury of being completely understood without explanation, like muscle memory for the soul.

Chapter Eighteen

IS THAT A RABBIT IN YOUR BAG?

"LET'S SHOW RACHEL THE HEART OF San Diego," said Karma. "Light the Gaslamp, baby!"

The foursome piled into Karma's van and headed down the island to Coronado Ferry Landing on First Street. The waterfront marketplace featured boutique shops, art galleries, restaurants, and the ferry shuttle to San Diego Bay. After a quick bite to eat of burritos, washed down with ice cold Pacificos, at Costa Azul, the girls boarded the Cabrillo ferry, bound for the Broadway Pier. Settled into their bench seat on the open-air deck of the eighty-five-foot boat, they gazed at the beautiful San Diego skyline. A gentle wind blew through their hair, and the smell of salt was in the air.

"I can't believe you guys grew up here," said Rachel. "It's so beautiful; it almost doesn't seem real!"

"Where did you grow up, Rachel?" asked Barbara.

"I grew up on a farm in the cornfields of Iowa," said Rachel. "I met Bob during spring break in Virginia Beach, Virginia, my senior year of college."

"Who's Bob?" asked Maggie.

"That would be Chainsaw to you," stated Karma.

"Oh … I only know the call signs," said Maggie. "Like most pilot wives, I'm the only one who calls my husband by his first name, George."

"Who's George?" said Rachel playfully.

"To the left is the Embarcadero," said Maggie. "Home to the *Star of India*, a one-hundred-fifty-plus-year-old sailboat that Karma, Barbara, and I got to spend the night on during an overnight field trip in fifth grade."

"Oh my God, that was so much fun!" yelped Karma.

"Maybe for you," said Barbara. "I spent most of the night barfing over the ship's side."

"Well, you seem to have your sea legs now … or should I say flight legs?" Karma laughed.

"We lived the life of a sailor," said Maggie. "We cooked in the galley, swabbed the deck, and raised and lowered the sails."

"My favorite was dog watch," said Karma. "It was the night shift, where we learned to tie knots, dance the jig, and sing sea chanties."

"Mine was speaking like a sailor," said Barbara. "The staff made it seem so real … and when we read the letters from home, my mom pretended to be Mrs. Alonzo Horton, the nineteenth-century real estate developer's wife. She talked about his purchase of nine hundred sixty acres on San Diego Bay for twenty-seven and a half cents an acre and her husband's desire to build a public city park, which later became Balboa Park."

The short fifteen-minute ride ended, and the girls departed the ferry on the Broadway Pier at the intersection of Broadway and North Harbor Drive.

"Ahoy, maties!" said Maggie as she glanced at Barbara. "Thar lies yer daddy's buildin', where we shall purchase our ball gowns."

The girls giggled as they walked down Broadway and stopped in front of Spreckels Theater.

"Let's peek inside this historic gem," encouraged Maggie.

The baroque-style theater, built in 1912, had served as a vaudeville opera house, then as a movie palace during the heyday of motion pictures, and now as a live arts venue. Entering the stately two-story grand lobby, the girls immediately turned to the skylight—a large, translucent onyx set of panels allowing light to filter into the lobby. Inside the theater, a large painted mural over the stage depicted two angels sprinkling a horn of plenty and the ancient sea god Neptune bringing San Diego the riches of the Pacific Ocean. A large, central, illuminated medallion in the theater's ceiling depicted dawn, and four smaller medallions featured motifs of air, water, fire, and earth.

"I just love this beautiful, old place." Maggie beamed. "To think that Al Jolson, Charlie Chaplin, Will Rogers, Judy Garland, and our own Marine band leader, John Philip Sousa, all performed on this stage is astounding."

"How do you know all this?" questioned Rachel.

"We're marching in my childhood playground," stated Maggie.

With that, an eruption of Sousa's march—"Semper Fidelis," the official march of the Marine Corps—burst out of the lips of the four friends. The acoustics were perfect in the old theater.

The girls marched out the door and up Broadway to Horton Plaza—the five-level outdoor shopping mall, which stretched across six and a half city blocks. Hours went by as the girls wandered through the mismatched, brightly colored levels, the long one-way ramps, and dramatic parapets, all in search of the "perfect" dress.

By eight p.m., bags in hand, they looked up at the historic Jessop's Clock. The gold twenty-two-foot outdoor clock with a pendulum stood proudly in the center court of the ground floor at Horton Plaza.

"Ladies … our work here is done," said Maggie. "Off to the bookstore for marital aids, or dating aids for Barbara, or personal aids for all of us."

Rachel looked perplexed at the irony of her statement. Karma and Barbara just laughed and shook their heads.

At the Fourth Avenue and F Street intersection, they entered a shop with a black-and-white sign that read *F Street Bookstore* above the door. The shop windows were wholly blocked out with red paper. The front door was covered with posters to obscure any view of what was inside. The sign on the door read, *You must be eighteen years of age or older to enter or purchase in this store.*

"This is unlike any bookstore I've ever been to," remarked Rachel.

Once inside, Maggie led the tour down the toy aisle and past the lotions and potions, the wall of dildos in every shape, size, and color imaginable; butt plugs; Ben Wa balls; Big O vibrating cock rings; videos; magazines; costumes; and an entire Bondage Discipline Submission Masochism section—displaying ball gags, wrist and ankle restraints, paddles, and whips—guaranteed to spice up your sex life.

"Might I suggest the rabbit?" said Karma as she held up a box with a bright pink plastic penis inside. "Plushy, soft, and incredibly powerful, it has multi-speed vibration and rotating beads and only requires three C batteries. It's also better than sitting on top of the clothes dryer!"

"I can't decide between the ultimate, fun restraint tool—gummy handcuffs—or Eat your Heart Out with a heart-shaped chocolate thong," remarked Barbara.

"I say double your pleasure and get them both," said Maggie. "You're guaranteed to have a sweet ending!"

After carefully considering the directions on the boxes, the girls made their selections and proceeded to the counter. The man behind the counter was in his early twenties, pudgy, and had straight, shoulder-length sandy-blond hair. His name badge said *Colt.*

"Let me guess … your last name is Dickman," said Karma.

"That would be the perfect porn star name!" said Barbara.

"Don't pay any attention to them," said Maggie.

Colt asked the girls if they were members of the Four Play Club.

"What is that?!" shrieked Rachel.

Colt explained it was a no-fee membership, which entitled the member to discounts on purchases after a specific dollar amount was spent in the store.

"It will only take a moment," explained Colt. "Just fill out this form with your name and address, and we'll mail you the card."

"Thanks, Colt," said Rachel. "I'm sure we all agree that it's probably not a good idea, given our husbands' jobs. Discretion and all."

"What do they do?" Colt asked.

"They're Marine fighter pilots," answered Rachel. "Oh, and Barbara is a Navy flight surgeon."

"Well then, they must know what the French call a great orgasm—*la petite mort*, the little death."

Karma mouthed, *What the fuck?*

Colt explained, "You know, the brief loss of consciousness when they do that G-force thing."

Barbara approached the counter and positioned herself in front of Colt's face. "For your information, pilots have tools to prevent them from blacking out during what you are referring to, called G-LOC. One is the G-suit, which squeezes their legs and abdomen like a blood pressure cuff. They're in peak physical condition because they work out and train hard. These three girls know more about riding the G-force than you can imagine. And let me tell you something else, Colt. It ain't petite."

Tumbling out the door, roaring with laughter, Barbara said, "I have a whole new appreciation for orgasms now."

"Whatcha got there, Rachel?" asked Karma. "It looks like a magazine."

"I thought it'd be fun to buy a *Playgirl* magazine," said Rachel. "We don't have bookstores like this in Iowa."

Karma reached into Rachel's bag and pulled out the magazine. She opened it up to the centerfold and burst out laughing.

"What's so funny?" asked Rachel.

"You can take the girl out of Iowa, but you can't take Iowa out of the girl!" Karma remarked. "Rachel, you purchased a gay porn magazine. I guess two heads are better than one!"

"Let's check out the Lucky Jeans store," said red-faced Rachel. "I looked it up, and it's on Fifth Avenue. I love the way the jeans fit. And who can resist the inside zipper tag that says *Lucky You* with the four-leaf clover?"

Maggie's heart began to race as they approached Fifth Avenue. The familiar brick facade of the Yuma Building loomed ahead, its twin spires silhouetted against the night sky. She could feel her palms growing clammy.

"You girls go on ahead," said Maggie. "I'll be right outside."

I can do this. I'm not that scared little girl anymore.

To the left of the Lucky Jeans store stood a three-story Victorian Italianate revival brick building. The front was ironclad and featured bay windows with red fire escape stairs between them. The top of the structure featured a hexagonal tablet with *Yuma Building* etched into the stone. In the northwest corner, Maggie pulled open the heavy, ornate door to reveal black-and-white honeycomb tiled flooring.

The weight of the door felt the same. How many times had she pushed through this door, terrified of what waited inside?

She entered the dimly lit foyer and quickly sat on a mission-style bench against the wall, facing an oil painting of the Grand Canyon. She stared at the painting for a moment, then closed her eyes. Her mind took her back over twenty years. She could smell the cigarette smoke in the foyer and hear the *Six Million Dollar Man* theme song on TV. She smiled, recalling Lou's hearty laugh and his daily words of endearment—*"Miss Maggie, you have a mighty fine day."*

Lou had been the only kindness in this place—the only one who saw her as a child.

Abruptly, her mood changed.

But Lou couldn't save her. No one could. She had to save herself. She fully understood the difference between loyalty and betrayal in relationships. She trusted no one. She relied on no one. She had to look out for herself if she was to survive.

She smelled the stench of alcohol and piss, the foul odor of filth and fear. The street was alive with people yelling and honking horns. Her dad coming home drunk, sometimes with a lady friend. Maggie, in her room, praying they would be gone when she had to leave for school in the morning.

Maybe she hadn't always made the right decisions, but she had done what she needed to do to survive. She was fifteen when she started smoking weed. She was sixteen when she first stole money from her dad's wallet while he was passed out. Seventeen when she started skipping school. Eighteen when she killed someone.

But she got out. She got out and never looked back. She made something of herself. She graduated from college. She married George.

She'd had a good life. So, why did this place still have power over her?

Her adrenaline rushed, and her heart pounded. She felt as if her body were being pierced, like arrows penetrating sandbags. She pushed open the door and escaped to the street, breathless and shaken. She sank to her knees as Karma, Barbara, and Rachel stepped out of the jeans store.

"Maggie! What happened?!" they demanded.

She couldn't tell them. She had never told anyone everything she'd experienced while living at the YB.

On the ferry ride back to Coronado, Rachel sat beside Maggie. Maggie rested her head on Rachel's shoulder, and Rachel gently rubbed her hair.

"My mother used to rub my hair like this to calm me down," said Maggie.

"I'm here to help, Maggie," said Rachel. "I don't know you as well as Karma and Barbara, but I sense your pain. My grandpa always told me that the pain won't go away until you have compassion for yourself. Forgive yourself, Maggie."

Forgive myself? But how? How do I forgive myself for the things I've done? For the person I became to survive?

For the anger and resentment she felt toward her dad, wishing he had been the one taken and not her mom? For running away and never looking back, not even to attend her dad's funeral? For the lies upon which she had built her new life?

She had a husband who loved her and friends who would do anything for her. And yet here she was, still that terrified girl. Still carrying the weight of choices no child should have to make.

But maybe Rachel was right. Maybe it was time to stop punishing herself for surviving.

At nearly ten o'clock p.m., the van arrived at the North Island gate. When it came to a stop, two sailors signaled for Karma to move it over to the side.

"I don't understand," said Karma. "What seems to be the problem?"

"We're doing a random check of vehicles this evening," said the petty officer. "I'll need your ID cards. Ladies, please exit the vehicle and stand in a line over here."

He pointed to a painted yellow line on the asphalt to the right of the vehicle.

"Please open the hood and the back hatch, ma'am."

The girls got out of the vehicle, presented their IDs, and lined up parallel to the van.

The second petty officer, standing nearby with his German shepherd, circled the vehicle, allowing the dog to access the van's interior.

"What's in these bags?" he asked as the dog pushed his nose into a bag.

Maggie quickly responded, "Dresses, shoes, and … toys!"

The petty officer completed surveilling the van and stepped to the side.

"You're free to go, ladies," said the petty officer who had initially greeted the girls at the gate. "Have a nice evening."

"Can you imagine if he'd looked inside the bags?" said Rachel.

"Thank God that detection dog is not trained to smell sex."
Maggie giggled.

133

Chapter Nineteen
PARTY LIKE IT'S 1999

THE THERMOMETER HIT NINETY-ONE degrees at five p.m. Yuma was living up to its reputation as the Hottest City in America. Hurl pulled the van into the Stones' driveway, and Karma jumped out of the passenger seat.

"Let's get this Marine Corps birthday party started!" she shouted to George and Maggie as they walked out the door.

Always the life of the party, Karma. Sometimes, Maggie wondered what it'd be like to be more like her. More carefree.

Hurl automatically opened the rear passenger doors. He jumped out of the driver's seat and rummaged through the cooler in the back, grabbing four cold bottles of Yards Brewing Company Jefferson's Golden Ale.

"Since we can't have a drink at Tun Tavern, the birthplace of the Corps, to celebrate the Marine Corps birthday, we'll bring Philadelphia to us," said Hurl.

These traditions held great significance for them. To George. Sometimes, Maggie felt like she was playing a part—the dutiful Marine wife who knew all the right things to say at the right times.

"How about a toast, Philly boy?" Hurl said to George.

"From the City of Brotherly Love comes this Ale of the Revolution," stated George. "We pay homage to our founding father and master brewer, Ben Franklin, for this powerful and complex golden ale, straight from the birthplace of our beloved United States Marine Corps."

"Oh … I have a Thomas Jefferson quote to add," said Maggie. "*Beer proves that God loves us and wants us to be happy.*"

"Maggie"—George laughed—"that is a misquote from a letter about wine by Benjamin Franklin."

George loved to correct Maggie. Not in a mean way. He thought it was endearing.

"It doesn't matter," said Maggie. "I like wine as well … and it makes me happy. You make me happy."

George gently kissed Maggie on the lips.

"My sweet Maggie," he said. "That's one of the many things you say that makes me laugh and love you more."

"Enough with the history lesson," said Karma. "We have a birthday to celebrate!"

Yuma was not known for its sophisticated restaurants, but Julianna's Patio Café stood out with its beautifully lit, secret tropical garden with live macaws and peacocks. Mexican tiles and wrought iron round tables dotted the patio. Soft white lights wrapped around tree trunks. Bright and colorfully painted flowers adorned the walls and fixtures. The Sonoran Desert sun flashed cascades of red, orange, and yellow fire as it set above the Gila Mountains.

Maggie, Karma, Rachel, and Barbara posed for photos in the garden. The women wore the dresses they had purchased in San Diego. Maggie wore a heavily beaded black halter top with a long, straight black skirt.

After dinner, the group attended the two hundred twenty-fourth Marine Corps birthday celebration at the Civic Center. The inside of the Civic Center resembled a dimly lit gymnasium, featuring aqua-colored steel fire exit doors and rows of long, rectangular tables with metal folding chairs tucked in. Despite the informal setting, traditional elements were present during the hour-long ceremony, which included a cake-cutting ceremony, a guest speaker, and the reading of the Commandant of the Marine Corps' Birthday message.

The band took the stage, dressed in an eclectic mix of 1970s fashion, featuring bell-bottom pants, frayed jeans, miniskirts, tie-dye, brightly colored polyester, patent leather boots, platform shoes, and huge black Afro wigs. Maggie remembered then that her dad had had a pair of bell-bottoms. He'd wear them when he was trying to pick up women. Said they made him look hip. God, she'd hated those pants.

The women joined the men, who were ordering drinks at the front of the bar.

"I took the liberty of ordering a round of gin and tonics for all," said George.

Gin still made Maggie's stomach turn. The smell of it on her dad's breath always meant trouble.

As he passed the drinks out, Barbara pointed to the stage. "Is that Nasty?" she asked gingerly.

"Yes," replied George, "along with Rosa and Marcie."

"YMCA" by the Village People piped in over the loudspeakers. Nasty, who looked nearly seven feet tall and wore a huge black Afro wig, marched in place to the beat of the music. Marcie and Rosa, posing as go-go dancers, flanked Nasty, their dark hair swirling about as their bodies gyrated to the music's beat. Marcie and Rosa moved center stage and began an erotic display of affection. Marcie, sticking close behind Rosa like a strip of Velcro, passed her hands seductively down Rosa's body. She split Rosa's legs open and ground into her from behind.

Something wasn't right. Rosa was smiling, but it didn't look genuine. That wasn't desire—that was obligation.

Colonel Gibbons abruptly pulled the plug on the sound system, and the ménage à trois onstage came to a crashing halt. "This celebration is officially over!" Gibbons belted out across the room, everyone standing in complete silence.

And just like that, the party was over. Authority stepped in. Rules were enforced.

He walked up to the stage, pointed his hand like a knife at Nasty, and said, "You, Major Wilson, will report for office hours at zero six hundred on Monday morning."

"I think something's going on with those couples," said Barbara.

"Well," said Karma, "rumor has it, they're swingers."

"I don't know," explained Barbara. "I think it's more than sport sex. There's something nefarious afoot."

It was always more than that. There was always something underneath—fear, control, desperation. Maggie understood the fear of losing everything if the truth were to come to light. She was making a valiant effort to steer the narrative and conceal the secret. If everyone knew what she had done, what would they all say? The knowledge that she had crossed an unbreakable moral line was more than just guilt over past transgressions. Barbara was right; there was always more beneath the surface.

Chapter Twenty
FALCON-77

THE GUYS WERE BUSY WITH classes, training flights, and exercises, with the MAWTS schoolhouse in session, while the girls followed their routines. Each morning during the week, Maggie and Karma walked Erin to Ronald Reagan Elementary School. Erin was in fifth grade. She had recently turned ten and was eligible for her dependent ID card—a rite of passage for every military child. Maggie loved Erin as if she were her daughter. She couldn't believe that Erin was the same age as when Maggie, Karma, and Barbara had first met. Maggie was Erin's godmother, whom Erin affectionately called Aunt Maggie.

Walking alongside Erin, Maggie sometimes felt a familiar ache twist inside her chest. The little girl's hand in hers was a bittersweet comfort—a reminder of what she had in her life and what she didn't. Maggie cherished these moments—the morning sunlight catching in Erin's hair, the excited chatter about school projects and playground politics.

Each day, as she watched Erin skip ahead, backpack bouncing, Maggie thought, *This is enough. I have a place in her life. It has to be enough.*

On the way back from school, the girls would stop for coffee at Karma's or sometimes at Rachel's if they happened to run into her while walking her young daughters to school.

Maggie treasured these coffee dates, the normalcy they provided, and the steady rhythm they brought to her life as a military wife. In these moments, surrounded by her friends, the weight of infertility seemed to lift, if only temporarily.

Mid-morning, the girls would head to the Yuma Racquet and Swim Club. If it was Monday, they had tennis lessons. Tuesday and Thursday were reserved for Rachel's aerobics class. Wednesday featured water aerobics, and on Friday, Maggie and Karma enjoyed swimming laps in the fifty-meter pool. Swimming always reminded the girls of their times together at Bud Kearns.

"I'm so glad Barbara's here with us," said Karma.

"I know," said Maggie, pushing wet hair from her face as she rested at the edge of the pool. "It's a dream to be stationed together. She said she'll try to get a free Friday to come swim with us."

Water had always been Maggie's sanctuary. The rhythmic strokes, the predictable lap after lap—it calmed the churning in her mind, drowning out the endless what-ifs that haunted her. What if the last in vitro fertilization (IVF) had worked? What if they could afford one more try? What if, what if, what if …

George and Maggie had tried for years to get pregnant. They met with reproductive endocrinologists at both Balboa and Bethesda Naval Hospitals. They endured countless diagnostic tests—an analysis of George's semen, blood tests, X-rays, and ultrasounds of Maggie's uterus and fallopian tubes.

For Maggie, each test was another invasion, another moment of hope, followed by crushing disappointment. She remembered staring at the ceiling during her X-ray procedure, the radiologist's voice distant as he explained the dye flowing through her fallopian tubes.

Please be open, please be open, she had silently pleaded, as if willpower alone could clear any blockage.

Diagnosed with endometriosis, Maggie underwent surgery to remove endometrial tissue. The recovery was painful, but she endured it with gritted teeth and forced optimism.

This will be worth it, she told herself. *This pain is temporary.*

However, the hoped-for pregnancy never came. Without success, the couple chose IVF treatments—a complicated process with many steps. Maggie endured numerous hormone injections, administered by George. She still remembered the first time he had trembled more than she did, his military steadiness deserting him as he prepared to stick a needle in his wife's abdomen.

"I can't do this to you, Maggie," he'd whispered.

"You can, and you will," she had replied, her voice steady, even as tears threatened. "We're a team, remember? Through everything."

After five unsuccessful attempts, years of emotional heartbreak, and physical exhaustion, they decided to give up. No longer pretending to be happy when friends shared their pregnancy news, only to cry privately afterward. This was their fate; they would remain childless.

The day they made that decision was surprisingly quiet. No dramatic tears, no shouting. Just a gentle, mutual surrender over coffee at their kitchen table. Maggie reached for George's hand, and they sat in silence for a long time, mourning a future that would never be.

Maggie and George devoted their time and energy to the military families under their command. It wasn't the life they had planned, but Maggie was determined to find purpose in it. The Marines and their families had become her surrogate children—each triumph celebrated, each struggle supported with a fierce maternal protectiveness.

Maggie found refuge in the structure and routine of military life, including the monthly officer wives' club coffees. She attended the April coffee, which was hosted by Candace and coincided with the start of the Weapons and Tactics Instructor (WTI) course at MAWTS.

"The guys check out for two months," Candace explained. "Top pilots in the Marine Corps come to participate in WTI for the intense coursework and advanced aviation training.

Between night flights and exercises, the sisterhood has you covered. Bunco nights and happy hours … time will fly."

"Yes, drunko nights," said Maggie, her laugh genuine despite the lingering ache. "I know it well. Who doesn't like to drink and throw the dice for money? And happy hour goes without saying."

The sisterhood. Those words meant everything to Maggie. These women—Karma, Barbara, Rachel, Candace—they were her lifeline. Where others saw only the childless officer's wife, they saw Maggie in her entirety—her strength, her humor, her uncompromising loyalty. On her darkest days, when the grief of infertility threatened to swallow her whole, they pulled her back from the edge with laughter, wine, and unwavering presence.

On a late Saturday afternoon, wives and their children gathered at Maggie's house for a potluck dinner while a significant training exercise was underway. George, the supervisor of flight, was on duty that evening at the MAWTS command post.

Maggie moved through her home with practiced ease, the perfect hostess filling wineglasses and making sure everyone had what they needed. She loved these gatherings—her large, empty house filled with noise and life. The children's laughter echoed through rooms that would never know the patter of her own child's feet, and somehow, that was okay. Not perfect, but okay.

Karma and Rachel sat in lounge chairs by the pool while Erin and Rachel's daughters played. Just before dusk, the thump of rotor blades could be heard in the distance. Two Ospreys flew over the yard. Everyone stopped to look at the sky and the newest Marine aircraft. The V-22 Osprey was a hybrid—a half plane, half helicopter designed to perform at forward speeds, like a fixed-wing airplane, with the flexibility of rotary takeoff, hovering, and landing.

"I wonder which one Barbara is in," said Maggie, shielding her eyes against the setting sun. A flutter of pride swelled in her chest.

"She was so excited to be flying in the newest bird in the Marine Corps," said Karma.

Maggie nodded, watching until the aircraft vanished from view. There was always that moment, the catch in her throat, as she saw the planes or helicopters disappear into the distance. Years as a military spouse had taught her to live with the ever-present knowledge that not every flight returned. It was the unspoken weight they all carried.

As the evening began to wind down, Maggie's phone rang. *George*, the caller ID read—nothing unusual there. He was probably calling to check if they needed anything before he headed home. But the moment she heard his voice, she knew.

There had been an accident. One of the Ospreys had gone down. The pilots were attempting a two-Osprey formation night assault landing on a civilian airstrip in Marana, Arizona. As the second Osprey descended into the landing zone behind the lead aircraft, one side of the plane lost lift. It'd flipped and plummeted nose-first into the ground, killing all nineteen aboard.

"Maggie," said George softly, "Chainsaw was the pilot of the plane."

"Oh God," said Maggie, her heart in her throat.

Chainsaw—Rachel's husband.

She turned to look at her friend, laughing by the pool, oblivious to how her world was about to shatter. Maggie's hand tightened on the phone until her knuckles went white.

"Keep Rachel there. I'll let the CACO know her location. I'll be home as soon as I can."

CACO was the casualty assistance calls officer. The official representative of the Marine Corps, tasked with notifying Rachel of her husband's death, helping her with funeral arrangements, and applying for military and government death benefits.

"George, was Barbara on the plane that went down?" Maggie's voice sounded strange and hollow, as if it belonged to someone else.

"I don't know."

Maggie hung up the phone, choking back tears. Her heart felt heavy as she thought of the nineteen families who would receive a knock on the door in the middle of the night from a Marine in uniform, a knock that would change their lives forever. She felt sick to her stomach, knowing Rachel was one of them. And what about Barbara? Had she been on the plane?

She stood frozen in her kitchen, the sounds of laughter and conversation suddenly obscene.

How do I do this? she thought. *How do I walk out there and destroy her world?*

But she already knew the answer. This was why they had the sisterhood. This was what it meant to be a Marine wife. You learned to be strong when no strength remained.

With a deep breath, Maggie steadied herself. Let Rachel have these last few minutes of her old life. The CACO will be here soon. For now, Maggie would protect her friend from the knowledge hurtling toward her like a missile.

Moving mechanically, she poured herself a glass of water, took a sip, and returned to the party. She caught Karma's eye and gave an imperceptible shake of her head, causing Karma's smile to falter. They had been friends long enough that no words were necessary. Something was wrong, very wrong.

"Hey, it's getting late," Maggie announced with forced cheerfulness. "Why don't we move inside for dessert? I've got that chocolate cake Rachel loves."

As the group gathered their things, Maggie approached Rachel. "Stay a while longer," she said. "The girls are having so much fun, and we haven't had a chance to catch up properly."

Grateful for the invitation, Rachel agreed. As the other guests departed, Maggie busied herself with tidying up, her mind racing. How long would it take for the CACO to arrive? How would Rachel cope with her daughters watching? Would

Barbara walk through the door, or was she among the nineteen?

When the doorbell rang an hour later, Maggie's hands shook so badly that she dropped the glass she was washing. The sharp crack as it shattered on the tiled floor seemed to echo the breaking of her heart for her friend.

The next moments unfolded with a surreal quality reminiscent of a nightmare—the somber-faced officers at the door; Rachel's slow comprehension, followed by a collapse; and the children's confusion morphing into fear. Throughout it all, Maggie, steady as a rock, held Rachel as she screamed, shielding the girls from witnessing their mother's raw grief while making calls, arranging for childcare, and thinking of everything Rachel couldn't.

It wasn't until hours later, when George finally came home and pulled her into his arms, that Maggie allowed herself to break.

"Barbara?" she asked against his chest.

"She's safe," George whispered. "She was supposed to be on that bird but got moved at the last minute."

The relief was so intense that it made her dizzy. Then came the guilt—how could she feel such joy when Rachel's world had ended? But that was the cruel calculus of military life—one family's miracle was another's tragedy.

Later that night, as Rachel finally slept, sedated in Maggie's guest room, Maggie slipped out with a glass of wine to sit by the pool. She stared up at the stars in the desert sky, at the universe that had denied her a child and had now taken Rachel's husband. None of it made sense.

But Maggie knew what came next. Tomorrow, and the next day, and the day after that, she would be there. She would ensure the girls had enough to eat and clean clothes to wear. She would stand beside her friend at the memorial service and support her if she faltered.

Because that was what the sisterhood did—they carried each other through the impossible.

A memorial service was held at the chapel aboard MCAS Yuma a week later. The chapel was a simple, rectangular structure with a tan and brown exterior, featuring a high tower steeple and a pointed, cone-shaped spire. At the front of the chapel stood a wooden altar on a raised platform with a thick wooden cross centered on the wall behind it. Nineteen wooden boxes were lined up on the platform. Atop each box was a set of desert boots, a rifle facing downward with a desert camouflage helmet placed on top, and a set of dog tags hanging from the rifle's handle.

Maggie helped Rachel dress that morning, her widow's fingers too numb to button her blouse or fix her hair. The girls were quiet, subdued in their dark dresses. Maggie explained to them, as gently as possible, what the day would bring.

"Your daddy was a hero," she told them, fighting to keep her voice steady. "Today, we get to say goodbye and tell him how much we love him."

Colonel Gibbons and Candace sat in the front pew. Rachel and her daughters nestled between them. The Stones and the McCauleys took seats behind the Gibbons and in front of the Wilsons and Hammocks. A few minutes later, Barbara slid in at the end of the aisle next to Maggie.

Maggie squeezed her hand and gently kissed her on the cheek, breathing in the familiar scent of her friend's perfume. "I thought I'd lost you too," she whispered, too quietly for anyone else to hear.

Barbara squeezed back, her eyes glossy with tears. "I know."

The randomness of it all made Maggie's head spin. One moment's decision—one officer saying, "You, not you"—had determined the difference between life and death.

The ceremony began with an invocation from the chaplain, followed by Bible readings. Maggie sat ramrod straight, her hand in George's, drawing strength from his solid presence beside her. She concentrated on the chaplain's words, refusing to let her gaze wander to the nineteen wooden boxes—nineteen lives, nineteen families shattered.

Outside the chapel, a bagpipe solo played "Amazing Grace," and Colonel Gibbons approached the podium to deliver the eulogy.

"On April 18, 2000, around eight p.m., nineteen Marines conducted training exercises near Marana Regional Airport when their Osprey V-22 tilt-rotor went down. The call sign for that flight was Falcon-77. Nothing can be said to lessen the emotional pain of those families who lost a loved one that day or for the Marines who'd had the privilege of serving with them. These Marines were incredibly brave, loyal, and patriotic Americans."

Maggie's eyes burned with unshed tears as she listened. The military had a way of making death sound noble, and perhaps it was. But as she sat here, watching Rachel's shoulders shake with silent sobs, there was nothing noble about it—just raw, terrible loss.

"The pilot of the aircraft was exceptional and accomplished, as were the flight crew and the fifteen Marine passengers. Freedom is never free. These Marines were part of a process that has made us a better fighting force, prepared to defend ourselves and our allies when needed. Losing a loved one is devastating to a family, and words cannot capture the horrific impact. The fallen filled many roles in life—son, brother, grandson, nephew, best friend, and Marine. Although insufficient, we can find solace in knowing that these men positively impacted their units, fellow Marines, and the community. May God bless these families. We will never forget their sacrifice. Semper fi."

The MAWTS sergeant major approached the podium and began the final roll call. "Lieutenant Colonel Stone," he shouted.

George quickly responded, "Here, Sergeant Major!"

"Major McCauley," said the sergeant major.

"Here, Sergeant Major!" Hurl responded.

The sergeant major called out, "Major Carter."

No reply.

After a few seconds of silence, he repeated the call, "Major Robert Carter."

Again, no reply.

After another few seconds of silence, he called out one last time, "Major Robert William Carter."

With the third absence of a reply came the painful reality that the Marine was gone.

The sergeant major repeated the sequence eighteen more times.

The congregation left the chapel to hear three rifle shots, signifying duty, honor, and sacrifice, followed by the bagpiper playing "Taps." Once outside, all eyes turned to the sky as a division of F/A-18 planes roared low overhead. One plane pulled up spectacularly from the rest, leaving its space in the formation empty. The missing-man formation was a bittersweet salute to the fallen.

Chapter Twenty-One
MEA CULPA

November 2009
MCRD, San Diego

THE RIDE BACK TO BASE from The US Grant was silent. Corporal Smith opened the car door for Brigadier General Stone. He exited quickly and entered the house, leaving the front door slightly ajar. Corporal Smith assisted Maggie as she exited the sedan and escorted her to the front door.

"Good night, Corporal Smith," said Maggie, forcing a smile that felt like glass cutting into her face. "Thank you for keeping us safe tonight."

"Good night, ma'am," he said.

The sedan pulled away from the driveway.

Maggie stood before the door. The image of George's face as he'd read the email from the inspector general consumed her thoughts. An investigation. Suspicious monetary transactions. Money she had paid to a blackmailer, payment after payment, thinking it would end. She paused, her hand trembling against the cool metal of the doorknob. Her stomach twisted into a knot so tight that she thought she might be sick right on the front doorstep.

Had it been nearly thirty years since that fateful night on Coronado Beach? Almost thirty years since the last time Maggie had seen Ian?

It had to be him. That bastard!

The weight of her secrets pressed down on her chest, making it hard to breathe. For years, she'd built walls around that night, tucking it away in the darkest corner of her mind. But now the walls were crumbling, and she couldn't hide anymore—not when it threatened everything she and George had built together.

In August 2008, the US Department of Defense had announced George's appointment as brigadier general, commanding general of MCRD, San Diego. Soon after, Swimbuddy1980@gmail.com sent a message with details about a night spent with Ian and Julia in 1980. The message threatened to reveal damaging information about the incident unless five thousand dollars was wired to an account.

Maggie was startled by the email, thinking it was from Ian. When she opened it that morning, seeing those words, it took her back to that night—details only Ian could know.

> *Dearest Maggie,*
>
> *Well, look at you now—a general's wife. You've come a long way from the skinny teenage girl with a shamrock tattoo. Do you still remember that hot August night when only two came out of the water? If you want to keep that little secret to yourself, you'll wire five thousand dollars to this account number: 127027867530952766.*
>
> *Yours truly,*
>
> *Swimbuddy1980*

Her first instinct was to delete it, as if it never existed. But the threat was too specific, too dangerous to ignore. She reacted out of fear and made the payment. She could not let anything compromise George's promotion. He had worked his entire career for this moment, and she wouldn't let her past mistakes destroy it. Stupidly, she thought the payment would suffice. It didn't. He demanded quarterly payments.

And then the letter arrived, timed perfectly to George's selection as major general. He was upping the ante and demanding monthly payments.

Every time a new email arrived, reminding Maggie of her upcoming payment, she felt her world shrink a little more. Each payment was another link in the chain binding her to that night.

Ian knew so much about her that it made sense to pay him to keep his mouth shut. Maggie handled the finances, so she knew there was only a tiny chance George would know about the money. If he did, she would tell him the money was being spent on her beauty regimen—massages, facials, Botox, skin treatments, skin care products, manicures, and pedicures. George was pleased with the results and would never say anything about the cost.

The lies had become so natural, and that was what scared her most. How easily she justified each deception, each misdirection. *For George's career. For our future. For us.* But the weight of those lies was now crushing her.

Maggie inhaled deeply and opened the door. Her heartbeat thundered in her ears as she walked through their home, aware that tonight would change everything. The click of her heels against the hardwood floor echoed like a countdown.

She found George in the Kennedy Room, sitting in the upholstered mahogany armchair with a claw-and-ball foot. His collar was open, and he held a glass of whiskey. His eyes lifted as he looked at Maggie with confusion. The sight of him—so strong, so honorable, and now so vulnerable because of her— nearly broke her.

"I have something to tell you. Please don't hate me," said Maggie, her voice barely above a whisper. She twisted her wedding ring around her finger.

The words hung in the air between them. *Please don't hate me.*

After nineteen years of marriage, after all they'd been through together, the thought of losing his respect terrified her more than any blackmailer ever could.

"Jesus, Maggie, you're scaring me," said George, setting his glass down with enough force for the amber liquid to slosh over the rim.

Maggie lifted a crystal double old-fashioned glass from the bar and poured herself a whiskey. She sat down across from George, close enough to see the worry lines etched around his eyes but far enough away that he couldn't reach for her hand. She couldn't bear for him to touch her.

Maggie took a sip of the whiskey, followed by a deep, shaky breath. "It happened a long time ago. It was the summer before my senior year of high school, and I had just turned eighteen. I met a guy going through SEAL training in Coronado. His name was Ian." Her voice sounded strange to her ears, detached, as if someone else was telling the story. "We dated for a few months. I caught him in bed with another woman, and that same night, all three of us went skinny-dipping in the ocean."

George opened his mouth to speak.

"Please, George, let me finish." Maggie raised her hand, knowing if he interrupted her now, she might lose her nerve entirely. "The sea was rough. Ian headed back to shore first. When he left, I confronted the woman. I lost my temper, and I started yelling and hitting her."

Maggie's voice cracked as the memories flooded back: the roar of the waves, the bitter taste of salt in her mouth, Julia's face—God, she could still see her face, illuminated by moonlight, eyes wide with fear.

"She pleaded with me to help her to shore. She said she was pregnant. I didn't help her, George!" Tears spilled freely now, hot against her cheeks. Her hands gripped the glass so tightly that she feared it might shatter. "I hoped she'd make it out of the water. Ian told me to leave the scene. So, I did. Several days later, the evening news reported her drowning."

Maggie looked directly into George's eyes now, needing him to understand the full weight of what she was confessing. "George, I think I left her to drown. I've been carrying this guilt all these years. God help me."

Maggie broke down sobbing, nearly thirty years of suppressed guilt finally breaking free. Her body shook with the force of it, the glass tumbling from her hands and rolling across the carpet. This was it—the moment she'd dreaded for decades. The truth was out, and there was no taking it back.

George moved out of his chair to comfort her, kneeling before her. His movement was so unexpected that Maggie flinched, certain he would turn away in disgust. Instead, he wiped the tears from her eyes and held her face between his palms.

"I don't hate you, Maggie; I could never hate you." His voice was thick with emotion, his eyes glistening with unshed tears.

The simple words broke something open inside her chest—not relief, but a crack in the wall of shame that had imprisoned her for so long.

"The blackmail started after you were promoted to brigadier general and we arrived at MCRD," she continued, needing to get it all out now. "Then, when you were selected for major general, the payments increased from quarterly to monthly. I'm so sorry, George. I should have told you sooner. It just snowballed, and I didn't know how to stop it."

"So, you've been making these payments for over a year." George's expression shifted, a flash of pain crossing his features as he realized the extent of her deception. "How much money are we talking, Maggie?"

"I've made six payments of five thousand dollars—thirty thousand dollars."

For a moment, Maggie saw the general in him—the strategist assessing the damage and calculating the threat. She held her breath, waiting for him to respond.

"Okay." His voice wavered slightly.

She knew it wasn't entirely okay—how could it be?—but they would face it together.

He pulled her into his arms, and Maggie collapsed against his chest, breathing in the familiar scent of his aftershave and whiskey. She sorely needed the calming rhythm of his steady heartbeat against her ear.

Wet with tears, she whispered against his shirt, "I should have told you years ago. I was terrified of losing you."

George's arms tightened around her. "You won't lose me," he said firmly. "But, Maggie, we need to face this. Together. No more secrets."

She nodded against his chest, knowing he was right. The thought of confronting what she'd done—possibly even charges—was terrifying. But the alternative—continuing to live under Ian's thumb, watching George's career and their life together unravel—was unthinkable.

"What do we do now?" she asked, pulling back to look at his face.

George's jaw tightened. "We fight," he said. "And we start by calling Hurl. We'll need legal counsel, and he'll know who to contact in the JAG's office."

JAG meant judge advocate general. They were Marine Corps attorneys who provided legal services to the Corps and its personnel. The JAG lawyer would give confidential advice, explain the legal process, and coordinate with NCIS and other law enforcement agencies during the investigation.

In that moment, looking at her husband's face—lined with concern but unwavering in his commitment to her—Maggie felt a flicker of hope. Whatever came next would be difficult, perhaps the most challenging challenge they'd ever faced. But for the first time in nearly thirty years, she wasn't carrying her burden alone.

The following day, Maggie, George, and Hurl met with three Naval Criminal Investigative Service (NCIS) agents and the JAG officer in George's office aboard MCRD. Maggie sat rigidly in her chair, hands clasped tightly in her lap to hide their trembling. She'd barely slept, replaying both that night in 1980 and her confession to George over and over in her mind.

Maggie repeated the story she had told George the night before. Each word felt like ripping off a bandage, exposing wounds that had never properly healed. As she spoke, she kept her eyes fixed on her hands, unable to meet the assessing gazes. Only occasionally did she glance at George, drawing strength from his steady presence.

Hurl looked on in utter amazement, his expression shifting from shock to concern as her story unfolded.

Maggie could read the questions in his eyes—*How could you keep this secret? How could you put George's career at risk?*

"The first thing I want you to do is stay calm," said the lead, Special Agent Morris. His voice was neither accusatory nor sympathetic. "General and Mrs. Stone, I understand how problematic it is for you to feel threatened by the blackmailer and the fear of potential harm to your reputation, personal life, and career. You've done the right thing by reporting this to the authorities. Blackmail is a federal crime. Mrs. Stone, I need you to stop engaging with the blackmailer and cut off all communication with them immediately."

"Absolutely, sir," she responded, a strange calm settling over her now that the situation was out of her hands. The relief of no longer managing this alone was almost dizzying.

"Next," Special Agent Morris continued, "I'll need proof of every interaction you've had with the blackmailer. Document their information, including name, user handle, and email address. Lock down all your social media accounts as well."

"Yes, I can provide that now," Maggie answered, reaching for her purse, where she'd stored a flash drive containing all the emails, payment records, and everything. "I feel pretty confident the blackmailer's name is Ian Murphy. He used the email address Swimbuddy1980@gmail.com. I met him in 1980 while he was undergoing SEAL training on Coronado Island."

Speaking his name aloud in this context—not as her first love, but as her blackmailer—sent a cold shiver down Maggie's spine.

How could the man who stole my heart do this to me?

"My team and I will begin investigating Mr. Ian Murphy," said Special Agent Morris. "We'll also try to get a lead on the account you wired the money to and the email address. Give us some time. We'll be in touch."

"Of course. Anything you need." Anger flashed through Maggie. "I want to catch the bastard!"

"Gentlemen," said George as he stood up and extended his hand to Special Agent Morris. Despite everything, he was still every inch the general, commanding respect, even as his personal life was being torn apart. Maggie had never loved him more than in that moment. "Thank you so much for your professionalism. I would appreciate your discretion in all matters of this investigation."

"Of course, sir," said Special Agent Morris.

"Hurl," said George, turning to his friend with a look that left no room for debate, "that also applies to you. Not a word to Karma."

"Understood, sir," replied Hurl. "I'll confer with the JAG officer and keep you informed."

Maggie's stomach clenched at the mention of Karma. Her oldest friend knew nothing about this latest part of her past surfacing. Karma knew about the drowning. She knew Ian had asked her to leave, to say she was never there. What would Karma think when the truth about the blackmail came out? Barbara?

As the door closed behind the gentlemen, Maggie turned to George, his face a mixture of concern, determination, and something else—something that looked almost like grief.

"We'll get through this," he said, crossing the room to take her hand. His voice was sure, but Maggie could feel the slight tremor in his fingers as they closed around hers.

"I'm so sorry," she whispered, the words woefully inadequate for the destruction she'd brought into their lives.

George squeezed her hand. "I know. But, Maggie, whatever happens next …" He paused, his gaze steady on hers. "We face it together. No more carrying this alone. Promise me."

Maggie nodded, tears threatening again. "I promise."

As they left the office, Maggie felt the sun shining brightly on the shadows of her secrets. The truth was out, but the consequences were only beginning.

Chapter Twenty-Two
WHEN THE PAST COMES CALLING

January 2010
Quarters One, MCRD

TWO BLACK SUVS PULLED INTO Quarters One's circular driveway. Maggie's heart raced as she spotted them through the window. Another meeting about the blackmail. Would they finally have answers? She straightened her blouse, took a deep breath, and opened the door before they could knock.

Maggie welcomed the NCIS agents into the parlor. She offered them coffee while waiting for George to finish a call in his office, her hands trembling slightly as she poured. The waiting was always the worst part. Minutes later, George walked into the room, his presence instantly calming her frayed nerves.

"Good afternoon, gentlemen," said George.

When the general entered the room, the NCIS agents put down their coffee mugs and sharply rose to attention.

"Good afternoon, sir," they chimed in unison.

"Thank you for allowing us to speak with you and Mrs. Stone, sir," said Special Agent Morris. "We have some updates we'd like to share with you."

Maggie's pulse quickened. Updates … was it good news or bad news?

"Wonderful," said the general. "Please be seated and proceed."

"We followed up with Mrs. Stone's person of interest, Mr. Ian Murphy. Mr. Murphy was, in fact, a recruit in Navy SEAL training at the Naval Amphibious Base Coronado, California, during the summer of 1980. There was a drowning involving Seaman Murphy and Ms. Julia Franco on the evening of Saturday, August 30, at The Dunes on Coronado Island. Ms. Franco washed up naked on the shores of Silver Strand State Beach three days later. An investigation into the water-related death was conducted at the time, and it was determined to be an accidental drowning. Seaman Murphy subsequently dropped out of the Navy SEAL program and returned to his home state of Massachusetts, eventually enrolling at Boston College, where he graduated magna cum laude in political science. He was then commissioned as an officer in the United States Navy. His current rank, assignment, and duty station are Commander Ian Murphy, Explosive Ordnance Disposal (EOD), Mobile Unit One, Naval Base Point Loma, San Diego."

"Oh my God," Maggie exclaimed, her voice barely above a whisper. The room seemed to tilt around her. "He's been here … for how long?!"

"Two years, ma'am," said Special Agent Morris.

Maggie got a sick feeling in her stomach.

Has he been watching me … following me?

Her thoughts raced back to memories from the past two years when she had sworn she felt watched. That prickling sensation on the back of her neck, which she dismissed as paranoia. Like the time she was at Balboa Naval Hospital for an appointment. She was heading to the elevator and thought she saw a blond gentleman reading the newspaper nearby.

Once she entered the elevator, he immediately took the stairs to exit. The newspaper had obscured his face, but something about his posture seemed familiar. Was it Ian, or was it just a coincidence?

She remembered the times when the phone had rung at the Quarters. She answered, her cheerful, "Hello?" met with silence.

"Hello? Hello! Is anyone there?"

No response. She would hang up, feeling unsettled but trying to convince herself it had just been a wrong number. Was it Ian?

Now, as she sat in her living room, surrounded by federal agents, those moments acquired a sinister new meaning. Her skin crawled at the thought of him watching her, tracking her movements, and invading her life while she remained oblivious.

"Did he mention that I was there that night?" asked Maggie, her voice rising with agitation.

"He did not," replied Special Agent Morris.

"Does he know I'm being blackmailed?" Maggie asked forcefully.

"No," said Special Agent Morris firmly. "He doesn't know the specifics of why we were questioning him or about the blackmail. Whoever the blackmailer is, they used an encrypted email account and a virtual private network (VPN) to hide their Internet Protocol (IP) address. When they connected to the internet, the VPN served as an intermediary, hiding the IP address and creating a secure tunnel where the data was encrypted. Websites only see the VPN server's IP address, not the blackmailer's. We'll have to obtain a court order to investigate this further."

Maggie struggled to process the technical details because of her increasing fear. Suddenly, it seemed as though the walls of their comfortable house were closing in on them, jeopardizing their safety and privacy.

"What about the account the money was transferred to?" George asked.

Maggie glanced gratefully at George. Always practical, always thinking clearly.

"The bank account is numbered," Special Agent Morris explained. "It's a bank account where the account holder's identity is replaced with a multi-digit number or code, making it anonymous. We've identified that the bank is in Tijuana, Mexico. We'll have to work with Mexican authorities to investigate further."

"What do we do in the meantime?" Maggie asked with a quiver in her voice.

"I'm glad you asked that, ma'am," said Special Agent Morris. "Would you be willing to meet Commander Murphy with a recording device to see if he'll give you any more information in person?"

The request hit her like a physical blow. *Meet him? Face-to-face?* Images from that night on the beach flashed through her mind—Julia, the waves, the darkness. Then, later, the news of Julia's body washing ashore. Bile rose in her throat.

"What about her safety?" said George, his voice carrying the fear he felt for her.

"We'll have a surveillance vehicle nearby the location with NCIS agents," Special Agent Morris explained. "We'll be able to hear their entire conversation. Mrs. Stone will be given a safe word. She'll use the safe word if she feels uncomfortable. It will alert us, and she can safely leave the premises."

Maggie's mind raced. Could she do this? Could she face Ian after all these years? The man who could be extorting her now. She trembled with fear, but would stop at nothing to protect George and their future together.

"What do you think, love?" George asked, his eyes filled with concern.

Maggie took a moment to gather her strength from within. She raised her chin a little and straightened her shoulders. Maggie's voice was steadier than she had anticipated as she stated, "I think I'll do whatever needs to be done to clear our names and put this whole ordeal to rest." She was still afraid, but now she was determined. "I know the perfect location for this meeting."

A plan started to take shape in her mind as she uttered the words. She knew exactly where to meet him—somewhere public enough to be safe but private enough for a real conversation. Somewhere she felt comfortable that would allow her to look him in the eye and face what had happened that night. Somewhere she hoped luck would be on her side—McP's Irish Pub.

Chapter Twenty-Three
SUNDAY—A NOT-SO-FUN DAY

A WHITE SURVEILLANCE VAN PULLED up a few blocks from McP's on Coronado Island the following Sunday afternoon. Inside the van, NCIS agents briefed Maggie and George. Special Agent Morris handed Maggie a cell phone.

"This is a specially modified cell phone," he explained. "Leave it out on the table. It'll record your conversation and transmit it to us in the van. Your safe word is *shamrock*. Do you have any questions before you go inside?"

"Can I order a drink?" she asked.

"Of course," replied Special Agent Morris.

"Love," said George, "I wouldn't have a martini. Maybe a glass of wine instead?"

"I love you, George," said Maggie. "Right now, I have so much adrenaline pumping through my veins that I doubt a double martini would even faze me."

It had been five days since she'd called Ian's office at the naval base.

Her hands trembled as she dialed the number she'd obtained from Special Agent Morris.

"Commander Ian Murphy's office," a crisp female voice answered.

"May I speak with Commander Murphy, please?" Maggie asked, her voice barely above a whisper.

"May I ask who's calling?"

Maggie hesitated. "Margaret … Maggie White." She used her maiden name—the name he would remember.

There was a pause, then rustling sounds.

"Commander Murphy speaking." His voice was deeper than she remembered, but still unmistakably his.

Maggie's breath caught in her throat. "Ian … it's me."

The silence on the other end stretched for what felt like an eternity. She could hear his breathing change.

"Maggie?" His voice cracked slightly. "Is it really you?"

"Yes," she said, feeling her heart pound. "I … let's talk."

"My God," he whispered. "After all these years. Where are you? How did you find me?"

"I'm in San Diego," she said, deliberately vague. "I saw your photo at McP's when I was there with … with friends." She couldn't bring herself to mention George. "I'd like to meet you there. Sunday at two p.m."

"Sunday at two," he repeated, sounding dazed. "Maggie, I can't believe it's you. There's so much I want to—"

"Sunday," she interrupted, afraid her courage would fail if she listened to him any longer. "We'll talk then."

She hung up quickly, her hands shaking so badly that she dropped the phone. What am I doing?

Now, as she sat in the surveillance van, those same doubts resurfaced.

Over the radio came the voice of the NCIS agent stationed outside the pub. "The suspect has entered the building," he reported.

Maggie kissed George and exited the van.

"Maggie!" shouted George. "You don't have to do this."

"Yes, I do," she answered.

"I love you!" said George, his voice quivering.

During her short walk to the pub, Maggie's head spun with thoughts. What if she didn't recognize him? What if she lost her temper and threw a drink in his face?

Oh my God, I can't believe I'm doing this.

That voice on the phone had transported her back thirty years in an instant. Why did he still have this effect on her?

Deep breaths ...

She threw her leopard-print wrap over her shoulder and walked fiercely through the pub's front door. Upon entering, she immediately headed toward the right rear of the room. Her eyes first fixed on the roaring fire in the fireplace, surrounded by kelly-green tiles. Then, she focused on the only booth in the bar to the right of the fireplace. Seated at the table—below a black-and-white photo of himself and his mentor, Declan Fitzgerald—was Ian, staring at her.

As Maggie approached the table, Ian stood up.

"Maggie," said Ian with an exuberant smile. "It's been thirty years, and you look the same."

Her heart skipped. He looked older—silver at the temples, lines around his eyes. But there was no mistaking him, still handsome in that dangerous way that had once made her heart race. The same Ian who had been part of the worst night of her life.

"Thank you, Ian," she replied, sitting directly across from him.

"You knew where to find me," said Ian.

"Of course. I've always loved this photo of you and Declan on the charter boat in Quincy. Declan, with his mouth open wide, holding a large striped bass with its mouth open wide. He seems like quite the character. I wish I'd had the chance to meet him. I would have liked him."

"I know he would've loved you," said Ian. "He passed away last year."

"I'm sorry for your loss."

"He was sixty-four years old," said Ian. "He died of cancer, but he'd had a good life. I was fortunate to have been part of it."

"I see you ordered us drinks already." Maggie gazed at the pints on the table.

"I hope you don't mind," said Ian. "I ordered two pints of Guinness ... for old times' sake. It feels good to be back. The place hasn't changed even though we have. What's more … we've been in the same town together, and we didn't know it. How crazy is that?"

Is that true? she wondered.

Or did he know exactly where she'd been all along?

"Pretty crazy," said Maggie. "You're not a SEAL. What happened?"

"After the accident, there was an investigation," Ian explained. "They determined it was an accidental drowning, and I was cleared of all suspicion. After that, my head just wasn't in the game. I couldn't do it. I went back to Quincy. I spent a lot of time with Declan. He convinced me to go back to school. I graduated from BC and was commissioned in the Navy as an EOD specialist. I might not be a SEAL, but I can still blow shit up!" he said with a chuckle. "What about you? A general's wife?"

He knows about George, she realized with a chill.

He'd been keeping tabs on her.

"I met George at G-LOC in the late '80s," she said. "We were married two years later. Lots of moves, deployments, and separations, but here we are … married almost twenty years."

"Any kids?" asked Ian.

"No … I guess that wasn't in the cards," she answered, feeling the familiar ache of that particular loss. Knowing she couldn't have provided Ian with a child either. "How about you … married … kids?"

"Well, no kids that I know of," Ian said with a laugh. "I never married … I guess you were the one who got away."

How dare he say that to me now? Anger flared inside her, hot and sudden.

"Really … Swimbuddy1980?" Maggie growled.

"What are you talking about?" Ian said with a startled expression.

"It was you at Balboa Naval Hospital," Maggie continued. "Right before I got on the elevator. Hiding behind the newspaper. How long have you been stalking me?!"

"Okay," said Ian. "I wasn't stalking you. I looked for you for years. I didn't know you had gotten married and changed your name until I saw the picture of you and your husband when he took command at MCRD in the *San Diego Union-Tribune*. I couldn't believe it. I had to see you for myself. It *was* me at Balboa."

"And the silent phone calls?" asked Maggie. "How many times did you dial me and not say a word?"

"I wanted to, but I just couldn't," he said. "I didn't know what to say. I just wanted to hear your voice."

"You didn't have trouble asking for money," Maggie snapped.

"What are you talking about?" Ian exclaimed.

He genuinely seemed surprised, but he was probably lying. Maggie was right about him watching her and the phone calls.

"You mean to tell me you aren't blackmailing me about the accident?" Maggie moved closer to Ian. "Swimbuddy1980 from an encrypted email account. Demanding that I wire money to an account in Mexico and threatening to disclose damaging information about me. George's promotion is held up because of you! You bastard!"

"Is this what this is all about?" said Ian. "NCIS questioned me recently about the drowning, but I didn't understand why. You think I'm blackmailing you about that night?"

"Aren't you?" Maggie asked, struggling to hold back the tears.

Ian gently cradled her hands in his and looked her straight in the eye. "I would never blackmail you," he said tenderly.

"I told NCIS I was there that night," Maggie continued. "Told them all about the fight in the water with Julia and how I pushed her head underwater. I glanced back and saw her head pop out of the water, but I left her and swam back to shore. Why didn't you tell them I was there?"

"I was protecting you."

"Protecting me from what?" she asked.

"The moon was full that night. I saw the two of you and what looked like an angry altercation. When you came back to shore without her, I panicked. I swam back out and couldn't find her."

Maggie jerked her hands back, shocked.

"Oh my God," Maggie said quietly. "You think I killed Julia?"

Tears streamed down her cheeks. Emotion flushed through her entire body, knocking her back in her chair. Feelings for Ian that she had repressed for thirty years surged back like a tsunami. All this time … he'd thought she was capable of murder? The man she'd once loved believed she could take a life.

"The ocean was rough that night," she said, her voice raw with emotion. "I barely made it back to shore. I was mad at her, and I was mad at you. She'd asked for help, but I left her behind. I'd left her there. I've been living with this guilt every day since then."

"It's not your fault," said Ian. "It was a terrible accident. I fucked up that night. If I could take it all back, I would. I wasn't going to drag you down with me."

"I returned to your house early the next morning to retrieve my bike. The house was dark, and your car wasn't there."

"I'd spent the night at Lance's. I didn't want to be alone."

"Did you know she was pregnant?" asked Maggie, a sting in her voice.

"No. Not then. I found out in the autopsy report the police shared. I'd cheated on you. It was wrong. I was an immature asshole. I'm not that same person. Maggie, please let me know how I can help. I've never stopped thinking about you."

Never stopped thinking about me or never stopped suspecting me? she wondered.

"Who else knew I was there? Did you tell Lance?"

"Yes, of course. But I trust him like a brother. You understand that. I'm sure Karma and Barbara know about that night."

"They do. I trust them implicitly. Did you see anyone else on the beach? There had to be someone there."

There was a tense silence between them. Maggie twisted her sterling silver cuff bracelet.

"You still have it," whispered Ian. "I've never stopped loving you."

"I wore it to remember. We had something good, didn't we?"

Am I still in love with Ian? He's like a magnet ... pulling at my heart.

Ian had rescued her when she was in a dark place of doubt, grief, and loneliness, struggling to cope with the emotional turmoil of losing her mother at fifteen. He shed light on her soul. He had filled the void of attachment and intimacy, if only temporarily. She realized now, sitting across from him, that it had been the emotional imprint of first love—that chemical feedback in her brain, stirred up by feelings of intense pleasure and attachment. Ian had been a safe harbor when she was adrift in an emotional storm.

During the past thirty years, she'd experienced the ebbs and flows of grief. She had become fiercely independent. She had developed a sharp awareness of her mortality, which drove her to live in the present. Losing her mother had made her stronger and more compassionate. She had spent her life chasing her mother's ghost. She had been her role model for being wise, kind, and purposeful. Maggie now knew who she was and had found her voice.

"I love my husband," she said.

Not because she knew he was listening in the surveillance van with the NCIS agents, but because it was true. Her love for George was real. It had been time-tested for nearly twenty years—for better, worse, richer, poorer, in sickness and health ... multiple deployments, separations, and moves. It wasn't easy. It took sacrifice, compromise, and strength to pull it together, even when things were easy, especially when things were hard.

"I am the one who got away," she said, finishing her last gulp of Guinness.

Maggie placed the glass on the table and walked out of the pub. Her feet moved quickly, and her heart pumped rapidly. As she approached the surveillance van, George threw open the horizontal sliding door and jumped out. Maggie fell into his arms. She tucked her face in tight against his chest as tears streamed down her cheeks.

In the coming months, NCIS determined Commander Murphy was no longer a person of interest.

Given there had been no criminal investigation into the drowning and that Maggie was not implicated, the inspector general of the Marine Corps placed George back on the list for promotion to major general.

The NCIS agents continued to investigate the blackmailer. They followed the IP address from the email to Jolt 'N Bolt, a twenty-four-hour internet café in downtown San Diego. They set up camera surveillance but were unsuccessful in gathering further information. The bank account was traced to Banco Azteca in Tijuana.

"The teller described a Hispanic woman in her late thirties or early forties," said Special Agent Morris. "The woman, using the alias Lana Bolsa, has been making quarterly withdrawals for over a year. A total of thirty thousand dollars."

"Agent Morris, you said alias," said George.

"Yes. *Lana* is the slang term for money in Mexico. *Bolsa* is the Mexican word for bag. Money bag. We followed up on the address she had listed for the account, but it turned out to be a dead end. The ID is fake."

"Obviously," retorted Maggie.

"Mrs. Stone, I understand your anger and frustration. We'll keep investigating. You mentioned in the pub that Karma and Barbara were aware of the incident. Commander Murphy indicated that he had told Lance."

"We've been best friends since we were children. It couldn't be either of them. And Lance—that bond of brotherhood is impenetrable."

"I understand your feelings, Mrs. Stone, but we must rule them out. Can you give us their contact information?"

"Yes, of course," said Maggie. "You'll have to ask Ian about Lance."

"We'll look at their finances in the meantime. We'll check if they've been depositing large sums over the past year and a half. There's good news, Mrs. Stone. You've stopped making the deposits, and the blackmailer hasn't acted on the threats."

"Yeah, lucky me," said Maggie.

"Agent Morris," said George, "we're thankful to you and your team for all your hard work. We have confidence in knowing you'll find the person responsible and bring them to justice."

"Thank you, sir. Mrs. Stone, we'll be in touch."

Chapter Twenty-Four
CHANGE OF COMMAND

MCRD, San Diego

GEORGE AWOKE TO THE SOUND of water running in the shower. He climbed out of bed and opened the shower stall door to find his wife nude under the showerhead. Her hands moved through her wet hair and down her neck. He stared longingly at her glistening body and her kelly-green shamrock tattoo. George quietly crept in behind her, his body brushing against her. He kissed her neck and shoulder and locked his arms around her.

"My God, you're beautiful," he whispered in her ear.

"Good morning, my love."

She turned around to face him, warmth spreading through her body at his touch. Her hands slid down to rest firmly on his ass. George placed his hands tenderly on her face and neck, gently pulling her lips to his. The warm shower water cascaded from their heads, past their shoulders, and down their backs as they embraced. Their bodies pressed against the shower wall, causing the glass to fog. Maggie lost herself in his arms, savoring the intimate moments that had become even more valuable as they prepared to move. She tried to memorize his touch, the reassuring familiarity of their morning routine that would soon be performed in a new house.

Afterward, Maggie slid into a silk kimono, and George wrapped a towel around his waist. The two retreated to the bed.

"I'm going to miss this old house," said George. His arms wrapped around her as her head rested on his chest.

"Me too," Maggie whispered, as a wave of nostalgia overcame her. How many mornings had they shared like this? How many memories were embedded in these walls? "To think this place wouldn't even be here without General Pendleton's perseverance. It's like a museum, filled with historical mysteries."

The thought of leaving imbued her with a blend of excitement and sadness. This house had been more than just a residence; it had served as their sanctuary during George's command.

"Speaking of mysteries," said George, "have you spoken to Karma or Barbara about the blackmail?"

Maggie tensed slightly at the mention of the blackmail, the intrusion of ugly reality into their peaceful morning. "I plan to talk to Karma after the ceremony today. Barbara's on East Coast time; I'll call her tonight." A knot formed in her stomach as she thought about confronting her friends. "George, I know in my heart it wasn't either of them." She needed to believe that and trust in the bonds she'd formed.

"Are you sure that's a good idea?" George asked. "Shouldn't you let the investigators deal with it?"

"Good, bad, indifferent—it has to be done." Her voice was firmer than she felt.

The thought of confronting Karma made her hands tremble slightly, but she concealed it by running her fingers through her damp hair. Her mind flashed back to the moment Karma had picked her up in Coronado that night. Could she have turned on her? Preying on her vulnerability? It couldn't be true. She quickly pushed the thoughts away.

Later, Maggie passed by the circular foyer table on her way to the kitchen. A card lay on the table—the invitation to George's change of command ceremony. She picked it up, running her finger over the embossed letters. All those months of preparation, stress, and anticipation culminated in today's event. Part of her couldn't wait for it to be over, for them to move on to their next chapter. Another part mourned the end of this period in their lives.

Corporal Smith entered the circular driveway and parked the black sedan in front of the Stones' quarters. When George and Maggie appeared in the driveway, Corporal Smith opened the car doors to allow them entry into the sedan.

"This will be our last ride with you, Corporal Smith," said Maggie, forcing cheerfulness into her voice despite the lump in her throat.

"If you mean your last ride with me as your driver, then, yes, ma'am."

"We'll make an aviator out of you yet," George added.

"With all due respect, sir," said Corporal Smith, "I prefer being infantry."

The sedan pulled up to the parade field. Maggie took a deep breath, straightened her dress, and mentally prepared herself for the public role she would play today. As they exited and walked to the VIP tent, her practiced smile returned—the one she'd perfected over the years as a military spouse and now as the general's wife. She squeezed George's hand briefly before they separated to mingle with their guests, drawing strength from his presence.

When the ceremony began, Maggie watched with pride as the band played "Waltzing Matilda." She caught George's questioning look.

"Maggie?" he said quizzically.

She nodded her head, a small smile playing on her lips. "I called in a favor. I wanted to commemorate our year in Australia when you attended school."

The familiar melody brought back memories of their time in Australia—one of the happiest years of their marriage, when they had been away from the pressures of command, just the two of them exploring a new country together.

Maggie hardly looked away from George during the ceremony. As he spoke, addressing the gathered troops with the assurance and command that had always drawn her to him, her heart swelled with pride. His words about pushing Marines hard in Iraq reminded her of when he had come home, exhausted from that deployment, revealing the toll it had taken on him, which he rarely showed to others.

When George concluded his speech, Maggie blinked back tears. This wasn't just the end of his command; it represented the closing of a significant chapter in both of their lives. She watched as he handed over the symbolic flag, a gesture that officially released him from the responsibilities that had dominated their lives for two years.

Hurl approached them afterward, and Maggie immediately noticed Karma's absence. A flicker of apprehension crossed her mind as she asked about her.

"She's at the Quarters with the packers," said Hurl. "They're loading the truck today. I apologize that she isn't here for the ceremony."

"No apology needed," said George. "We've all been there. It's a stressful time."

"Congratulations on your new command," said Maggie, keeping her voice steady despite her mixed feelings about Karma's absence. Was it truly about the packers, or was it connected to the blackmail issue?

"Thank you," said Hurl. "I'm honored to have been selected. Looking forward to going back to Okinawa."

"How's Erin doing in law school?" Maggie asked, deliberately changing the subject to something less fraught.

"She's just about finished her first year at the University of San Diego."

"She's doing great," said Hurl. "Straight A's, and she was awarded another scholarship for her second year."

"Well," said Maggie, "she certainly doesn't follow in her mother's footsteps concerning studying and getting straight A's." The joke came easily, masking her internal turmoil about the conversation she needed to have with Karma.

"She's a good girl," said Hurl.

"Yes, she is," Maggie answered, feeling a pang of guilt for her suspicions about Karma while discussing her daughter.

After posing for pictures and chatting with guests, George, Maggie, and Hurl headed toward the reception.

"I'm going to drop by the house and see how the packing is going," said Maggie, her heart pounding at the thought of confronting Karma face-to-face. This might be her only chance before they moved. She needed to confirm Karma wasn't the blackmailer, to eliminate another person from her search for the real culprit behind this constant nightmare. "I'll meet you at the O'Club in a bit."

"Sounds good," said George, giving her a look that told her he understood her real intention.

"See you there," said Hurl, oblivious to the real reason for her detour.

As Maggie walked away, she took several deep breaths to steady herself. The blackmail situation was a dark cloud hanging over what should have been a celebratory time. Whatever she discovered at Karma's house, she knew it would bring some closure. The end of George's command wasn't the only chapter closing today.

Chapter Twenty-Five
PIECES OF THE PUZZLE

MAGGIE ENTERED THE MCCAULEY QUARTERS to the sound of paper crackling and the ripping of packing tape. Her shoulders tensed at the noise, each tear of tape reminding her of her many past moves and the many still to come. She found Karma seated at the kitchen island, reading *People* magazine.

"Hey, doll. What's up?" said Karma. "Sorry I didn't make the ceremony. Will you forgive me?"

As if that's the thing I need to forgive today, Maggie thought, forcing a smile. "Of course. Moving overseas is a big deal. You have the express shipment, the storage shipment, and the main shipment. The sooner you get your crates on the ship, the better." Her voice was light yet rehearsed—the practiced tone of a military wife who had given this advice countless times while hiding her burdens.

"Would you like a cup of coffee? I just made a fresh pot."

"That would be lovely. I could use the caffeine jolt before I head to the club for the reception." Maggie's fingers fidgeted with her necklace, her heart beginning to race. *Just say it. Just ask her directly.* "Karma, have you heard of an internet café downtown called Jolt 'N Bolt?"

"It's a catchy name, but I've never heard of it. What's so special about it?"

Maggie swallowed hard, her mouth suddenly dry. "Nothing. But I need to ask you a question, and I want you to be honest." Her voice dropped, each word heavier than the last.

"Jesus, Maggie, what's this about?"

Maggie inhaled deeply before speaking. She felt her pulse in her temples, the question she'd feared asking finally rising to her lips. "The night Julia drowned … do you think I killed her?" The words hung in the air like a confession, leaving Maggie vulnerable.

Karma paused for a moment.

"I think anyone is capable of anything. It was a night of shocking information. She told you she was pregnant. So, yes, the thought did cross my mind."

Maggie felt the words like a slap to the face. *She indeed thought it, after all these years of friendship.* A cold emptiness spread through her body. "Karma, I must be a terrible person if you can think that about me." Her voice trembled, the hurt raw and unfiltered.

"Thinking and knowing are two different things. I know you didn't do it. It was a terrible accident."

Maggie exhaled heavily, feeling relief and renewed fear clash within her as she fell into an embrace with Karma. The touch of someone who truly understood was both terrifying and comforting. But she didn't know everything.

"I'm being blackmailed." Her words were spoken with a directness that stemmed from her honesty.

Karma pulled away to face Maggie. "About the drowning?"

"Yes." Maggie's voice was low, silent suffering echoing in that single word. "It started when George took command of MCRD. I've been wiring payments to a bank in Mexico." She felt lighter and heavier with each admission, the shame of confession counterbalanced by the relief of sharing.

"Does George know? John?"

"Yes. NCIS is involved." Maggie's jaw tightened, a flash of anger replacing the vulnerability in her eyes. "I've stopped making the payments, but the bastard's taken thirty thousand dollars from us. I want to find this person." Her voice hardened with determination.

"Seems like Ian would be the perfect person of interest."

"NCIS tracked down Ian and cleared him. They will be contacting you and Barbara. I wanted to speak with you both first. I'll call Barbara tonight." Maggie observed Karma's face, studying for signs of deception or knowledge. "Honestly, I never suspected Barbara. You, on the other hand ..."

"Well, thanks for that vote of confidence." Karma grinned.

So, we're back to jokes, Maggie thought with relief, mingled with lingering hurt. *Maybe some friendships can survive even this.*

At that moment, Hurl entered the kitchen.

"John," said Karma, "what's the matter? You look baffled."

"I just got off the phone with my monitor at Headquarters Marine Corps," explained Hurl. "My orders have been changed. We're no longer going to Okinawa, Japan."

"What do you mean, we aren't going to Japan?" Karma questioned. "Everything we own is boxed up and sealed in crates on that moving truck out front."

"The colonel slated to get Marine Aircraft Group (MAG) 14 turned down command," said Hurl. "I'm taking the command now and deploying with General Stone from Carolina to Afghanistan for a year."

"Wow!" said Karma. "Today is full of surprises."

Afghanistan. George. Maggie's mind raced with the implications, worry for her husband mixing with the selfish relief that this conversation would have to be cut short. She needed to get back to the reception before her absence was noticed.

George walked into the kitchen unexpectedly, and Maggie felt her stomach drop. Even after all these years, his presence still commanded her attention immediately. The way he carried himself told her something had changed.

"General," said Hurl. "Why aren't you at the reception? Has something happened?"

"I received a call from Special Agent Morris."

George glanced at Karma and then at Maggie. She gave him a slight nod, her eyes communicating more than words could.

"It's okay. She knows." Maggie's voice was steady now as she drew strength from George's presence.

"The team finished the financial reviews of Karma, Barbara, and Lance and found no unusual transactions or discrepancies," George continued. "What is interesting is … they've reopened the investigation into Julia Franco's death."

"What? Why?" Maggie's question came out sharper than intended, fear clutching at her throat. After all this time, after everything they had been through …

"New evidence has surfaced," George explained. "In the initial toxicology report, Julia showed traces of marijuana, alcohol, quaaludes, and cocaine in her system. Her parents didn't think much about it since she was known to experiment with drugs. It wasn't until her parents moved into a retirement home that they found the journals sent to them from Julia's room in Coronado. Special Agent Morris believes a potential third party is involved. The Drug Enforcement Administration has joined the investigation. Special Agent Morris asked me if the name Levi meant anything."

Karma's eyebrows rose as she turned to face Maggie, their eyes meeting in mutual understanding, with a shared history suddenly illuminated from a different angle. The name Levi struck Maggie like a thunderbolt, and pieces of a puzzle she hadn't even known she was solving fell into place.

"I think we both have the same possible suspect in mind." Her voice was low but certain, connecting dots across decades.

Maggie grabbed George by the arm, her fingers digging in slightly. She needed his strength and wanted to end this conversation before more was revealed. "George, let's return to the O'Club and join our guests."

As the Stones exited the McCauleys' quarters, Maggie leaned her head back and shouted, "See you in Carolina." The words were cheerful, but there was steel beneath them.

Whatever came next, they would all face it together—bound by secrets, service, and survival.

185

Chapter Twenty-Six
WELCOME TO CAROLINA

May 2010
MCAS
Cherry Point, North Carolina

THE INVITATION RESTED ON THE kitchen counter amid the clutter and chaos of yet another move to a new house. Maggie stared at it with a mixture of pride and apprehension. Another promotion, another move, another war.

George E. Stone to the rank of major general … 2nd Marine Aircraft Wing (MAW) Change of Command Ceremony … Thursday, the 27th of May at ten in the morning … Cherry Point, North Carolina.

Under gray skies, Maggie stood beside George as they approached the white VIP tent. Her heart fluttered with a familiar cocktail of emotions—pride entwined with fear, excitement mixed with dread. The aircraft lined up on the tarmac loomed like giant sentinels—EA-6B Prowlers, Cobras, F/A-18s, UH-1N Hueys, and MV-22s. Squadron commanding officers and their troops were perfectly aligned—reminders of the danger George would soon face in Afghanistan.

Nearly twenty years of this, she thought, smoothing her dress. *Twenty years of ceremonies and goodbyes.*

George wore his desert camouflage, the uniform of the day, though he would soon wear his desert flight suit into battle. Maggie's fingers brushed against his arm as she memorized the feel of him beside her, whole and safe. For now.

"Ladies and gentlemen," the announcer's voice boomed, "please take your seats. The promotion ceremony is about to begin."

Maggie settled into the padded chair, her posture perfect. She had learned to wear composure like armor. Inside, her stomach twisted with the awareness that this ceremony was not just a celebration; it was a prelude to separation.

Behind them sat Anna Reed, Karma, and Erin. Maggie drew comfort from their presence—these women who understood what it meant to love someone who belonged first to their country and Corps.

Barbara was there, too, with her new husband, Jack. She had recently taken command of the Naval Health Clinic aboard the base. Barbara and Jack had met at the Blue Jay Café on Broad Street in downtown New Bern, North Carolina. She was looking for a place to rent when Jack recommended a quaint, recently renovated historic home on Pollock Street. He assured her that the landlord was a friendly local gentleman with a knack for fixing old houses. The gentleman had, of course, been him. Maggie envied their fresh happiness and remembered when she and George had been newlyweds before the weight of rank and responsibility settled on their shoulders.

As she scanned the crowd, Maggie's heart lifted at the sight of familiar faces. She leaned toward George. "It's so great to see Sneaky Pete and Candace," she whispered, genuine warmth in her voice, which was low and intimate. The sight of old friends soothed her anxiety. "I'm glad Sergeant Major Reed agreed to follow you. I just love Anna. I didn't know the Hammocks and the Wilsons were here. God knows what drama those couples will bring to the command."

"Yes," replied George, motioning to the seats behind them. "Be nice. So far, they've stayed clean and out of trouble. Let's give them the benefit of the doubt."

Maggie and George waved to Marcie and Rosa, and Maggie flashed back to the ball in Yuma, when Marcie, Rosa, and Nasty had been onstage.

I hope you're right, dear.

"It's a Yuma reunion," she said jubilantly, her voice colored with nostalgia.

These were people she had known for years. Not to mention, Karma and Barbara would be here for the deployment.

"At this time," said the announcer, "the generals will take their positions."

Maggie watched George walk away, her chest tightening. Even after all these years, she still found him handsome in uniform, proud of how he carried himself. But today, pride was shadowed—each step toward his new rank brought him closer to Afghanistan. The Marine forces had grown to over nineteen thousand, and the Battle of Marjah had started in February with fierce fighting. Marines constantly faced challenges from improvised explosive devices (IEDs) to insurgent ambushes and sniper fire.

The ceremony continued with General Gibbons taking the microphone. Maggie straightened in her seat, ready for the public performance that being a general's wife required.

"Good morning, everyone!" General Gibbons called out. "Thank you for joining us on this special Carolina morning."

As he spoke of George's accomplishments—the medals, the deployments—Maggie's mind flashed with images from their shared past. Behind each accolade lay a memory—nights she had stayed up, waiting for a call to know he was all right, and holidays celebrated through unreliable Skype video connections.

"I would be remiss if I didn't mention his beautiful bride, Margaret," General Gibbons continued. "She's been faithfully by his side to support him and the Marines and families in his care. This summer, the Stones will be celebrating their twentieth wedding anniversary. That deserves a round of applause."

The audience clapped enthusiastically, and Maggie smiled. Twenty years—how many of those had they *actually* spent together? She pushed the thought away; it was unfair on this day of celebration.

When her name was called, Maggie rose smoothly, her movements graceful despite her racing heart. This was the moment she both treasured and dreaded—standing before everyone as the supportive wife, pinning the stars that would take her husband away from her.

Walking toward George on the tarmac, Maggie felt everyone's eyes on her. She had chosen her outfit carefully—elegant yet appropriate, fitting her role. A navy-blue sleeveless sheath dress with her Ann Hand Marine Corps brooch pinned proudly over her heart.

Maggie's fingers trembled as she pinned the silver stars to his collar. Their eyes met, and everything she couldn't say aloud passed between them in that glance.

I'm proud of you. I'm scared for you. Come back to me.

She smiled for the camera, a genuine smile this time, allowing her love for George to shine through. Whatever fears she harbored about the future—about Afghanistan, about the blackmail that still hung over them like a shadow—those could wait. This was his moment.

Maggie took a deep breath to regain her composure as she sat down again. She heard George's confident and powerful voice as he took his oath. The sight of him accepting his flag— the symbol of his new rank—filled her with a mixture of pride and sadness, knowing what would come next.

We'll get through this, she promised. *We always do.*

And when the announcer's voice proclaimed, "Ladies and gentlemen, it is my privilege to introduce Major General George E. Stone," Maggie stood with everyone else, applauding the man she loved, her face betraying none of her mixed emotions.

Chapter Twenty-Seven
FEEL THE BERN

MAGGIE WRAPPED HER HANDS AROUND her coffee mug, letting the warmth seep into her fingers as she sat with George on the back deck of their new home. The historic white colonial on the Neuse River was a stark contrast to their quarters in San Diego, with its wooden dock extending into the river where George's new twenty-six-foot Sea Ray waited for its maiden voyage. At George's feet, three-month-old Smokey—their black German shepherd puppy—dozed contentedly.

"I'm excited to take everyone out today," George said, reaching down to scratch behind Smokey's ears. His face displayed the easy contentment of a man settling into a new beginning, his new home, before deploying in nine months.

"So am I," Maggie replied, trying to match his enthusiasm. "It'll be nice to catch up with Erin. I'm looking forward to getting to know Jack as well." She was genuinely curious about Barbara's new partner, this man with deep roots in a place unlike their nomadic military existence.

"Jack seems perfect for Barbara," George observed. "Kind, sensitive, comfortable with all the military jargon and ceremony." His voice took on a wistful quality. "I'm a bit envious of his deep hometown roots. What must it be like to be settled and not move constantly?"

Maggie laughed, hiding her complicated feelings about their transient life. "George," she said, "you would go crazy in a small town. Besides, home is wherever the Marine Corps sends us."

"Right you are, Maggie. Spoken like a true military wife."

She hesitated before asking the question that had lingered since they'd left California. "Have you heard anything from Special Agent Morris?"

George's expression tightened immediately. "Not since my last conversation with him in San Diego," he answered, his fingers tracing the rim of his coffee cup. "He was very interested in Levi Siegel and his drug dealings in San Diego in 1980. He said he would be in touch, but it would probably be several months at the very least before we heard back."

With the mention of Special Agent Morris, Maggie's stomach clenched. She had hoped to leave San Diego and the investigation behind.

Levi Siegel. The name alone brought back memories she would rather forget. Karma's relationship with Levi, the drug dealer for Julia. Was he the blackmailer?

When will this end? she thought, the coffee suddenly bitter on her tongue. She'd thought leaving San Diego would make things easier. Who was she kidding?

The arrival of their friends mercifully interrupted her spiraling thoughts. The McCauleys, along with Barbara and Jack, appeared, their voices carrying across the lawn as they approached. Smokey sprang to life, barking excitedly, his tail wagging in frantic circles. The dock creaked beneath their feet as they loaded coolers, canvas tote bags, and towels onto the boat.

George settled into the cockpit with Smokey on his lap, ears perked and alert. Maggie joined Karma, Barbara, and Jack on the bench seats behind George. Erin claimed the bow, stretching out to face the sun, while Hurl, ever the daredevil, trailed behind on waterskies.

"Welcome to the family," Karma said to Jack, her voice warm with the easy acceptance that had drawn Maggie to her years ago. "Has Barbara told you all about her San Diego friends?"

"Yes, she has," Jack replied with a genuine smile. "It's nice to put faces to the names. It sounds like you all have quite a history together."

"That we do," replied Karma, exchanging a knowing look with Barbara and Maggie that spoke volumes about the shared experiences that Jack could never fully understand.

As Jack described his historic New Bern home—its Georgian architecture, the visit from President Monroe, its listing on the National Register of Historic Places—Maggie studied him. He spoke with the confidence of someone whose identity was firmly rooted in a single place—a concept almost foreign to her after years of military relocations.

The Sea Ray cut through the Neuse River, its wake creating a silver ribbon behind it as it passed waterfront homes with covered porches and private docks. At Union Point Park, where the Trent River merged with the Neuse, they docked at the octagon gazebo and unpacked lunch on a picnic table. Maggie distributed submarine sandwiches and potato chips while George handed out beers and sodas from the cooler.

When Karma pointed out a nearby bear statue, Jack easily slipped into the role of tour guide.

"New Bern was settled in 1710 by Swiss and German adventurers, led by Baron Christopher de Graffenried from Bern, Switzerland," he explained. "*Bern* is the old Germanic word for bear, and the bear became the city's symbol." His knowledge was comprehensive, detailing everything from the city's three-hundredth-anniversary celebration to the origin of Pepsi-Cola in a local pharmacy.

Their day unfolded leisurely—cruising to Beaufort, where the women shopped along Front Street while the men relaxed at Clawson's pub; exploring the isolated barrier island of Shackleford Banks with its wild horses and pristine beaches; collecting seashells and swimming in the warm saltwater. By late afternoon, sunburned and pleasantly exhausted, they collapsed into the boat for the journey home.

As George steered the boat back toward their dock, Maggie settled in the bow with Karma and Barbara. Behind them, Erin, Hurl, and Jack laughed as Smokey bounded between them, shaking sand from his fur.

"Erin looks great, Karma," observed Barbara. "I adore that girl and admire everything she has accomplished."

"She's remarkable," said Maggie. "So disciplined and studious. Are you sure you're her mother, Karma?"

"I have the C-section scar to prove it," said Karma, maternal pride evident in her voice. "John and I are very proud of her. With all the transitions—moves to new duty stations, new schools, new friends every couple of years—she survived." She paused, her expression turning reflective. "Do you ever think it's worth it? The military lifestyle."

"You mean the stress of multiple moves, the long separations during deployments, constantly adapting to new environments and friends, all while single parenting half the time?" Barbara replied with gentle sarcasm.

"I think we agree this life is stressful, and we have little control," said Maggie, looking out at the water. "We have to be flexible and accept change readily." She considered the deeper question. "Is it worth the heartache? The tears? The fear? The worry? That may not be as easy to answer as *what* is worth it."

She felt something settle within her as she continued, "The pride in knowing my husband is doing what he loves and defending our country. The satisfaction of knowing my life has a purpose and meaning as I watch over the families in our command. The comfort of knowing I have strong friendships with people who know exactly what I'm going through and support me." She looked at her friends, these women who had become her anchors. "This is what makes my life rich. You are my family. You make my life rich."

"Okay, enough sentimentality," said Karma with a laugh that didn't hide her emotion. "Barbara, grab us some beers out of that cooler."

As the sun began to set, painting the river in gold and amber, the Sea Ray returned to its dock. Maggie found herself smiling amid the comfortable silence of treasured friends. The day had been about making memories with the family she had chosen for herself.

She had learned long ago that home was not a place. It was the people. It was the feeling of strength she felt, knowing they loved, supported, and cared for her. Despite the shadows from San Diego that still haunted her, despite the uncertainty of what Special Agent Morris might uncover about Levi Siegel, despite the knowledge that living here, too, would eventually end, she knew with absolute certainty …

It was worth it.

Chapter Twenty-Eight
KON'NICHIWA, OKINAWA

August 2005
Okinawa, Japan

THE AIRBUS 321 ENTERED ITS approach into Naha Airport in Okinawa, Japan. Maggie glanced out her cabin window as the plane descended, her heart fluttering with excitement and apprehension. This was really happening. They were actually moving to a tiny island on the other side of the world.

"Oh, George," she said, her voice tinged with wonder, "look at the crystal-clear emerald-green water. I'm eager to get scuba certified and explore the underwater world. You did research it, didn't you?" *Please say yes. I need something to look forward to in this upheaval.*

"Of course. Marine Corps Community Services (MCCS) has Professional Association of Diving Instructors (PADI), and their instructors are among the best in the business. On my bucket list are the *USS Emmons*, which sank during World War II, and Miyako Island for cave dives that bring you through tunnels into an underwater bathed in blue light. But the most challenging dive is Cape Hedo Dome. The massive air pocket cave inside the cliff is only accessible from under the water."

Maggie smiled, feeling a small surge of relief. Trust George to have done his homework. At least this was one adventure she could look forward to. "Sounds spectacular. What types of sea life will we see?"

"Manta Scramble, off Ishigaki Island, is a great dive spot to see manta rays. Yonaguni Island is home to mysterious underwater ruins and is a popular spot for spotting hammerhead sharks. The Kerama Islands are where humpback whales come to breed in the winter season. With two hundred of the world's eight hundred species of coral and excellent water visibility, I assure you, my love, you will be pleased with your underwater escapades."

Hammerhead sharks? A nervous tingle ran down Maggie's spine. Maybe she would start with something less intimidating …

The plane touched down on the runway with a jolt that rattled Maggie's entire body.

"Did we just land in the middle of the ocean?!" said Maggie abruptly, her voice rising with sudden panic.

Oh my God, they were surrounded by water. This couldn't be safe.

"Yes, we did," replied George. "Airports on reclaimed land are common in Asia due to limited land availability and population growth. Artificial land solves the problem by allowing the airports to expand and accommodate more passengers and aircraft. It's impressively innovative."

Maggie's stomach lurched as the plane taxied to the terminal. The sight of water on three sides of the aircraft made her uneasy. She gripped the armrest tightly, her knuckles turning white. Artificial land? That didn't sound reassuring *at all.* This move was different—more different than she had prepared for.

After passing through customs, the Stones headed to the baggage claim area. Maggie's legs felt wobbly, partly from the long flight and partly from the rising sense of disorientation. Everything was so foreign—the signs, the language, the crowds.

Standing at the baggage carousel, they encountered a petite woman wearing a yellow sundress, holding a sign that read, *Welcome, Colonel & Mrs. Stone.* Her dark chestnut-brown hair was swept into a side ponytail. Maggie and George approached the woman.

"Colonel and Mrs. Stone," she announced with a Southern accent. "I'm Charla Ross. My husband, Dave, and I are your sponsors. We hope to make your transition to Okinawa a smooth one."

A Southern accent? She seems friendly, thought Maggie with unexpected relief.

"Thank you, Charla," said George. "Please call me Rocky. Is your husband Razor?"

"Yes, sir," said Charla.

George's face lit up with recognition. "I knew it. We were students at WTI in '86. He's well known in the Hornet community for his razor-sharp turns and maneuvers and his sharp instincts. I'm looking forward to seeing him again. Charla, this is my wife, Margaret."

"Please," said Maggie, extending her hand to Charla, "call me Maggie."

George was already in his element, connecting with old colleagues.

"Charla," said George, "what unit is Razor with?"

"He has command of Marine Wing Headquarters Squadron-1," replied Charla. "What about yourself?"

"Taking command of MAG-36."

After loading their extensive luggage pieces into Charla's van, the trio headed north on Route 58 on the Okinawan Expressway. George sat in the front passenger seat and engaged in a deep conversation with Charla. Maggie was sandwiched between luggage in the second row of the van. Her head was foggy with jet lag.

Of course George got the front seat while I'm crammed back with the luggage, she thought with a flash of irritation that she immediately felt guilty for. *Stop it, Maggie. You're just tired and overwhelmed.*

She noticed that Charla's steering wheel was on the right side of the car and that she was driving on the left side of the road. Above the expressway, green road signs were written in kanji and kilometers. Everything was backward and unreadable. How was she supposed to get around here on her own? Maggie felt her anxiety spike.

A rickety old truck pulled out in front of Charla's van. It carried three large bulls in the wooden pen in the back. Charla braked suddenly, sending Maggie lurching forward.

Good Lord!

"Welcome to Okinawa drivers," said Charla. "It seems overwhelming, but you'll be behind the wheel in no time. Just wait for typhoon season. That's when things get spicy."

"Typhoon season?" Maggie's eyes widened, her voice faltering slightly.

"Hurricane season on steroids."

First sharks, now typhoons? What else hadn't she prepared for?

What have we done? thought Maggie, a knot forming in her stomach.

This wasn't just a new base. This was an entirely different world.

The van ascended a narrow hill in the seaside town of Chatan. Maggie peered through the window, trying to absorb the unfamiliar landscape—a blend of Japanese buildings and what appeared to be American-style establishments.

"I thought you might like some comfort food to help alleviate the jet lag you're probably feeling right now," said Charla.

Comfort food. Yes, please, Maggie thought gratefully. Something familiar would be heaven right now.

The Railcar Diner was perched on a hill overlooking the East China Sea. It was a 1950s-style silver car, modeled after original train dining cars, with a neon sign flashing *24 Hours*. When they entered the diner, an Elvis Presley tune played on the old-fashioned jukebox in the corner. The floor featured black-and-white checkered vinyl tiles. Japanese diners sat beside Americans, enjoying their burgers, fries, and shakes.

This is surprisingly normal, Maggie thought, feeling some tension leave her shoulders. *Maybe it won't feel so strange living here after all.*

Charla, Maggie, and George sat on a row of red vinyl barstools along the counter. Photos of American film and music stars, along with movie posters, decorated the walls. The only difference between an American diner and this place was the hum of several slot machines lining the perimeter.

Gambling in a diner? Different, Maggie noted with surprise.

After they ordered cheeseburgers, fries, and root beer floats, Charla took a packet from her handbag.

"This is your first order of business," she said. "It's your study guide for the Japanese road test. When you're ready, I can take you to Camp Foster to get the US Forces Japan Operator's Permit. Then comes the fun part. We go shopping for your island cars."

Driving test? In a foreign country with unfamiliar rules and signs I can't read. Maggie felt her anxiety spike again. *Deep breaths. One step at a time.*

"I heard they have funny names for the cars here," said Maggie, trying to sound casual despite her mounting concerns.

"Naked, Life Diva, and Mira Cocoa are just a few of the cars you'll see." Charla chuckled. "You don't need a fancy car. We all drive beaters with dents and rust from the salty sea air. You need a reliable one with cold air-conditioning. The roads are narrow, there's a lot of traffic congestion, and, except for the expressway, the speed limit is thirty-seven miles per hour."

Narrow roads, congestion, strange rules. Maggie's hands fidgeted with her napkin. She was going to be stuck at the house for months before she worked up the courage to drive.

"How long have you been on the island?" Maggie asked, hoping to gauge how long it might take to adjust.

"We've been here a year," Charla stated.

"Well then, you must know our friends, the McCauleys. He's the commanding officer of VMA-208. His wife is Karma, and they have a sixteen-year-old daughter named Erin."

"Yes, of course," Charla replied. "Erin is friends with my daughters. Harper is Erin's classmate, and Charlotte will be a senior this year. Karma is a hoot. She's so much fun at karaoke at the Butler Officers' Club on Friday nights."

"She's always the life of the party," said Maggie, a fond smile softening her features despite her exhaustion. "Where are you from, Charla? I love your accent."

"I'm from Kingsville, Texas," Charla said proudly. "I come from a long line of ranchers and rodeo competitors. I grew up as a buckle bunny, as the cowboys call us. My childhood was spent calf roping and barrel racing my way across Texas. I was even a rodeo queen."

"Wow, look at you, hot stuff." Maggie giggled, genuinely impressed and momentarily forgetting her worries. *A real Texas rodeo queen!* "How did you meet your husband?"

"I met Dave at Jimmy D's Saloon in Old Town Kingsville," continued Charla. "He was a flight instructor at the Naval Air Station. He approached me, introduced himself, and offered me a Kamikaze shot. We often hung out there, drinking, listening to live music, and circling on the dance floor. Now, nearly twenty years later, we're living halfway around the world."

Twenty years, Maggie thought with a pang. George and she had been married for fifteen years, and that seemed like a long time.

"Allow me to pay the bill," said George when the trio finished their lunch.

"Thanks, Rocky. Do you have yen?" Charla asked.

"*Hai.* Yes," George answered with a grin.

Show-off, thought Maggie with a mix of affection and exasperation.

Of course he was already prepared with local currency and phrases.

George returned from the cashier. Maggie and Charla were still seated on the barstools.

"What took you so long?" Maggie asked.

"I had some change, so I tried my hand at a slot machine."

"And?" Maggie inquired, raising an eyebrow.

"Not profitable, but fun. This place is fantastic. They even have a vintage pink rotary phone at the cashier's stand."

"It works," Charla piped. "I used it when I brought my daughters here for breakfast and forgot my phone and yen. The only number I knew from memory was Dave's office. Thank goodness he had just returned to the office from his night flight. It wasn't a pleasant call."

"Well, you can call me next time," said Maggie, surprising herself with the offer. *Look at me, making connections already.* "When I get my Japanese phone."

"Deal," Charla replied.

The van traveled back down the hill to the WestPac Inn aboard Camp Foster. Maggie stared out the window, taking in the lush greenery and the strange architecture, feeling as though she were on another planet.

So much to learn, so much to adapt to, she thought with a mixture of dread and a tiny spark of curiosity.

Charla helped the Stones unload their luggage into their hotel room. Lastly, she retrieved a rectangular white plastic laundry basket from her van and walked toward the Stones' room.

"I leave you with this," she said, handing the basket to George. "It's your welcome basket. It's filled with American snacks, copies of the *Okinawa Living* magazine, a cheat sheet with common Japanese phrases, Japanese Pocky candy, Japanese Orion beer, and a bottle of sauvignon blanc, which is not Japanese."

Wine! Maggie perked up. That was exactly what she needed after this day.

George set the basket on the floor, startling a gecko that dashed across Maggie's flip-flops. She screamed, leaping back and almost crashing into the wall.

What the hell was that?

"Geckos are good luck," said Charla. "It's the centipedes and *habu* you have to watch out for. More on that later. The humidity is dangerous here. You'll want to invest in dehumidifiers for your home to protect your furniture and clothing from mold. American shopping is limited to the exchanges on the bases, so if you don't want to dress like everyone else on the island, dehumidifiers are a priority."

Centipedes? Habu? What is a habu? Maggie's mind raced. And now she had to worry about mold destroying their things? And limited shopping? The list of concerns was growing by the minute.

"Thank you for the lovely basket, Charla," said Maggie, pulling out the bottle of white wine with barely concealed eagerness. This was getting opened the minute she left. "Can we get nice bottles of wine here? I thought the heat might make it difficult." If she couldn't have familiar surroundings, at least let her have decent wine.

"Oh, girl, the Okinapa Wine Festival is just around the corner," Charla replied enthusiastically. "Butler O'Club transforms into a wine lover's paradise with opportunities to sample fine wines from around the world. There are food pairings and entertainment. Amazing ice sculptures. I was sipping wine next to a priest from the chapel last year. You're going to love it."

Wine festival? Now that's something I can look forward to, thought Maggie, a genuine smile spreading across her tired face.

"With that introduction, how can I not?" said Maggie.

"You know it," Charla quipped. "I'll be back at noon tomorrow to take you to get your Japanese cell phones. You'll be my lifeline when I can't get ahold of Dave. A deal's a deal."

Charla jumped in her van and started moving. She stopped the vehicle and yelled back to Maggie, *"Toire wa doku desu ka?"*

"What does that mean?" said Maggie, her brow furrowing in confusion.

"Where is the bathroom?" yelled Charla with a twinkle in her brown eyes. "That's the first one you need to learn!"

Charla waved as she drove away.

Where is the bathroom? Maggie repeated the phrase silently, trying to commit it to memory. She supposed that was essential.

As she watched Charla's van disappear down the road, Maggie felt a surprising warmth bloom in her chest, cutting through the fog of jet lag and anxiety.

This is the beginning of a beautiful friendship, she thought.

And for the first time since landing, she felt like maybe, just maybe, this new chapter might turn out all right.

Chapter Twenty-Nine
COWs

CHARLA SET OUT EARLY WITH Charlotte and Harper to pick up Karma, Erin, and then Maggie. It was to be a girls' day. Charla, Karma, and Maggie would join their husbands at the Okinapa Wine Festival in the evening while Charlotte, Harper, and Erin babysat the children of parents attending the festival.

Maggie climbed into the van, wearing a sundress and flip-flops. After weeks of her unpacking boxes and navigating the bewildering maze of military housing procedures, along with overseas rules and regulations, this outing felt like her first real opportunity to unwind.

The first stop of the day was Kanda's Art Gallery. The quaint yellow stone house with wood-framed windows and a red-tiled roof showcased Japanese prints, including woodblock, etching, mezzotint, stencil, and lithograph. Maggie lingered by a delicate cherry blossom print, entranced by its simple beauty.

"I should add this to my collection," she mused. "I love adding art pieces to remember each place we've been stationed."

Next, the van made its way toward the Sunabe Seawall and entered the parking lot of Cocok Spa.

"Maggie," said Charla, "you're in for a treat. Up these stairs is the best pedicure, nail design, leg massage, and overall relaxing experience you could ever imagine."

"I've been dreaming about this," Maggie admitted with a warm laugh. "I'm exhausted from unpacking boxes and setting up the house. My feet are begging for mercy."

Stepping inside the spa, the girls were transported to an Indonesian paradise overlooking the East China Sea. A thatched circular pole held brightly colored nail polish bottles. Exotic fabrics, draped below the ceiling light fixtures, diffused the light. The girls sat in a row of plush leather recliner chairs with sheer privacy curtains between them. They received laminated menus written in kanji and English, and their feet were placed in warm buckets of water.

Maggie sank into her chair with a contented sigh, overwhelmed by the luxury. As she wiggled her toes in the warm water, she thought, *This is heaven.* She started to release the tension she had been holding in her shoulders.

"Here's the perfect one for you, Erin," said Karma. "It reduces menstrual and premenstrual pain and stress and helps ease pain from PMS."

"Mother!" said Erin, irritated. She got up from her chair and walked away in a fury.

Karma leaned toward Maggie and said, "She's been so moody lately."

"Well, she is a teenager," Maggie said, her voice gentle and understanding. Although she wasn't a mother, she viewed herself as Erin's doting godmother and aunt.

"I know," said Karma, "but her grades have dropped. I try to speak nicely to her, and I can never say anything right."

"Do you think she's doing drugs?" asked Maggie, immediately regretting her bluntness. *Why did I say that?*

"God, I hope not. She'll end up in a Japanese prison. Not only do you not drink and drive here, but Japan also has zero tolerance for illegal drugs."

Erin returned to her chair, holding an ice cream cone in her hand.

"Where did you get that?" Maggie asked as she flipped through the thick book of nail designs, eager to change the subject.

"From the vending machine," replied Erin.

"Does the vending machine dispense wine?" asked Charla.

"It does," replied Erin.

"Well, giddyup, girl, and get me a glass of white."

"Charla," said Karma, "you're driving. Erin, you can give that glass of wine to me."

"Vending machines," Maggie said, her eyes lighting up with genuine fascination. "You can get anything from vending machines—eggs, cigarettes, beer, batteries, umbrellas, underwear … and the list goes on. I've seen Japanese vending machines in the strangest places. I understand them being in hotels and restaurants, but I'll be driving down a desolate road, and out of nowhere, there's a vending machine." She had been keeping a mental list of all the unusual things she had seen since arriving in this foreign country.

"That's just as strange as how you get directions to Camp Courtney," replied Karma. "Turn right at the stoplight. Drive down the winding road until you see the red Coca-Cola vending machine. Then turn left. When you come to the intersection with the bull—a real bull, I might add—turn right."

"What happens if the bull isn't there?" asked Maggie, her eyebrows shooting up in genuine concern. The navigation challenges had been one of her biggest anxieties since arriving.

"You get lost," said Karma. "If you're lucky enough to have a navigation system in your car, it's in Japanese, but at least you can follow the breadcrumbs on the screen. If you're like most of us, you have your cell phone, which you can only use to send and receive calls because everything is in Japanese."

Bulls as landmarks, Maggie thought, feeling a fresh wave of uncertainty about her ability to navigate independently. Add that to her list of strange things.

"So, COWs," said Charla, "are we excited about the upcoming conference?"

"COWs?" asked Charlotte quizzically.

"Commanding Officers' Wives," said Charla. "Our quarterly conference is coming up next week."

"Have you had a chance to look at the schedule?" asked Maggie, perking up.

"Yes," said Charla. "It looks pretty good. Standard ethics training, Family Readiness Program update, a combat stress and posttraumatic stress brief with a mental health nurse guest speaker, MCCS update, turnover file workshop, social media/public affairs, and entertaining with the 100-yen store."

The 100-yen store sounds perfect, Maggie thought, excited to add local flair to her home.

Feeling relaxed, renewed, and refreshed, the girls walked out of the spa with nail art designs featuring Hello Kitty, flowers, polka dots, sea turtles, palm trees, or butterflies.

Maggie admired her nails, adorned with delicate cherry blossoms that matched the print she had seen at the gallery. It felt like a small celebration of her new life here, something beautiful amid all the chaos of transition.

"Off to lunch at Yogi's House," said Charla.

Yogi's House was a favorite restaurant for both Okinawans and Americans. It was a small establishment with only a few seats at the bar and several low tables, featuring tatami mats for seating. The walls were adorned with photos of Yogi, the owner, alongside Okinawan and American celebrities and diners. Yogi had lived in the United States for twenty years, refining the art of sushi to appeal to Americans. During his time in the US, he'd created the California roll, which became his trademark.

Maggie hesitated at the entrance, carefully observing the others as they removed their shoes. *Don't mess this up,* she thought anxiously, worried about committing some cultural faux pas. She had been practicing with chopsticks in private for weeks, determined not to embarrass herself.

"Good afternoon, ladies," said Yogi, wearing his signature white chef jacket and round sushi cap.

"*Kon'nichiwa.* Good afternoon, Yogi," replied Charla. "These are my friends—Karma and her daughter, Erin. You know my daughters, Harper and Charlotte. This is Maggie. She's new to the island, and I wanted to be the first to bring her here."

"*Hai,*" said Yogi. "Yes, welcome to the island, Maggie. Charlasan, what would you like to order?"

"The original California roll," said Charla. "The Chatan roll, swordfish sashimi, and a bottle of awamori."

"Is that sake?" asked Maggie, leaning forward with interest. Her mother would've frowned on day drinking, but Maggie was determined to embrace local customs. When in Japan …

"It's island sake," said Charla. "A distilled liquor born in the islands of Okinawa."

"Charlasan," said Yogi, "you must try the fugu sushi. Our blowfish is very fresh and tasty."

"And deadly," replied Charla. "I've read about fugu poisoning from the toxic fish's liver, ovaries, and skin."

Maggie's eyes widened as a brief image of George receiving notification of her death by poisoned fish flashed through her mind. *Not exactly the way I planned to make an impression,* she thought, forcing a brave smile.

"Charlasan, I'm a specially trained and licensed preparer. Have no fear."

"Only if you show us your fearless stance," said Charla.

Yogi hoisted his samurai sword from his side holder and raised it above his head. "*Banzai!*" he shouted.

"Well, I feel better," said Karma. "He's going into battle with the blowfish. Speaking of fish, Charla, you should come diving with me and Maggie. You can see the fish up close and personal."

Maggie brightened, delighted to begin scuba diving on the island. She had recently completed her PADI Open Water diving classes.

"No thanks," said Charla. "The closest I need to get to fish is looking at them through the glass at the Churaumi Aquarium or eating fresh and tasty ones here at Yogi's House."

"Where's your sense of adventure?" Karma teased.

"I leave the adventure to you, Karma."

"Oh, Charla, I think you'd love it," Maggie said enthusiastically. "The reefs here are spectacular, and I've heard the blue cave is magical."

She felt relaxed and unguarded. As stressful as military life could be, she loved how quickly they formed bonds and support networks.

Thank you, Charla, for making me feel so welcome.

Chapter Thirty

OKINAPA

MAGGIE FIDGETED WITH HER PENDANT necklace as she approached the Butler Officers' Club alongside the other two couples, all dressed in cocktail attire. She felt a bit nervous about meeting new people yet excited at the same time.

"Look how wonderful they've transformed the club," she exclaimed.

She glanced at the long tables with their burgundy tablecloths, each holding bottles of wine with a description printed on it. Black-clad attendants were waiting to pour samples. She was particularly drawn to the artistic dolphin ice sculptures that glistened in the center of the room, surrounded by appetizers and floral arrangements.

Someone invested a lot of money to make this look impressive, she thought.

The three couples each picked up their tasting glasses, etched with *Okinapa Wine Festival*, and started sampling the wines. Maggie swirled her glass as if she knew what she was doing, even though her palate couldn't tell the difference between a ten-dollar bottle and the fancy vintage they were serving.

Karma purchased an eighty-dollar bottle of Argentinian Malbec and invited Charla and Maggie to join her on the patio.

Eighty dollars for wine? Maggie thought.

She followed. Saying no to Karma was like trying to stop a moving train.

As they navigated through the crowded club, Karma bumped into a woman who introduced herself as Erin's English teacher.

"Will ten o'clock work?" the teacher asked after requesting a meeting for Monday morning.

"Yes, that'll be fine. Thank you, Mrs. West," Karma replied, maintaining her composure, though Maggie could see the slight tightening around her eyes.

Once the teacher walked away, Maggie turned to Karma. "What was that about?"

"Erin's English teacher wants to meet with me and John on Monday morning. Something about her journal entry."

Concern overtook Maggie. Erin was a good kid. What could be in that journal?

"Maybe you'll discover why she's been acting so strange lately," Maggie suggested, remembering how Erin had acted earlier in the day, hunched over her phone with that faraway look teenagers got when something was eating at them.

"Yeah, maybe." Karma's voice had that forced lightness Maggie recognized all too well. She was worried but determined not to show it.

They settled at an outside patio table and uncorked the wine. The band, The Sushi Rolls, performed popular American party music, and the crowd loved it.

Charla excused herself to visit friends at a neighboring table, promising to bring another bottle when she returned. Maggie envied her easy sociability; connections that took Maggie months to build seemed to fall into Charla's lap like ripe fruit.

When the band played "Macarena," Karma jumped up from her chair and started dancing. For a split second, Maggie hesitated—she hated dancing, hated drawing attention—but something about the wine and the night air pushed her forward. She joined Karma, following her movements as she went through the familiar arm positions and hip shaking. Her body moved stiffly at first, then more freely as she let go of her self-consciousness. For once, she didn't care what anyone thought of her making a fool of herself.

Charla returned with another bottle of wine, her cheeks flushed with excitement and a hint of alcohol. "I saw the guys when I went inside to get the bottle."

"Let me guess," Maggie said, knowing exactly what she'd find if she went looking. "They were huddled in a corner, talking shop."

Always the same with military men—couldn't let go of work, even at a party.

"Uh-huh," Charla confirmed. "They just don't have an off button. We're having much more fun out here. Karma certainly is."

Maggie rolled her eyes, watching Karma twirl with abandon. "She's in a drinking mood tonight." She recognized the signs—she'd seen this version of Karma before, pushing it too far, running from something.

"Aren't we all?" Charla replied. "I hope the girls make good money sitting tonight. It looks like most of the housing area is here. I see the girls' soccer coach. I'll be right back, y'all."

After Charla left, Karma mimicked her. "*I'll be right back, y'all.* Is she going to talk to everyone in the club tonight?" There was an edge to her voice that Maggie didn't like.

"Karma, stop," Maggie said, feeling protective of Charla. "She's a social butterfly. She loves people." *Unlike you and me,* she thought, but didn't say.

Karma and she shared a certain cynicism that Charla didn't seem to possess.

"She's nau-se-at-ing," Karma slurred, stretching out the syllables.

A knot formed in Maggie's stomach. This was going beyond tipsy and into something uglier.

"Are you jealous?" Maggie asked, trying to keep her tone light while watching her carefully.

"Of her? Hell no."

Karma laughed as she poured more wine into both their glasses, sloshing liquid onto the table. "Let's finish off the bottle the Yellow Rose of Texas bought us."

Maggie accepted the glass but only pretended to sip. Someone needed to stay clearheaded, and it clearly wasn't going to be Karma tonight.

When the band returned from their break with "I Like to Move It," Karma raced to the space in front of the stage. Maggie's heart sank as Karma dropped to her knees and started doing the worm dance, arching her back and rocking forward. She wanted to look away, but couldn't; it was like watching a car accident in slow motion.

God, we're not twenty-two anymore, Maggie thought. *Tomorrow, she'll feel this in every joint, not to mention her dignity.*

She saw George, Hurl, and Razor enter the patio area, and relief washed over her. Hurl approached his wife and picked her up from the floor, his expression a complex mix of embarrassment and concern that Maggie recognized as *my spouse is making a scene* look.

"It's time to go home, Karma," said Hurl.

With a noticeable slur, she answered, "Wine not!"

Her loud cackle carried throughout the O'Club, making Maggie cringe internally. She caught George's eye across the patio and gave him the slight headshake, which they'd developed over years of silent communication—meaning *not good.*

The group gathered their belongings and made their way back inside toward the exit. Maggie stayed close to Charla, distancing herself from Karma's increasingly erratic behavior. Karma insisted on saying goodbye to her "spirit animal"—the dolphin ice sculpture. Maggie anticipated what would happen before it did, having known Karma for a long time. As Karma pushed away after planting a kiss, she slipped and fell, taking the sculpture down with her. Ice shattered everywhere, fragments scattering across the floor like confetti from a burst party balloon.

"Dolphin down," Razor quipped.

Maggie didn't laugh. There was nothing funny about watching her friend spiral.

Hurl looked concerned, his military composure cracking. "Maggie, what is going on with her tonight?"

"You have a meeting with Erin's English teacher on Monday morning," she explained, keeping her voice low. "Erin wrote something of concern in her journal." She didn't need to elaborate; they all understood how teenage troubles could drive a parent to seek comfort at the bottom of a bottle.

Maggie wrapped her arm around Charla and whispered, "Is there a substance abuse brief at the COWs conference?"

They both laughed, but for Maggie, beneath the joke lay real worry. This wasn't the first time Karma had gone overboard, and patterns were emerging that Maggie couldn't ignore.

They headed toward the exit with George and Razor following behind them. She could feel George's hand at the small of her back, steady and reassuring. His touch always grounded her when chaos swirled around them.

Hurl helped Karma up again, wrapping his arms around her as he guided her out. Her mascara had smudged, giving her raccoon eyes that made her look vulnerable despite her bravado.

As they passed through the exit doors, Hurl sighed philosophically, "Into each life, a little rain must fall."

And some of us, Maggie thought, watching Karma stumble against her husband, *are caught in a downpour without an umbrella.*

Monday's meeting with the teacher suddenly seemed very far away, and she wondered what storms were brewing for all of them in this tight-knit military community, where secrets rarely stayed buried for long.

Chapter Thirty-One
THE TRUTH REVEALED

AFTER KARMA'S URGENT CALL, MAGGIE'S hands shook as she clutched the steering wheel and hurried to the McCauley residence. The fear in her friend's voice had been unmistakable. Something was terribly wrong.

When Hurl met her outside with watery eyes, her stomach dropped. She'd known this family for years—watched Erin grow from a little girl with pigtails into a thoughtful teenager. Whatever had happened must have been devastating for Hurl to look so broken.

As she sat on the sofa beside Erin, Maggie tried to prepare herself. Nothing, however, could have prepared her for what Karma had to say.

"Erin was sexually assaulted at a high school party on the island."

The revelation hit Maggie hard. She felt sick, then furious, then heartbroken—all in a matter of seconds. Maintaining her composure for Erin's sake required every ounce of self-control she had. As Erin described what had happened, Maggie fought back tears, focusing instead on being present and strong when this girl needed strength around her.

"It's not your fault," Maggie echoed Karma's words, meeting Erin's gaze directly, imploring her to believe it.

Inside, Maggie was screaming. The injustice of it—that Erin should blame herself while the perpetrator walked free—made her want to punch something.

When Erin revealed it was Tommy Kirkdale, Maggie couldn't contain her shock. She knew of the Kirkdales—everyone on base did. The golden boy with a decorated father. The perfect military family image. Her outburst stemmed from a place of protective rage, though she immediately regretted adding to Erin's burden.

"Tommy's father is Colonel Kirkdale," she said softly, thinking of the power dynamics and the uphill battle ahead.

This poor girl, she thought, as if the trauma itself wasn't enough to bear.

During the NCIS agents' questioning, Maggie observed how Erin seemed to shrink physically, folding into herself with each probe into that terrible night. Maggie wanted to stop the interrogation and shield Erin from reliving it all. Instead, she quietly passed tissues and offered water while Karma placed a steady hand on Erin's back—small gestures that said, *I'm here. I believe you.*

When the agents revealed Tommy's claim that the encounter had been consensual, rage flashed through Maggie again.

"That's not true," she yelled, unable to contain herself. "She told him no!"

The moment the words left her mouth, she regretted drawing attention to herself when Erin needed to be the focus. But the thought of that boy lying, of getting away with what he'd done, made her blood boil.

Later, as the agents explained the unlikelihood of a successful case, Maggie watched Erin's face fall. She recognized that expression—the realization that justice might be unattainable. Maggie had seen it before in other women's eyes, had felt it herself. The systems meant to protect often failed those who needed them most.

After the agents left, Maggie stayed behind. She helped Karma make tea while Hurl sat with Erin.

"What can I do?" Maggie asked Karma quietly in the kitchen, tears finally breaking free now that Erin couldn't see them. "Anything. Everything. Just tell me."

"You're already doing it," Karma replied, squeezing her hand. "Being here. Believing her."

Maggie noticed Karma's shoulders slump, the day's weight crushing her usual confident posture. In the quiet aftermath of the NCIS agents' departure, Maggie could see her friend's mind turning inward, toward darker thoughts.

"Do you think I'm being punished?" Karma looked at Maggie with a pained stare.

Maggie felt her heart constrict at the raw vulnerability in Karma's eyes. This wasn't just a mother's grief for her daughter's trauma; there was something deeper, something haunted in that question.

"Punished? For what?"

"Sins of the mother. Terrible things I did in my past."

"Oh, Karma," said Maggie, draping her arm around her and holding her close. The familiar weight of Karma against her shoulder brought back memories of crises they'd weathered together, other confessions in the dark. "I'll admit, you don't have the cleanest record, but, good God, no, what happened to Erin is not payment for your sins."

Maggie felt the tremor that ran through Karma's body, the silent sob she was struggling to contain. How many times had they held each other like this through the years? Through deployments, losses, and the peculiar loneliness that could only be understood by military spouses.

"None of this would've happened if I hadn't hooked my wagon to Levi."

The name sent a chill down Maggie's spine. It belonged to their shared past, a chapter they rarely discussed.

"Levi," said Maggie, her voice careful. "What does this have to do with Levi?"

"Maybe Julia wouldn't have died. He was supplying her with the drugs."

Maggie tensed, memories flooding back—Julia's face in the water—but she pushed them aside. Tonight wasn't about their complicated past; it was about Erin.

"Levi very well might have had something to do with Julia dying, but it had nothing to do with you." Maggie squeezed Karma's shoulder firmly. "For now, you need to focus on supporting Erin. We all do. I will be by your side the whole time."

She meant it. She would be there for this family she loved, regardless of the secrets that still held them together or the shadows from their past that continued to loom large.

"I love you, Maggie," said Karma, hugging her tightly. "You know I would do anything for you."

"I know. I love you too, Karma."

The fierce protectiveness that had characterized their friendship for decades returned to Maggie. They had witnessed each other's best and worst sides. They had shared their burdens and kept each other's secrets. What she and Karma had created was unique and valuable in the military, where friendships were frequently short-lived due to deployments and moves. Years of loyalty that had been tried and tested were contained in those few words. As always, they would confront whatever lay ahead, whether it was the aftermath of Erin's assault or the ghosts of Levi and Julia.

That night, as Maggie drove home, she pulled over twice when tears blurred her vision too much to continue. She thought about Erin, about all the young women navigating a world that too often hurt them, and then asked why they hadn't been more careful. She made silent promises to herself—to check on Erin daily, to stand by Karma and Hurl, and to bear witness to Erin's pain and her healing.

Maggie wouldn't let Erin face this alone. Female solidarity wasn't just about pretty words; it was about showing up, time and time again, in the most challenging moments. It was about sitting in the discomfort of another's pain, for leaving them to bear it alone was unthinkable.

The next morning, Maggie would arrive at the McCauley home with breakfast, with books that had aided her through her darkest times, and with a playlist of songs about resilience. She would continue to show up, day after day, for as long as it took. Because that was what women did for each other when the world failed them—they created safety where there was none, they believed when others doubted, and they held space for both rage and healing.

For now, however, Maggie drove home in the dark, already planning how to build a cocoon of female support around Erin and Karma, with Charla, Charlotte, and Harper Ross, along with every woman she knew who understood what it meant to face trauma and come out, not unchanged, but undefeated.

Chapter Thirty-Two
OCEAN LOUNGE

MAGGIE BOOKED A PRIVATE SCUBA diving tour for herself and Karma on the island's northern part. She gripped the steering wheel of her white Nissan Fairlady Z tightly as she drove, Karma's words playing in her head.

"None of this would've happened if I hadn't hooked my wagon to Levi."

"Maybe Julia wouldn't have died …"

Her repressed thoughts of Julia's drowning flashed back in her mind. The ocean, with its vastness, was a terrifying reminder of how quickly it could claim a life.

I can do this. I need to do this.

It was early in the morning when she picked up Karma. The sports car drove north on the Okinawa expressway toward Nago/Ishikawa. Shortly into the hour-long drive, Maggie glanced at Karma, noticing the dark circles under her eyes and how her usually vibrant friend seemed somewhat diminished.

"I know this has been a traumatic experience," said Maggie, falling naturally into the caretaker role she'd inhabited since childhood. "But you've been in bed for weeks."

"I know," said Karma. "Thank you. I needed this. It's been a stressful couple of weeks."

"My pleasure, my friend. How's Erin doing?"

"Remarkably well. She likes her therapist. She visits her once a week at the naval hospital. We decided not to press charges. Erin's been through enough. She needs to heal."

"Is Tommy still on the island?"

"Yes. His parents think he's done nothing wrong. I hope John never runs into him. I'm afraid of what he might do if he sees him face-to-face."

"She's a strong girl, Karma. She'll get through this … you all will."

Maggie's thoughts drifted to Julia as she spoke words of reassurance. How many times had she told herself the same thing after the accident? *You'll get through this. You're strong. You'll survive.* But surviving wasn't the same as living—a distinction she was only beginning to grasp.

"I keep thinking we shouldn't have come to Okinawa. None of this would've happened."

"I'll share some advice that Lou gave me years ago. Bad things happen, Karma. It could've happened anywhere, not just because you're in Okinawa. You'll learn from this experience. You'll rise like a phoenix from the ashes— stronger, smarter, and more powerful."

If only I could believe that myself, Maggie thought, remembering how she'd repeated Lou's words like a mantra after Julia's death.

"Lou said that. Was he standing and pulsing his fist like a preacher at a sermon?"

"No." Maggie smirked. "He was in the wooden rocker. You idiot!"

Karma reached for Maggie's hand. "Thanks, Maggie. Thanks, Lou. I get it. I'm just being a smart-ass."

The sports car pulled up in front of a two-story black building with blue logo flags reading *Ocean Lounge.* The girls headed down to the docks toward the dive shop. The weather-worn exterior, with its bleached wood from the sun and sea and rusted metal windows, was a testament to its centuries-old existence. Inside, the shop smelled of mildew and fish, but it had a slightly rustic mom-and-pop feel. The walls were lined with diving and snorkeling equipment hanging from hooks—masks, snorkels, fins, wet suits, regulators, and tanks.

Maggie's heart raced as she looked at the equipment. She was really doing this—her first open water dive.

A short, dark-haired, dark-skinned man with a stocky build greeted them.

"Good morning, ladies," he said. "You must be Maggie and Karma, my first dive of the day. My name is Rex. I'll be your guide."

Rex had a round face, defined brow, and deep-set eyes, indicative of a native Okinawan.

"Do you have your C-cards?" he asked.

"Yes," Maggie replied, handing over their certification cards.

She'd gotten certified when she first arrived on the island, but only been in a pool. Karma had begged her to try open water diving, but Maggie had always found excuses. *Too busy. Next time.* She was doing this for Karma now. She needed to help her friend with a distraction from the pain of Erin's assault.

Rex examined the cards, noting they were both PADI Open Water divers, the lowest level of certification.

"Karma, your paperwork said you have six prior dives, but I saw that this will be Maggie's first open water dive."

"Yes," said Maggie, masking her anxiety with enthusiasm. "I am so excited." *And terrified.*

"Great. You'll love it. When booking the tour, you mentioned you have wetsuits, masks, fins, and booties. Let's get the rest of your gear."

Rex handed each girl a tank, a buoyancy control device (BCD), and a regulator. As Maggie took the equipment, her hands trembled slightly. She thought of Julia, water filling lungs, darkness, and silence. She took a deep breath.

I can do this. I will do this.

The three loaded into a fifteen-foot outboard boat and set out for a fifteen-minute ride to the nearby islands of Minna and

Sesoko. The boat stopped at Minna Island, also known as Minna-jima among the locals. Rex cut the engine.

The gentle rocking of the boat soothed Maggie. Water had always been her sanctuary before Julia's accident—a place of peace and clarity. It was complicated, filled with beauty and danger, much like life.

"Minna-jima has been a crucial navigation point for centuries," Rex explained. "During the Battle of Okinawa, the Marines captured the island to establish a firebase in support of the invasion of Okinawa. Thanks to its C shape, it is often called Croissant Island."

Maggie and Karma gazed at the white sand beach and the emerald-green water.

This is nothing like the gray waters where Julia drowned, Maggie reminded herself. This was different. She was different.

"To avoid upsetting the boat, you two will back-roll off opposite sides when I give the word," Rex instructed. "Surface and give me the okay signal. Then I'll join you and descend to sixty feet."

Karma and Maggie put on their gear. As Maggie prepared to enter the water, she felt a panic grip her chest.

Julia couldn't breathe. The water wouldn't let her breathe. She forced the thought away and focused on her training.

They submerged in the warm, pristine blue-green water on Rex's count. Maggie felt the cool embrace of the ocean against her skin through the wetsuit—a sensation vastly different from the suffocating panic she had imagined. Rex waited for the girls to give the okay signal before entering the water. The trio descended thirty feet.

Colorful coral reefs popped within the crystal-clear water with shades of blue and emerald green. Anemonefish, eagle rays, trevally, and pipefish whisked past the divers. It was beautiful.

Why had she waited so long to experience this? The answer came unbidden—because she had been afraid. And still scared.

When they dropped deeper to sixty feet, the distinctive white sandy bottom spread endlessly. Schools of snapper darted in and out of isolated coral reefs. Maroon-red lionfish with white stripes propelled through the coral, reflecting light in brilliant purple, blue, green, and red hues.

For the first time since Julia's death, Maggie felt a sense of wonder displace her grief. The ocean that had taken a life was now showing her another side of itself—a place of vibrant life and color.

Forty-five minutes later, Rex motioned the girls to return to the surface. Once inside the boat, Maggie and Karma gushed enthusiastically about the magnificent underwater world.

Rex piloted the boat toward the second dive site, Sesoko Island, which was connected to the main island by a distinctive bridge.

"Sesoko-jima used to be a quiet fishing village. It's fallen prey to tourists now that it has become easily accessible by car. However, the underwater topography, shaped by ancient volcanic activity, has remained largely untouched. This dive will be more challenging, with tunnels, caverns, and swim-throughs."

Maggie felt a flutter of apprehension. *I've done well so far. I can handle this.*

"Your English is perfect, Rex," Karma remarked. "Did you study in the United States?"

"I did. I studied marine biology at Scripps Institution of Oceanography at the University of California, San Diego."

Karma caught Maggie's eye; they exchanged looks and shouted, "We're from San Diego!"

"What a small world," said Maggie. "You must have loved the La Jolla tide pools."

"Point Loma is the best. But I liked La Jolla and Swami's Beach in Encinitas."

"Were you born in the US or Japan?" Karma asked.

"Born in Okinawa. My mother is a native Okinawan. She was working as a translator on the Marine Corps base when she met my American father, a retired Marine Corps master sergeant. He runs the recreation and fitness programs for MCCS."

"What did you love most about San Diego?" Maggie asked enthusiastically. "The surf, the weather, the food?"

Without missing a beat, Rex answered, "California women."

Karma and Maggie laughed.

Rex explained that after graduating from UCSD, he'd returned to Okinawa to help his uncle out by running tours at the Ocean Lounge.

"I work weekends running tours now that I've finally landed my dream job as a researcher at the Okinawa Institute of Science and Technology. I've always loved the sea—diving, snorkeling, boating. I get to spend my days diving for hours on beautiful reefs. I play detective, collecting samples and analyzing them back at the lab. Life underwater is magical—so beautiful and tranquil. The soft hues of the coral blend like a Monet painting. Did you know there are seasons underwater— spring, summer, fall, and winter—each with flora and fauna? A stingray glides past me, and I can examine the intricate lines on its body. I'm amused by a sea star doing backflips and excited and exhilarated when observing sharks in their natural habitat. It's so much fun; I don't even feel like I'm working."

His words, like the Pied Piper's magic flute, lured Maggie and Karma into the quiet beauty of the undersea world. Maggie listened, entranced. She had always been the one to lead, to take responsibility, to fix things. But here, underwater, she would have to follow—to trust Rex, to trust Karma, to trust herself.

Rex approached the second dive site, cut the engine, and dropped anchor. He then explained the dive details.

"Like I said earlier, this dive will be more challenging. You will both back-roll off the sides, just like the first dive. Once below the surface, I'd like to take underwater photos of you. Then we'll head to the first swim-through. Starting at sixty feet on the wall, we'll go about thirty feet to a vertical chimney that pops out at twenty feet on top of the reef. Are we ready?"

"Hell yeah!" the girls shouted.

Maggie's enthusiasm masked her growing unease. A chimney. A tight space. Underwater. She pushed the fear down.

You're doing this for Karma. You're doing this for yourself.

As they descended, sea life exploded around them. Rex photographed magnificent sea turtles paddling past them. The girls were suspended beside an octopus, watching its boneless body stretch long and thin as it jetted away. Rex led the way into the long, dark, cave-like swim-through, followed by Maggie and Karma.

The tunnel had many small cracks where sunlight shone through. Vast schools of tiny fish surrounded the divers. As Maggie wove in and out of swim-throughs, she felt like a fish. She passed a green moray eel, sea snakes, and clownfish. For a moment, she forgot her fear, forgot Julia, forgot everything except the mesmerizing beauty surrounding her.

The divers approached the vertical chimney that would pop them out above the reef. Maggie followed Rex into the tunnel. On the way up, Maggie was startled by a fish that appeared right next to her face. She quickly turned to the left to see what kind of fish it was. She didn't realize her second-stage hose had just snagged on an outcropping. When she turned her head, it pulled her mouthpiece from her mouth.

Maggie stopped. Stunned. Her eyes widened, her heart pounded, and she clenched her fists. Time seemed to slow as her mind raced.

Oh my God, what do I do?! I can't think straight.

Images of Julia flashed before her eyes—Julia begging for help to get back to shore.

Is this how it felt for Julia? This panic? This terror?

Maggie tried to locate the hose by corralling it with an arm sweep, but the tightness of the chimney made that impossible. Near panic, she remembered her octopus—a backup air source—and pulled it out of its D-ring on her chest, put it in her mouth, and cleared it. She finally had air again and could begin to calm down.

She was not Julia. This wasn't the same. She had air, she had training, and she was not alone.

Once outside the chimney, she felt clearheaded—until she didn't. She began to ascend too quickly, and her body felt eerily lightweight. The pressure change popped her ears painfully.

This wasn't good. If she rose too rapidly, she'd get the bends.

Maggie knew that if she ascended too quickly, the surrounding water pressure would decrease too fast for the gas bubbles in her body to dissipate. The bubbles would enlarge, creating a potentially fatal block to her blood flow. The spots in her vision were already evidence of what was happening.

I need help. I can't do this alone. The thought was foreign to Maggie, who had always been the helper, never the helped.

Karma emerged from the chimney. Maggie turned to her, shaking both hands rapidly in circles, palms facing forward, fingers extended.

Karma quickly recognized that Maggie had lost buoyancy control. She grabbed her, dumped Maggie's BCD and her own to arrest the ascent, and stabilized them both.

As Karma took control, Maggie felt a strange mix of terror and relief. It was both terrifying and liberating.

Rex realized Maggie was in distress. He swam toward the girls and escorted them to the surface. Maggie hastily removed her mask and mouthpiece. Rex climbed back into the boat, assisting Maggie and Karma safely into the hull.

"Maggie, what happened?" Rex asked breathlessly.

"It started in the tunnel. I lost my mouthpiece due to a close encounter with a fish. Then I started rising rapidly. I knew I was in trouble. Thank God Karma came to my aid." The words felt inadequate to describe the brush with mortality she'd just experienced.

Was this how it had been for Julia? The question haunted her. *Only I didn't save her.*

"Nice job, Karma," said Rex. "I'm sorry, Maggie. I probably pushed the envelope with that last tunnel, especially with you being a newbie."

Rex helped Maggie remove her shoulder straps and tank. She was shaking uncontrollably and short of breath. He wrapped a towel around her, grabbed a water bottle from the cooler, and handed it to her.

"I think that's enough excitement for today," said Rex. "Sit back, relax, and enjoy the short ride back to the dock."

As the boat sped back to shore, Maggie stared at the endless blue surrounding them.

Water gives life. Water takes life. She had experienced both truths today.

She glanced at Karma. They had both faced darkness— different kinds, but darkness nonetheless—and they were both still here, still breathing.

Back at the Ocean Lounge, Karma and Maggie headed to the locker room to shower and change.

Maggie was in the shower when Karma shouted, "See you upstairs, doll."

With her eyes closed, warm water cascaded over Maggie's head and shoulders, rinsing away the salt and sea. Her muscles relaxed, and her heart ceased racing. She inhaled through her nose and exhaled gently through her mouth, feeling the day's tension drain away with the water.

Water cleanses. Water heals.

She let the tears flow then, mingling with the spray of the shower—tears for Julia, tears for herself, tears for all the fears she'd faced today and all the ones still waiting.

Maggie grabbed a towel and dried off. She combed her wet hair, got dressed, and headed upstairs. Karma was seated at the bar, enjoying the panoramic view of the East China Sea through the floor-to-ceiling windows.

"I took the liberty of ordering us martinis," said Karma.

"What a morning!" Maggie exclaimed, taking a seat next to Karma. "Thanks for having my back."

"You know I'll always look out for you, Maggie, but I think you need to take a refresher course in underwater hand signals."

"What?"

"Yes, what? What was that Jazzercise routine you pulled underwater outside the tunnel?"

"I know … I panicked. But you didn't. You knew exactly what to do."

Maggie felt a newfound respect for Karma. She'd always seen herself as the caretaker in their friendship, but today had shown her that relationships weren't one-sided. Sometimes, the strong one needed strength from others.

"Don't sell yourself short. You're stronger than you think. You were the strong one helping me through this terrible ordeal with Erin."

"That's what friends are for." To save each other, in all the ways that mattered.

"Will this incident scare you away from diving?" Karma asked.

"Only if I'm diving without my buddy. You saved my life today. I'm forever grateful."

The words felt inadequate for the profound shift Maggie felt. Perhaps that was the lesson Julia's death had been trying to teach her all along—*no one survives alone.*

"*Kampai.* Cheers," said Maggie, clinking her glass against Karma's glass. "We'll be here a few hours while I burn off this alcohol before the drive home."

"Me too," said Karma. "Or I'll be charged with irresponsible behavior, according to Japanese law."

"*Irresponsible* and *Karma* in the same sentence have nothing to do with Japanese law." Maggie laughed.

Karma smiled, pulled out the underwater photo Rex had taken of the girls, and handed it to Maggie.

Maggie gazed at the photo, at two friends suspended in blue infinity, connected, even in the vastness. She thought of Julia, and for the first time, the memory didn't bring only pain. Perhaps this was what it meant to rise like a phoenix—not to forget, but to transform the pain into something that could sustain flight.

"We'll always have the Ocean Lounge," Maggie said softly, a promise to Karma, to herself, and to the memory of Julia—that life would continue, that connection would endure, that water, like grief, could both drown and sustain.

Chapter Thirty-Three
It's Only Kinky
the First Time

July 2007
Love Hotel Alley
Japan

MAGGIE TOSSED A DUFFEL BAG, boom box, and picnic basket into the trunk of her Nissan. A giddy excitement boiled up inside her chest as her heart raced with anticipation. Even after seventeen years, she still got butterflies, planning surprises for him.

"George, are you ready for your anniversary surprise?" Maggie inquired, trying to keep her voice steady despite her growing excitement. She had been planning this for weeks, researching the perfect location and gathering all the necessary items.

"Sure thing. I can't wait to see what you have planned for this evening."

Still plays along with my schemes after all these years.

Excitement spread through her body at his willingness to follow her lead, even when he had no idea what she was planning.

The Stones hopped into the two-door coupe. Maggie sat behind the wheel and handed George a sheet of paper, her fingers tingling slightly as they brushed against his. She hoped he didn't guess where they were going too quickly. She wanted to see his face when he realized. Their two years on this island were about to end, and this, like scuba diving, was on her bucket list.

"George, can you please read these directions to me?" Her voice carried a hint of mischief that she couldn't quite suppress.

George opened the piece of paper. "*Head east on 330. At the intersection with 20, take a right. At the sixth stoplight, take a right. Follow until you pass a golf driving range and the Birdland Café, then take a left. When you pass a pink-and-white apartment building on your right, take the next left onto Route 22.* What kind of directions are these, and where are you taking me?"

"Love Hotel Alley." Maggie smiled, her voice dropping to a sultry whisper.

Gotcha. She felt a thrill of satisfaction, seeing his shocked expression.

"Maggie, no! I'm not spending our anniversary evening in a no-tell motel with possible bedbugs and someone else's pubic hairs on the sheets."

Maggie bit back a laugh. So predictable. "George, I promise you, it's not like that," she said, her tone gentle but firm. "Japanese families live with several generations of family members under one roof. Couples visit the love hotels for privacy. It's part of the culture and not frowned upon as sleazy, fleabag hotels, like in the States. They have paper-thin walls, remember?" *I've done my research, my love. Trust me on this.*

"Yes. Shoji screens. I get it."

Route 22 was lined with neon signs advertising various hotel establishments. Roughly twenty-five hotels lined the Okinawan Vegas-style strip. Maggie's eyes widened with delight as they drove past each hotel, uniquely themed. This was even better than the pictures online. Her pulse quickened with each colorful establishment they passed.

"The vacancy sign is on at The Mint House," said Maggie, pointing eagerly. "Let's drive in and see what's available." She wondered what themed rooms they had; she hoped there was something perfect for them.

The Nissan pulled up to a kiosk with a bank of TV screens displaying various themed rooms. Lit rooms were vacant, and dimmed rooms were occupied. Maggie leaned forward, her eyes scanning each option with mounting excitement.

"It looks like we've got a jail cell for the Cops and Robbers Room, and abundant foliage and animals in the Tropical Jungle Room. The Chocolate Room is available if you want to sleep in a chocolate clamshell or bathe in a chocolate-filled bathtub. In need of a consultation? The Clinic Room with a stethoscope, X-rays, and an examination bed is open. Or there's the Bali Hai Room with a Polynesian vibe and walls filled with Bali sunsets and beaches." Her voice rose enthusiastically as she described each room, imagining the possibilities.

Maggie knew George wasn't sold yet, but he'd get into it once he saw the right room.

Maggie looked over at George, who was shaking his head. A flicker of disappointment passed through her, but she quickly recovered. Patience. The perfect place was here somewhere.

"Okay, let's move on and see what else this alley offers." Her tone remained upbeat; she was undeterred.

The white sports car continued along Route 22. It passed a silver flying-saucer-shaped object in front of Hotel UFO. An alien-themed hotel that promised a night that was out of this world. In front of Hotel Avalon was an artificial waterfall with water cascading down. A building shaped like a ship advertised the Pirate Ship Hotel, and an Arc de Triomphe graced the entrance to Hotel Silk Road.

Maggie's breath caught in her throat. *That's it!* "Hello, Hotel Silk Road. This is exactly what I was looking for," she said, unable to contain her excitement. Her voice dropped to a seductive purr. "Your fantasy begins in the French Riviera, my love." Perfect—elegant but still exotic and romantic.

"My fantasy?" said George. "Since when is this *my* fantasy?"

"You can thank me later." Maggie laughed, a knowing glint in her eyes. *Oh, you'll thank me later.* A delicious shiver of anticipation ran down her spine.

The coupe pulled into the kiosk at Hotel Silk Road. Maggie chose the Monte Carlo Room with a private indoor pool. This was going to be amazing. She pulled the car into the assigned garage and pressed a button on the wall to close the garage door and unlock the room's door. A sign, written in kanji with pictures, was affixed to the wall, instructing them to remove their shoes before entering.

When they entered the room, the colors red, white, and black materialized—a prominent Japanese combination, representing strong emotions, like happiness, joy, love, and sexual desire. Maggie felt a surge of satisfaction as she absorbed the details. A large roulette wheel, providing light, hung directly above the king-size bed. There was a red leather sofa, a round glass coffee table, and two chairs shaped like life-sized horse chess pieces—one black and one red.

Maggie set up the boom box, pulled a few items of clothing out of the duffel, and went into the bathroom to change. The bathroom walls were wallpapered with playing cards—black queen of clubs, black king of spades, red eight of hearts, red ace of diamonds. A door in the bathroom led to the pool.

This is it. Time to transform. She took a deep breath, steadying her nerves. Despite their years together, she still felt a flutter of vulnerability about revealing this side of herself. *He's going to love this. WE are going to love this.*

Maggie stepped out of the bathroom, dressed as a French maid. She wore a white lace-neck collar, an off-the-shoulder black minidress with white lace trim, and a white satin apron. A black lace headpiece was delicately placed atop her auburn hair, pulled up into a French twist. Black fishnet stockings, attached with a garter belt and straps; a black thong; and black stiletto heels completed the outfit. She held a white feather duster in her hand.

She was ready for business.

I feel ... powerful.

The costume gave her a confidence that radiated from within—a delicious blend of vulnerability and strength that made her skin tingle. She stepped over to the boom box and pressed play. Immediately, the spiritual and sensual melodic sound blend of Enigma's *MCMXC* album erupted. Gregorian Latin chants fused with electronic synthesizer, begging for an emotional and soon-to-be physical release.

Perfect ambiance. The music sent a delightful shiver down her spine, matching the rhythm of her desire.

Maggie pulled a chilled bottle of Taittinger Brut and two Baccarat crystal flutes from a picnic basket.

Thank you, Okinapa. She silently expressed gratitude to the wine festival that had helped her prepare this perfect evening.

She uncorked the bottle and poured the champagne into the glasses, watching the bubbles dance with satisfaction. Every detail mattered.

"*Bonsoir, monsieur.* Good evening, sir," she said, her voice adopting a playful French accent. She had been practicing. "*Mon nom est Margaux. Voudrais-tu du champagne?* My name is Margaux. Would you like some champagne?"

She handed a glass to George, seated on the leather sofa. Her fingertips brushed against his deliberately as she passed the glass, sending a pleasurable current through her arm.

Maggie removed cheese, crackers, and a wooden board from the basket and artfully displayed them on the glass coffee table. Each placement was measured, unhurried. She wanted him to watch every move she made.

"Are you going to pull a rabbit out of that basket next?" George asked.

"Given the *Alice in Wonderland* ambiance," said Maggie, a sultry smile playing on her lips, "you might expect that. However, tonight is not about child's play. Let me introduce you to my kinky boot box."

Her heart raced as she prepared to reveal the next part of her surprise. Would he think it was too much? No—seventeen years deserved something extraordinary.

Maggie opened a large rectangular box with *FRYE* written on the side. She unfolded the packing paper to reveal a black flogger with a six-inch handle and suede strips at the end; a black riding crop with a braided leather handle; five pink plastic butt plugs, ranging in size from three and a half inches to five and a half inches; a pair of stainless steel nipple clips with rubber tips and black and red beads dangling from the ends; Kama Sutra Honey Dust body powder; a black silk blindfold; and water-based lubricant.

"May I interest you in a game, *mon cheri?* My dear." Her voice was honey sweet but underlined with a current of desire that made her body warm. *Please say yes. Please join me in this fantasy.*

George took a sip of his champagne. "But of course, my love."

She tingled with excitement. *He's with me. He's in.* She felt almost dizzy with anticipation.

Maggie unfolded a game board entitled Sweet Surrender, the Game of Dominance & Submission. She placed a black and red game piece and a die on the board, her fingers trembling with excitement.

"Let's begin," she said, rolling the die. It landed on a six.

She moved her red piece six places and landed on a Dom square. She took a card from the Dominance pile. It read, *Pretend you are a drill sergeant and your partner is a recruit.*

Perfect! Start with something he can relate to.

She straightened her back, adopting a stern expression, though her eyes danced with mischief.

"Drop and give me ten, Marine!" Her voice rang out with mock authority, though underneath, she was thrilled at taking control, at George's willingness to play along.

George dropped to the floor and did ten push-ups.

George rolled the die, which landed on a three. He moved his black game piece three spaces and landed on a Sub square.

He took a card from the Submission pile and read it. *"Bend over, grab your ankles, and beg your partner to spank you."*

"Mi amor. My love," said Maggie, her voice dropping to a sensual whisper. This was getting good. "We must remove your clothing for this to be done right."

Maggie pulled George's T-shirt up over his head. She then helped him to his feet, unbuttoned and unzipped his shorts, and slipped them off his feet.

"My underwear too?"

"Oui, oui. Yes, yes," said Maggie as she slipped off his white Hanes briefs.

Seventeen years, and he still took her breath away.

George bent over, grabbed his ankles, and said, "Please spank me."

Maggie picked up the riding crop and smacked it against George's butt. *Maybe that was a bit much to start with.*

"Really?!" he said.

"Too hard?" Maggie giggled, a mixture of amusement and concern in her voice.

She needed to be more careful. This was supposed to be fun for both of them.

She picked up the suede flogger and smacked George on the ass again, gentler this time, observing his reaction.

"Better?" Her voice was softer now as she checked in with him.

"Yeah," he said, his voice steadier now. "That's better."

Maggie rolled a one on the die. She moved her red game piece to the next square, Sub, and pulled a card from the Submissive pile.

Perform a sensual dance for your partner and ask if they enjoyed it.

Now it was her turn to put on a show. A thrill of exhibitionism ran through her.

"This calls for a new soundtrack," she said as she popped a Janet Jackson CD in the boom box and hit track two, "That's the Way Love Goes."

Maggie swayed and stepped to the beat of the music. She removed her neck collar, feeling her pulse quicken as she began to undress. His eyes hadn't left her once. She pulled down one side of her dress, then the other, and shimmied out of it. Next, she removed her lace headpiece, undid her pinned hair, and let it fall gracefully around her face.

She strutted about the room, wearing her black thong, black fishnet stockings with a garter belt and straps, and black stiletto heels. Occasionally, she would strike a pose and say, "*Aimez-vous?* Do you like it?" Her voice was breathy, warm with yearning and the excitement of being watched, of being desired. She relished the way George was looking at her, like it was their first time all over again.

George rolled the die again. He moved his black game piece four places and landed on a Sub square. He picked up a Submission card.

Get on all fours and pretend you're a dog. Allow your partner to walk you around the room and ensure you are a good doggy.

"I draw the line on this one!" George exclaimed.

"Oh, George!" Maggie's tone was affectionate, but slightly disappointed. She knew that might be pushing it, but it was worth a try. "Just pick another card."

George read another card, "*Wearing a blindfold, with your hands tied behind your back, beg your partner to do as they desire with your body.*"

Maggie motioned for George to take a seat in the red horse chair. This was perfect—exactly what she'd hoped would happen. A delicious anticipation built within her as she prepared for the next phase. She removed her heels, garter belt, and stockings and used one of her stockings to tie George's hands behind his back. She placed the silk blindfold over his eyes.

"What do you say, George?" Her voice was now a husky command, confidence flowing as she took control.

"Please fondle me?"

"Oh, c'mon, George. Say it like you mean it." She wanted to hear him ask for *it*. She felt powerful, desirable, in complete command of the moment.

"Suck my cock … *please.*"

"Well, that's a start." A smile of satisfaction curved her lips. *There he is—my George, finally letting go.*

Maggie picked up the feather duster and Kama Sutra jar in one hand and grabbed the nipple clips with the other. Her heart pounded with anticipation as she prepared to please him. She had been dreaming about this moment.

She dipped the white feathers in the coconut-pineapple powder and dusted George's body. She dusted George's nipples and licked them before clamping the tweezer-like clips. The taste of the sweet powder, mixed with the salt of his skin, sent a jolt of desire through her. She wanted to taste every inch of him.

"Let me see you shake those black and red beads," Maggie commanded, her voice thick with arousal.

George did not move.

"Do it, or I will smack you with the riding crop." *Don't make me ask twice.* The dominance in her voice surprised even her, but it felt right, natural at that moment.

George complied and swayed his chest from side to side, and the beads moved like a pendulum.

"That's better," said Maggie, a note of approval warming her voice.

He looked incredible like this—vulnerable, trusting, hers.

She lightly dusted his penis before wrapping her mouth around it, savoring his taste, his warmth, the sound of his pleasure. This was better than anything she had imagined.

"*Oui, oui,*" said George.

"Yes, it's a wee-wee." Maggie giggled, her eyes sparkling with mischief. Still couldn't resist making him laugh, even now.

"Ohhhhh," moaned George as Maggie continued to suck and delicately rub his testicles.

George arched his back and moaned louder. Maggie stopped abruptly, concern immediately replacing desire.

Something's wrong.

"Is that a good moan or a bad moan?" Worry creased her brow.

"Ugh," George replied. "I think I tweaked my back."

Maggie quickly untied George's hands and removed the nipple clips and the blindfold.

Poor baby. I hope he's okay.

Her heart filled with tender concern, all thoughts of role-play instantly forgotten.

"Clint Eastwood said it in *Heartbreak Ridge*," said George. "Improvise, adapt, overcome. Nothing a little zero gravity can't fix."

Relief flooded through her. Always her resilient George. A smile of affection and understanding spread across her face.

Maggie removed her black lace thong. She helped George to his feet and assisted him as their nude bodies headed to the pool through the bathroom. It was not exactly how she had planned it, but maybe it was even better. Tenderness replaced the heated passion of moments ago, a different but equally powerful form of intimacy.

George kissed Maggie on her head.

"Happy anniversary, Maggie."

"Happy anniversary, George." Her voice was soft, filled with seventeen years of love, adventure, and the promise of many more.

This was what mattered—not the perfect fantasy, but the two of them, together, rolling with whatever came their way. Contentment settled over her as she held him close.

Chapter Thirty-Four
CASINO ROYALE

September 2010
Camp Lejeune, North Carolina

TEMPERATURES DROPPED INTO THE seventies and low eighties in coastal Carolina. The leaves of elm and maple trees turned various shades of yellow, orange, red, purple, and brown, creating picture-perfect landscapes. George and Maggie were settled into their new home aboard MCAS, Cherry Point. George was busy acclimating to the new command and focused on getting his Marines ready to deploy to Afghanistan. Maggie met with the Family Readiness Command Team, which consisted of Family Readiness Coordinators (FRCs) for each subordinate command.

Maggie knew from past deployments how important it was to strengthen bonds with spouses and families and to support them as they faced the challenges of the military lifestyle. The FRCs would provide regular communication, resources, and referral information, deployment support, and unit-sponsored social events. While she put on a brave smile during these meetings, a knot of anxiety tightened in her stomach each time deployment was mentioned. Another separation loomed ahead—more nights alone, more holidays missed, more worrying about George's safety while flying missions. Maggie would never hear about the successful ones. It was the mishaps that were reported at home. The ones that required the wives to rally around the fallen or injured Marine's wife. She'd been through this before, but it never got easier.

Thunderstorms rolled in, and the wind whipped through as George and Maggie dressed for their evening event. Maggie smoothed her emerald silk gown over her hips, the color highlighting the green in her eyes. She fastened the pearl necklace George had given her for their tenth anniversary, her fingers lingering on the cool, smooth surface. Tonight was supposed to be about building camaraderie, but Maggie felt the familiar weight of expectation settle on her shoulders. As the general's wife, she had a role to play—supportive, gracious, discreet. Sometimes, she felt like she was wearing a mask, hiding her true feelings behind a practiced smile. Her desire was to be at home with George, all alone, wrapped in his arms, knowing he was safe and sound.

Men in tuxedos, Marines in their evening dress, and ladies in their finest gowns flowed into the club, passing the display of luxury cars at the entrance. Clicking roulette wheels, shouts from the craps tables, and the shuffling of cards in the hands of dealers transformed the club into the sights and sounds of a Las Vegas casino. Showgirls, wearing rhinestone-encrusted bikinis and huge feather headdresses, walked among the crowd, selling ten thousand dollars in fake chips for twenty-five dollars.

Maggie and George worked their way through the room, shaking hands with fellow Marines and their spouses. Maggie's smile never faltered, though her cheeks ached with the effort.

"Sergeant Major Reed," said George. "How are you this fine evening?"

"Very well, sir."

"Where is your lovely bride?"

"She's over at the craps table with Mrs. Wilson."

"I understand they're both from the same town in Texas."

"Yes, sir. Their families have been friends for years. It's a tight-knit Puerto Rican community in Laredo."

"Enjoy your evening, Sergeant Major."

"You as well, sir, ma'am."

Maggie smiled warmly at the sergeant major, genuinely fond of the man. She admired his steadfast devotion to the Corps and his wife. As they moved away, she squeezed George's arm, drawing strength from his solid presence beside her.

The aroma from the all-you-can-eat buffet lured the Stones into the dining room. They each filled a plate and sat down at a table with Karma, Hurl, Barbara, and Jack.

"I'm glad we're all together," said George. "I have an update from Special Agent Morris."

All eyes were on George as he continued. Maggie's heart raced; she dreaded yet needed to hear more about the case that had followed them to their new duty station.

The NCIS agents had examined Julia's journals and confirmed she had purchased illegal controlled substances from Levi Seigel. They believed her body had developed a tolerance to the small initial doses, leading her to require larger amounts over time. On the morning of the accident, they thought she'd ingested a potent mix.

"Karma," said George, "DEA and NCIS are aware of your relationship with Levi in 1980, and they will contact you for further questions. They are also tracking down Levi to charge him with involuntary manslaughter."

In 1985, Levi had been arrested for possession of controlled substances with intent to distribute and served ten years in prison. After his release, he had gone off the grid—erased his digital footprint, no driver's license, no phone, no email, no credit cards.

A wave of sadness swept over Maggie. Karma had been right about Levi. Julia never would have met Levi, her drug dealer, if Karma hadn't dated him and brought him to McP's. She couldn't stop picturing Julia, reduced to desperate journal entries, chasing a high that would ultimately contribute to her death. The tragedy of it all tightened her throat.

"Well, Karma," said Maggie, unable to contain the sharp edge in her voice, "you picked a winner."

She regretted the words as soon as they left her mouth, but the pain and anger demanded release. George shot her a warning glance, but she looked away, unwilling to apologize just yet.

"Maggie," said Barbara, "stop it. Karma feels terrible about what happened to Julia."

"Of course I do," replied Karma. "I just wish what happened had stayed in the past."

Maggie bit her tongue, fighting back a retort. To Maggie, it seemed like Karma was more concerned about her reputation than mourning a lost life.

The Hammocks and Wilsons passed by the table. After a few informal exchanges, they moved on. Maggie watched them with a practiced eye, noticing the slight distance between Marcie and Banana, the way Nasty's hand lingered a moment too long on Marcie's lower back.

"I still think there's something strange going on with those couples," said Barbara.

"Last week," said Jack, "I was running along Union Point Park and saw Marcie Hammock and Tom Wilson in an intimate embrace under the gazebo."

"Hmm," Maggie said. "I'm not sure I want to know what that was about."

Her mind flashed to previous duty stations, other scandals that had rocked tight-knit military communities. Although affairs were not unusual, they were always followed by destruction. Even the strongest marriages were strained by the military lifestyle. Long separations, frequent moves, the constant pressure. Maggie understood the temptation to seek comfort elsewhere, even if she'd never condone it.

George stood up from the table. "Let's head to the back bar and cigar lounge."

Maggie rose, grateful for the change of scenery. The evening's conversation had left her emotionally drained, and the weight of unspoken words hung heavy between her and Karma. She slipped her hand into George's, drawing comfort from his steady presence. As they walked away from the table, Maggie resolved to focus on the evening ahead, on supporting George as he built relationships with his new command. The investigation, Karma, the Hammocks, and Wilsons—all of that could wait for another day.

Chapter Thirty-Five
MAJOR GENERAL &
MRS. DOOLEY

GEORGE AND MAGGIE CONTINUED THROUGH the Paradise Point Officers' Club, heading toward Follow Me—the bar and cigar patio named after the motto of the 2nd Marine Division (MarDiv).

Maggie, still reeling from the news about Julia, walked beside George, her emerald silk gown whispering against the polished floor. The weight of unresolved tragedy followed her like a shadow, even in this glittering setting.

"Good evening, Major General and Mrs. Stone," said Brigadier General Lee Sterling, the 2nd Marine Logistics Group (MLG) commanding general.

"Nice to see you, Lee," said George as he shook hands.

"Allow me to introduce my wife, Valerie," said Lee.

"Valerie, so nice to meet you," acknowledged George. "This is my wife, Margaret."

"Good evening," said Maggie, sliding effortlessly into her role as George's wife. "I met Valerie at Mrs. Dooley's welcome coffee. Nice to meet you, Lee." She smiled warmly, though beneath the polished exterior, she felt the strain of maintaining appearances when her thoughts were elsewhere.

"How is your evening so far?" asked George.

"Quite well," said Lee. "Valerie has been killing it at the craps table."

"Hopefully, some of that luck will rub off on us." Maggie smiled, thinking how they could use some luck, not for gambling, but for resolving the mess they'd inherited with Julia's death and Levi's disappearance.

"Lee, have you had a chance to speak with Major General Dooley this evening?" asked George.

"Yes, sir. Valerie and I paid our respects to the general and Mrs. Dooley in the bar a few minutes ago."

"That's exactly where we're headed. You and your bride have a wonderful evening."

"Evening, sir."

Major General Nathan Dooley was the 2nd Mar Div commanding general and the commanding general of II Marine Expeditionary Force (MEF) Forward. His wife, Martha, was the nurturing mother figure for the spouses.

Martha had recently invited all the commanders' spouses to her home for coffee. She'd even poured out of a silver pot into china cups with saucers. Martha was a classic example of Southern hospitality. She had a pleasant air about her. When you had her attention, you entirely had her attention. She made you feel like you were the most important person in the world. Maggie adored her, finding in Martha the mentor she'd always sought in the military community.

Major General Dooley could command a room. His silver-gray hair, ruddy complexion, and steel-blue eyes projected confidence, authority, and charisma. His wife, Martha, at five feet three inches, stood a foot shorter than him, and she was soft-spoken with a Southern lilt. Her dark brown hair, with distinguished hints of gray, was cut in a classic chin-length bob.

"Sir, ma'am," said George. "So nice to see you this evening. This is quite an impressive event."

"I have my staff to thank for that," Nathan replied in a thick New York accent. "We're lucky to have such talented people on the division staff. George, you do know the chips are fake, right?"

"Yes, sir." George snickered. "That Aston Martin DB5 parked out front is not fake. I wouldn't mind taking that for a spin."

"Tell you what," said Nathan. "If you play your cards right, you just might. Would you like to join me on the patio for a cigar?"

George and Nathan excused themselves and retired to the patio. Maggie watched George go, a flicker of anxiety crossing her features. Soon, he would be deployed again, and these casual moments would become precious memories to sustain her through long, lonely nights.

Martha and Maggie walked up to the bar to order glasses of wine. A Korean woman with short black hair and a friendly heart-shaped face greeted the ladies, already preparing the wineglasses.

"Good evening," she said. "Will you be having the usual?" she asked while automatically grabbing a bottle of sauvignon blanc.

"Oh, yes, Min," said Martha. "You take such good care of our husbands and us."

"No general is driving home drunk on my watch," said Min. "I make sure they eat something and drink plenty of water while they drink at my bar."

"That's more than we can accomplish." Maggie laughed. "Thank you, Min. Things will get more tense as they ramp up for this deployment." The word *deployment* caught in her throat slightly, bringing with it the reality she'd been trying to push away all evening.

"After twenty-five years working behind this bar, I know that to be true. The bar gets crowded, and the drinks get stiffer."

Martha and Maggie picked up their glasses and moved to a quiet table in the corner. Gloria Estefan played the lyrics to "Here We Are" over the speakers.

"Gloria Estefan always makes me long for home," said Martha.

"Are you from Miami?" asked Maggie, grateful for the distraction of conversation.

"Tampa. My father is a citrus grower. He built his business in the 1960s. He has six thousand five hundred trees on forty acres in Hillsborough County, where he harvests multiple citrus acres of grapefruits, oranges, kumquats, and tangerines."

"Did you work in the family business?" asked Maggie, imagining the sun-drenched groves, so different from the military bases that had become her shifting home.

"Oh God, no. I attended the University of Tampa, got my master of science in exercise and nutrition, and worked at Tampa General Hospital until I met Nathan."

"That begs the question," said Maggie, "how does a citrus grower's daughter from Tampa, Florida, meet up with a Marine from Brooklyn, New York?"

"I grew up in Hyde Park. I would love to take you there. It's a quaint neighborhood with historic Victorian homes and bungalows. I met Nathan in 1977. My next-door neighbor, Charlie, brought his roommate from The Basic School (TBS) in Quantico, Virginia, home for Easter. Nathan was gregarious, charming, and so polite. It was love at first sight. After we met, he graduated from TBS and was sent to Okinawa. We had a two-year engagement. I learned from the very start that separation would be a constant."

Maggie nodded, a familiar ache in her heart. Separation was the thread that wove through every military marriage. With another deployment looming, that familiar dread was returning, settling in like a cold front.

"You both are a shining example of what a strong relationship looks like," said Maggie. "You've experienced a lot and complement each other well." She hoped her marriage had that same resilience. Twenty years of following George from base to base, country to country, had tested them both.

"Thank you. Yes, Nathan and I have been through a lot together. Raising four children in the military is no easy feat. You know that old saying … what doesn't kill you makes you stronger."

"True." Maggie laughed, though she remained serious. "You're a strong role model for spouses. We're lucky to have you."

"Maggie, you, too, are a strong woman. You show genuine care for the families and understand the importance of building a network of support. Just remember, strength isn't in handling everything alone."

Martha's words touched something vulnerable in Maggie. How many times had she tried to bear her burdens alone, not wanting to burden George with her fears while he was focused on his command responsibilities? She had not heard from the blackmailer since she had stopped payments and reported it to the authorities nearly a year ago. Now, with the unresolved situation involving Julia's death and Levi hanging over them, she felt that familiar impulse to shield George from her worries.

Martha paused, taking a sip of wine.

"Let me tell you about the time I thought I could handle a burst pipe, three sick kids, and a battalion fundraiser all by myself. That's a lesson in knowing when to call in reinforcements."

Maggie glanced at George across the room, standing next to Nathan on the patio. She smelled the distinct note of cigar smoke—a blend of leather, wood, and spice. Her thoughts traveled back to her early years with George, who had always been devoted, earnest, and determined. He had only gotten better with age.

She watched him now, engaged in conversation with General Dooley, his posture straight, his attention focused. In less than six months, he would be in Afghanistan, facing dangers she couldn't bear to imagine. And here she would be, holding everything together, just as she always did. Only this time, she'd also be dealing with the aftermath of Julia's death and the hunt for Levi Seigel.

The thought of Levi sent a chill down her spine despite the warm room. She desperately wanted him found, not just for justice for Julia, but to end the threat of blackmail that loomed over their new beginning here. What secrets had Julia written in those journals? Karma had ended her relationship with Levi right before the tragic accident. She had no idea what Levi knew or who else he might have told. The uncertainty gnawed at her. Until Levi was caught and the whole truth about Julia's death came to light, Maggie couldn't shake the feeling that danger still lurked, waiting to destroy the life they'd built.

Nathan and George approached the table.

"Ladies," said George, "it's time for Major General Dooley to say a few words. Please join us as we head into the casino room."

As they walked away, Maggie leaned closer to George, drawing comfort from his familiar scent of aftershave, mixed with the faint trace of cigars and whiskey. Everyone appeared so relaxed. If only they were aware of the situation. In a silent affirmation that he could sense Maggie's troubled thoughts, George squeezed her hand. She returned the pressure, grateful for his intuitive understanding.

Major General Dooley stood on a platform in the center of the room. Behind him hung the 2nd Mar Div insignia, which featured the Marine Corps' official colors of scarlet and gold. The insignia displayed a spearhead-shaped scarlet background with a handheld torch. A scarlet number two was superimposed upon the torch, and the torch was encircled by five white stars in the arrangement of the Southern Cross Constellation.

"Ladies and gentlemen," began Major General Dooley, "on behalf of the Second Marine Division, thank you for joining us this evening for Casino Royale. I hope you're having a good time and winning lots of money. The person who wins the most money tonight will walk away with the grand prize—a weekend in South Carolina, learning how to drive the Aston Martin DB5 parked out front. Major General Stone has expressed his interest in driving it. Let's see if his luck plays out tonight."

Maggie smiled up at George, trying to focus on this moment of lightness.

"A few weeks ago, we activated II MEF Forward. In less than six months, we'll deploy to Afghanistan as a Marine Air-Ground Task Force. Our commanders are here tonight, representing ground combat, aviation combat, and combat logistical support, to form a Marine-unique war-fighting team. Keeping Helmand Province stable and incorporating Afghan forces into operations to rid the area of insurgent fighters will be a complex endeavor. Marines have a proud legacy of winning battles. It's an honor and a privilege to serve with the caliber of Marines and sailors here tonight. I would like to thank the spouses and families for their sacrifice. It's not easy to watch your loved one deploy for a year into harm's way. We appreciate the challenges you'll endure while we're gone. We know that you'll care for each other because that is what Marines do—we care for each other. Thank you, and enjoy the rest of the evening."

Maggie's hand tightened on George's arm. Nathan's comments about family sacrifice weighed heavily on her mind. A year, one full year without George, worrying every day about his safety in a war zone. The speech had made the deployment real in a way nothing else had. Less than six months—all they had left before separation became their reality again. Less than six months to find Levi, to end this nightmare she and George had been living for the past two years, to establish a strong support network for the spouses who would rely on her leadership during the deployment.

As applause erupted around her, Maggie maintained her composed smile, but her heart was racing inside. She looked around at the sparkling room, the laughing couples, the air of celebration, and felt oddly disconnected from it all. How could she focus on casino games when their lives were about to be upended once again?

"You okay?" George whispered, his breath warm against her ear.

"I just want it all resolved before you go," she whispered back, the words slipping out before she could stop them. "Levi, the blackmail, all of it. I can't bear the thought of dealing with that alone while you're gone."

George's arm tightened around her waist. "They'll find him," he promised. "If Levi is the blackmailer, we'll face it together. Just like we always do."

Maggie nodded, drawing strength from his certainty. Together—that had always been their way. But soon, they would be worlds apart, and the thought terrified her more than she could admit, even to herself.

Chapter Thirty-Six

SEMPER FAMILY

January 2011
Training House
Cherry Point, North Carolina

"DON'T DISAPPOINT ME, KARMA," SAID Maggie, pulling her silver convertible Ford Mustang into the training house parking lot.

Families attended pre-deployment briefs and concentrated on organizing their affairs and solidifying their family care plans. The combat deployment was scheduled to leave in six weeks. The L.I.N.K.S.—Lifestyle, Insights, Networking, Knowledge, Skills—training program had been designed to assist families with this unique way of life. L.I.N.K.S. training empowered Marines and their families by providing the tools and resources necessary to navigate the military lifestyle. L.I.N.K.S. was also one of the many advisory roles Maggie had assigned to Karma.

Maggie had learned over the decades as a Marine wife that preparation for deployment was essential to family stability. She'd seen too many marriages crumble under the weight of unmanaged expectations and poor communication. Her role as a general's wife came with responsibilities she took seriously, though she still felt the familiar knot in her stomach whenever deployment approached.

George would be gone for a year. Three hundred sixty-five days of sleeping alone, worrying, and maintaining perfect composure were expected of her position.

Maggie slipped quietly in through the back door of the house. The training facility was indeed a home. Its comfortable surroundings included couches, soft lighting, and the sweet smell of cinnamon rolls flowing from the kitchen. Even the classroom was warm and welcoming. Karma was at the podium.

Maggie observed the comfortable setting. The military could be impersonal and harsh; this environment offered the perfect counterbalance. She positioned herself near the back wall, standing with perfect posture—a habit forged through years of attending military functions, where she was constantly being observed.

"Hello, everyone," said Karma. "I'm here to talk to you about emotions and deployment. I know many of you are in the pre-deployment phase. I can relate. I am as well."

"Good start," said Maggie softly to herself, her tension easing slightly.

Karma had a way of being brutally honest, which Maggie both admired and feared. These young Marine wives needed authentic guidance, not sugarcoated information, but Maggie worried Karma's unfiltered approach might overwhelm the already-anxious spouses.

"So, how many of you think this deployment will not happen?" Karma continued. "It's not real? Well, girlfriend, it's real. It's happening. You need to prepare."

Oh God, don't spook them, Maggie thought, her jaw tightening.

Even after all these years, she still caught herself hoping each deployment would somehow be canceled. It was a foolish thought she'd never admit to anyone—not even George.

"Your Marine has completed a power of attorney and a last will, as if that doesn't make it real. You still think, somehow, this whole thing will be canceled. Normal. You're walking down the cereal aisle at Piggly Wiggly, and you see Frosted Flakes—your husband's favorite cereal—and you break down crying. Am I right?"

Maggie's throat constricted as memories flooded back—years of deployments, countless breakdowns in grocery stores, at gas stations, in parking lots where no one could see her. She'd mastered the art of the two-minute cry—allow the tears, then wipe them away, reapply lipstick, and move on.

Several of the participants nodded.

"He's getting ready to leave, and you're having less sex than ever. What is up with that? You're tense, you're angry, you're frustrated. Meanwhile, your Marine is excited! You'd think he'd just won the lottery by the way he moves about with a spring in his step, smiling all the while. You want to shake him and say, *Don't you know you're leaving me?!* Sisters, that is pre-deployment emotions."

Maggie winced inwardly. *Too much information, Karma.* But she couldn't deny the truth in those words. Even now, with George busier than ever preparing for deployment, she found herself resentful of his laser focus on the mission, his ability to compartmentalize their impending separation. At the same time, she lay awake at night, contemplating a year without him.

"I hope it gets better," said one of the participants.

"Oh ... it does," Karma replied. "He leaves."

The participants laughed. Maggie allowed herself a small smile. There was relief in the goodbye, though she'd never admit that to George. The anticipation was always worse than the reality.

"What a relief it is to say goodbye," Karma continued. "The anticipation is over. Then you feel guilty about the relief. Normal. You might have trouble sleeping. You might feel overwhelmed by all the new responsibilities. You might be angry at the Marine Corps for making him leave. Normal. You will eventually become comfortable and capable in your new roles. You'll feel self-confident and independent. You can eat cereal for dinner every night if you want. You are not alone. You have this group around you who will experience the same. You have the names of support groups and services. You'll get through this."

Maggie nodded slightly, recalling her growth. She had transformed from a scared eighteen-year-old girl, uncomfortable in her skin, into an independent, strong woman. Like most women, she would struggle when George returned and disrupted her carefully built routines, but that was the cruel irony of military life—you learned to live without them, and then you had to learn to live with them again.

"What if I don't feel all these emotions?" a participant asked. "Is that normal?"

"Absolutely," Karma replied. "Each of you is unique. You may feel some, all, or none of these emotions. If you feel you're having difficulty being separated from your Marine, please reach out to loved ones, friends, your FRC, or a counselor. You're not alone. Please take a moment to turn to the person next to you and tell them, *You're not alone*."

Maggie swallowed hard, fighting unexpected emotion. *You're not alone.* How many times had she needed to hear those words over the years? As a general's wife, she was expected to be the pillar of strength, the one everyone else leaned on. But who did she lean on? George was her rock, but when he was gone, she carried the weight of her fears privately.

Karma continued with the session. "It's been three hundred fifty-one days, but who's counting? They're coming home in two weeks. You're excited but nervous. You think, *Will he still love me?* You start buying all his favorite foods, such as Frosted Flakes, and change back to pre-deployment patterns. It's finally the big day. Homecoming. You dress your finest and prepare for your Marine's arrival on the flight line. The C-17 touches down on the tarmac. The doors open. It's raining men. Hallelujah."

The participants cheered, and Maggie felt a rush of delight as her mind drifted back to past homecomings. The butterflies never went away, not even after all these years. Each reunion carried its unique mix of excitement and anxiety—the strange dance of reconnecting with someone who was both intimately familiar and temporarily foreign.

"Now the new normal begins," said Karma. "You will not want your in-laws and family members showing up at your house in the first few days or weeks. You and your Marine may need time to adjust and reintegrate after being apart for a year. It may take time and patience to feel comfortable again. Your Marine may feel out of place. He hasn't been a part of your daily life. You'll continue to adjust as you share roles, responsibilities, and decisions again. As we discussed earlier, each person may deal with these emotions differently. Remember, you're part of the Marine Corps family. Stay involved with the Marine Corps family. We'll support you. Lean on us because that's what we do … we care for each other. Thank you for joining me today. Let's take a break before we begin the following module: Operations Security and Personal Safety."

Maggie walked toward the front of the room, keeping her expression neutral, even as she mentally reviewed Karma's performance. She'd done well—honest without being alarmist, informative without being condescending.

"Nice job, Karma."

"Well, thank you."

"I forgot how much you love being the center of attention."

"Yeah, that's me. Attention whore. Wait … that is me." Karma laughed.

Maggie shook her head and laughed. Their relationship had always been complicated—a blend of genuine affection and professional obligation, underscored by Karma's inability to filter herself and Maggie's compulsive need to maintain appearances.

"Mrs. Stone," said one of the participants. "You and your husband spoke to us at our pre-deployment brief. I'm Sarah

Kane. My husband, Corporal William Kane, is an aircraft mechanic with VMA-223."

Maggie extended her hand, automatically shifting into her public role—gracious, composed, and attentive.

"So nice to meet you, Sarah. Thank you for introducing yourself."

"I wanted to thank you for recommending this course. It's a lot of information to take in as a new Marine wife, and sometimes, it feels a bit overwhelming, but I'm glad I came."

"I'm so glad you came too, Sarah." Maggie felt a genuine connection with the young woman, remembering her first deployment as a newlywed—the terror, the loneliness, the uncertainty.

"I feel more connected, like I have a place in all these charts and graphs. I feel like a part of the Marine Corps family, which is nice since our family is growing." Sarah patted her slightly bulging belly.

Maggie's heart constricted. A pregnancy during deployment was one of the most challenging scenarios for a military spouse. She'd counseled dozens of young wives through similar situations, but the emotional toll never lessened.

"Congratulations! You must enroll in the New Parent Support Program. They offer a great Baby Boot Camp. The Navy-Marine Corps Relief Society (NMCRS) offers a monthly Budget for Baby class. You'll receive a gift bag full of baby supplies and a handmade quilt, donated by NMCRS knitters nationwide. Please don't hesitate to reach out to our 2nd MAW FRC, Hope Gold. You know what we say—semper family."

The resources flowed automatically from Maggie's lips—the culmination of two decades of supporting military families. She wished someone had been there to guide her through her early years as a Marine wife, when she'd stumbled through each challenge alone, determined not to appear weak or unprepared.

"I don't know much about a general's wife, but I didn't expect to see you show up so much. You're your husband's number one supporter. It shows in your eyes, your words, and your actions. You truly care about the Marines and their families."

"Oh my goodness," said Maggie, blushing.

The genuine compliment caught her off guard. For a moment, Maggie felt seen, not as Mrs. General Stone, but as Maggie, a woman who had built her life around service to others without expecting recognition.

She hugged Sarah. "Thank you for your kind words. I hope you stay active and reach out if needed."

"I will, ma'am. Thank you."

Maggie exited the training house and headed toward her car. Her phone rang, but she didn't recognize the number. She felt a faint wave of unease—unknown calls rarely brought good news in military life.

"Hello? This is Maggie."

"Hi, Maggie. This is Rosa Wilson."

Maggie paused, surprised. Rosa Wilson, Nasty's wife—the commanding officer of MAG-29. They had a cordial but distant relationship, the kind maintained through obligatory social functions and polite small talk. Rosa and Nasty were known for their unconventional lifestyle—rumors of them being swingers had circulated through officer circles for years.

"Hi, Rosa. Is everything okay?" Maggie kept her voice even, though her instincts told her something was very wrong.

"Well, I was hoping you could meet me for a coffee," Rosa said anxiously. "I wanted to talk with you about something."

Maggie's stomach tightened. This was not a social call. This was trouble, and with deployment just weeks away, trouble was the last thing anyone needed.

"Of course, Rosa. How about the Blue Jay Café on Broad Street? I can be there in thirty minutes."

"That works. Thank you."

Maggie ended the call. She hesitated before opening her car door. A fixed look of concentration on her face. She and Rosa were never close. Rosa had sounded agitated, even a bit fearful. This most definitely was not going to be a pleasant conversation.

As she drove, Maggie's mind raced through possibilities. Financial problems? Domestic violence? Health crisis? Whatever it was, the timing couldn't be worse. With deployment looming, every problem was magnified.

Maggie parked in downtown New Bern. She approached the café to find Rosa at a small outside table. The woman looked haggard, her normally perfect makeup applied hastily, her eyes rimmed red. Maggie's sense of foreboding deepened. She walked inside to the counter to order an Americano, using the brief moment to compose herself, to prepare for whatever was coming. Cup in hand, she sat down across from Rosa.

"So, what's going on?" Maggie asked, keeping her tone neutral, even as she braced herself.

Rosa blurted out, "Tom's having an affair with Marcie Hammock."

"Oh ..." said Maggie quietly, her mind immediately calculating the ripple effects.

Marcie's husband, Colonel Matt "Banana" Hammock, was George's assistant wing commander. Colonel Tom "Nasty" Wilson was the commanding officer of eight squadrons. Both men were integral to the upcoming deployment. This explosive situation was occurring weeks before the deployment.

"Rosa, that's ... are you certain?" Maggie asked gently.

"I found texts. Explicit ones." Rosa's hands trembled around her coffee cup. "And then hotel receipts. When I confronted him, he didn't even deny it. He said it just happened and that I was too stupid to notice he was unhappy." Her voice broke. "Twelve years of marriage, Maggie. I gave up a lucrative modeling career to follow him in the Marine Corps. And this is what I get."

Maggie reached across the table to squeeze Rosa's hand. "I'm so sorry."

"I know everyone thinks we're swingers," Rosa explained. "We are. We're also good friends with the Hammocks, but this is different."

Maggie maintained her composed expression, though internally, she was reeling. Despite the rumors, hearing Rosa's confirmation of their lifestyle was jarring. She'd never judged them—what happened between consenting adults was their business—but the confirmation still caught her off guard.

"How so?" Maggie asked, her voice steady despite her racing thoughts.

"This isn't consensual. This is secretive. They've been hiding this relationship."

The distinction was clear to Maggie. This wasn't about sex; it was about betrayal, about broken trust, even within their unconventional boundaries.

"Does Banana know?"

Maggie's heart sank. Matt Hammock was a talented officer, respected by George. If this situation affected his performance, it could impact the entire deployment.

"Yes, he knows," Rosa said heatedly. "He walked in on them when he came home during his lunch break two days ago."

"What did he see?" Maggie asked, needing to understand the full scope of the situation.

"He saw them fucking each other in his bed. He grabbed the side table and threw it, shattering the sliding glass door. Then he stormed out and called me."

Maggie flinched internally. This was worse than she'd imagined. A physical altercation, property damage. This could easily escalate into a command problem, requiring George's direct involvement.

"I'm going to have to tell my husband," said Maggie, her stomach churning at the thought. She dreaded being the one to bear such news.

George was already under immense pressure. This situation would force him to make difficult decisions about his command team at the worst possible time. Banana was integral to the mission's planning and execution. Replacing him would create significant disruption.

Rosa closed her eyes and lowered her head. When she lifted her head, tears were in her eyes. "I wanted you to hear it from me first. I know the general needs to be informed about this. It's … it's a breach of military code. But I also needed someone who understands this life to talk to."

Maggie nodded; her heart was heavy. "You did the right thing, coming to me. This is serious, Rosa. I'll speak with George."

Maggie felt a pang of sympathy. Despite her misgivings about Rosa's lifestyle choices, the woman was suffering. In this moment, she wasn't the provocative, boundary-pushing wife; she was simply a woman betrayed, seeking support.

"I'm glad you told me."

"Thank you, Maggie."

Maggie stood up and hugged Rosa, fighting back her anxiety about what would come next. Her mind was already racing ahead to the conversation with George, and she was planning how to present this explosive information.

"It will be okay. You'll get through this." Her words felt flat, but it was all Maggie could offer.

The truth was messier; this situation could derail careers, damage reputations, and add unnecessary stress to an already-challenging deployment.

Maggie sat back down as Rosa left the café. She stared into her coffee cup, mentally rehearsing how to break this news to George. He would be furious—not just at the breach of trust, but at the timing. Just weeks before deployment, he would be faced with a potential powder keg that could affect unit cohesion and mission readiness.

Worse, Maggie knew this would burden George with precisely the kind of distraction he didn't need when preparing to lead Marines into a combat zone. His focus should be on the mission, on bringing everyone home safely, not on managing personal dramas among his staff. She resented Rosa for putting her in this position, even as she understood the woman had needed someone to confide in.

Moments later, Barbara walked past on the sidewalk.

"Maggie, what are you doing here, all by yourself?"

"I just met Rosa for coffee," said Maggie, her voice light, hiding the turmoil beneath.

"Rosa Wilson? That's interesting."

Barbara was a dear friend, but military protocol was clear—this situation had to be handled discreetly, contained before rumors spread through the tight-knit community.

Maggie quickly changed the subject. "I dropped in on Karma's L.I.N.K.S. session earlier today."

"How was she?"

"She was perfect."

"You sound surprised. Maggie, you know she's comfortable in front of an audience."

"Don't I know that?"

Running into Barbara was a relief—a momentary escape from the weight of Rosa's revelation.

"There were a few Navy spouses at the L.I.N.K.S. training today."

"I'm happy to hear that. We have quite a few corpsmen and a handful of doctors deploying."

"What brings you downtown?"

"I just picked up my ring," said Barbara, her face beaming. She extended her hand to Maggie. "Jack bought me this beautiful channel-set diamond eternity ring to celebrate our first anniversary."

"Jack's a good man, Barbara. I'm so happy for you."

"See you Sunday for dinner?" Barbara smiled.

"Sure thing!" Maggie smiled back.

As Barbara walked away, Maggie felt a pang of melancholy amid her genuine happiness for her friend. She was struck by the striking contrast between the two women. Barbara was triumphant, full of hope, and celebrating the beginning of her married life. Rosa was desolate, devastated, and reeling from the discovery that her husband had been unfaithful. Life was full of surprises, and this was one surprise she was not looking forward to sharing with George.

Maggie sat motionless, staring at the pedestrians as they passed by. She dreaded tonight's conversation with George. He would be late, of course—these days, he rarely made it home before nine. She'd have dinner waiting, a glass of whiskey ready, and then she'd have to destroy whatever brief respite he might have found in her company.

She could already predict his reaction—first disbelief, then anger, then the cold, analytical military mind taking over, evaluating options and consequences. He'd pace the living room, whiskey in hand, cursing Nasty for his recklessness and poor judgment. He'd weigh the impact on the deployment, on unit morale, on mission readiness.

Maggie hated adding to his stress, knowing he already carried the weight of every Marine's safety on his shoulders. This was the part of being a military spouse no one prepared you for—being the bearer of bad news, watching the person you loved shoulder impossible responsibilities, and being powerless to lighten their load.

She sighed, finally rising from her seat. Better to get it over with. She'd prepare George's favorite meal, create a peaceful environment, and deliver the news.

As she walked to her car, Maggie reflected bitterly on the irony. Just hours ago, she'd been watching Karma teach young military spouses how to handle the emotions of deployment. How fitting that she was now facing her emotional challenge— one that no class could have prepared her for.

Chapter Thirty-Seven
FAREWELL

MAGGIE HEARD GEORGE'S CAR PULL into the driveway later than expected, but earlier than she'd feared. She'd spent the afternoon since her meeting with Rosa in a haze of anxiety, rehearsing how to deliver the news. His favorite meal—grilled salmon with roasted vegetables—was warming in the oven. A glass of Macallan 18 waited on the kitchen counter.

She met him at the door, taking his cover and briefcase. The exhaustion in his eyes made her heart ache. Another fourteen-hour day, preparing for deployment.

"You look like you could use this," she said, handing him the whiskey after a brief kiss.

George accepted it gratefully. "You're a mind reader." He took a long sip, closing his eyes momentarily. "Something smells amazing."

"Dinner's ready when you are. Why don't you go change?"

Minutes later, they sat across from each other at the dining room table. Maggie had barely touched her food, her stomach in knots.

"All right, out with it," George said, setting down his fork. "You've been watching me like a hawk. What's going on?"

Maggie took a deep breath. "I met with Rosa Wilson today."

George's expression remained neutral, but she saw his grip tighten on his whiskey glass. "And?"

"She came to me with something … concerning." Maggie chose her words carefully. "She told me that Nasty is having an affair with Marcie Hammock."

The silence that followed was deafening. George's face remained expressionless, but Maggie saw the slight twitch in his jaw.

"Does she have proof?" he finally asked, his voice measured.

"She says Banana caught them together. In *his* bed." Maggie kept her voice steady. "Two days ago, during his lunch break."

George pushed his plate away and stood abruptly, walking to the window. His back to her, shoulders rigid. "Tell me everything."

Maggie recounted her conversation with Rosa, omitting nothing not even the admission about their swinging lifestyle. As she spoke, she watched George's posture grow increasingly tense.

"When he found them, Banana threw a side table, breaking the sliding glass door," she concluded. "Rosa says he called her right after."

George turned to face her, his expression now intense. "Weeks before deployment. Goddamn weeks." He drained the last of his whiskey. "My assistant wing commander and my MAG-29 commanding officer. Perfect."

"I'm sorry," Maggie said softly. "I know this is the last thing you need right now."

George began to pace, his military mind visibly processing, calculating. "If this gets out—when this gets out—it'll be a disaster. Unit cohesion, chain of command, not to mention Article 134 of the Uniform Code of Military Justice regarding adultery." He ran a hand through his hair. "Christ, I can't replace either of them this close to deployment."

"What will you do?"

"I'll have to speak with both of them. Separately." He stopped pacing. "I need to contain this before it gets out of control."

Maggie watched him transform before her eyes—from her exhausted husband to the major general, the commander responsible for thousands of Marines. She'd seen this metamorphosis countless times over the years, but it never ceased to both impress and sadden her.

"I'm sorry to add this to your plate," she said, standing to clear the barely touched dinner.

George caught her hand as she reached for his plate. "No, I'm sorry. This isn't your burden to carry." His voice softened. "Thank you for telling me. It couldn't have been easy."

"It wasn't," she admitted. "But Rosa needed someone to confide in, and you needed to know."

He pulled her into an embrace, his chin resting on the top of her head. "What would I do without you?"

"Let's hope you never have to find out," she murmured against his chest, finding comfort in his heartbeat.

They stood like that for a moment, finding brief solace in each other before the storm that was sure to come.

"I'll speak with Matt first thing tomorrow," George finally said, pulling away. "Then Tom."

Maggie nodded, recognizing the determination in his eyes. "Just remember, you're deploying soon. Try not to let this consume you."

"Easier said than done." He attempted a smile. "But I'll try."

Later that night, as George slept fitfully beside her, Maggie stared at the ceiling, her mind racing with worry—not just for the Wilsons and Hammocks, but for George. He carried so much on his shoulders already. She feared this additional weight might be the one that finally crushed him.

George and Maggie planned their farewell dinner at their favorite waterfront restaurant, Persimmons. The warm ambiance, calming river view, and stellar cocktails and food pairings provided the perfect setting for celebrating birthdays, holidays, anniversaries, and other special events that they would *not* be spending together in the following year.

Maggie gazed across the table at George, memorizing every line of his face. After twenty years of marriage and seven deployments, she thought this part would get easier. It never did. Each goodbye carried the same weight of uncertainty, the same knot of fear that settled in her stomach and refused to dissolve. She'd become an expert at masking her anxiety—a skill all military spouses eventually mastered.

The Stones ate silently over plates of salmon, grits, and seared scallops, indulging in the moment's serenity. The deployment was in a few days, and Maggie's thoughts raced.

Please, God, bring him back to me safe and unharmed.

Her mind replayed the conversation with Rosa Wilson weeks earlier. The woman's tearstained face haunted her. She'd come to Maggie, desperate and broken. Rosa's revelation about Nasty's affair with Marcie Hammock hadn't shocked her as much as it saddened her.

"Maggie? Where did you go just now?" George's voice brought her back to the restaurant.

Over coffee and a shared piece of Key lime pie, Maggie worked up the courage to ask about the situation. She smiled faintly. "Just thinking about Rosa. What will happen?"

"I must tell you, Maggie, that was not a pleasant conversation with Colonel Hammock or Colonel Wilson. I called Matt into my office. I informed him that there were allegations of inappropriate behavior between his wife, Marcie, and Colonel Tom Wilson. Matt swore nothing was going on between his wife and Tom. He said the couples were very close and their relationship was not inappropriate. I called Tom into my office. I told him there were allegations that he was in an inappropriate relationship with Marcie Hammock. He swore there was no inappropriate behavior between him and Marcie.

He echoed Matt's words about the couples being close friends. Maggie, it felt like their responses were rehearsed, almost scripted. I believe Rosa's telling the truth, but I can't prove it. Unfortunately, I'm compelled to drop the investigation."

"Poor Rosa," Maggie sighed. "I wish you could've seen how distraught she was when she told me."

"If it makes you feel any better, I looked Tom in the eye and said, 'I know you're screwing around with Colonel Hammock's wife. If I can prove it, you're done. You're looking at a court-martial.' I reminded him of Article 134 violations and then kicked him out of my office."

"Thank you, George. Either these couples will work it out or they won't. God knows how this will end. I doubt well."

George leaned forward; his voice was low. "The Corps loses good officers, families fall apart, and careers end in disgrace. If Tom doesn't end this thing with Marcie, someone will eventually report it through official channels. Matt might be willing to look the other way now, but when his pride catches up with his denial …"

"Matt might snap," Maggie finished the thought. "They're both living on the same base, working in the same Marine aircraft wing. He could destroy Tom's career—or worse."

"Exactly. I've seen officers come to blows over less. I've done what I can, Maggie. Now we have to let them make their choices."

Maggie sighed. "I know," she said softly. "It just breaks my heart to see this happening again."

Maggie's convertible pulled up in front of the 2nd MAW headquarters building with George in the passenger seat and Smokey in the back seat. The car stopped. George opened the door to allow Smokey to exit and pulled his military-green parachute bag and duffel bag from the back seat. He tossed the bags onto the curb. Maggie got out of the car and embraced

George. Her head was tightly against his chest, and his arms were lovingly around her. She looked up into his eyes.

"Here we are again," said Maggie, swallowing the lump in her throat.

Each goodbye felt like ripping off a piece of her heart, but she wouldn't let him see her fall apart. Not now. He needed her strength.

"What is this … our eighth deployment?" George asked with a laugh.

"Stop!" said Maggie. "I don't even want to know how many. Just promise me you'll come back to me."

"Always do," said George.

His hands cupped the back of Maggie's head and tilted it back. His eyes searched her face as he pulled her closer. His lips gently touched Maggie's.

"I love you," he said.

"I love you too," said Maggie, memorizing the feel of him, the scent of his aftershave, the strength of his arms wrapped around her.

Smokey whined. George bent down to hug and pet him.

"Okay, boy," said George. "I love you too. Take care of Mom for me."

George stood back up. Maggie grasped George's hand and gently released it. She stood on the curb beside Smokey and watched George enter the headquarters. Then she returned to her car, opened the door for Smokey to join, and sat quietly behind the wheel.

Deep breaths in, deep breaths out. It was no use; the tears cascaded down her face.

She would get through this … she always did. She had to be strong for these families. They sacrificed so much, and they were so young.

God, help me.

The familiar ache of separation settled over her like a heavy blanket. No matter how many times she'd done this, the pain never lessened. But experience had taught her that the only way past the pain was through it. She allowed herself these vulnerable moments before she needed to be strong for the other spouses.

Maggie dropped Smokey back at the house and headed toward The Public House, an all-ranks club located aboard MCAS Cherry Point. As she pulled into the parking lot, buses lined up outside the entrance. Inside the club, families gathered to say goodbye to loved ones who would be deploying. Young children played Xbox, Nintendo, and PlayStation at the gaming station. The children zigzagged between the ping-pong and pool tables, unaware of the tears and hugs in the lounge area. Parents, grandparents, and siblings loaded paper plates with sub sandwiches, pizza, and chips. They grabbed sodas and water from large coolers to pass the time and fill the silence before the inevitable departure.

Maggie scanned the room, her eyes automatically cataloging who might need extra support in the coming months—the pregnant spouses, the mothers with multiple young children, and the newlyweds experiencing their first deployment. Her role was to guide them through this journey.

FRCs mingled about the room, introducing themselves to family members. Maggie found the 2nd MAW FRC, Hope Gold, speaking with Sarah Kane.

"Hello, ma'am," said Sarah as Maggie approached.

"Sarah, it's so good to see you," Maggie replied. "And you as well, Hope."

"Mrs. Stone," said Sarah. "I'd like you to meet my husband, Bill."

"Nice to meet you, Corporal Kane," said Maggie. "We'll take care of your wife. She's part of our semper family." She meant every word. The military family support network had been there for her through countless deployments.

"Ma'am," said Hope, "I was just telling Corporal and Mrs. Kane, if they would like, we can set up a web camera for the birth. Corporal Kane might be able to watch the live birth. If not, he would be able to watch the video."

"That's wonderful," Maggie exclaimed. "What do you think, Corporal Kane?"

"I'm speechless, ma'am. Thank you for taking care of my wife. It's an honor to serve with your husband."

"Well, don't you worry," said Maggie. "You keep those planes in the air, and we'll take care of the home front. That's the deal."

"Deal accepted, ma'am."

"Marines," Sergeant Major Reed bellowed. "We'll begin loading the buses in five minutes. Now's the time to say your goodbyes and move to the front of the building."

Families hugged their loved ones and said their final goodbyes. Marines gathered up their belongings and loaded them onto the buses. Both sides of the buses were lined with families waving American flags. The loudspeakers blared Lee Greenwood's "God Bless the USA" as the buses headed toward the flight line to await charter flights to Afghanistan.

As the last bus departed, Maggie caught a glimpse of Anna Reed and Rosa Wilson in an emotional embrace. Maggie walked toward them.

"Rosa, how are you?" Maggie asked, noting the younger woman's composed demeanor despite her reddened eyes.

Without saying a word, Rosa hugged Maggie.

"I'm so sorry," said Maggie, returning the embrace with genuine warmth.

"I'll get through this," Rosa said tearfully. "I've been through worse, believe it or not."

"You know Anna and I are here to support you," said Maggie, locking eyes with Anna.

"I do," Rosa said. "And I appreciate that. I've decided to go home to Texas."

"When do you leave?" Maggie asked gently.

"Next week. I've already started packing." Rosa's voice grew stronger. "Tom knows. We had one final conversation before he left. He didn't even fight for me to stay, Maggie. Just said maybe it was for the best."

Anna squeezed Rosa's shoulder supportively.

"I wanted to tell you in person that I'll always be grateful for your friendship," Rosa continued. "You showed me what a strong military marriage looks like. I just wasn't lucky enough to find that for myself."

"Life doesn't end with divorce, Rosa," Maggie said softly. "Sometimes, it begins again."

Rosa nodded, a flicker of hope crossing her face. "My sister says the same thing. She's already preparing me for my real estate license exam. I'll throw myself into a career again, rebuild my life."

"What about …" Maggie hesitated. "What happens if Tom tries to reconcile when he returns?"

Rosa's eyes met Maggie's, resolve replacing the tears. "I married Tom too quickly. I was dazzled by the uniform and the prestige. But I've spent the past twelve years feeling like I was living someone else's life. This affair hurts—God, it hurts so much—but it's also given me clarity. My marriage has been over for years. I didn't want to admit it."

Maggie's heart sank at this revelation. "I had no idea."

"No one did. I was very good at playing the dutiful officer's wife." Rosa wiped away a stray tear. "But I'm done pretending. I deserve better than living in his shadow, always wondering who he's with when working late."

"I wish you all the best, Rosa. This life … it isn't for everyone."

"You and the general make it look easy," Rosa said with a sad smile.

Maggie shook her head. "It's never easy. We just decided a long time ago that we were worth fighting for. Every single day."

Maggie sighed deeply. She couldn't save everyone, but she could be there to pick up the pieces. It was the role she'd accepted as the general's wife. She squared her shoulders and turned toward a group of new spouses who looked lost.

One day at a time—that's how we all get through this.

Chapter Thirty-Eight
LOVE, DECEIT, AND A HAND GRENADE

April 2011
II MAW Conference Room
MCAS
Cherry Point, North Carolina

MAGGIE SAT IN A CHAIR, staring listlessly at the television screen on the wall, waiting for George to appear on the Tandberg screen from Afghanistan. Her stomach was in knots, and she knew full well that she was only summoned here when something was wrong. The screen crackled, and George appeared, wearing his desert flight suit behind his desk.

"Oh, George," she gasped. "You look so thin."

"I'm fine, my love," George said reassuringly. "God, it's so wonderful to see you. I miss you."

"I miss you too, George. Only ten more months to go … yes, I'm counting."

George chuckled briefly. Then his face turned serious. He leaned back in his chair; his eyes had that faraway look they got when he was recalling something important. He clutched his coffee mug. "There's been an incident at Camp Leatherneck you need to know about. Tom Wilson and Matt Hammock are involved."

Maggie took a deep breath. Waiting to face her fears, she realized that this relationship had come to a head.

"Matt Hammock had just finished his evening run around the base and headed to the shower trailers," George began. "He turned on the water when an explosion blew him out of the shower stall and onto the ground outside. Poor guy was completely unconscious—naked, bleeding, and covered in burns with bits of metal and wood scattered all around him."

"Oh my God," Maggie whispered, covering her mouth with her hand.

According to George, the first person on the scene had been Colonel Tom Wilson, who claimed he'd been coming back from the gym. He'd used his shirt and jacket to try to stop Matt's bleeding until the medics arrived and rushed him to the hospital at neighboring Camp Bastion.

"The whole base went on high alert," George said. "Everyone thought it might be the start of an enemy attack. NCIS Agents Horn and Harris flew in from Kabul to investigate. At first, it seemed like a possible terrorist attack, but why target a shower trailer with just one person inside? That's when things got interesting."

"Oh my God, George," Maggie exclaimed, leaning closer to the screen.

"The agents discovered that no one at the gym remembered seeing Wilson there that night, despite his claim," George continued, sipping his coffee. "And when they searched Wilson's quarters, they found love letters and explicit photos with Matt's wife, Marcie. After hours of questioning, Wilson finally confessed," said George. "He had thrown the grenade into the shower where Matt was.

"It's what we feared, Maggie," George said, shaking his head. "They made their choices. Unfortunately, they were bad ones."

George explained how Matt had blamed himself for prioritizing his Marine Corps career, thinking Marcie could handle the deployments and separations. She couldn't. She needed constant attention, which Matt couldn't provide while serving in the military.

"In the end," George concluded, "Matt will be medically discharged. He's decided to move back to Columbus, Ohio, with Marcie to start a new life. Rosa filed for divorce and moved back home to Texas. And Wilson himself? He's to be court-martialed, dishonorably discharged, and locked up in the Camp Lejeune Brig, awaiting trial for attempted murder."

"Do you think Matt should have taken Marcie back after everything?" Maggie asked, still trying to process it all.

George shrugged and said, "Love makes people do strange things. Matt probably felt he'd failed her in some way. But I think we both agree—no marriage troubles justify attempted murder. Wilson crossed a line that night in the desert that changed many lives forever."

Maggie wiped away a tear, thinking of Rosa and what she must be going through. Tom had thrown away everything—his marriage, his career, his freedom—all because of an affair.

"How is everyone else handling it?" Maggie asked.

"It's been tough on the whole unit," George said, rubbing his eyes. "Matt was well liked. So was Tom, for that matter. No one saw this coming, though looking back, there were signs. People are second-guessing themselves, wondering if they could have prevented it."

"You couldn't have known," Maggie assured him.

"Maybe," George replied. "I just keep thinking about what a waste it all is. Marriages, careers, destroyed in an instant."

The screen flickered slightly, reminding them of the thousands of miles between them.

"Stay safe, George," Maggie said softly. "I need you to come home to me."

"I will," he promised. "Nothing will keep me from coming home to you, Maggie. Ten more months."

"Ten more months," she echoed.

As the screen went dark, Maggie sat there in silence, thinking about Marcie and Matt, Tom and Rosa, choices and consequences, how quickly life could change, and George, so far away in that dangerous place and how desperately she wanted him home.

Chapter Thirty-Nine
LOVE LETTERS

May 2011
Postmarked Letter from Helmand Province,
Afghanistan

My dearest Maggie,

I flew to Kabul yesterday, the capital of Afghanistan. In 2001, five hundred thousand lived there. Now, in 2011, three million live there.

Snow-capped mountains ring the city this time of year. The city is six thousand feet, almost the same as Colorado Springs. Kabul is a mix of Tijuana, Mexico, and Naples, Italy, except it is more crowded and dirtier. It is the world's third most polluted city—smoke, fumes, and pollution everywhere. There is no rhyme or reason to the traffic patterns. Drivers who get frustrated with traffic change lanes and head into oncoming traffic!

The streets are lined with small shops, selling everything from meat to fruit to blankets and cooking supplies. The people are a mix of Pashtuns, Tajiks, and other

Central Asian ethnicities. Some have Western European features, others appear Russian, some look Iranian, and others have Asian characteristics. They are not large, but wiry, slim, bearded, and in good physical shape. Several lieutenant colonels and colonels I've met are veterans of the 1979 to 1989 Soviet– Afghan War.

Last night, I returned to Camp Leatherneck, where I live. This base is in the middle of the desert, a one-thousand-six-hundred-acre outpost in the middle of nowhere. We have four gyms, six dining facilities, a ten-thousand-square-foot post exchange, three chapels, and a twenty-four-hour call center. The base is large enough that I can go for a four- or five-mile run daily. It's an excellent way to start my day, to clear my head. The mornings are relatively cool, though I know that will change as we move into the summer months.

We've been here almost three months. The days are long, but the weeks go by fast. My Marines are doing great things!

I miss you terribly!

Love,

George

P.S. Hug Smokey for me!

June 2011
Postmarked Letter from Cherry Point, North
Carolina

Dear George,

Happy birthday! I bet you never thought you'd be turning fifty-one in Afghanistan. I miss celebrating holidays with you. So far, we've missed Valentine's Day, Presidents' Day, St. Patrick's Day, Easter, April Fool's Day (if you count that one), and Memorial Day.

At least for Memorial Day weekend, I wasn't alone. I rented the general officers' beach house at Onslow Beach aboard Camp Lejeune. I invited the wives and children of the MAW commanders to spend the day at the beach. Sgt. Maj. Reed's wife, Anna, and their two daughters joined us. What a day it was! The weather was gorgeous. The kids ran in and out of the water all day while the moms sat in chairs, wearing big, floppy hats. I enjoyed watching the older boys carry the smaller children on their backs into the water. Boys and girls were boogie boarding, tossing footballs and Frisbees, and burying one another in the sand. Martha Dooley joined us for a few hours. At dusk, the older boys cast their fishing lines. One of them caught a baby shark.

Our thoughts were not far from those of our patriotic husbands and fathers. But that day, we came together to relax, laugh, and spend time with the women and children who understood what it was like to be separated from a family member in harm's way.

Charla called me the other day. She and Razor will move into their quarters on Parris Island, South

Carolina, in August. She has invited me to visit over Labor Day weekend. I'm unsure I can wait that long, knowing she is only six hours away. Razor will be the commanding general of MCRD, Parris Island, where Marines are made! I fondly remember our time at MCRD, San Diego.

I can't tell you enough how proud I am of you, George. Your bravery, your service, and your sacrifice do not go unnoticed. I watch how you care for and mentor your Marines, passing down actions and core values that make you the remarkable man that you are. The man I fell in love with.

Please stay safe and focus on your Marines' mission and safety. Know that you are missed greatly, but that those you have left behind care for each other and will continue until you return home.

All my love,

Maggie

P.S. What's pink and wet and misses you? Smokey's tongue, of course. What did you think it was?!

September 2011
Postmarked Letter from Helmand Province, Afghanistan

My dearest Maggie,

We are finally getting a reprieve from the heat. In June, the hottest month, it was in the mid-120s. The summer heat reminded me of Yuma—except there was no pool to jump into. Like my time in Iraq, the summer season is the hardest.

Work has been all-consuming. This job is complex and challenging. I am very fortunate to have great Marines with me. They amaze me every day. They get up at 0500, work out, turn wrenches, fix engines, move fuel, and load aircraft—fourteen to sixteen hours a day. Most of the Marines are in their early twenties. They are selfless, motivated, and extremely loyal to each other. My pilots are doing fantastic work. To date, they have completed one thousand two hundred sorties. They are protecting Marines from the sky. I have been doing this for twenty-nine years and have never seen Marines as good as these. Marines are focused and responsible when they are busy, challenged, and in the fight. The new technology has been excellent, with iPads used during helicopter flights and unmanned helicopters for cargo deliveries. We can deliver aviation fires quickly and reduce the threat of IED bombs to ground convoys.

We have integrated with the British forces. They do things differently and talk funny, but working with them has been a pleasure. As tempting as it is, they have a bar in their headquarters. You have to love the Brits!

The other day, I joined several Afghan officers for dinner. The waiters served a plate the size of a Frisbee with a thick bed of native rice, covered in a lamb concoction, like a Greek lamb stew. Delicious! Speaking of Greeks, I have been to places in Afghanistan where historians believe Alexander the Great fought, camped, and transited from 330 BC to 327 BC. I'm still determining how the ancient Greeks walked through this land without sunscreen, bottled water, and sun hats!

I miss you so very much. The only saving grace here is that the days fly by due to the pace and tempo of operations.

Love,

George

P.S. I miss my French maid from Okinawa. Will Margaux be performing again upon my return, sans the back spasm?

Chapter Forty
THE BEST-LAID PLANS

November 2011
Camp Lejeune, North Carolina

BIRTHDAYS ... A TIME OF CELEBRATION. For the spouses of II MEF Forward, who had endured months of separation, the upcoming two hundred thirty-sixth Marine Corps birthday did not seem like a cause for merrymaking. Maggie knew this ball season was going to be a tough one.

God, these women look so tired, she thought, watching fellow spouses trying to maintain brave faces despite the hollow look in their eyes.

Spouses had been dealing with their share of deployment blues and concern for their Marines in harm's way for nine months. The traditional ball celebration would bring back memories of happier times, dressed in formal gowns and escorted by their Marine in dress blues and evening dress. She couldn't just let them wallow in misery. They needed something ... different. Special. She set out to do something about it, her mind racing with possibilities as she picked up the phone.

Maggie formed a committee with her fellow general officer wives, Martha and Valerie, and COWs from Mar Div, MAW, and MLG. At the first meeting, there was a lot to discuss.

"Thank you, Maggie, for spearheading this committee," said Martha. "It's important for us to reinforce the traditions of the Marine Corps. Our husbands will celebrate at Camp Leatherneck, so why shouldn't we? It should be something different so that even though spouses will feel like a part of them is missing, they can still have fun."

Always so proper, Martha.

She was right. They needed this to be special, not just another reminder of what they were missing.

"I agree," said Maggie, feeling a surge of determination as she spoke. "It doesn't matter their age, their husband's rank, if they're male or female; we're all going through this together. We hope to impress the spouses, especially the younger ones, with the special and strong nature of our relationships. No one understands what they're going through better than us. We truly are a semper family." Her voice carried the passion she felt. This wasn't just about a party; it was about survival, community, and supporting one another when the weight became too much.

"What shall we call the event?" asked Valerie. "We can do something more creative than just the Deployed Spouses' Ball."

This is your moment, Maggie. Don't second-guess yourself. Her heart fluttered with a mix of nervousness and excitement.

"I have something to pitch to you," said Maggie, her voice gaining confidence as she pushed forward. "I just finished reading Fiona Kelly's *Nights in Bamiyan.* Ms. Kelly's novel, inspired by her experiences as a nurse in war-torn Third World countries, is about her work in a small medical clinic in Bamiyan, Afghanistan. There are themes of sisterhood and perseverance that I think will resonate with the spouses. And then there's the symbolism of the lipstick. Her main character feels indestructible when she wears her lipstick. It gives her strength and endurance. So, here goes ... what do you think about the Lipstick and Camouflage Deployed Spouses' Ball?" *Please like it, please like it*, she silently pleaded, her nails digging into her palms as she waited for their response.

"We love it!" the ladies resounded.

Relief washed over Maggie, loosening the knot in her stomach. They liked it! It might work.

"Wouldn't it be great if Fiona Kelly were our guest speaker?" asked one of the MLG spouses.

"That's a great idea," Maggie piped up, feeling optimistic. "Let's reach for the stars and see what happens. All we can do is ask."

The worst she could say was no, but wouldn't it be amazing if she said yes?

"What are we thinking about the attire?" Valerie asked.

"Well, if we stick with the theme," Maggie answered, her mind already visualizing the possibilities, "we could go in modified military attire. In the wing, we have flight suit parties. You can make a dress from a flight suit or add a camouflage belt or clutch purse to a cocktail dress."

George would laugh his ass off, seeing me in a cammie cocktail dress, she thought with a bittersweet pang, missing his laughter.

"Maggie," said Martha, "we must not disrespect the uniform. Might I suggest we consult with the lawyers in the JAG office?"

Always the rule follower, Maggie thought, suppressing a snort.

But Martha's caution was warranted. The last thing they needed was a scandal involving disrespect for the uniform.

"We'll establish guidelines," said Maggie. "We don't want to offend anyone, nor do we want to disrespect the Marine Corps. I'll follow up with the JAG's office. The MAW will coordinate with facilities and the club system to manage the venue, food, pricing, and other details. I was hoping Mar Div would coordinate the color guard, the cake ceremony, and the entertainment."

"We got it," said Martha.

"My daughter is in the Junior ROTC program at Lejeune High School," said a Mar Div spouse. "Perhaps we can ask the cadets to perform the ceremony."

"Excellent idea," said Maggie, feeling enthusiastic as the plans began taking shape. This was happening. They were doing this. "Valerie, would the MLG take on marketing and publicity, including creating a logo for the event and a program for the evening?"

"We're more than happy to help," said Valerie.

"Lastly," said Maggie, her lips quirking into a self-deprecating smile, "I could not sew a dress if my life depended on it. As the MAW representative, Karma, do you think L.I.N.K.S. could assist us with a dressmaking clinic for the event?"

"I'll look into it tomorrow morning," said Karma.

"Thank you, ladies," said Maggie, feeling genuine gratitude. "We're off to a great start. We'll meet again in a few weeks."

We just might pull this off, she thought as the meeting dispersed, a flicker of pride warming her chest despite the persistent ache of George's absence.

At the next committee meeting, the ladies provided updates on their assigned tasks.

"We were able to secure Marston Pavilion aboard Camp Lejeune," said Maggie, unable to keep the excitement from her voice. "It's a beautiful, newly renovated facility overlooking the New River and Wallace Creek. We sat down with the head chef for the club. We selected a menu that included chicken Wellington, wild rice pudding, seasonal vegetables, a garden salad, and a birthday cupcake for dessert. We thought signature cocktails would be fun, so we created a Cammie Cosmo and Lipstick Martini."

Those cocktails might be the best idea I've had in months, she thought with an internal chuckle. *Lord knows we could all use a drink or two or three.*

"That's wonderful, Maggie," said Martha. "The Lejeune High School Junior ROTC color guard, which is all female, will present the colors and assist with the traditional cake ceremony. The 2nd Mar Div Jazz Ensemble has agreed to provide music during the cocktail hour. Popular local DJ Devil Dog Jam has generously donated his services to our event."

An all-female color guard—perfect.

"Our FRC, Hope Gold, has a girlfriend who's a professional photographer," Maggie added. "She's also donated her services to offer commemorative photos."

"We've been working with the talented staff in the MCCS marketing department," said Valerie. "We've designed a logo we hope you'll love. It features a hot-pink script font for *Lipstick and Camouflage*. A horizontal tube of hot-pink lipstick, housed in a camouflage case, is positioned in the middle."

It's coming together! Maggie felt a surge of satisfaction, her chest swelling with pride.

"We're working with marketing on getting newspaper articles published in the base paper, *The Eagle*," Valerie continued. "They'll also assist us with the printed program for the event."

"I spoke with L.I.N.K.S.," said Karma. "They'll offer a complimentary glamouflage dressmaking clinic. Seamstresses will be on hand with sewing machines to create outfits with material the spouses provide."

"Along those lines," Maggie added, her expression serious, "I spoke with the JAG's office. Only uniforms that are unserviceable, ripped, faded, or unwearable can be used. No Marine Corps medals or ribbons are allowed. Regulations governing Marine Corps uniforms state that wearing parts of the uniform does not constitute misuse. Active-duty Marines cannot wear altered uniforms, but the same restrictions do not bind spouses."

Martha will be relieved.

"Wonderful," said Martha. "Let's keep it classy, ladies."

And there she goes, Maggie thought with an endearing smile. *Predictable as sunrise.*

"Since this is a Deployed Spouses' Ball," Maggie continued, feeling a warm glow of accomplishment, "we've been approved for Family Readiness funds from the MAW, Mar Div, and MLG to help offset the costs and bring the ticket price down to a reasonable twenty dollars a ticket. Complimentary childcare will be offered at the Tarawa Terrace Child Development Center. Finally," said Maggie, barely containing her excitement, "I'm excited to announce that Fiona Kelly has agreed to be our guest speaker for the event."

Holy shit, we got her!

"I'll handle all VIP escort services for Ms. Kelly. I've reserved rooms at the Chesty Puller Guesthouse on Camp Lejeune for the evening."

"Will Mrs. Gibbons be speaking at the event?" Martha asked.

"Yes," said Maggie. "Candace has agreed to say a few words as a special guest and as the II MEF commanding general's spouse."

"Ladies, thank you for all your hard work," said Martha. "This will surely be a unique event. Our husbands will be proud."

They will be proud, Maggie thought, a bittersweet ache growing in her chest.

On the night before the Lipstick and Camouflage Deployed Spouses' Ball, Maggie was summoned to the 2nd MAW headquarters building for a secure phone call from George. Her heart raced as she hurried down the hallway, a mixture of dread and hope churning in her stomach.

Please let him be okay. Please don't let this be bad news.

Maggie picked up the phone, her fingers trembling.

"George," said Maggie hesitantly. "Is everything all right?"

"Yes, my love," said George reassuringly. "I just wanted to give you a heads-up on a few developments. The NCIS special agents finally tracked down Levi. He was living and working as a ranch hand on a horse ranch in Alpine, California. They questioned him about the drugs he'd provided to Julia. Are you sitting down? He admitted that Karma had given him extra money to increase the doses."

Karma? The name hit Maggie like a bombshell.

The room seemed to tilt, and she had to steady herself against the desk, her knuckles turning white as she gripped the phone. Her stomach twisted into a tight, painful knot.

No. No, no, no. Not Karma.

"Why would Karma do that?" Her voice came out strangled, barely audible.

The bitter taste of betrayal flooded her mouth.

"Levi said he'd told Karma he saw Julia and Ian in bed together. He said Karma intended to get Julia hooked on the drugs so that Ian would disapprove of her behavior and stop seeing her."

The room swam before Maggie's eyes as nausea rose in her throat. She pressed her palm against her sternum, as if trying to hold herself together physically.

She killed her. Karma killed Julia out of some twisted sense of loyalty.

Images flashed through her mind like a film reel—Karma smiling, Karma drinking cocktails at the Rendezvous Lounge, Karma sharing their diving photo from Okinawa, Karma nodding solemnly when they discussed the blackmail. All the while, she'd harbored this terrible secret.

"Oh my God, Karma." The words escaped as a choked whisper. "Loyal to a fault." Her voice broke on the last word, bitter irony coating her tongue. "Do they think Levi is the blackmailer?" She could hear her heartbeat pounding in her ears, drowning out everything else.

"The agents questioned Levi extensively. They don't believe he's our man."

Maggie's legs threatened to buckle. If it wasn't Levi, who was the blackmailer? There was something she was missing. Had someone else been there that night, lurking in the shadows?

She sank into the nearest chair, her body suddenly heavy.

"Oh, George," she whispered, a tremor coursing through her entire being. Her mind replayed the terrible scenario on repeat—Karma calculating, planning, watching as Julia had spiraled into addiction. "This is horrible. What does it mean?" Her voice cracked as tears stung her eyes.

Julia was dead. Snuffed out because Karma had been obsessed with … what? Protecting Maggie?

"It means Karma is going to be arrested and charged with involuntary manslaughter."

Maggie's hand flew to her mouth to stifle a sob. Her world narrowed to pinpricks of light as darkness encroached from the edges of her vision.

Manslaughter. Prison. Dear God.

"When?!" The word exploded from her, raw with panic.

Images of Karma being led away in handcuffs during the ball, of the shocked faces of the other spouses, of all their hard work collapsing into chaos flashed through her mind.

Not during the ball. Please, not during the ball.

"I asked the agents to wait until after the Deployed Spouses' Ball tomorrow night. They agreed. They'll be arresting her the morning after the ball. Maggie, everything I told you is confidential."

"I understand," Maggie whispered, though she felt she understood nothing anymore.

Her mind reeled with the impossible task ahead—to stand beside Karma, smile, and celebrate, all while carrying this terrible knowledge. Her throat constricted painfully, making it difficult to breathe. She'd be laughing, drinking the Cammie Cosmos, while Julia lay cold in the ground. Maggie felt a wave of revulsion so strong that it left her shaking. Thank God Barbara would be there, and she had invited Charla. Maggie would need their support even though they wouldn't know it.

"I have some other news. Unfortunately, Hurl didn't make brigadier general."

"Well, given the circumstances now, that's probably for the best." Probably better for Karma, too, considering where she was headed. "Wow, this is a lot to take in."

"I know, my love. Hang in there. I'll be home before you know it."

"You'd damn well better." Her voice took on a fierceness that surprised even her. *I need you here. I need you to be safe.*

"There's the feisty girl I know and love." George chuckled.

Maggie paused before answering, emotion overtaking her.

"Please, come home safe." *I can't do any of this without you.*

"That's the plan," said George.

"I love you, George." *More than you know. More than I can say.*

"I love you, Maggie. I'll see you soon."

"What the fuck just happened?!" cried Maggie as she hung up the phone. The sound tore from her throat, raw and primal, echoing in the empty room like the cry of a wounded animal. Her breath came in painful, sharp gasps as her whole body shook violently.

As the full horror of George's revelations swept over her in unrelenting waves, the walls appeared to close in around her. She staggered backward, knocking over a chair with a clatter. Her legs gave way, and she slid down against the wall, drawing her knees to her chest. Hot tears spilled down her cheeks, but she barely noticed them.

Karma. Her childhood friend. Her loyal and dear friend. She loved her, trusted her, and confided in her. And all the while … when Karma had picked her up that fateful night, she was so supportive. Reassuring Maggie it was a terrible accident. Karma never criticized Julia. She'd always convinced Maggie that Ian loved her and loved her alone. How would she face tomorrow? How would she smile and clink glasses and pretend she didn't know Karma had blood on her hands?

A sob broke free, then another, until she was weeping openly, her shoulders shaking with the force of her grief.

"Damn you, Karma," she whispered fiercely into the empty room.

Slowly, with trembling hands, she wiped at her face, smearing tears across her cheeks. The ball was tomorrow. Hundreds of women were counting on her. George was counting on her. She couldn't fall apart now.

Deep breaths, Maggie. Just breathe.

She forced herself to stand on unsteady legs, smoothing her clothes with shaking hands, trying to compose herself. There would be time to process this later, to rage and grieve and try to make sense of the senseless. But not now. Now, she had to be strong—for the spouses, George, and herself.

One day at a time, Maggie. Just like always. One impossible, unbearable fucking day at a time.

Chapter Forty-One

LIPSTICK AND CAMOUFLAGE
DEPLOYED SPOUSES' BALL

MAGGIE AND CHARLA WERE SEATED in the lobby of the Chesty Puller Guesthouse, a two-story red-brown brick building overlooking the New River.

Maggie wore a black spaghetti-strap gown and a green camouflage bolero jacket with *Stone* embroidered in hot pink on the right breast pocket. She wore a green camouflage cover with a tiara on the front brim.

This feels surreal, Maggie thought, tugging at her bolero jacket. Her stomach churned with anxiety.

She glanced at Charla with gratitude. Thank God she was here. Maggie would never get through this night alone.

Charla was dressed in a tan flight suit, fashioned into a short dress with tan camouflage trim at the collar and sleeves and ruffled at the bottom. Fiona entered the lobby, wearing a black cocktail dress and a green camouflage belt. She was petite with lily-white skin and straight, shoulder-length, dark brown hair with bangs.

"It's a lovely evening, ladies," said Fiona.

"You're Irish," said Charla, surprised.

"Originally from outside Dublin," said Fiona. "I live in Boston now."

Maggie introduced Fiona to Charla, her voice steady despite the storm raging inside her. Maggie had to focus on being a good hostess.

"Fiona, we're so happy you could be here with us tonight," Maggie said, bringing a smile to her face. "Ladies, shall we head to the curb and await our ride?"

A black limousine pulled up in front of the guesthouse. Candace, Martha, and Valerie were seated inside. The limo driver opened the door, allowing Fiona, Maggie, and Charla to enter. Maggie introduced Fiona and Charla to everyone. Champagne glasses were poured, and toasts were made.

Just breathe. Smile. Act normal. Maggie took a long sip of champagne, welcoming the cool liquid down her throat. *Maybe alcohol will make this charade easier.*

"Fiona's fiancé, Andrew, was with the Royal Marines during Desert Storm," said Maggie, grateful for the easy conversation topic.

"He has fond memories of the Marine Corps," said Fiona. "Proud to serve, as your husbands are."

"Does that mean you understand our jargon and acronyms?" Valerie asked.

"Oh, of course." Fiona chuckled. "I know the Royal Marines say, *Per Mare, Per Terram—By Sea, By Land.* Your Marines say, *Semper fi.*"

"Thank you, Candace," said Maggie, "for treating us to this limo for the evening." *Small talk. Keep making small talk. Don't think about tomorrow.*

"It's my honor," said Candace. "It's a special evening. You ladies deserve to ride in style. We have something else to celebrate. Pete tells me Lee has been selected for major general, and Nathan and George have been nominated for lieutenant general. Cheers, ladies!"

"A toast," said Martha, raising her glass. "To Fiona, our honored guest. By Sea, By Land. Semper fi."

Maggie raised her glass with a practiced smile.

The limousine pulled up to the entrance of Marston Pavilion, a restored Georgian-style white building. The ladies exited the limo and entered the foyer, where over two hundred guests filled the room, smooth jazz set the tone, and cocktail glasses clinked with merriment. Custom-made camouflage attire and hot pink dominated the room.

They did it, Maggie thought with a bittersweet surge of pride as she surveyed the scene.

Despite everything, they had created something beautiful tonight. Her eyes stung with unexpected tears that she quickly blinked away.

Maggie escorted Fiona and Charla into the room. Their first encounters were with Karma and Barbara. Karma wore a khaki-green dress with hot-pink patent leather boots and a feather boa wrapped around her neck. Barbara looked sharp in her dress blues.

Maggie was struck with force by the sight of Karma. *How dare she stand here like nothing's wrong? How dare she smile and laugh?* Her jaw clenched so tight that it ached, and she fought the urge to scream the truth to everyone in the room.

"What are you doing here, Charla?!" said Karma venomously, her jealousy of Maggie's relationship with Charla in Okinawa surfacing.

Of course she starts drama. Of course. Anger flashed hot through Maggie's veins.

"Charla is here because I invited her," said Maggie, her voice clipped and cold. "Razor took over as commanding general of MCRD, Parris Island. She's here to show her support." *And to keep me from falling apart, you murderous bitch.*

"Will wonders never cease?" Karma quipped.

"Shame on you, Karma," said Barbara. "Charla and her daughters were so supportive of everything you went through with Erin in Okinawa."

"What do you know?" Karma asked. "You don't even know Charla, and you weren't in Okinawa at the time."

"I know enough," said Barbara.

Maggie couldn't do this. She couldn't stand there while Karma acted like she had the moral high ground. She was going to vomit. Maggie's hands trembled, and she clenched her fists to steady herself.

"This is not the time or place for any of this," Maggie reprimanded, summoning every ounce of control she possessed. "Especially in front of our guest of honor. Pull up your big-girl panties, Karma, and move on."

It was her last night of freedom, and she was spending it creating drama. If she only knew what tomorrow would bring.

Karma lifted her chin and walked away, arms sweeping by her sides.

That's right; walk away while you still can. Maggie took a deep breath, maintaining her composure.

"Fiona," said Maggie, deliberately turning her back on Karma's retreating figure, "I would like you to meet Barbara, one of my oldest and dearest friends. She's a Navy doctor and the commanding officer at the naval clinic at Cherry Point. Several of her spouses have doctors or corpsmen deployed."

"It's a pleasure to meet you, Doctor," said Fiona. "You're a woman after my own heart."

"Barbara," added Maggie, "I'd like to introduce you to Charla properly."

Barbara hugged Charla. "It is so nice to finally meet you, Charla. I've heard so much about you and your adventures with Maggie in Okinawa."

"Likewise," said Charla. "Now that we're stationed in South Carolina, I hope to get to know you better. That is, if Maggie invites me up to play."

"That's a promise," said Maggie, a genuine smile breaking through her tension for the first time that evening. She would need all the true friends she could get after the storm that was coming.

Barbara excused herself to visit with the Navy wives. Maggie, Fiona, and Charla headed to the bar and stood in line behind Sarah Kane and Hope Gold.

"Fiona," said Maggie, slipping back into her role as hostess, "I'd like to introduce you to Sarah Kane and her Family Readiness Coordinator, Hope Gold."

"Nice to meet you, ma'am," replied Sarah.

"A pleasure to meet you," said Hope.

"Mrs. Stone," said Sarah, "thank you for putting this evening together. This has been a hard deployment. I'm happy to be here rather than sitting at home, crying."

This is why we are all here, for women like Sarah. Focus on that, Maggie. Her heart softened as she was reminded of the purpose behind all their work.

"Sarah was six months pregnant when her husband deployed," Maggie explained. "With the help of her FRC, her husband was able to watch the birth on an internet video."

"How grand," said Fiona. "How was the experience?"

"When I went into labor," Sarah continued, "I called Hope."

"I was shocked when I got the phone call," Hope explained. "She was two weeks early. That rarely happens with a first baby. I contacted her husband's unit to let them know Sarah was in labor. Then I headed to the naval hospital to support Sarah and set up the internet camera."

"I was in labor for ten hours," Sarah groaned.

"That's not unusual," said Fiona. "First-time mothers average eight to eighteen hours in labor."

"That wasn't the worst of it," said Sarah. "The internet kept dropping. I thought he might miss the actual birth! But he didn't; he saw the baby before I did. It was amazing!"

"How's the baby?" asked Maggie, genuinely interested despite her inner turmoil.

Life goes on. Even amid all the ugliness, beautiful things still happen.

"She's doing great. She's six months old. We named her Melodie. Hope has been a godsend. You weren't kidding when you said I am part of the semper family."

Maggie, Fiona, and Charla grabbed their cocktails and moved about the room, speaking with spouses and admiring one another's outfits.

"Take a look at this supermodel," Maggie exclaimed, forcing enthusiasm into her voice. "Fiona and Charla, this is

Anna Reed, the wife of my husband's right-hand man in Afghanistan, Sergeant Major Reed."

Anna stood six feet tall in heels. Her distinctive dark-skinned face included high cheekbones, full lips, and captivating hazel eyes.

"I just love your outfit," Charla gushed. "A simple black cocktail dress with neck detail that accentuates your décolletage. The camouflage scarf cinched around your tiny waist and the camouflage bow in your long black hair … simply stunning."

"Wow," Anna replied. "I need to hang out with you ladies more often."

"Anna," said Maggie, her voice softening with genuine emotion, "I can't tell you enough how comforting it is to know Sergeant Major Reed has my husband's back overseas."

"The same can be said about General Stone," said Anna. "Roy respects him greatly. Maggie, thank you for your selfless service. You have a great heart for your husband, our Marines, and our families. My daughters remember their wonderful time at the beach house on Memorial Day weekend."

"It's my pleasure," Maggie said, embracing Anna. "Have you heard from Rosa Wilson?"

"Yes. I spoke with her the other day. She called to wish us a happy birthday and said to enjoy a Cammie Cosmo for her. She's doing well. She got her real estate license and is kicking ass in Laredo."

"That warms my heart," replied Maggie, and she meant it. At least some stories had happy endings.

Valerie approached the ladies. "Maggie, sorry for the interruption," she said. "Can I steal you and Charla away for a photo?"

"Of course," Maggie replied, though her stomach twisted at the thought of posing with Karma. These photos would be a grotesque memento after tomorrow. "Fiona, will you be okay on your own?"

"Absolutely," said Fiona. "I'm sure Anna will keep me company."

Maggie and Charla navigated through the crowd to the photo area. In the center, a navy-blue leather couch was placed atop a decorative rug. Desert camouflage netting served as the backdrop, with an American flag flanked by the flags of the Navy and the Marine Corps. Maggie and Charla joined the others for the photo shoot.

Smile for the camera. Pretend everything is normal. Maggie positioned herself as far from Karma as possible, her face aching from the strain of her artificial smile.

After the traditional ceremony recognizing the two hundred thirty-sixth birthday, which Maggie observed in a haze of detached grief, the attendees moved to the Tinian Room for dinner. They stopped by the bar to refill cocktails and admire each other's custom outfits.

Another drink. She needed another drink to get through this. Maggie accepted a fresh Cammie Cosmo, the cold glass a welcome anchor to reality.

The attendees enjoyed a plated dinner, followed by a birthday cupcake dessert. Maggie barely tasted her food, pushing it around her plate while nodding at appropriate intervals in the conversation.

After Candace's brief speech, welcoming everyone, it was Maggie's turn to take the podium. As she stood, a strange calm settled over her. This, at least, she could do. This was real—Fiona's work, her compassion, her courage. She took a deep breath and approached the microphone.

"I'm thrilled and honored to introduce tonight's guest of honor," Maggie began, her voice strong and clear despite her inner turmoil. "Fiona Kelly is a modern heroine. She has put herself in some of the world's most demanding and heart-wrenching situations, serving as a nurse in Third World countries. She has written extensively about refugees and has appeared on numerous television and radio programs. Ms. Kelly lives in Boston, Massachusetts, as an emergency room nurse at Boston General Hospital. While these credentials are impressive enough, her debut novel, *Nights in Bamiyan*, is based on her experiences as a nurse following the 9/11 attacks. Ms.

Kelly's novel opens a window into the lives of women half a world away. We discover that despite cultural differences, we share qualities, such as strength, resiliency, and the power of friendship. The world is filled with miracles and inspiration. We are fortunate to have one with us this evening—Ms. Fiona Kelly."

Strength. Resiliency. Friendship. The words echoed in Maggie's mind as she stepped back from the podium, her eyes deliberately avoiding Karma's face in the crowd.

It was Fiona's turn to step to the podium.

"You spouses rock," she said with enthusiasm. "When Margaret Stone emailed me about speaking to you tonight, I had to pull my guy, Andrew, over to the computer and ask him, 'Are you seeing what I'm seeing?' He confirmed this fabulous invitation, and here I am. I'm thrilled and honored to be here with you tonight to share my experiences."

Fiona spent the next ten minutes sharing a slideshow of her time working for an international aid organization at a medical clinic. Her photos evoked strong emotions from the attendees. Eyebrows rose and lips pursed when photos showed Fiona tending to patients with disease and devastating injuries. Spouses' eyes danced at photos of Fiona playing with local children. Eyes gleamed with pride when pictures of service members securing the perimeter emerged on the screen.

Maggie watched the presentation with a mixture of admiration and profound sadness. *This is what service means. Not betrayal. Not death.*

"What the service members do is important not only for the United States, but for the world," said Fiona. "When they show up, they don't just protect us; they rescue everyone. When our military arrived, hope was renewed for everyone. Farmers are harvesting crops again, and children, including girls, attend school."

Fiona finished her presentation to a standing ovation. Maggie clapped until her hands hurt, grateful for the genuine moment of inspiration amid her nightmare.

Martha, Maggie, and Valerie approached the stage.

"Thank you, Fiona," said Maggie, her voice thick with emotion, "for joining us tonight and for sharing a firsthand account of the value of what our service members are doing overseas."

At least this was real. At least this mattered.

"As a token of our appreciation," said Valerie, "we'd like to present you with personalized camouflage." Valerie presented Fiona with a custom-made green camouflage clutch handbag with a pink embroidered *Kelly* name tag.

"We have a saying in the military—*go big or go home*," said Martha. "Please accept this rather large gift so you'll always remember your time with us at the Lipstick and Camouflage Deployed Spouses' Ball." Martha handed Fiona a life-sized cardboard cutout of a hot-pink lipstick in a camouflage case.

"Enjoy the rest of the evening, dancing to tunes spun by DJ Devil Dog Jam," said Maggie, summoning one last smile. A few more hours. Just a few more hours, and this charade could end. "Thank you for being a part of this unique celebration. Have a safe journey home."

As the music started and the dance floor filled, Maggie slipped away to the edge of the room, finding a quiet corner, where she could lean against the wall and finally drop the mask just a fraction. Her eyes found Karma across the room, laughing and dancing without a care in the world.

"Karma's sure having a good time," said Barbara, stepping in next to Maggie.

"Doesn't she always?" said Maggie curtly. "Do you ever wonder what it must be like to be Karma? Not a care in the world, no regrets, no worries."

"Maggie, you know that's not true. She has her moments when she's empathetic. She's a loyal friend. Remember our pact—always to protect each other?"

"She's loyal to her family and friends, but at what cost?"

"Maggie, are you okay?" Barbara asked with sincerity and concern in her voice.

"I'm fine. I'm just exhausted. I love you, Barbara," she said, bringing her into a warm embrace. "You're loyal and kind and trustworthy—all the qualities that make you the special person you are and why I'm so lucky to call you my friend."

"I love you too, Maggie. Well done tonight. You celebrated the spouses most uniquely and lovingly. I'm so proud to be your friend."

Enjoy tonight, Karma. Tomorrow, everything changes.

Chapter Forty-Two
THE MORNING AFTER

MAGGIE ENTERED THE CHESTY PULLER Guesthouse lobby with a knot in her stomach. She spotted Karma and Charla seated on the couch, enjoying coffee. After last evening's heated exchange, the sight of them sitting near each other, though not speaking, surprised her. She felt a pang of guilt, mixed with frustration. Karma's jealousy of Maggie's friendship with Charla had festered since Okinawa. Maggie had seen this pattern before—Karma's fiery nature would explode, then settle like a dormant volcano, always leaving destruction in its wake.

I hope she's calmed down this morning. Things are about to heat up, Maggie thought as she poured herself a cup of coffee.

Her hands gripped the warm mug, drawing comfort from its heat while gathering courage. She sat across from Karma and Charla, the silence between them heavy and stifling.

Fresh from her morning run, Barbara burst into the lobby with Saturday's edition of *The Eagle* tucked under her arm. The newspaper landed with a soft thud on the table in front of Maggie. As Barbara walked away to get coffee, Maggie unfolded the paper and felt her heart plummet.

"Oh God," she gasped, blood draining from her face as she stared at the headline—"Deployed Spouses' Ball Aftershock: Did the Party Girls Go Too Far?"

There they were—a candid photo of Maggie, Martha, Valerie, Candace, and Charla. All five generals' wives smiling in their custom camouflage outfits, with Cammie Cosmos raised in celebration, utterly unaware of how their joy would be twisted.

Maggie's eyes darted across the article, each word feeling like a personal attack.

> *Last evening, more than two hundred wives of II MEF Forward Marines and sailors, including the wives of prominent general officers, attended the Lipstick and Camouflage Deployed Spouses' Ball, held at Camp Lejeune's Marston Pavilion. The spouses dined, danced, and drank in clothes custom-made from camouflage uniforms, adorned with feathers, sequins, ribbons, and pink tulle fringe. Some argue that the military costumes are in poor taste and violate regulations regarding the proper wear of military uniforms.*
>
> *"Cutting up camouflage uniforms that symbolize the United States Marine Corps is disrespectful," said an anonymous source, "especially since their Marines and sailors are deployed in harm's way. These women have not earned the right to wear the uniform. Next thing you know, they'll be wearing their husband's rank!"*

A hot flush of anger rushed through Maggie's body. After all the planning, all the support and camaraderie they'd offered each other, this was how someone had repaid them? By twisting their intentions? By suggesting they were disrespectful to the institution they'd poured their hearts and souls into?

"Wow!" said Barbara. "I didn't see that coming. As an active-duty naval officer, I agree that my wearing a modified uniform would have been disrespectful. Last night, I saw nothing but love and respect for the Marine Corps and the Navy."

"I'd love to know the name of the anonymous source," Maggie said, her voice low and dangerous, fingers tightening around the newspaper. She could feel her blood pressure rising. "Was that rat bastard a wolf wearing sheep's clothing among us last night?"

"I wonder if the wolf was wearing a pink tulle fringe?" Charla joked.

Despite her anger, Maggie couldn't help but grin at Charla's attempt to lighten the mood. That was one thing she'd always appreciated about her friend—her ability to find humor in difficult situations. Maggie's mind was already racing ahead to damage control.

"I'm calling *The Eagle* and demanding they print a rebuttal," she declared, her voice gaining strength with her resolve. "At the very least, I'm writing a letter to the editor."

"Karma," said Barbara, "you're quiet."

The observation sent a chill up Maggie's spine. She looked at Barbara, and then they turned to Karma. In that split second, as Maggie studied Karma's face—the averted eyes, the slight flush of her cheeks—realization crashed down on her.

"It was *you*!" Maggie screamed, built-up tension erupting like a geyser. Her entire body shook with rage and betrayal. She slammed her fist on the table, sending coffee sloshing over the rim of her mug. "What is *wrong* with you? After everything we've been through together, all these years—your mom's illness, my mom's death, deployments, Erin's assault—and *this* is how you repay friendship?"

Hot tears pricked at the corners of Maggie's eyes, but she blinked them back furiously. She wouldn't give Karma the satisfaction.

"You don't know what it's like, watching you and the other general officer wives, including the newly minted Yellow Rose of Texas, prancing about the room," Karma shot back, rising to her feet to meet Maggie's fury with her own. Her face contorted with years of suppressed resentment. "Everyone praises you when the wives who do the real work must watch their husbands get passed over for promotion. You have *no idea* what that feels like, do you, Maggie? To watch your husband sacrifice everything and get *nothing!*"

"Is that what this is about?" Maggie finally asked, her voice barely a whisper. "Hurl getting passed over for brigadier general? You destroyed something that meant so much to us because you're bitter?"

As Charla tried to intervene with Southern grace, explaining the promotion statistics, Maggie watched through blurred vision. All these years, she'd thought of Karma as a friend, a sister who had her back. And all along, this resentment had been festering like an infected wound.

"Leave her out of it, Karma," Maggie said firmly when Karma mocked Charla's attempt at empathy. She felt protective of Charla, who was only trying to help. "I had a phone call with George the other day. He told me he was given the brigadier general select list and would notify those in the 2nd MAW. I'm sorry Hurl didn't make the list."

Her words were sincere despite her anger. She knew the disappointment of dashed hopes, how it felt to watch your spouse work tirelessly without receiving the recognition you believed they deserved. But to betray friends over it? That she couldn't understand.

"Thank you," said Karma brusquely.

Something in the air changed. Maggie felt it before she saw the reason. Her throat constricted, and she struggled to swallow as she spotted Special Agent Morris at the lobby entrance. A cold dread settled in her stomach, much worse than the anger from moments before.

"There's something else," said Maggie softly.

She'd known this moment was coming, dreaded it, hoped against hope it would never arrive.

NCIS agents entered the lobby. Special Agent Morris approached Karma.

"Karma McCauley," said Special Agent Morris. "You're under arrest for involuntary manslaughter in the death of Julia Franco."

Maggie felt the room spin slightly. She watched, frozen in place, as Karma stood up from the couch, eyes fixed on the floor.

"I was hoping this day would never come," Karma said quietly.

"Oh my God," Barbara shrieked. "Karma, what did you do?"

"I did it for you, Maggie," said Karma, finally meeting Maggie's eyes with a look that chilled her to the bone. Her voice cracked, her facade crumbling at last. "I knew Julia was sleeping with Ian. I didn't want you to find out. I didn't want you to get hurt. I thought if Julia depended on the drugs, Ian would tire of her. I never meant for her to die."

"*For me?*" Maggie's scream tore from somewhere deep in her gut, primal and wounded. She lunged forward, grabbing Karma's shoulders and shaking her before Barbara could pull her back. "You killed a woman, and you dare to say it was *for me?*"

Maggie's entire body convulsed with sobs. The revelation about Ian's infidelity had cut deep—a betrayal within a betrayal—but it paled in comparison to the horror of what Karma had done.

"How dare you use me as an excuse for murder?" Maggie's voice dropped to a dangerous whisper, her fingers digging into her palms. "Who gave you the right to play God with someone's life? Did you know Julia was pregnant?"

Tears streamed down Karma's face now too. "Of course not. What kind of monster do you think I am? I knew Ian was seeing her behind your back. I couldn't stand by and watch you get hurt. Not after everything you'd been through. You had been a shell of yourself after your mother died. Ian brought you back to life. We had Maggie back again. I didn't want that to end because of a New York bimbo."

"Stop it!" Maggie screamed, her voice raw. "How could you? How could you?" The words tore from her throat between gasps. "I trusted you with everything!"

Maggie couldn't stand still as Special Agent Morris cuffed Karma and read her rights. The storm of emotions—shock, disgust, grief, and betrayal—took over her body as she paced wildly around the lobby. She rubbed the back of her neck vigorously, as though she could somehow erase what she had just heard, her face burning hot with anger and shame.

Maggie gave Karma a final look as the agents eventually escorted her out. Thirty-eight years of friendship flashed between them in that moment—all of it tainted now.

"I'm sorry, Maggie," Karma whispered, her face crumpling. "I'm so sorry."

As the door closed behind them, Maggie's legs gave way, and she collapsed onto the couch. The strength that had carried her through so many challenges deserted her completely. Her body shook with sobs so violent that they were almost silent, stealing her breath. She pounded her fist against the cushion in helpless rage.

Barbara and Charla moved to sit beside her, offering physical comfort that could barely penetrate the storm of emotions raging through her. Barbara wrapped an arm around Maggie's shoulders while Charla pressed a tissue into her trembling hand.

"She ruined Ian's career," Maggie choked out, mascara streaking down her blotchy face. "She killed a woman, and she did it, thinking it was for me!" Her voice broke on the last word, dissolving into raw, guttural sobs. "God help you, Karma. God help you."

Fiona entered the lobby, breaking the heavy silence.

"Jesus, Mary, and Joseph," she exclaimed. "Has there been a death?"

"Of a friendship," Barbara answered. "Yes."

Maggie sat in stunned silence, her world irreparably altered. The Deployed Spouses' Ball drama seemed trivial now, a petty squabble compared to the weight of a lost life and the twisted version of loyalty that had led to it. Everything she'd thought she knew about Karma, about friendship, about the community they'd built together was shattered.

"What a morning this has been," Barbara announced, squeezing Maggie's hand. "I could go for a Cammie Cosmo."

Maggie felt a spark of gratitude for Barbara's steadiness, her ability to acknowledge the gravity of the situation while gently suggesting they move forward.

"The O'Club is open for brunch," said Charla. "I hear Min mixes up exceptional mimosas and Bloody Marys. We can all relax before we put Fiona back on a plane to Boston."

"Perfect," said Fiona. "Ladies, I'm going to miss you! Never a dull moment round here."

Maggie nodded mutely, knowing she would go through the motions for her friends' sakes, but inside, a voice kept repeating, *She did it for me. She did it for me.* She wasn't sure she could ever come to terms with the burden of that knowledge.

Chapter Forty-Three
WHAT THE WATER KNEW

January 2012
Little Creek Naval Base
Norfolk, Virginia

MAGGIE DIALED THE NUMBER. HER heart pounded in her chest as she listened to the ring. One, two, three times.

Maybe he won't answer. Perhaps this is a mistake.

She nearly hung up when a familiar voice came through the line.

"Captain Murphy speaking."

Maggie swallowed hard, and her throat suddenly dried. "Ian? It's Maggie."

A pause. She could hear his sharp intake of breath.

"Maggie? Hi. How are you?"

"I need to see you," she said, her voice steadier now, more determined. "It's about the blackmail. NCIS told me they updated you."

Another pause, longer this time.

Maggie closed her eyes, picturing his face, wondering what he was thinking.

"Of course," he finally said, his tone shifting to something more formal, professional. "When?"

"Tomorrow. I can be there by noon. It's about a three-hour drive from North Carolina." She bit her lip, wondering if she should have waited longer.

"That works. Come to the EOD Group Two building at Little Creek. I'll make sure they're expecting you."

"Thank you, Ian." She hesitated, a thousand unspoken words hanging between them. "I'll see you tomorrow."

After hanging up, Maggie stared at the phone in her hand. Was this finally the end? She gazed out the window, feeling like she was standing at the edge of a cliff, about to step off into the unknown.

Maggie's convertible pulled into a visitor spot in front of the EOD Group Two building aboard Little Creek Naval Base in Norfolk, Virginia. No turning back now. She took a deep breath, smoothed her hair, and stepped out into the crisp, coastal air.

After entering the building, she was escorted by a sailor to the office of the commodore—Captain Ian Murphy. With each step down the corridor, her anxiety mounted.

"Maggie," said Ian, standing up from behind his desk. "So good to see you."

Her heart skipped. He didn't look much different from the Ian she'd met at McP's two years earlier—the same Ian, with the wild intensity in his eyes, who both frightened and excited her.

Ian walked out from his desk to embrace Maggie. She stiffened slightly before allowing herself to relax into the familiar embrace, memories flooding back with his scent—salt and sea; he'd been surfing that morning, she was sure of it.

"Thanks for meeting me," she said, her voice wavering slightly. "I needed to see you in person."

"Of course. Anything I can do to help. Please take a seat."

Maggie surveyed Ian's desk, trying to read who he had become in the life they hadn't shared. His personalized EOD nameplate was prominently displayed. Mission briefing folders and a bomb disposal robot remote control were stacked on both sides of the desk. On the wall behind him hung certificates of commendation, plaques, and unit mementos. On the credenza below, framed photographs of Ian with teammates and dignitaries were lined up.

"How's George?" asked Ian.

George. My anchor. "The deployment is almost over. I can't believe how long and fast it can feel simultaneously," she replied, her voice softening with genuine affection. "He's doing well. Thank you for asking. What is it you do here?" *Keep it light.*

"In a nutshell, we perform combat operations worldwide. We clear explosive threats—chemical, biological, radiological, nuclear, and sea mines. We parachute in for distant targets and dive under the sea to disarm weapons."

"So, basically, you've advanced to blowing shit up on land, sea, and air worldwide. Congratulations!" Maggie heard her voice take on a sharper edge than intended, her anxiety wearing thin on her nerves.

"Thanks, Maggie." Ian's eyes narrowed slightly. "What's up? You didn't drive three hours just to talk about me."

Here goes. Maggie's heart hammered in her chest, but her voice remained steady. "NCIS told me they filled you in on the latest updates on the search for the blackmailer."

"Yes. They found Levi. Sorry to hear about Karma. NCIS doesn't think either of them is the blackmailer."

"No. Which brings me to my question." Maggie leaned forward, her eyes locking on to a photograph of Ian and Lance on the credenza. "Are you still in touch with Lance?" *Please say no. Please tell me I'm wrong.*

Maggie had not seen Lance since their days together when he and Ian were going through SEAL training. She remembered his quick wit and language skills, which always mesmerized the women at McP's. Her thoughts flashed back to their trip to Baja, Mexico, and Lance's reckless driving habits. That didn't make him a blackmailer. She needed to find out what he knew, what Ian had told him about that night.

"Of course. He's my best friend. He finally left the West Coast and was assigned to SEAL Team Two, Naval Special Warfare Group, just down the road. You think *he's* the blackmailer?"

An invisible weight pressed down on Maggie's chest. Lance. Could it be Lance?

"I don't know. Did you ever talk about that night with him? What did you tell him?" Her voice dropped to just above a whisper, as if speaking the words too loudly might conjure the past right into the room with them.

"Maggie, that was over thirty years ago. I'm sure I mentioned it to him. Maybe I told him you came out of the water after me and that there was no sign of Julia. I don't know."

"It's bad enough I carry the burden of that night all those years ago. For the past four years, I've had to add the shadow of the blackmailer. I need it to end, Ian. Four years of living with this nightmare. It has to stop. I know NCIS cleared Lance from suspicion, but I have a gnawing feeling about this. Please … will you help me find out if Lance is involved?" Her voice cracked slightly, revealing the desperation she'd tried so hard to hide.

Maggie checked in to an oceanfront suite at the Hilton in Virginia Beach. Ian planned to meet Lance for breakfast at a diner the next day.

Maggie rose at six a.m. the next morning. Nervously, she clicked the TV remote, flipping through news channels at a cyclic rate. She paced the room, her palms sweating.

Is this it? she thought, her stomach churning with each passing minute. *Will this finally be over?*

The weight of three decades of guilt and fear pressed down on her shoulders, making it hard to breathe. She paused at the window, watching the waves crash against the shore.

Water cleanses. Water heals.

She felt tears start to form in her eyes. Not yet. It wasn't over yet.

At ten a.m., there was a knock at the door. Her heart leaped to her throat.

This is it.

She opened it to find Ian with an unreadable expression on his face. Maggie invited him to sit on the balcony overlooking the Atlantic Ocean, her legs feeling like they might give way beneath her as she fell into the lounge chair.

"Do you prefer the Atlantic or Pacific Ocean?" asked Maggie, desperate for anything to delay what she knew was coming.

"Well, they're different. I'm not sure which I prefer. I know I need to be in the ocean. To feel the cool water on my skin. Taste and smell the salt. Hear the waves. Marvel at the sight of the distinct and varied shades of blue. I don't think I can live without it."

"Neither can I. We always shared that feeling, didn't we?" She sounded wistful, mourning for what could have been in another life—one without that night, without Julia.

Ian gazed into her eyes, cupped his hands around her face, and kissed her softly. Maggie's heart ached with a bittersweet longing for what they'd once had, what they had lost.

"That we did," he said sadly.

"What happened this morning?" whispered Maggie, the question hanging above them like a guillotine blade.

There was a silence between them. The silence rendered the feeling that all was lost. That life would not be the same from this moment forward. The solemn silence that signified the end.

"We met at our usual diner just outside the base," began Ian. "After a while, I brought up the night of the accident. I said I wished I could take it all back. I asked him if he remembered me mentioning it to him. He said, 'Not much.' He told me he thought you had drowned Julia to get her out of the picture. He said he knew I was seeing Julia on the side. I told him he was wrong … that you didn't kill Julia. That someone was blackmailing you. I looked at him and said, 'Lance, that someone is you.' I threw it out there. Waiting for him to tell me I was wrong. I wanted him to tell me I was wrong. But he didn't. He asked, 'How long have you known?' "

Maggie's blood ran cold. Lance. All this time.

"I'm so sorry, Ian," she managed. "This must be such a shock."

"Over the years, Lance had accrued gambling debts," Ian continued. "In 2008, while stationed in Coronado, California, he became aware of George's promotion to brigadier general. He devised a scheme to defraud you to pay off his debts, acquiring the help of a woman in Mexico to carry out his plan."

Ian sat forward with his hands clasped in front of him. "I mean it, Maggie." Ian's eyes watered. "I wish I could take back that night with all my might. I never should have cheated on you. I was an immature idiot. I never wanted it to end this way."

Maggie leaned her head on Ian's shoulder, years of shared history and secrets binding them together in this moment. Her voice came out in a near whisper, shaking with decades of buried guilt. "I'm still haunted by that night. I was so mad at her. When she told me she was pregnant, something inside me snapped. I pushed her head down under the water. I wanted her to die." The confession burned her throat like acid. "After a moment, I came to my senses. I released her, and her head popped above the water. She was a weak swimmer, and I didn't help her. Ian … I think I killed her." There it was—the truth she had carried all these years.

"No, Maggie. You didn't kill her. I did."

Maggie sat upright and faced Ian. Her eyes searched his face, wide with disbelief. *No. No, that's not possible.* She felt dizzy, unsure if she wanted to hear what he was about to say.

"I swam back out to find her. She was struggling in the water. She begged me to help her back to shore. I wanted to make it all go away. I knew I'd fucked up, but I wanted it all to go away. It didn't take much effort to push her head underwater."

Maggie and Ian sat in silence. Maggie tried to digest everything she had just learned. In a flash, she experienced shock, denial, and anger. Her mind reeled as pieces clicked into place—the way Ian had never seemed distraught enough, how quickly he'd moved on. All these years ... she had been carrying his guilt. His crime.

"Ian ..." Her voice was soft but steady, the weight of thirty years lifting from her shoulders with each word. "I'm going to call NCIS now."

Ian's shoulders slumped, but he nodded, a tear sliding down his weathered face. "I understand."

As she reached for her phone, Maggie felt a strange sense of peace. The ocean waves crashed against the shore below, constant and eternal, just as they had been that night three decades ago. Just as they would be long after all of this was over.

"All this time," she whispered, her fingers hovering over the keypad, "I thought I was the monster."

"We were both monsters that night, Maggie. But you found your way back. I never did." Ian reached across and squeezed her hand. "I'm sorry for letting you carry this alone all these years."

Maggie watched from the doorway as NCIS officers escorted Ian out of the hotel lobby in handcuffs. A silent recognition of everything they had been to one another, everything they had lost, and the truth that had finally freed her came as their eyes locked one last time.

Maggie stood by herself on the beach that night as the tide receded and night fell. She considered how water could give birth to life, hold secrets for decades, and then release them to the surface. How the truth always came back, like the tide itself.

Chapter Forty-Four
WELCOME HOME

February 2012
Cherry Point, North Carolina

BOTH BASES, CHERRY POINT AND Camp Lejeune, were buzzing with anticipation of II MEF Forward's homecoming. Houses were being cleaned and were ready for loved ones' return. Grocery shopping for favorite foods was on the rise. Outfits were picked out for the special day. Children received haircuts. Even furry family members were washed and groomed for the big day.

Entrances to both bases were plastered with *welcome home* signs tied to the chain-link fences. Maggie drove along the fence line of Cherry Point, her heart fluttering with nervous energy.

I've waited so long for this moment, she thought with anticipation as she pulled off to the side of the road.

"Don't you look fine?" Maggie said, grabbing Smokey's face and planting a kiss. "Smartly groomed with a patriotic American flag bandanna. Dad will be so happy to see you."

She popped the trunk of her Mustang, pulled out her sign, and tied it to the fence. It read, *I can't wait to lick you! Love,*

Smokey. She chuckled to herself, imagining George's face when he saw it.

A little humor has always helped get us through the separations.

Maggie's Mustang V-8 engine rumbled as she pulled into a parking spot near the flight line. The vibration beneath her seemed to match her racing heartbeat. Families gathered this brisk February morning, carrying homemade *welcome home* signs, handheld camcorders, and cameras. She exited the car, headed toward the hangar, and immediately ran into FRC Hope Gold.

Thank God for people like Hope, who have kept me sane during this deployment.

"How's it going, Hope?" she asked, trying to keep her voice steady despite the emotion building inside her.

"Going great, ma'am. It's the big day, and it's finally here."

"How many on the first flight?" Maggie asked, excitement in her voice.

"We have four hundred sixteen Marines on the first returning flight and many more incoming flights for the next eight hours. There are plenty of snacks and refreshments for the celebration. Sarah's on the flight line with baby Melodie. Have you met Melodie?"

"No, I haven't. I can't wait to meet her," Maggie replied, her eyes brightening. "This is so exciting! Thank you, Hope, for being so professional and caring for our families."

These reunions always hit her hard, especially when she saw babies meet their fathers for the first time …

"Ma'am, I love my job and these families."

Maggie kissed Hope on the cheek before releasing her grasp, drawing strength from the connection. She then floated out to the flight line, goose bumps on her arms as she glanced at all the families anticipating the arrival of their loved ones. Her heart swelled with empathy for each of them.

She couldn't believe a year had passed, wrapping her arms around herself against the February chill. She wished she could say it had gone by fast. Some of these Marines and sailors would come home to meet their son or daughter for the first time. Some would go home to find out their wife was divorcing them because they couldn't bear the separation. It was a stressful life, not for everyone. Maggie swallowed hard, thinking of the marriages she'd seen crumble under the weight of separations. But for those who prevailed, it was a life rich in friendship and shared experiences.

Try to hold it together, Maggie. She blinked rapidly, fighting back tears that threatened to spill over.

The charter 747 aircraft touched down on the tarmac just before noon to the sound of cheers. Maggie's breath caught in her throat, and she pressed her hand to her chest, feeling her heart pounding. Families patiently waited as the plane door opened and the maintenance crew on the ground rolled the boarding stairs into place. One by one, Marines wearing desert flight suits deplaned and formed a formation on the tarmac. It seemed like hours, though only minutes passed before Sergeant Major Reed stood before the formation.

He debriefed them and then shouted, "Dismissed."

The Marines responded with a resounding, "Ooh-rah."

On that cue, families raced to meet them. Maggie stood rooted to the spot, overcome with emotion. Young children, some dressed in replica desert flight suits, some holding Daddy dolls, with the image of their Marine in uniform, jumped into the arms of their fathers. Wives fell into the embrace of their husbands. Maggie stood back and witnessed Corporal Kane hold Melodie in his arms for the first time. Tears streamed down her face unabashedly.

This is what makes it all worthwhile, she thought. *This moment right here. The pain of separation gives way to the joy of reunion.*

George's plane would be the last one to land. At nightfall, Maggie loaded Smokey in the front passenger seat of the Mustang and drove to the 2nd MAW headquarters building. Her stomach was in knots, a mixture of excitement and nervous energy.

Smokey was the first to enter George's office. He ran straight up to George, wearing his desert flight suit. George knelt down and vigorously rubbed Smokey's midsection. He glanced up to see Maggie smiling through tears.

There he is, she thought, her heart nearly bursting with love. *My George. Home safe.*

Relief and joy coursed through her veins.

The Mustang reverberated in the garage at the Stones' quarters. George dragged his duffel bag and parachute bag into the living room, then removed his cover. It was like watching a transformation. From Marine to husband. From warrior to lover.

Once inside the house, Maggie instructed him to pull the chilled bottle of champagne out of the refrigerator and pour two crystal flutes while she went to retrieve Margaux. After everything they had been through, this reunion felt different, especially with her secrets coming to light in the past four years. Deeper somehow.

A few minutes later, the crackle of vinyl emanated from the living room record player, followed by the mezzo-soprano voice of Edith Piaf singing "La Vie en Rose." Maggie stepped into the kitchen and transformed into Margaux, the French maid. A flutter of nervous excitement passed through her body. This was their ritual, their way of reconnecting after long separations. It felt both familiar and new each time.

"*Mon cheri,*" said George. "You're back."

"*Oui, monsieur.* I have missed you!" Maggie replied in her French accent, feeling a blush rise.

Nearly twenty-two years, and he still made her feel like a newlywed.

George handed Margaux a glass of champagne. She clinked against George's glass and took a sip, the bubbles dancing on her tongue. A powerful realization struck her as she looked at him over the rim of her glass.

She had never loved George as much as she did now. The thought came unbidden but with startling clarity. George, who'd never questioned her nightmares, who'd held her through the panic attacks, who'd loved her despite sensing there was something she wasn't telling him. George, her rock. Her gratitude for his unwavering support nearly brought her to tears again.

"I'm sorry about everything about my past coming back to haunt me … us." Her voice quavered with emotion as she dropped the Margaux persona for a moment. "I promise no more secrets, George." She meant it with every fiber of her being.

George lifted Maggie onto the countertop. He removed the hairpins, removed her lace headpiece, and ran his fingers through her hair. Then he gently kissed her forehead and cradled her face softly in his hands. Maggie savored his tenderness as she leaned into his touch.

"I want you to know that the best thing that ever happened to me was meeting and marrying you," he said. "You've been an incredible partner for close to twenty-two years. I wouldn't be where I am today without you. I love how you look—classy and beautiful—and your passion. I love you with all my heart."

"Oh, George," said Maggie. Her face beamed, and her cheeks glowed with happiness.

How did I get so lucky? she wondered. After all she had been through, all she had hidden, to find this man who loved her completely …

The couple embraced in an intense kiss. Maggie slipped out of her black minidress, delighting in the hunger in George's eyes.

"*Monsieur*," said Maggie, slipping back into her Margaux character, her voice husky with desire. "*J'ai une surprise pour toi.* I have a surprise for you. Follow the clothing trail, and don't forget to bring the champagne."

They had earned this night—this reunion, this celebration of surviving another separation.

"Promise, no bondage?" said George.

"*Oui, monsieur*," she replied with a mischievous glint in her eye.

George wandered through the house, picking up a white lace-neck collar, black stiletto heels, black fishnet stockings, and a garter belt. Smokey followed closely behind. George stood outside the bedroom door and bent down to lift a black lace thong off the floor.

"I'm sorry, boy," he said, looking at Smokey. "You're going to have to sit this one out."

George opened the bedroom door with an armful of clothing and the champagne bottle and flutes in his other hand. He closed the door with a kick of his foot and placed the items on the nightstand. He zipped out of his flight suit and joined Maggie, who lay naked in the bed, her skin tingling with anticipation.

George swept his fingers across Maggie's body. He traced her nipples and used his index finger to trail down her abdomen toward her pubic area. Suddenly, George went utterly still, and his mouth fell open.

"George, what is it?" Maggie questioned, alarm instantly replacing desire.

"I'm not sure. You'd better look."

Maggie hopped out of bed and stood in front of the full-length mirror, her heart sinking as she saw what had caused George's reaction.

"Oh my God," she said, mortification washing over her. "This was supposed to be the surprise. I had a Brazilian wax, but I've had an allergic reaction. It was supposed to be a landing strip for your return flight home. Get it?" She forced a laugh through her embarrassment. "Instead, it's a bumpy, pimple-like red rash."

So much for the perfect homecoming night, she thought ruefully.

"It's the thought that counts, my love." George chuckled. "I'll get the cortisone cream."

Maggie watched him go, shaking her head but smiling. This was real love. The kind that survived deployments, secrets, and Brazilian wax disasters. They were going to be just fine.

Chapter Forty-Five
TEARS OF SORROW, JOY, AND HOPE

April 2012
Paradise Point Officers' Club
Camp Lejeune, North Carolina

THE DEACTIVATION CEREMONY OF II MEF Forward marked the end of a chapter, the closure of a year of waiting, of worrying. Maggie's heart pumped with pride as she and George entered the reception area, soft jazz floating through the foyer. The ceremony room was filled with Marines and their spouses, all dressed in their finest, but Maggie's eyes remained fixed on George—her George, home safe.

"I see Barbara and Jack," Maggie said, spotting familiar faces across the room.

She guided George through the crowd, feeling a surge of pride as heads turned toward him. Her husband. Her hero.

"Welcome home," Barbara exclaimed, wrapping George warmly.

"Welcome home," said Jack, shaking George's hand firmly.

Maggie watched the interaction, her chest tight with emotion. How often had she imagined this moment during those long, lonely nights? The homecoming, the celebrations, the chance to exhale fully again.

"I hope your orders send you to DC," Barbara continued, "because that's where I'm headed. I've been selected for rear admiral, and I'll assume the role of surgeon general chief."

"Congratulations!" Maggie's excitement burst forth genuinely. "This is good news. We're so proud and happy for you, Barbara."

When the announcement came to be seated, Maggie settled in beside George, her thigh pressed against his. Even now, she couldn't bear the thought of space between them. She half listened to the speeches, the formal words blurring together as she studied George's profile. The tiny lines at the corners of his eyes that hadn't been there before. There was a slight tightening of his jaw when specific locations were mentioned.

Maggie watched as the unit's colors were cased, a lump forming in her throat. What had he seen that he would never tell her? What memories would wake him in the night—of flight missions that had failed or mishaps that had occurred? Had he witnessed Marines killed in IED blasts? She pushed the thoughts away. He was home. That was enough. That had to be enough.

The ceremony continued with commendations and announcements of new assignments. When George's promotion was announced, Maggie felt a flutter of excitement and apprehension.

Lieutenant General George E. Stone's next assignment would be in Washington, DC.

Later, at Follow Me Bar, Maggie couldn't contain her excitement about their next chapter.

"DC, here we come!" Barbara yelled, wrapping her arms around Maggie and George.

"Do you know where you'll live?" Jack asked.

"The deputy commandant for aviation has an assigned house on the compound at Marine Barracks Washington," said George. "It's the oldest Post of the Corps."

"Oh, Maggie," Barbara squealed. "We'll live right down the street from you at the Navy Yard. Jack will have to come down for major construction projects, but we're hoping he'll spend most of his time in DC."

"We're heading there next week to look at Quarters Two," Maggie added, her voice brightening. "It was built in 1907; it has four stories, and it's over six thousand square feet. There's an enclosed porch facing the parade deck and gardens on both sides."

"There are so many great restaurants on Eighth Street," said Barbara. "Rose's Luxury and Trattoria Alberto. And historic bars on Pennsylvania Avenue—Tune Inn, Hawk 'N' Dove, and Mr. Henry's, where Roberta Flack debuted her singing. I'm sure the young ones don't even know who she is."

"We'll be there for the Evening Parade season," Maggie continued, picturing herself in that grand house, hosting dinners, making new connections. "I'll be able to hear them practice daily and just walk out my front door to attend the pre-ceremony parties."

"Do you think you'll get tired of hearing all that commotion?" Jack asked.

"Possibly," Maggie answered truthfully. Every military sound reminded her that George was home, safe from deployment while serving as deputy commandant for aviation. "I want to pinch myself. I can't believe I'll live on such a historic post."

The conversation flowed around her—congratulations and laughter, stories and inside jokes. Maggie smiled and nodded, but part of her mind remained elsewhere.

"I propose a toast," said Barbara. "To new beginnings ..."

"To new beginnings," echoed Maggie, clinking glasses with the women who had become more than friends. They were her support system, her lifeline, and now they were moving forward together.

"You've all earned this," Maggie said, looking around at the faces of those who had sacrificed alongside her. "Not just the Marines who deployed. All of us who kept things running on both sides."

"Hear, hear." Min raised her glass from behind the bar. "To the strongest military spouses I've ever known."

George lifted his cover from the wall hook, bid his goodbyes, and motioned to Maggie to head for the exit. As the Stones passed through the foyer, they encountered Hurl. Maggie's stomach tightened.

"How's Karma doing?" Maggie managed to ask, feeling George's concerned glance.

"She's out on bail," Hurl said. "She's been extradited to California to stand trial."

"And Erin?"

"It's been hard on her, but she's strong. Her firm has agreed to represent Karma. Her lawyers are hoping to obtain a lesser charge, possibly a dismissal, given Ian's testimony."

Maggie stood frozen as the warm salt of tears welled in her eyes. When Hurl moved toward her and wrapped his arms around her, she allowed herself to be held, feeling the empathy in his embrace. Some wounds never fully healed; they just became part of you.

"Please tell her …" Maggie started, then paused. The pain was too much, too deep, too unmanageable to put into words. "Please tell them both I'm thinking of them."

"Keep us updated on her progress," George said, his hand reaching for Maggie's as Hurl departed.

"Semper fi, General," said Hurl, saluting George.

"Semper fi," said George, returning the salute.

Maggie left the Officers' Club, feeling the bittersweet pull of endings and beginnings. "I couldn't agree more," she said when George mentioned the mixed feelings of departure. "But I'm so excited for what lies ahead."

In an intimate moment outside, Maggie traced her fingers gently across George's brows, down the sides of his face, and to the tip of his chin. She softly kissed his lips and said, "Enjoy the ride!" Her touch conveyed everything words couldn't.

Outside, the evening air caressed Maggie's face as George drove them away from the Officers' Club. The silver Mustang convertible hugged the waterfront road, lined with pine trees, and she leaned back, letting the wind tangle in her hair. The Carolina sunset painted the sky with brilliant oranges and reds, reflected on New River's surface.

When George clicked on the radio and The Byrds' classic melody "Turn! Turn! Turn!" drifted from the speakers, Maggie glanced at George and smiled. He had come back home. He had come back to her. No spoken words were needed as the beautiful and timeless lyrics sank in. She struggled against the tears—tears of sorrow for all that had been lost, tears of joy for all that remained, and tears of hope for what was yet to come.

Acknowledgments

To all my Semper Sisters—I've written this novel for you, the military spouses, to commemorate your strength, your courage, and your willingness to follow your Marine to every clime and place. Our sacred friendships are what make the Marine Corps journey rewarding and possible.

To my late parents, who taught me to live life to the fullest and were incredible role models for a happy marriage.

To my Marine, Mike—My anchor, my heart, my soul, and my best friend for thirty-five years. Every day, I fall more in love with you.

To Jimmy and Jack—My greatest inspirations for all that is good in this world. I love you both to the moon and back.

To Shannon—You have always loved and supported my family through our military adventures. You have been there for me in the highs and the lows.

To Jill and J.P.—Thank you for your love and support.

To Roberta Gately—When you said yes to being the guest speaker at our Deployed Spouses' Ball, it began a beautiful friendship. Your book, *Lipstick in Afghanistan*, was a comfort to read while our spouses were deployed in harm's way.

To my editor, Caroline Tolley—It took me a while to find my path to you, but when I did, it made all the difference. I am deeply grateful for your insightful guidance and support.

To Jovana Shirley—Thank you for copyediting, proofreading, and creating the beautiful interior formatting.

To Monika MacFarlane—You created the gorgeous cover design. It was love at first sight!

To Pascal Albright—You are an exceptional multimedia editor. How did I get so lucky?

To Bob, who is smiling down from heaven, and Joe Malloy, Cricket and Chuck Hudson, Denise and Joe Mortensen, D'Arcy Neller, Helen Toolan, Krista Crosetto, Sharon Henry, Dawn Rowe, Joe Finley, Camille Weier, and Kristin Holsworth—Thank you for supporting me, reading early drafts, and being such good friends!

To authors Andrew Kaufman and Jessica Park—Your support, guidance, and friendship are invaluable.

To Jenna Tomasello at The Painted Lady—I adore my shamrock tattoo!

To DTC HH Club—Thank you for your support and friendship … and so many laughs.

About the Author

SUZANNE DANA IS BOTH A general's daughter and a general's wife. She graduated from San Diego State University with a degree in journalism and a secondary education credential in English. As a general's wife, she moved nineteen times and supported her husband through eight deployments, including those to Iraq and Afghanistan. She currently sits on the Marine Corps Scholarship Foundation board as an adjunct director. She enjoys photography, travel, water sports, and volunteering at a local women's shelter. She resides in Arizona with her husband.

The General's Wife is her debut novel.

For more information, please visit her website at www.suzannemdana.com, or follow her on Facebook/Instagram at authorsuzannedana.

To enhance your reading experience, listen to *The General's Wife* Playlist. Scan the QR code or visit www.suzannemdana.com.

www.ingramcontent.com/pod-product-compliance
Lightning Source LLC
Chambersburg PA
CBHW020236010826
48973CB00006B/1529